BONE-MEND
and SALT

By E.A. STEWART

ACCIDENTAL HERETICS SERIES
Book 1: *Bone-mend and Salt*
Book 2: *Trebuchets in the Garden*
Book 3*: Crux Lunata*
Book 4: *Song of Valerós*
The Mad Woman of La Catalane: A Novella
The Blue Door… and More Accidental Heretics Tales

LEGENDS OF VALERÓS SERIES
Wheel and Serpent: 1
Traitor: 2
Hero: 3

RAIN CITY INCIDENTS SERIES
(As Annie Pearson)
The Grrrl of Limberlost
Artemis in the Desert
Nine Volt Heart
The Pirate King

Bone-mend and Salt

Salt

ACCIDENTAL HERETICS: BOOK 1

E.A. Stewart

Jūgum Press

For Jacyn, who wanted to read a story.

Characters

House of Valerós
Pèire Leteric, an old crusader, seigneur of Valerós (pronounced like pear)
Beatriz, Pèire's granddaughter; Isabella's sister
Felicia, a ward in Pèire's household; Beatriz's half-sister
Isabella, Pèire's granddaughter
Katelina of Naxos, duenna to Beatriz and Felicia
Sebastián, Isabella's son; heir to Valerós, Fontcours, and Montcava

Also at Valerós:
Anselm, the Valerós chaplain; a former crusader
Benito, master at arms
Ermessen, a kitchen matron
Guillem, marshal of the Valerós knights

House of Don Miquel on Cyprus
Don Miquel de Morella y Cyprus
Numa, wife of Don Miquel; a Kurdish noblewoman
Tomás, son of Numa and Don Miquel
Chrétien, Tomás's foster-brother

House of the Montcava Seigneurs
Durán, a Montcava footman
Eloïse, dòmna of Montcava
Louis, a Montcava cousin; Hélène's brother
Nicolau, Eloïse's older son
Renoud, Eloïse's younger son

Among the French Crusaders
Gerard, Viscount de Chartrain; a crusader
Hélène, wife to Hugues de Beaurain; a Montcava cousin
Hugues, Marquis de Beaurain; a crusader
Jean-Luc, a former knight
Yves, Jean-Luc's brother

People in the South

Anfos, a woodcutter, and his wife Maria
Avraham, a scholar and merchant in Toulouse
Clémence, a secular priest
Lubos, a wayfarer
Pare Abát, "Father Abbot" of St-Féliz

Historic Figures

Arnau Amalric, a Church prelate
Folquet de Marselha, Bishop of Toulouse
Innocent III, papal head of the Holy Roman Church
Pedro II, King of Aragón, Count of Barcelona; called *"El Católico"*
Philippe II, King of France; called "Philippe Augustus"
Raymond VI, Count of Toulouse
Simon de Montfort, French army leader; now Viscount of Carcassonne
Thedisius, pope's legate and aide to Arnau Amalric

In the Languedoc, 1210

AT THE BEGINNING OF the thirteenth century, what we call the Languedoc wasn't part of France. People there didn't speak French. The Count of Toulouse held territory under the kings of Aragón and France. Count Raymond found himself crosswise with the new pope, Innocent III, who commanded him to suppress the communities of people that the Church called heretics, who had lived in the area for a century. The pope also (not coincidentally) sought proper tithes to the Church from this wealthy land, wanted to nominate the bishops, and presented a host of other continuing and expanding complaints.

The diplomatic exchanges continued for several years, as these things do, but then the pope's emissary, Peter of Castelnau, was murdered near the Rhône River. The pope blamed Raymond and asked Philippe II of France to bring an army to force Raymond to comply.

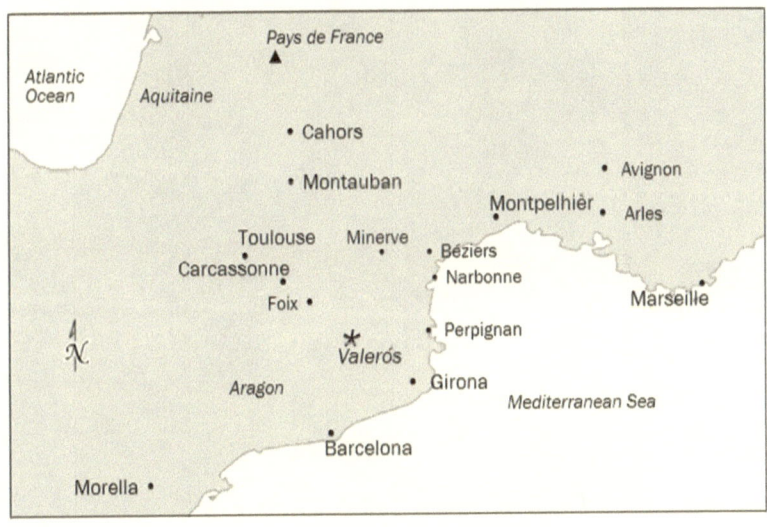

The Languedoc • 1210

In 1209, a French crusader army arrived, believing they served God like earlier crusaders had by colonizing territories in the Outre-mer, the lade of Crusader States and other territories across the

Great Sea. Béziers was burned and sacked. Tricked into surrender, the inhabitants of Carcassonne were turned out of the city.

But French knights came south to fight for forty days, promised forgiveness of their sins and whatever booty they might win. At the end of the crusading season, they went north again. Over the winter, the remaining French forces experienced more defeats than advances, either in territory or in restraining the so-called Cathar heretics, Christians who believed a Good God ruled heaven and a Dark God made the material world.

In the spring of 1210, French forces prepared to ride south again. Simon de Montfort, a leader of the French army, was named Viscount of Carcassonne. However, the king of Aragón had not yet accepted his oath.

Meanwhile, people wanted to plant crops, care for their animals, prune their vineyards and orchards. They waited for the Count of Toulouse and their seigneurs to restore peace to the south.

Bone-mend and Salt

PART ONE
Wolves in Spring

Noble generosity and giving with a true heart,
Good banter and "You are truly welcome!"
A grand house, and good pay,
Gifts and gear, and living the right way...
I wish you would take this away,
With nothing retained
In this world of trouble
After this evil-starred year
That seemed so good at the beginning.

— Bertran de Born
"Mon chan fenis ab dol et ab maltraire"

In Part One

1

1

Badly Knit Bones

Tomás in the Pyrenees foothills,
31 days before Pentecost, April 1210

PRIESTS SMELL AS BAD as any other men.

This one, a gold-sniffing renegade, even worse.

That's all Tomás had learned after traveling from Toulouse with a pack of priests for a fortnight. Over those fourteen nights, he moved closer to the gold-sniffing priest whose pocket Tomás wanted to examine. Each night, as Tomás watched from a neighboring camp-fire, that rogue took a packet of letters from his satchel and wrapped it in the corner of his blanket to make a pillow.

The formerly handsome Tomás de Morella y Cyprus, a mercenary with no current master, needed those letters. The bishops' court in Toulouse gave him until Pentecost to render proof of how his father had been wrongfully dispossessed. A year ago, in his quest for that proof, Tomás had been thrashed by his enemies. His broken limbs and ribs recovered slowly. Now, all he wanted in this life was to redeem his father's honor, to restore his father's rightful inheritance, and to wreak havoc on his enemies.

After trading places among slumbering pilgrims that night, Tomás spread his camp kit close enough to pry the packet from the sleeping priest's possession. Edging toward where the odiferous man slept, Tomás paused, lying still as a stone for sixty heartbeats before wiggling a hair closer, while a toothache plagued him and the poorly healed scars on his face begged to be scratched.

His badly knit bones ached from sleeping on bare ground, like a dog the devil kicked. Listening to night-sounds in the Pyrenees foothills, Tomás endured long, painfully cold moments as he crept closer to the satchel he longed to steal. He breathed through his mouth to avoid the fetid smell of garlic and unwashed renegade priest. After an eternity, he moved his hand to—

"*Peccador! Maricón!*"

The priest cried out in fear of being molested.

Burning and aching in every bone, Tomás disappeared among the sleeping pilgrims. Without gaining the letter he needed from the gold-dousing priest's satchel.

Back inside his own bed-roll, Tomás rewrapped the leather binding that hid the bonfraires brand on his wrist, and then checked that his best dagger remained tucked in his boot.

Maricón? Your dreams are grand, you goat-legged weasel.

■

Tomás in Famagusta, 1209

The notoriously handsome Tomás de Morella y Cyprus arrived in Famagusta with his milk-brother Chrétien. As they sprinted up the narrow streets, the men who stepped aside recognized them instantly: Tomás, the compact, umber-dark man in embroidered black fustian like his father always wore, and his extraordinarily tall Celtic foster-brother in woad-dyed blue, long pale hair streaming behind as he ran. Men hailed them, sending respectful wishes that Jesus in heaven might bless Tomás's father.

"Tomásino! Chrétien!"

Their mother Numa stood under the orange tree by the villa gate, exactly where she had waved farewell six years ago.

"*Kalila!*"

She opened her arms to embrace Tomás, calling him *sweetheart*, as you would a child. He shivered in shock, because her slender body now felt bony and brittle. Her dark hair was streaked with grey. Chrétien had his turn, kissing his foster-mother hello, bending down to murmur in her ear and make her smile, however briefly. Then they crouched at a bedside where the scent of orange trees and jasmine drifted in from the courtyard but never masked the stench of illness.

Tomás's father—Don Miquel, a knight from Aragón, a hero and captain of knights under crusader-lords in Syria and Jerusalem—

was finally dying of the gut wound assassins had delivered fifteen years ago. He lingered, waiting for Tomás to bring word of long-desired revenge.

"I failed you, Father. I haven't yet found your enemy." Tomás told their hunting stories, reciting the list of men they still sought as possible enemies, concluding with Pèire Leteric and Hugues, the Marquis de Beaurain.

"May all the angels weep as they dance in the golden heaven. No." His father denied Tomás's claim with a familiar epithet. "It's not Hugues. Not Pèire. Don't waste your time. I want your oaths. Swear to me what you'll do after I'm gone. Tomás? Chrétien?"

His mother, Numa, cried out. "No, Miquelito! You have already stolen their youth. Not more years of hunting."

Chrétien embraced Numa. "We haven't suffered, Mother. We are happy to do as our father asks."

"I want all the Montcava sons dead, too," his father said. "Long ago, I was betrayed by that family. They took away the Fontcours estate I won as a crusader. Clean out the whole nest of scorpions—land, name, honor. Destroy the Montcavas. Take back our lands."

"Father, I swear it."

"Swear as our bonfraires do."

His clawlike hand grasped Tomás's wrist, rubbing the welt where Tomás had been branded when he joined his father's brother-hood of knights. Breaking such an oath, the old man said, meant yielding your immortal soul.

"*Sodalitas, fidelitas, virtus.*" Tomás repeated the oath. "On my honor, my life is given to your revenge."

Chrétien repeated the same oath.

His father pulled Tomás closer. "God won't condemn you for what you must do."

"No?" Tomás puzzled. Miquel had left their religious schooling to Numa.

"God doesn't care about us," his father said. "I learned that over all these long nights."

Numa drew a sharp breath, as if his words hurt as much as his dying and leaving her.

The old man said, "If He had a care, He'd never have let those wolves, the Knights of the Lunate Cross, come to be. Our enemy is one of them." Crux Lunata, the league of enemies that Miquel had frightened his sons with since the cradle.

"Please, Miquelito," Numa begged. "You must have faith in the goodness of our Lord."

"*Kalila*, my darling Numa, faith is fine if you need it." Miquel coughed, wrenching his hands from Tomás's clasp. "A sword is always better. Especially if you are hunting wolves."

·

Now, across the Great Sea, high in the Pyrenees foothills, with about thirty days of hope left that the bishops' court might restore what was stolen from his father Miquel, Tomás sought ground that might be kind to his bones, while expecting another night of painful sleep and planning his next incursion against the gold-bug priest. His sore tooth throbbed.

The cry of a nighthawk sounded like his father laughing, just beyond the thorn hedge.

2
A Wild Man

Jean-Luc at Valerós
Easter Monday, late March

"IT'S JACQUES THE GIANT!"

The children in the village outside Castell-de-Valerós called the man names, threw clods, and then ran away to hide, dodging behind trees. The huge, bearded man ignored their taunts and set up camp by a stream. The children crept back for another look.

He wasn't a real giant, just tall and strong, with ice-blue eyes like slices of the sky shining amid his stork's nest of beard and wild hair, both dark as charcoal from road dirt.

"*Bon día, mon amics.*" The giant greeted them in the common tongue of the south, except he talked through his big broken nose.

He trapped a rabbit faster than any of their fathers could, and then he showed the boys how to tie knots for a trap like his and how to set the bait. He laid twigs to start his campfire in a peculiar way, but it flamed up instantly at his touch. He set his portable forge in the fire and used it to bake bread from dough that he'd set to rise in his pack.

A brave boy whose father was a bordonier, a freeholder who fought in the last crusade, asked, "Do you know magic, senhór?"

"I'm just a smith," he replied, shaking his big head. "But the fire-spirits and I have a special understanding."

The fire-spirits must not be kind, the boys decided, because an angry burn crawled up the giant's right arm. He shared his bread-cakes and told the boys about the Outremer, where Saracen servants fanned Frankish lords and served glorious food that Christians on this side of the Great Sea never dreamed of. While the rabbit crackled,

7

roasting over the fire, the smith told bloody stories about the siege of Jaffa, when the Angevine King Richard and the Franks' King Philippe strove to reclaim Jerusalem.

The boys forgot their chores, so the girls tattled on them. Consequently, the Valerós marshal and parish priest came to greet the giant camped by the stream.

"I'm Father Anselm and this is Marshal Guillem. Valerós welcomes former crusaders needing work and shelter."

"I'm no crusader," said the giant. "My name is Jehan of Breton. I'm a smith who's lost his master."

The marshal frowned, his great moustaches twitching as if he smelled a falsehood.

"Our smith fell ill this past fortnight," the priest said. "You might be the answer to our prayers." The marshal stroked his moustache, seeming to think as the smith did: the big man had never been the answer to anyone's prayers.

·

On Easter Monday, the man who claimed to be Jehan of Breton crawled up to the loft over the castle's smithy forge, dragging the new blanket and clean straw ticking the marshal had given him.

However, once alone, he was the spy Jean-Luc who served Viscount Gerard de Chartrain from the Pays de France. He probed the corners of the loft, which smelled of mice. He tried to open the hatch under the eaves. Nothing could get in without coming up the loft ladder, so he lay down, too tired to sweep out the corners.

This high in the Pyrenees foothills, the nights were still bone-freezing cold and heat from the forge dissipated quickly. Jean-Luc felt grateful for vermin-free straw and a wool blanket, because old injuries pained him. Each time he rubbed the gnarled tissue on his arm and the long scar on his thigh, a host of memories sprang free. He fingered the boar's-tooth charm on the string around his neck and stared up at the rafters, because if he closed his eyes, he'd once more see that church in Constantinople, where an icon of a sad-eyed Madonna fell into his lap from the hands of a dead man. His night terrors started there, back when he'd been a knight of the Cross with a real name. When he was a soldier, not an itinerant smith who

8

spied for a French lord, to learn how things stood with certain seigneurs amid the chaos in the Languedoc.

At dawn, he stoked the forge fire so it would blaze hot when he
returned from matins. Then, as Jehan the smith, he knelt in the chilly
stone chapel to pray amid strangers. He prayed that he might finish
his business here by Pentecost, as his lord required, and then that
he might resume searching for a man—any man—who would swear
to the truth and redeem Jean-Luc's name and honor.

The marshal knelt beside him, his elbow prodding the smith
when he folded his hands. The nudge left Jean-Luc aware that this
castle housed an inordinate number of battle-tested crusaders, and
likely each of them lay awake at night nursing wounds and regrets
and betrayals.

Pray for us, O Holy Mother of God, that we may be made worthy.

3
Duty

Isabella outside Valerós
30 days before Pentecost

IN THE BEST PART of spring, when scrub oaks showed sufficient leaf to prove they still lived and the morning air smelled of golden broom and wild thyme, a pack of wolves came down from the high mountains to feed on the new lambs.

A young shepherdess from a village in the hills beyond Castell-de-Valerós had her arm mangled when she fought an adolescent wolf stalking her flock. The villagers sent a message to the Valerós steward. Something must be done.

Isabella of Valerós (she'd cast off her dead husband's name) served as steward for her grandfather, Pèire Leteric, the baron of Valerós. Duty called Isabella to protect the sheep and their shepherds, so she'd asked the Valerós marshal to hunt down the pack.

Before dawn, she pulled on a leather jerkin and leggings, braided her unruly hank of copper hair, stuffed it into a man's felted cap, and ran to the stable, where three house-knights and a small band of bordoniers loaded ponies and traded jibes. These freeholders served as soldiers, tree-fellers, or huntsmen, doing whatever Isabella or their seigneur Pèire Leteric asked — and were more than happy to hunt a pack of wolves.

The horses stamped and blew a white mist with each breath. Isabella, lanky and taller than most, looked over the men's heads to find their leader.

"No, ma dòmna." Marshal Guillem addressed her as "my lady" but shook his head when he saw her standing there, ready to ride. "You can bully us down on the farms. But you are not coming today."

He spoke with the burr of the Norman courts in Sicily. His accent and drooping moustaches, long hair, and silver-streaked beard made him seem exotic for a backcountry castle. Six years before, when Guillem came with Pèire to rescue Isabella and her son, their crusader battle scars and broken noses seemed like the faces of angels to her. They brought her back home from the hell she'd endured as a young wife in Toulouse.

And here, at Valerós, she wasn't going to be denied the greatest excitement of this spring season. "I can hurl a javelin as well as any bordonier. And sit a horse better than you, Marshal Guillem."

"Pèire Leteric will have my hide on a stick and wave it like a knight's banner if anything happens to his grandchild."

"I'm not a child. At my age, Pèire had fought in the Outremer for a dozen years."

"At your age, Pèire Leteric had trained under the best knights in Christendom. And not coincidentally, he was a…" Guillem stopped before finishing his thought and took a different tact. "Fine. But keep that hawk's nose you inherited from Pèire out of trouble."

She could have argued that she'd also inherited a hawk's eyesight and reflexes, but she'd won her point, and so she did as Guillem wanted when he mounted his horse and pointed to where she should ride beside him.

．

From Castell-de-Valerós, you can see halfway to the Outremer. Hewn from living rock, the castle's stone walls and alleys meandered among the cliffs and granite outcroppings. Some heathen shepherds time out of mind first stacked stones on that hilltop. The Romans built upon their work. Pèire Leteric and his uncle Sanç had expanded and refortified it. Across the valley lay the much smaller castle at Arracheuse, which had belonged to Isabella's father and which her son Sebastián would inherit when he turned sixteen.

The crusade that foundered in Constantinople had ended her father's life and relieved Isabella of an unworthy husband. She came back to Valerós with her six-year-old son, ready to live a sane life again, warmly welcomed by her real family and hearing Pèire's complaint that her father had mortgaged Arracheuse to finance going on crusade, and then didn't bring home any golden booty. *"It'll take a generation before Arracheuse regains its former wealth."*

However, the bordoniers who returned from that ill-fated crusade preferred farming to fighting, and so pitched in to work under Isabella's leadership. They built a new olive press, and now Arracheuse produced more olive oil than the villages needed. They took the valley's novelty crop, peaches, to sell in Narbonne, where the castellans and the bishop's stewards paid half the fruits' weight in silver, earning as much as the olive oil. She practiced a few other endeavors to pay off that mortgage before her son came of age.

Riding out the Valerós gates, Isabella peered down into the valleys, assessing the handiwork of a double score of sheepherders and several scores of bordoniers who kept vineyards and olive groves, fields of woad to sell to Narbonnese dyers, and orchards with pears and peaches grown from Outremer stock that Pèire carried home. She intended never to leave this glorious world.

The trail wound up into the hills. They traveled from dawn into the heart of the morning until they reached the meadow where the shepherdess had been attacked. The bordoniers didn't take long to find spoor leading to the wolves' den.

"We approach the den in an arc, like this." Marshal Guillem used a twig to draw a plan in the dust. "Each animal emerging from the den will have a pair of hunters to reckon with."

In Guillem's plan for the wolf hunt, a small X stood for Isabella at the far end of the arc, off to the side near the marshal's own mark.

"You succeeded in keeping me out of the way," she said.

Pleased at the compliment, Guillem stroked his moustache, but then saw she meant otherwise. "I have to answer to Pèire Leteric."

"Therefore, my sole task will be to tell the story of your glory?"

"Yes, please. Like your grandfather tells a good story."

"But I'm also as useful as anyone here." She held his stare, hoping to imitate the way Pèire Leteric could freeze a man in his tracks. However, the marshal didn't flinch, though he clearly recognized how much she resembled her crusader grandfather.

"Because you're reasonably handsome compared to Pèire, that fierce look doesn't scare me," Guillem said. "However, you may do what you like. You always do. But stay on your horse."

"Easy, Al-Malik."

She patted her horse while the men moved through the granite rockfall and gorse to surround the wolves' den. Guillem waited nearby while his strategy unfolded. But the dogs disrupted the plan, surging ahead in a pack, baying as they swarmed the den. When Guillem cursed the hounds, a hare darted out. His horse lurched, tossing Guillem onto a granite outcropping. Blood flowed from the cut on his head as he leaped up to reach for his spooked horse.

Isabella startled like the rabbit, heart pounding. She hated blood.

"Do we need full armor just to ride in these hills?" Guillem joked as he calmed his horse.

Then Al-Malik became restless, ignoring Isabella's whispers. He snorted and tossed wildly. She turned to Guillem.

"What do you think—"

A wolf stalked the marshal, preparing to leap.

"Guillem!"

She hurled her javelin, striking the wolf in its thigh. The marshal's horse bolted when the lanced wolf fell upon the surprised marshal. She vaulted off Al-Malik, drew her dagger, and thrust it into the wolf's heart. The animal yelped, its howl a piercing misery. Guillem threw the dying animal off him and sliced its throat with his own dagger.

After they gulped several breaths, Guillem cleaned his dagger and hers in the dust.

"I fought in the Outremer with counts and kings," he said. "I was there when Saladin joined the peace at Ramla. Then I climb this little hill and need a woman to save me."

"It was luck," she said.

"Lucky for me, ma dòmna, you know how to use your javelin."

Isabella flushed, but didn't look at him. The blood.

"Let's call our debts even," she said. "You once saved me from that nest of Montcavas in Toulouse."

"We saved you from a piss-ant, not a wolf," he said.

For the rest of the hunt, Isabella kept to the edge, like Guillem had drawn in his plan, and watched while the men encircled and destroyed the three remaining adult wolves. But she didn't follow the bordoniers who entered the den to kill the cubs. She was working here to protect Valerós, but she didn't need to go that far.

Setting out on the ride home, the bordoniers sang for the sake of the day's victory, though they chose a nursery song.

> I saw the wolf before the wolf saw me.
> I'll kill the wolf before the wolf kills me.
> God take the wolf and God save me.

Lubos in the City

BACK IN THE TEEMING southern cities, strangers brushed against you in the streets and fly-swarmed alleys. Lost in the crowds, Lubos struggled to hear the voices of his guiding angels and spirits. He missed their music as much as he missed his woman Aykuna's suppers of fried bread with spicy sausages, or bouncing the girls on his knee, begging him to tickle them until they wiggled and sobbed with joy, their tiny bones under linen shifts as fragile as the bones of a small bird you might hold in your hand.

But Lubos soldiered on. A funny way to say it since he had abandoned soldiering after that war. He continued to keep his kit in order. He kept his body clean like Aykuna taught him, saying he looked so handsome when his face was shaved. He marshaled the silver Père-Izsák had given him and chanted the names of men his dear father asked him to find. It was taking a long time.

Last winter, beside the Rhône, the dawn frost had rimed the skeletons of trees and decaying rushes, making them even more beautiful than other dead things. Lubos said the prayer Père-Izsák taught him, and he rubbed the lunate cross the priest had pricked into his arm with a needle and ink, marking the crescents in red at each end of the X.

"It is what sons owe their fathers, like what knights owe their lords." Père-Izsák talked about honor as he tapped the cross into Lubos's flesh. He explained that he wasn't a priest like those men in brown robes. He was God's knight, a leader among soldiers, like Lubos had once been. "You must help the spirits to keep turning the wheels of God's creation."

Lubos had completed the first task Père-Izsák commanded. He rode out on horseback along the Rhône river and ran a man through with his sword.

"Priests know when they've been selected for sacrifice," Père-Izsák had said when he told Lubos what he must do. "You can tell by what they say when you set their souls free."

15

And yet, the priest he sacrificed hadn't uttered a word when Lubos sliced his middle. He just died.

Another of the priests riding there cried, "*Ai Dèu, Pèire!*"

In the silver dawn, Lubos galloped away, confused, the frigid air frosting his bare face and turning to ice in his lungs. Pèire was the next name on Père-Izsák's list. Or was it Pedro? Or were all the men in the south called Peter?

4
Fishers of Men

Isabella outside Valerós
30 days before Pentecost

AT MIDDAY, CROSSING THE last hill but one, Isabella urged her horse ahead. She wanted to celebrate the success of the morning's hunt.

"Let's race. I'll be at Valerós before any of you."

Benito, the Valerós master at arms, called out, "Senhóra Isabella, Pèire wouldn't approve." Isabella considered Benito the best example of Catalan knights; dark, handsome, tidy, thoughtful. However, he did not rule her. She urged Al-Malik ahead.

"What can happen here in the lower hills?" Marshal Guillem said. "We killed the wolves. Let her go."

Launching the race, she rode off the soft Turkish saddle, curled along Al-Malik's side like a Seljuk horse-archer, or so Pèire said when he taught her to ride that way.

"Go fast, Al-Malik."

When she rounded a turn, she urged Al-Malik onto a lower path she often rode with her son Sebastián, a path that Guillem claimed was merely a sheep's trail. Midway along the narrow path, her horse kicked loose a hail of rocks, which knocked several boulders free and raised a cloud of dust. As Al-Malik skittered away from the landslide, she urged him forward to a flattened space under a large oak. He reared and threw her off.

Stunned and bruised, she called to the nervous horse. Dust filled her throat from the fall, her voice a jagged gasp. She reached for Al-Malik, but the earth abruptly dropped away. Her stomach lurched, and she struggled as a hempen net jerked her into the air.

"*Bon Dèu!*"

17

Dizzy and angry, she saw only rocky ground, far below.

"The Scripture is without error!" a man's voice called. "Jesus said, 'I will make you fishers of men,' and lo! The nets were let down and caught a man."

She thrashed in the net, turning to see a tall, slender stranger who gazed up, a fishpole over his shoulder. His long blond hair hung free as if he'd just risen from sleep. He didn't look like a hunter who'd set a trap. She called out, her voice husky and yet breathless.

"Blessed Savior and the golden angels! Let me down!"

"I don't see how I can, my friend. You are too high."

"*Punxor!* Why the devil did you set this trap?" she shouted, cursing like one of Pèire's bordoniers. "I could have been killed!"

"It's not my trap. I only came up here because the rockslide ruined my fishing. Though your curses would also scare the fish."

"*Ai Dèu*, damn the fish!"

"The rockslide already did."

"Get me out of here, senhór." She intended the same voice Pèire used to command his men, while trying to calm the panic she felt from dangling so high.

"You shouldn't have got up there if you can't get down," the fisherman said.

"I didn't choose to be here, *baquelar*." The man drove her to curse in a fury, which at least relieved her panic.

"We none of us choose, do we?" he asked. "Aren't we all just sent wherever God flings us?"

"Am I being punished by God? For what?" she cried.

Enraged, she reached for her dagger to tear the cage open, but lost hold of the blade. She tumbled over in the next, ending up staring up at the oak canopy, forcing her mind to rational thought. Who had laid this trap? Men use metal traps to catch a wolf, not hemp. The only purpose for such a trap was to catch or kill a human.

She quelled panic. No one rode this decrepit trail except Isabella and her son Sebastián.

Who wanted her captured? Or killed?

She tussled with the net, like a fly caught by a giant spider. On the ground below, despite his laconic talk, the stranger studied the tree and the nearby rock face, seeking a way to help her.

He carefully folded his faded, crimson silk surcoat and set it beside his fishpole. The embroidered linen sleeves of his quilted undershirt had been patched, as if he'd assembled his wardrobe from the back-alley rag-pickers of Narbonne, where crusaders sold their Outremer silks for coin to travel home. But he couldn't be that destitute, because his silver-handled dagger and embossed leather belt could buy passage all the way to the Pays de France, or wherever this man called home.

His hair flying behind him like a banner, he ran and leaped to grab the lowest branch of the tree. But, tall as he was, he couldn't reach the lowest branch.

"It appears God is not yet done with you today, my friend."

"Catch my horse and stand on him."

"I don't see any sign of your horse," he said.

"Then we'll have to wait until my men circle around the upper trail." She let loose of the death-grip she had on the net, preparing to wait for Guillem.

"Your men?" he asked. "People say Pèire Leteric leads all the men in these parts."

She sank into the net, disappointed that even a stranger knew her privilege to lead a band of men came from her grandfather.

"I'm the steward at Castell-de-Valerós," she said. "Until my son comes of age."

"*Ai*, you're married. That's a pity." He attempted another leap. And once again failed to seize a branch.

"Not married." Isabella was glad to be distracted from fear by his casual chatter. "I was freed by the blessed angels of mercy. And shall stay free ever more."

Her horse reappeared, stamping and snorting through foam-flecked nostrils.

"Here's your savior," the man said. "A beautiful animal."

"His name is Al-Malik."

"A king, eh?" He spoke softly, soothing the horse, which let him move closer. Soon, Al-Malik was nuzzling the man's hand, while Isabella remained unnerved, pondering who laid this trap for her.

Or for Sebastián, who also rode this trail.

The fire of her old terrors kindled once more, the nagging fear that her dead-husband's family still pursued her, determined to snatch Sebastián from her.

While Isabella's fear about the meaning of the trap increased with every heartbeat, Al-Malik let the stranger mount him and circle under her. In a swift, graceful movement, the fisherman stood in the saddle and then scrambled out along the branch from which she hung. His weight tipped the net closer to the ground.

"Put your hands over your head to protect it," he said. "Ready?"

When he cut her down, she rolled in a ball so her shoulder took the force of the fall. She lost her breath, but her leather hunter's clothes offered good protection. As she wrestled with the net to tear it away, the ground still seemed to sway. She sat down to keep from falling.

"That can't have been pleasant." The man dropped from the tree and sat beside her. "I walked right past here this morning. I might have been hanging there waiting for you to ride by. I'd have been less brave than you."

He leaned back on his elbows. One of his long legs brushed her knee. She rather liked being called brave, especially since inside, her heart hammered still. *A trap for me? Or Sebastián?*

"Who are you?" she asked. Even without considering the crimson surcoat, the way he commanded Al-Malik indicated that he was a soldier. "You aren't a squire from around here."

"A squire? I'm a bit old for that." He had a handsome face for a northerner, only slightly marred by a cynical smile. "*Ai*, the south has strange ways. Young donzels become knights while your squires grow old in the same station. Your seigneurs collect rents on the ovens, pastures, and vineyards that surround their castles, but refuse to bow to any king."

"*Òc*. It's called our domus, our entire household, for which the seigneur has special duties to uphold paratge, the honor of our grandfathers, going back generations." She let the conversation go on, while he revealed that he didn't know the south and its ways; therefore, he wasn't an unlikely Montcava mercenary sent to hunt her down. And yet…

He prattled on. "People here say *òc* as if they're coughing, instead of saying *si* or *oui* like most Christians do. And your mothers are all goodwomen who ignore popes and priests."

"My family calls Pedro d'Aragón king," she said. "Our villages say their Creed and baptize their babies. And they're mountain people who speak Catalan more often than the common tongue of the south."

"Ah, you bow to the pope's will. How unusual here."

She didn't care to discuss her family's alliances or beliefs with a stranger. She had no reason to trust him, though his chatter distracted her from the fear that still throbbed inside. "Tell me your name."

"I'm Chrétien, a jongleur. I make my way in the world by singing troubadours' songs. The minstrels I travel with are camped in a swale around the bend."

"Then perhaps you'll come to Castell-de-Valerós tonight? We haven't had entertainment since All Saints."

If she was wrong about him being a soldier, then as a jongleur he'd be accustomed to court life, which explained why he felt free to sit beside her and chat so easily. The troubadours and singers she'd known in Toulouse were impoverished cousins of the lords and ladies who supported them.

"You're worried." He examined her more closely. "Even though you're safe on the ground."

"I'm wondering who set that trap. Who seeks to harm…me."

"You could run away with us. Cast off such worries." Stretched out beside her, Chrétien returned to the laconic, teasing manner as when he first came upon her. "If you can't sing, you can do horse tricks. Or swing from a net."

"Why would I run away from the most beautiful place on God's earth? All I want in life is to make Valerós prosperous and safe."

"All you want? You don't want another marriage, with more children to succor your old age? I'm not partial to such connections myself," he said. "If you know what I mean."

"Yes," she said, though unsure. As friendly as he was, she still felt wary of him, even if he hadn't set that trap. "But truly, the safety of Valerós is all I care about. Its villages, its people. Fruitful crops and market days that bring joy to everyone."

"Then you won't run away with me?" he teased. "You're break-ing my heart, you know."

"I'm not known to be a heartbreaker."

Following a whistle, Chrétien stood. "Here are my friends."

Half a dozen men spilled into the clearing. That motley band of minstrels passed through Valerós every year, the last time at Mid-summer's Eve. They'd play music and offer foolish tricks at dinner that night, while she discussed with Pèire Leteric whether Sebastián needed stronger protection. And whether the House of Montcava was reviving its desire to destroy her.

The crowd of friendly, jostling minstrels helped calm her turbu-lent fears. When she stood to greet them, her cap fell away. Her hair tumbled down, free of its braid.

"It's the senhóra of Valerós!" one of the minstrels exclaimed.

"You're not a man." Her rescuer Chrétien frowned. Then he smirked. "The disappointment is crushing. If you were a fish, I'd throw you back."

5

Bel Respos

Isabella at Valerós
30 days before Pentecost

PÈIRE'S MEN SHOUTED FROM the walls of Valerós as she approached with Guillem. The gates creaked open. The stable boys ran to help with the horses, crying, "Bonjorn! Bonjorn!"

"You went after those wolves, didn't you, *xiqueta?*" Pèire called from where he sat in the courtyard, lingering with his family after midday lunch. "Looks like you both got mistook for prey."

With his piercing eyes and bushy, snow-white eyebrows, Pèire resembled an emperor or stern saint like on the icons he brought home from his travels. Scarred head to toe from blade, Greek fire, and iron-and-clay grenades, Pèire sat under the arbor, holding court.

Beatriz and Felicia, her sister and stepsister, sat across from Pèire, with Katelina beside him as usual. The girls still called Katelina duenna, although she was now just a close friend. The three women wrinkled their noses at Isabella and Guillem, who were filthy with road-dust and wolf-blood.

"The wolves are all dead." Guillem stroked his drooping moustaches, which always meant he had a story to tell. "Isabella took down one of them with her javelin to save me."

Beatriz folded her hands in quick prayer. Gentle Felicia cried out in dismay when Isabella described the wolf attacking Guillem. Katelina, as usual, kept her feelings to herself.

Guillem cleared his throat. "A man-trap snared Senhóra Isabella on that rotten sheep's trail where she likes to ride with Sebastián."

Pèire rose out of his seat, growling in anger. "Not on my land!"

"Our men are seeking the trapper." Isabella told the story quickly, not wanting Guillem to suffer Pèire's wrath for letting her ride alone. "Perhaps it's just mischief. Perhaps it's…"

"Perhaps it's your old enemy, the House of Montcava." Katelina finished the thought, the only person in the world who'd heard the entire story of what Isabella suffered in Toulouse.

Isabella heard her fears expressed perfectly. But Pèire growled again, in his heaviest backcountry Catalan accent. "That miserable piss-ant? Renoud of Montcava ain't coming near here for fear of having his balls and bowels served to him on a platter."

Katelina urged food and drink on Isabella, who accepted the cup of watered wine and settled down with her family, feeling the day's terrors and challenges shrink to a size she could manage.

"How are you, *xiqueta*?" Calm, sensible Katelina had a way of making Isabella feel as if she were under the woman's protection. As she spoke, Katelina concentrated on the needlework in her lap, turning it to see better in the afternoon light, her many bracelets ringing like music. A dark-haired lady from an island near Greece, Katelina had been first nurse, then tutor, and now companion for Beatriz and Felicia. And Isabella's only true friend. Katelina managed Pèire's household and, Isabella believed, she shared Pèire's bed. Katelina behaved in most ways as his wife, but she was Orthodox; he'd be excommunicated if he married her.

"This girl works too hard," Pèire said. "If we don't stop her, she'll set my men to work cutting back more forest for a new vineyard."

Isabella said, "Tomorrow they're starting work on a bigger mill over the stream by Arracheuse. We need a new mill more than another vineyard. Where's Sebastián?"

"He has chores with the men," Pèire said. "That boy is how old? Twelve? People here are too inclined to treat him like a child."

"He's small for his age," Katelina said. Isabella kept quiet.

"I'm small for my age," Pèire said, "and I'm old as the hills. That boy needs to get used to a harder life, eh, Guillem?"

Guillem didn't answer, being busy trading looks with Felicia, who tried to keep a sober face under his scrutiny, but mostly failed. Guillem made the barest gesture and Felicia rose, insisting that his wounds must be looked to.

Pèire snorted. "Thanks to that wolf, our Felicia gets to play nurse to a weary soldier."

Felicia didn't blush, familiar with Pèire's teasing. She'd come to the family as a baby when Isabella's father married a widow from Béziers, who'd left him widowed again when Beatriz was born.

"You called me a fool at Candlemas when I declared our Felicia should consider Guillem," he said to no one in particular. "I'm as good a fortune-teller as that soothsayer who harassed us in Jaffa."

"You just noticed what everyone knew at Twelfth Night," Katelina said. "Felicia made up her mind before you gave it a thought."

"You taught these girls their *alpha, beta, gamma*," Pèire said. "Our Felicia just used common sense, the way you trained her."

He sipped the wine Beatriz poured for him and patted her hand. To him, Beatriz remained the coddled baby. "Now if only you'd teach them to do as they're told without plaguing me dawn to dark." His eyes glinted in the way they did when he teased. "All your quarreling in Greek won't make a man happy."

"Felicia is beautiful enough to keep any husband satisfied," Beatriz said. As much as she worshipped Katelina, Beatriz refused to adopt her Greek methods for enhancing beauty. "Good housekeeping will have to be enough to satisfy whatever husband Grandfather chooses for me."

Katelina scrunched her elegant nose. "If Senhór Pèire decides that man will be the ancient Dolcet de Cambia from the upper hills, like he swears he will, I'll need to share a great deal more of my housekeeping hints with her. Dolcet allows dogs in his dining hall."

"*Ai, bel respos,*" Pèire sighed, calling Katelina's jibes *good conversation*. Jibing with the women in his own domus served as a distinct pleasure for the old man.

Sitting peacefully under the arbor, they watched the new smith in the stable yard below who was busy mending the tongue of a wool-wagon. With their own smith ill since Easter, Pèire now relied on an itinerant giant of a man who'd appeared at their gates as if delivered by angels.

After the smith heaved a load three times his own weight, Pèire said, "With this new crusade coming, I'd trade any five of my men for a knight so strong."

25

"What? Why?" Isabella hadn't heard Pèire mention that damnable, false crusade since Twelfth Night.

Beatriz glanced between them. Seeing that Pèire and Isabella were launching a discussion she loathed, Beatriz left to deliver instructions to the kitchen. Katelina poured more wine in her own cup.

•

"Grandfather, Valerós has a coterie of crusader-knights and a valley full of bordoniers. Why do you want more men? You said last year that this French enterprise will never touch us, because the Church only wants to punish Raymond of Toulouse."

"Last year." Pèire turned his palm down, as if emptying a cup.

"*Òc.*" She switched to the common tongue of the Languedoc, which they did when discussing that wretched French invasion. "We had plenty of food last year to share with people seeking refuge from Béziers. And land to share with Catalan mercenaries who bivouacked here. We'll do as well this year."

"We don't know what the coming crusading season will hold." Pèire poured wine for Isabella and passed her a plate of feta, bread, and olives.

"Most of the French army went home last autumn," Isabella said. "Everyone says they complained that the south is too hot. They didn't earn enough booty or gain significant territory. Why would they come back? Just to burn more heretics?"

"Perhaps," Pèire said. "We can't understand the ways of the pope or *francimand* knights. Or knights like Simon de Montfort who lost their fortunes in the last crusade."

"Why have you changed your mind, Grandfather?"

"I've been thinking on it every time we get news from Narbonne. Since Benito came home yesterday with stories about how it goes, I been thinking harder."

Benito had traveled to Narbonne to do certain market chores for Isabella, and he hadn't told her new stories, though he'd ridden with her all day on that wolf hunt.

"You're Pedro d'Aragón's seigneur." Isabella refused Pèire's offer to pour more wine for her, intent on their argument. "The pope didn't call on him to fight here. And if Pedro does come to aid any of his counts and viscounts, he has his own armies."

"Who knows how it stands now?" Pèire slathered a small loaf of brioix with feta, using an ancient and useless dagger as a dinner knife. "Narbonne and Montpelhièr belong to Pedro's family. The Count of Toulouse is married to Pedro's sister. The counts and viscounts are under Pedro's protection."

"And we pay taxes to Pedro. What happens in Toulouse is not our business."

"Sebastián's other lands are just outside Toulouse," Pèire said. "And the new viscount of Carcassonne will wants much higher taxes from us for Arracheuse. So, he's bound to ask my loyalty oath." He held a finger up when Isabella started to object. "Where Simon comes from, they don't ask oaths from women."

Isabella didn't argue. Pèire's prejudice against Angevines and Normans was firmly set after King Richard's disgraceful actions in the Outremer. No one ever mentioned that several of the men Pèire trusted most were Normans, like his marshal and the parish priest. Among the new invaders, Simon de Montfort, the new viscount of Carcassonne, was a zealot, eager to rid the Languedoc of its goodmen and goodwomen, whom the pope called heretics. She sought a new argument.

"No one would ever dream of calling Valerós a heretic stronghold." When Pèire didn't respond, she said, "We are too far from where the invaders are crusading.

"You and I aren't fools, *xiqueta*. We need to prepare this castle and the villages for a siege. We can't pretend it isn't possible."

She hadn't won a single point with Pèire, yet she said, "We aren't going to war."

"That's my fondest hope." Katelina's words sounded empty of reassurance.

"At least you won't have to worry about that scorpion Renoud coming from Toulouse to bother you." Pèire laughed. "He's too much of a duck-hearted coward to leave the Montcava villa, what with *francimand* knights out to rob and burn the countryside."

Like water pouring from a sieve, pleasure drained out of the peaceful moments under the courtyard arbor. Pèire's last jibe didn't strike Isabella as humorous. Even with all the extra water, the wine turned bitter in her mouth.

Katelina's bracelets jangled as she settled her hand on Isabella's. "We'll just do what we must, *xiqueta*. Keep going forward. Do the next most important things to be done. Perhaps you should help Guillem with provisioning the castle for a siege."

"The most important thing," Pèire said, "will be scrounging silver to pay taxes for Arracheuse. Damn that *punxor* for mortgaging the place, when every dancing angel in heaven could see he'd never be any kind of crusader."

"Senhór," Katelina's voice held caution, "you are talking about Isabella's departed father. May his soul find peace in heaven."

"Indeed." Pèire lifted his shoulders, pretending he wasn't conceding to correction. "But our Isabella knows the real world for what it is. There's no use pretending. Or hiding truths from her."

Isabella shoved her wine cup aside, preparing to return to her chores. While wanting badly to pretend.

That Valerós could hide from the coming war.

That the tax collector wouldn't arrive—at least, not before she'd done all she could to scrounge silver

That Montcava scorpions didn't intend to kill her. Or steal her son.

Pèire rose, either tired or bored of the conversation. "I'm going out. My new horse needs riding, and I'd like to take a look-see at that mantrap that caught you."

"You are off to work, Isabella?" Katelina asked after Pèire had left them.

"I'm going to sharpen quills and work in the scriptorium. We'll gain a little silver that way, too." She'd learned copyist skills in Toulouse, and now replicated the worn Gospel scrolls Pèire bought in the Outremer. Benito, the arms master, sold her copies whenever he was in Narbonne. It wasn't a deceit, she reasoned, because each copy contained a true Gospel, only made to look ancient.

For that afternoon, inking another Gospel of St-John was the best way to go forward. To help pay their taxes.

6
Strangers at the Gate

"COME HELP THE SENESCHAL welcome tonight's guests, Isabella."

Near sunset, after Pèire had brushed down his new horse, he guided her toward the gate, his boney fingers grasping her elbow, a stick in his other hand, though he needed no assistance walking.

"Since the snow melted, we've had a flood of pilgrims to feed. With Angevines and *francimand* knights all over God's creation nowadays, I want to know everyone's true business. Else they can find a rock pile outside and bivouac there."

At the gate, Pèire hailed the minstrels Isabella had encountered earlier in the day.

"That man looks like a Norman." Pèire pointed his stick at the tall jongleur who'd rescued her earlier. The jongleur stood with an unstrung rebec over his shoulder, a reasonable instrument for a traveling musician; another minstrel carried the fishing gear.

"He speaks both Catalan and the common tongue. Though with an accent." Isabella didn't mention her lingering distrust for the man. Pèire would uncover danger before she did. "He's the jongleur who freed me from the trap this morning."

"He looks Norman," Pèire insisted quite loudly. "Even a Norman can be trained to speak properly and climb trees."

The jongleur overheard, as Pèire intended. "Please, senhór, a Norman or his Viking cousin had his way with one of my ancestors. But my mother is a Celt, left behind in Narbonne by crusaders sailing for Jerusalem. She prays to St-Patrick and St-Brigit."

"And your father?" Pèire asked.

"I never met the man, so I can't speak for him."

Pèire laughed. "You sing? I've known Celts who can make the birds cry themselves green with jealousy."

The visitor bowed. "Chrétien of Narbonne. A singer of troubadours' songs, at your service."

Given the jongleur's accent and his earlier comments about strange southern ways, Narbonne was not his natal city, though he probably had a Celtic mother. Isabella caught the odor of horse from his clothing, more than came from his brief ride on Al-Malik.

"Troubadour or tramp?" she asked.

Chrétien-of-not-Narbonne bowed again. "My songs could make the Queen of Jerusalem into an honest woman. Or teach the Angevine John Lackland to be an honorable king."

"That's a proud boast. Let's hear you at supper." Pèire greeted the other minstrels, taking their leader by the hand and thanking them for helping Isabella.

A flock of pilgrims and Cistercian monks crowded at the gate to beg shelter, the usual travelers that the past century of crusades had created: pale northerners mixed in with dusky southerners, Moorish men whose forefathers had been left behind generations ago after invading Christendom as far as Poitiers and Provence. Pèire walked down to greet them. Isabella drew her cloak around her shoulders to ward off the chill as the sun disappeared. When she moved to follow Pèire, a man in a scribe's brown robe stepped in front of her.

"My humble apologies," she started to say.

He whirled around, his dark eyes smoldering, a Moor with a trim beard and long hair prematurely streaked with white. He might once have been handsome, but his chisel-planed face now had a vicious gash across the right cheek and a deep cut in the left eyebrow. Another scar slashed through his lip, twisting his mouth into a savage expression. He carried the satchel of a scribe but was an entirely different species from the well-fed priests and clerks among the pilgrims. The broad shoulders under the rough wool robe and his fighter's stance indicated that he'd trained for a different vocation.

The scribe avoided her eyes as she apologized, and he made a sign with his fingers to ward off evil. He must be one of the Perfected goodmen the Church called heretics, who feel polluted by the touch of a woman. The idea disgusted her.

"I'm sure you are capable of bringing evil on yourself. Without my help." She pulled her cloak close, piqued by his rudeness, and went to join Pèire at the line of pilgrims and monks.

"Grandfather, did you see the Moor who..." she began.

Unexpectedly, Father Clémence appeared, that hulking mass of spleen who had been her confessor in Toulouse. He abruptly brushed aside the scribe in a plodding intent to reach Isabella, who recoiled from him just as Sebastián had done as a small child.

You no longer have power over me.

She fought the disgust creeping up her spine at the sight of him. The man who'd heard every one of her secrets and offered only condemnation, never forgiveness, never holding out his hand to protect her from the travesties in the Montcava villa. She'd wished him to the devil then, when she was too young and nursed fantasies about expediting his demise. People said Clémence went to Constantinople after the Normans took that city. Too bad he wasn't buried there, like her husband Nicolau had been.

Clémence bowed when Pèire approached. "God be with you, Pèire Leteric. I have messages for you from Simon de Montfort."

So, the call to crusade had come to their domus, in the misshapen form of Father Clémence. Isabella next had to suffer the clasp of the priest's wart-plagued, damp hands in greeting.

"Senhóra Isabella," Clémence droned, "they still miss your son at the House of Montcava. I'm here to persuade you to return home."

She grimaced, hoping it looked like a smile. *The Montcava household will still be missing my son long after Satan lets Judas escape the precincts of hell.*

·

A bevy of snowy-frocked Cistercian monks, plump and sprightly as partridges, engaged the seneschal's attention. Pèire became bored.

He walked with Isabella to the parapets above the gate, where they watched the seneschal hail the last of the visiting pilgrims.

"Look below. Your boy escaped Benito's watch again."

Sebastián darted among the visiting pilgrims, following that hostile scribe with the white-streaked hair. The boy snatched something shiny off the cobbles and sprinted up the crooked alley behind the smithy. The scribe chased after him.

Her body juddered with fear again, like when the net jerked her toward the sky. Here was danger. If the Montcavas sent anyone, she believed it would be a mercenary behind a mask.

Sebastián was quick, but the scribe leaped against the alley wall and landed yards ahead, like a cat pouncing on prey. He pinned the boy to the wall. Undaunted, Sebastián dropped what he'd grabbed and twisted free, then dived into an archway that led to the cellars under the castle.

The scribe retrieved what Sebastián dropped, a steel dagger, which the scribe tucked into the top of his boot. The last of the afternoon sun lit his ravaged face, turning it the color of burnt umber. He glided back up the alley. Back at the gate, the scribe met the Celtic jongleur and the motley minstrels, abandoning the Cistercians he'd come with.

Pèire whistled softly through his teeth. "I bet the wolf you hunted walked the same way."

Still struggling with fear, she pointed to the two men below. "Those men are dangerous. That scribe and the jongleur. They aren't what they seem."

"Those two?" Pèire sniffed. "I bet they're gamblers running from bad debts. *Xiqueta,* I saw you with that miserable priest. Was I wrong about the Montcavas? Bad news?"

"He says Sebastián's uncle Renoud wants him in Toulouse. Perhaps those two men are Montcava agents."

"Only if God has surrendered this green earth to the devil himself." Pèire seemed thoughtful, still inspecting the night's visitors. In what passed as a whisper, he said, "Sebastián had best come along when you marry."

"But I'm not marrying anyone." His words vibrated in her ear, compounding confusion with the day's fears.

"Given the threat from Simon and the *francimand* invaders, I need to protect all of you. My old comrade Gerard de Chartrain will be here by Pentecost. He's Philippe's viscount, and as your husband, he can protect you. And Sebastián's estates."

"You agreed before that I can protect Sebastián's estates myself." She kept her voice steady, not wanting to sound like a beggar. The dread in her belly wanted her to drop to her knees and beg.

"I believed that last year, *xiqueta*." Pèire didn't look her way, as if he knew how he'd betrayed her trust. "But I've been thinking—in ways I haven't had to do since I came home from the Outremer. I need a battle strategy for you."

"Battle strategy." She echoed back the words he'd formerly used to describe his life in the Outremer. *"We were forever calculating battle strategy."*

"These invaders aren't like us, my girl. Men here respect a woman as regent or steward. But with this new crusade, you need a husband to protect your land from those bandits. And we've always known that if Renoud made a case in the courts, he could force your boy to return to Toulouse."

Her insides tumbled, her belly wanted to give up its lunch. She sought an argument that didn't sound as frantic as she felt. "Does Katelina know your plan?"

He made a familiar gesture of dismissal. "She insists that God didn't make you for marriage, so I had to make this plan on my own. It'll take a bit, but she'll come around."

The feeling that rose highest at that moment? Betrayal. Her belly screamed for justice. "Grandfather, you said just today there was no use hiding truths from me."

"That's why I'm telling you now, *xiqueta*."

"And you told us that your friend Gerard went to a monastery after his wife died. Why would he want to marry now?" *Why would he want to marry me?*

"He's doing me a favor, for old time's sake. Gerard is ancient as the hills, like me. He's not looking to make babies. He won't make your life hell."

She knew hell. Hell was the prison of marriage to a stranger. She dug deeper for an argument to persuade him while resisting the frisson of fear and disgust that wouldn't go away. "When Eleanor was my age, she'd ruled the Aquitaine for six years. She rode at the head of her own army on crusade to Jerusalem."

"She did it to show off her Amazon costume." Pèire, amused by his own story, didn't notice the storm of emotion that gripped Isabella. "Knights had to protect Eleanor instead of fighting Saracens. Here, our seigneurs appreciate women who can keep accounts and manage the domus. But no more queens, not after the mess when Jerusalem had only queens. No, it's the wrong time for you, and I'm sorry for it."

As horror and dismay flowed through her bloodstream, she bucked up, the way she'd learned to do while paralyzed by fear in Toulouse. The only way to go was forward, with bravado.

"I can do more than the queens of Jerusalem could ever dream." She immediately regretted boasting to her grandfather, who had led men through the gates of hell in the Outremer and brought them safely home. "I have no reason to fear the French invaders. We are innocent of any crimes the pope called to be cleansed in the Langue-doc. If you lend me your knights, I can protect Sebastián's land. Including the Fontcours and Montcava estates in Toulouse."

Pèire sighed, which meant he was out of patience. "Gerard is the best of men. You'll have all the power you need with him as your protector."

"It's my duty to protect others here at Valerós, not to be pro-tected by a stranger." If she said it over and over, it might quell the fear that struck her at Pèire's brutal decision. Marriage? She pre-ferred any other danger. Even invading crusaders. Or a wolf den. Or mantraps.

He rubbed her shoulder gently, the way he did when he taught her to ride, encouraging her to get back on a horse after a bad fall. "You're brave enough to do your duty come Pentecost, *xiqueta*."

34

7
Under a Scarred Birch

Jean-Luc at Valerós
30 days before Pentecost

WHEN THE CASTLE VILLAGE HAD finished the day's chores and no longer needed him to mend a kettle or shoe a horse or repair armor, Jean-Luc walked to the terraced garden below the castle. Given a few more warm days, the gardeners could harvest the early lettuces and set the sun-loving plants to grow. In the dying afternoon light, the place was deserted. He came to find solitude and to harvest comfrey to treat the scar on his thigh, which plagued him in the cold. It felt like a chilblain, gnawing at the core of his being.

Sheltered by the terrace's upper wall, a nice patch of comfrey had appeared after the snow melted. He tucked a handful of the scratchy leaves into a pocket of his jerkin and sat on a bench in the purpling light to listen to the sounds echoing from the castle: wooden wheels on cobbled streets, the calls as the guard changed on the parapets, the chanting of the priest calling people to vespers. An aged birch tree stood by the wall, its heart scarred by fire, but tender frills of green at the tips of scorched branches yearned to unfurl and declare spring.

Twenty days since arriving at Easter, and Jean-Luc still had more questions than answers to send by courier to the viscount. Was Pèire Leteric of sound mind? His men still capable fighters? Were Pèire's villages filled with heretics? Was Pèire's daughter a shrew? A ninny? He hadn't gotten close enough to the family to learn much.

In the nearby woods, mistletoe hung from the highest branches of the oak trees that nestled among sweet chestnut, mountain ash, and stone pines. He wanted a few pieces of mistletoe for a potion to relieve pain, plus a few twigs to protect against new wounds. He searched his memory for the best times for gathering mistletoe. Was it the sixth day after the new moon?

Then he cursed his foolishness. How in Our Lord's holy name had he got so superstitious as to care about the proper day for cutting twigs to protect from wounds? His dagger was sufficient protection.

On the terrace below, an animal rustled in the vegetation and then yelped in surprise.

"*Ai, Dèu!*"

It wasn't a creature but the muffled cry of a woman or a child.

Jean-Luc leapt over the wall to the lower terrace where shadows wrestled amidst the rushes near the pond. He grabbed for the larger form, instinctively protecting the smaller one. As he held the man against the wall with one hand, he thrust the child—a young boy— behind him. The attacker had the look of a Frankish man but wore a quilted Greek corselet and struggled to reach for a short-sword at his waist. He fended off Jean-Luc's knife with a studded gauntlet and then pushed to escape Jean-Luc's grasp.

Jean-Luc grabbed a garden stake and took a pikeman's stance to fend off the swordsman, sliding in the garden-muck as he sought his footing.

"Cuckold!" The man shouted a string of profanities that Jean-Luc didn't completely understand. The bastard's sword pommel clattered as he freed it from its Eastern scabbard, telling Jean-Luc this was no great swordsman.

Jean-Luc didn't stand a chance against the blade, so instead he used his greater height to bring the long pole down on the man's arm. He delivered a second stroke with too much force and heard a crack when he whapped his foe's arm, breaking the stake, but perhaps not the man's arm. Yet Jean-Luc succeeded in beating the man back.

The attacker sprinted over the stone wall in retreat.

Jean-Luc jumped onto the wall to follow, nearly colliding with that child, and then swayed to gain his balance atop the stone wall.

"Watch out!" The child shrieked like a swordmaster yelling on the practice field.

The brigand sliced upward with his dagger.

"*Merde!*" Jean-Luc cried, as the sting turned to pounding pain in a heartbeat. He struggled to keep his place on the wall as the brigand ran for the woods. Tumbling back into the garden, Jean-Luc fell into brambles and then tried to stand but couldn't. The attacker had cut deeply into his thigh.

The boy bent over him, his pale face and copper hair ghost-like in the disappearing light, grey eyes curious instead of frightened. Pèire Leteric's grandson, always where he shouldn't be.

"Go back to the castle, donzel." Jean-Luc spoke calmly, as if he watched this scene from across the way. "Tell the marshal to come."

"But Marshal Guillem will chastise me for being outside the castle at night."

"Tell someone else." Jean-Luc gasped. "Please. I need help."

The boy disappeared into the shadows, although it seemed he ran the wrong direction for the castle gate, while Jean-Luc pressed the vein to try to stop the dark-on-dark stain flooding his breeches.

At least it was the same damned thigh.

8
Ululations

ISABELLA SEARCHED FOR SEBASTIÁN in the kitchens first, and then the stables, where the younger boys were listening to gruesome stories the stable master told about the Siege of Acre. When she climbed the steps up the castle walls to ask the guards, she spied Sebastián in an alley down below, a bundle of rags and mud.

To her dismay, that scribe once again had a predator's grip on Sebastián's shoulder, headed toward the passage that led under the ramparts and out of the castle.

She cried out, an ululating alarm, and then leaped from the walls, landing on the scribe's back. He rolled over onto her and reached for the dagger in his boot, but got his hand tangled in his long robe. Isabella had room enough and time to thrust her knee into his groin.

"*Jhezu del tron!*"

The man's arms wrapped around her as he folded in pain. Pinioned in a hot embrace, she felt the power of his shoulder muscles as he panted near her ear like a lover, his breath perfumed with cloves. She lifted her knee again, to move him off her. The man who was stealing her son away.

"Stop, Mother!" Sebastián cried. "He's helping me."

"Infernal angels!" The man choked, writhed. She shuddered, alarmed to have that man on top of her.

"The smith fought a brigand. He's wounded," Sebastián said.

A guard lifted the scribe to his feet. Isabella wanted to rub her skinned knee, but instead drew herself up to her full height.

"What are you doing with my son?"

"Helping him to—"

"What in the name of all the golden angels is going on here?" Pèire came down the alley, followed closely by Felicia and Beatriz. "The smith is bleeding in the garden." Sebastián had his eyes on the scribe, who nodded, which seemed to restore the boy's bravado. And which destroyed Isabella's sense that she was protecting her son. "A man grabbed me. He cut the smith. Badly." Sebastián's voice rose, its pitch matching the wild fear still beating in Isabella's heart. *The Montcavas had come for her son!* "We need to go help him now."

Pèire's frown meant future trouble for Sebastián. "Guillem, find the smith. Only the golden angels know how he's faring."

"We'll help." Beatriz dragged Felicia by the hand. "We'll have to stitch him up. And Isabella is squeamish."

I'm not squeamish, Isabella protested silently. *I just hate blood. I have every reason to hate it.*

After Guillem left with four of his men and the two sisters, Pèire's hand settled on Sebastián's shoulder.

"Is there not a rule?" Pèire said mildly.

Sebastián drew up like a soldier and looked at the scribe while he spoke. "I'm not to be outside the walls alone after dark."

"And, donzel, what are the consequences?"

"I shall be confined to the barracks and submit to Master Guillem in the morning. And I am sorry, Master Scribe, for the trouble I caused you." He bowed to Pèire and then walked up the alley toward the barracks without looking back.

"Grandfather," Isabella heard beggary in her voice, "that priest warned us. His uncle intends—"

"Òc." Pèire waved a hand, which always meant stop speaking. "Guillem will attend to it. We need to properly greet our guests." He took the scribe's hand in a Catalan greeting. "For the love of the dancing angels, forgive us. Please tell us your name."

"I'm called Tomás of Barcelona." He spoke in an accent unlike what she'd heard in Barcelona.

Unnerved that Pèire didn't seem to share her alarm, that the Montcavas had sent at least one man to grab her son, Isabella imitated his greeting, though she still suspected that this scribe was another agent pursuing her. She held out her hand in the traditional

Catalan way. "I am so sorry for your injury, Master Scribe. It seems you were right to ward off evil."

The scribe nodded at her apology but didn't touch the hand she offered. Like a goodman who felt polluted by a woman's touch.

"What set you out on the road from Barcelona, Master Scribe?" Pèire's voice dripped honey as bait for truth or lies. Isabella listened closely. Perhaps he was as suspicious as she was. "A vocation for the Church, eh?"

The scribe bent his head in assent. "My father is a seigneur with little land to divide among his many sons. Fortunately, I'm not made for a worldly life."

He spoke in a mellifluous, smoky tenor. His long fingers, ink-stained nearly to the second knuckle, showed no writer's bunion, and the ink didn't hide the fine web of scars on the backs of his hands. The only part of the scribe that wasn't false was his burnt-umber skin.

Pèire said, "Come with us to dinner, Master Scribe, and tell us your story. One season we fought alongside knights from Barcelona against the Angevines in Gascony. Did we meet your father there?"

"My father is not an adventurer." Master Tomás named his father, offering the most common name south of the Dordogne River. She marked another lie while studying the scars on his face.

"Which order will you join, Master Tomás?" Pèire asked, still pouring on the honey. "The Knights Templar? The Hospitallers of Jerusalem? The Ransomers?"

"I'm just a humble scribe." The man didn't see that Pèire was having him on—since a man of God isn't perpetually poised to grab the steel blade in his boot. Yet Pèire wasn't yet demanding truth from a visiting liar.

"I pray God helps you find your way in these confusing times." Isabella did not mask her disbelief.

The scribe glanced at her, his eyes blazing. He still stood too close: she smelled cloves again, like when his breath had been hot in her ear during their mistaken embrace.

Pèire strolled up the street, his arm around a man who might be a Montcava agent. Isabella brushed away the sense of being betrayed by the only man she loved, her grandfather. She knew that he'd defend his family against all enemies. But still…marriage as a battle strategy?

She needed to defend against the House of Montcava now. She couldn't wait for Pentecost and Pèire's ill-considered battle strategy. The day presented enormous evidence of imminent danger.

A mantrap that was surely meant for her. Or Sebastián.

Clémence's dire warning, that Renoud wanted Sebastián.

Sebastián grabbed by a brigand in the garden.

Pèire welcoming a man too likely to be a Montcava agent.

She needed to prepare to fight back now, not wait through most of the spring, until Pentecost brought an elderly stranger who might save her, at the worst cost she could imagine.

Katelina was her only ally. Perhaps Katelina could convince Pèire not to cast her off to the care of strangers. However, it struck Isabella, like a bright light in the dark of night, that she must do once more what she'd learned in Toulouse: turn fear into anger and keep that anger until she had a plan. Until she knew how to go forward.

9

Aqua Vitae

Jean-Luc at Valerós
30 days before Pentecost

JEAN-LUC SUCKED IN THE cool mountain air when he again failed to stand. He crawled on his elbows toward the garden gate, which seemed leagues away. But then he grew sleepy and warm, until it wasn't important to go anywhere.

He wanted to greet the dark angels when they came, but before he could speak, one angel touched his leg. He cried out to the Holy Virgin Mary to intercede.

"God forgive me," he whispered. "I did not believe in you."

When Jean-Luc woke, the angels were replaced by mortal women who stitched his leg while one of Pèire's men held him down on a narrow cot.

"Here, man, bite on this." The soldier placed a leather truncheon between Jean-Luc's teeth. "Seems you've had this kind of needlework done before."

Worse than the stitching was the sting each time they poured an evil-smelling concoction over his wound. The two small women worked together, his gore smearing their aprons. One woman held his flesh while the other sewed. When they finished, one woman left, pleading fatigue. The soldier removed the truncheon. He handed Jean-Luc a flask.

"Pèire Leteric's aqua vitae." He grinned. "You should be honored that he chooses to share with you."

The remaining angel and the bordonier shifted him in the cot and replaced the bed linen. Only one linsey-woolsey square preserved any modesty. As he reached to keep the covering in place, she

42

had the good grace to turn her head, but he saw her suppress a smile. He'd surrendered his modesty before he awoke; they had stitched far up his groin.

"Your breeches are hopeless," she said. "We shall find you another pair before you need them."

She handed him a flask of water. Pretty in a common way, her face reflected the glow of the torchlight. From her inquisitive smile and the way she tilted her head, regarding him in the manner of a lively, curious wren, she seemed to be asking a question, but he didn't understand what she said.

"What's your name?" He couldn't speak above a whisper. The aqua vitae left him light-headed; he had too little blood left to mix with strong drink.

"Call me Felicia," she said.

"*Merci beaucoup, doux ange,*" he said. A sweet angel had come for him, when before he'd only known devils.

10
Crusaders at Supper

Isabella at Valerós
30 days before Pentecost

ISABELLA SAT FOR DINNER in the great hall, where Katelina and Beatriz contrived to feed everyone each night. Pèire didn't like dining alone, so they fed tables-full of knights, donzels, and bachelor bordoniers as if Valerós were the standing camp of a small army. With pilgrims and guests, the room buzzed, every table and corner filled with people who must be fed.

It was Friday and now that Lent was over, Pèire had given up deprivation for the remainder of the year. He dug in with relish when the kitchen girls brought broiled trout stuffed with black mushrooms, and then sheep's cheese with crusty brioix still hot from the brick ovens. They carried bowls of spring chicory and purslane in olive oil, plus garden rocket, lightly fried to tone down its bitterness. The old herb woman in the kitchens called it an aphrodisiac, so it was never served without Pèire joking at some man's expense.

Pèire's favorites were foods he'd brought home from the Outremer: dried peaches stewed and softened to accompany the trout; chickpeas ground into a garlicky paste and spooned onto unleavened bread; cracked semolina berries floating in oil with mint and onion. And palm-dates, the only food Pèire paid good silver for, buying them off the ships at the Narbonne docks. They tasted like burnt sugar, so chewy one needed hot wine to wash away the sticky remains.

Isabella sat by Katelina at Pèire's table, pretending to be calm, with ordinary life spinning around them. The world had turned upside down since breakfast, like tumbling in a mantrap.

At the end of the room, Tomás the scribe watched her, his hand at his side again making a sign to ward off evil. She knew what he saw: a woman past the flush of youth, without adornment, dressed in pale grey and fawn, because she hadn't the patience for baubles. As her husband Nicolau had often commented, she resembled Pèire too much for anyone to find her beautiful.

A twitch flickered across the scribe's scarred lips.

"That man wants you," Katelina whispered.

"You've never been so wrong. He's laughing at me."

"You didn't learn to flirt properly. It's a failure in my teaching," she said. "Drop your gaze when you catch his eye. Then look up and smile. Touch your head covering, the way a young girl touches her hair. Then look away again."

"I'm not looking away," Isabella said. "He's a sneak, a liar, and he's challenging me."

Katelina laughed. "You know, with those white streaks in his hair, he might be any age between thirty and fifty. But when he moves, you can tell he isn't more than twenty-five. A man like that would have challenged me, too, when I was your age."

Pèire summoned the jongleur, repeating what he always said to minstrels, "We'll have *cançós de guerra* now, no *amor* rubbish."

Katelina demurred as usual, but *cançós de guerra* was what they always had. Chrétien paid truth to his boast, with *cançós d'Arturo* that jongleurs had been singing for many seasons, changing his voice for each character, so one might believe it was Lancelot's own beautiful tenor and Guinevere in a lovely falsetto. He used familiar tunes like *"Reis Glorios"* and *"Parti de Mal"* to move from one part of a story to the next, and therefore had most of the room sighing when he stepped down for a cup of wine.

The girls at the serving table abandoned their work to flock around the jongleur like bees on borage, chatting and smiling until the kitchen matron chased them back to work. Left alone, the jongleur leaned over for whispered conversation with the scribe. When Tomás rose from the table, Chrétien's arm fell from his companion's shoulder in a tender gesture and his eyes followed the scribe across the room.

"So that's how it is with the jongleur," Katelina said. "But the scribe prefers women."

"No, he makes a sign to ward off evil when he sees me."

"Most men would, after finding your knee in their privates."

"He did it when he first saw me. It's infuriating."

"Trust me. That man was born to make love to women. You can have him for the asking."

"Your talent as a procuress is wasted on me. And the scribe says he's not made for a worldly life."

Katelina laughed, though more of a cough, shaking her head. She reached for the brioix, her bracelets and rings jangling.

"If that's true, save him from making a terrible mistake. Enjoy yourself for a few days."

Isabella tore at her own bread. "It's unthinkable. If he's anything, he's an itinerant mercenary. If he has a master, it's likely as not the House of Montcava who sent him here to spy or to steal Sebastián. He lied to Pèire, claiming to be from Barcelona but he speaks Catalan as if he were raised where no one else ever heard of that tongue." As she shredded the scribe's character, the brioix was reduced to crumbs on her trencher. "Now, if I met a warrior as great as Pèire…"

"If you met a warrior determined to live an honorable life? Who'd go into the world as your comrade? Or haven't you decided what you want most?" Katelina turned serious. "Perhaps fifty years ago Pèire was no greater than that handsome scribe over there."

"A scribe? That's the face of a battle-wrecked mercenary."

"Why can't you take your eyes off him, *xiqueta?*"

The scribe poured wine and whispered to Chrétien-of-certainly-not-Narbonne. The jongleur caught her staring and raised his goblet. Isabella grasped her cup and toasted the two of them for being more bold-faced liars than she ever hoped to be.

"Do you want me to ask why they lied to Pèire?" Katelina continued to tease—because Isabella hadn't yet told her how the world had changed. When Isabella didn't answer, Katelina touched her hand. "Don't let today's calamities and Pèire's talk of war affect your good sense. Tomorrow we will—"

"Katelina, my confessor in Toulouse—remember my stories of his cruelties? He's here. With a warning that Renoud wants Sebastián, and me, to return to Toulouse."

"*Ai.* The devil hasn't taken that priest to his bosom yet?"

"I wished for that every single day when I lived in Toulouse."

"But you know, *xiqueta,* Pèire will continue to fight Renoud. Valerós will always rise above the House of Montcava."

"But Pèire didn't tell you." Isabella got the words out slowly; the horror still churned inside. "His battle strategy for this crusade?"

"Which I pray will keep Pèire out of battle," Katelina said. "I pray three times a day that he won't be called into this travesty with the French invaders."

"He's asked Gerard de Chartrain to marry me, to take me away. For my protection. And Sebastián's. Against Renoud, and to save Sebastián's lands from the invading French."

Isabella's attention drifted for a moment, back to that lying scribe who might have come to capture or spy on her. But he was whispering with the Celtic jongleur.

Katelina looked suitably shocked at the news. Pèire had indeed held this from her. "I didn't know."

"He didn't tell you because he thought you'd disagree."

"I very much do disagree. What a terrible idea."

"Can you stop it, Katelina?" Now that she'd started to beg, the words flowed, relating the abhorrent news. "Gerard is coming at Pentecost, but I will not be trapped in marriage again. The notion leaves me physically ill."

"Stop it?" Katelina frowned, as if confused.

"You can always persuade Pèire. And you know how marriage failed me before. You know why I'm terrified."

"I know you—well enough to know that you are never truly terrified. You always find a way to go forward."

"Please, Katelina. You are my only ally in this. Only you know what happened to me in Toulouse."

"Which you made me swear never to reveal to Pèire." She stirred the remains of dinner on her trencher with her jewel-handled dinner knife. "Do you want me to tell him now?"

47

"What? No. Just convince Pèire that his strategy with his friend Gerard is a bad idea."

"But I can't." Katelina had lost every bit of the lighthearted way she'd begun at dinner, when she's been intent on boosting Isabella's spirits. "If it's Pèire's battle strategy, I swore an oath not to interfere. And I must help if he asks."

"Battle strategy? We aren't at war. This is my life. You must—"

Katelina grasped Isabella's hand, silver rings digging into flesh, and dragged her to stand at the same moment that the knights and squires in the hall jumped up. Even Pèire rose and faced the door.

An older knight stood under the arched entrance to the great room, obviously French from his dress and the livery of the two men with him, and as noble as a king. The French invaders had indeed come for Pèire.

"Pèire, you old rascal." The magnificent knight spoke in the common tongue of the Languedoc, with a French accent. "May I beg a meal and doss here for the night?"

At Isabella's side, the fearless Katelina choked a sob.

11
Susurrus of Prayer

JEAN-LUC CLOSED HIS EYES, hoping exhaustion would carry him beyond the usual plague of bad dreams. He hadn't drifted far, however, when his angel returned to sit by his side. He didn't have
strength to speak, so he drifted again.

An angel lifted his hand to slip her warm, dry palm under his
while stroking his arm as his mother did when he and his brother
had spotted fever. His angel whispered a prayer. In his drifting confusion, it sounded like Greek rather than Latin. When she rested
her hand on the tangled scar on his arm, her touch felt like comfort.
Which he could never have.

The angel prayed. The sea rocked him.

■

His brother Yves dropped to the deck beside him, and they crouched
together on the transport ship floating outside Constantinople in the
pre-dawn. Jean-Luc listened to the soft susurrus of his men's prayers
as waves gently rocked the ship. With no wind rising, the air lay
heavy with the odor of huddled, unwashed men; sweat from last
night's labors mingled with the sour smell of nervous anticipation.

"We shouldn't be here, brother," Yves said. The chainmail of his
long hauberk rang like tiny bells as he settled on the deck alongside
Jean-Luc. Like him, Yves was too tall to stretch out his legs; they both
sat cramped, waiting for the battle to begin.

"Hush, Yves, our men will hear." He fidgeted with his boar-tooth charm, ending a prayer.

"I am whispering, little brother," Yves said. "Don't turn twitchy on me now. It's not like you. Besides, our men can only hear the speech we just shouted for them: '*Deus vult!*'"

Jean-Luc swallowed, his throat hoarse from oratory. As captains and brothers, they always worked in unison. Except for now, when neither brother could stop picking the same quarrel. The only difference between them had ever been that Yves went on crusade for the joy of battle, while Jean-Luc did it to expiate sin. Yves liked to fight, and Jean-Luc couldn't stop sinning. This crusade to Constantinople did not serve either of their needs So they quarreled.

"We gave our oath, Yves."

"God doesn't care about oaths to faithless Venetians." Yves whispered "I'm here because you are."

Since Antioch three years ago, Yves's face no longer mirrored his brother's. A glass grenade of wet Greek fire—naphtha, pitch, and sulfur—had enveloped Yves in flames. Jean-Luc rolled him in the sand to smother the fire, lucky that he'd escaped with only his arm burned. But now children ran in fright when they saw Yves, and some women turned their heads away. Yves laughed at that: *A good woman can tell I've still got what matters.*

"We swore allegiance to Hugues de Beaurain." Jean-Luc named the French lord they'd served since they were squires, against whom Jean-Luc repeatedly sinned: he was in love with his lord's wife. "Hugues says this battle will make our reputations as captains."

"We earned reputations as captains and sinners long before now," Yves said. "Hugues may be the greatest crusader knight, but God knows we should never have come to Constantinople."

They'd began arguing when the Venetians and Franks rioted in Zara, when many knights either left for home or sailed on to Syria. The remnants of the army, including Hugues's men, made a detour to assert the power of the Holy Roman Church over schismatics in the east. All Jean-Luc wanted was to be united with Yves again.

"At least we're on the outside this time, Yves. That's better than when we were stuck inside Jaffa, when the Saracens held siege."

"Listen, little brother. You've been in this city before," Yves said. "What happens when every ignorant Alfons and Gombal in this army sees the treasures of Constantinople?"

"The Normans and Venetians signed the pact last night. Our men will take all booty to the priests." Most soldiers fought for booty, to pay the cost of crusading and to go home rich. "We can keep order among our men, Yves. We fared better in the Zara riots than other captains."

"We had better odds then. I just promised the men all my share of the booty if they stick with us inside the city walls. Make the same promise, Jean-Luc. We don't want any share of this. It's a black mark on our souls to take the Cross and then kill Christians for booty."

"You never cared about your soul before," Jean-Luc said.

"And you didn't go crusading to get rich, little brother."

"Fine. I'll promise my men the same."

"And then we go home," Yves said. "Our father will find me a dim-sighted French bride too blind to see my face." He shifted on the deck of the transport, and his chainmail rang again. "I hate the cold winters in the Pays de France, but I'm tired of fighting for a pack of greedy crusaders and priests. It's enough to turn me into a Bogomil heretic or goodman from Toulouse."

Jean-Luc shivered. His brother's views were dangerously heretical. "A goodman gives up women, war, and meat."

"Fine, then not a heretic. But I'm going home after this. Are you ready to give up playing mercenary for a pack of priests?"

"What do we know about anything except *sodalitas, fidelitas, virtus*?" Jean-Luc quoted the oath of their brotherhood, the bonfraires.

Yves grasped Jean-Luc's hand in the sign of the bonfraires. "We have the rest of our lives to find out." He started to move away, his chainmail ringing in the darkness. "We won't quarrel again, little brother. It makes us both unhappy."

Jean-Luc fingered the boar's-tooth charm again. He prayed *Mater mitis, sed viri nescia*, the way his mother did when she slipped the charm into his hand twenty years ago and kissed him goodbye.

·

"Hush," the angel by his bed said. "I'll say the prayer for you."

Pray for us, O Holy Mother of God, that we may be made worthy.

51

12
Cançós de Guerra

Isabella at Valerós
30 days before Pentecost

THE KNIGHT IN THE archway towered over most men in the room, his silver-white hair glinting in the candlelight like an angel's halo.

"Who is it?" Isabella whispered.

"Hugues, the Marquis de Beaurain." Katelina breathed the name as if it hurt.

"Why are you upset?"

"Surely, he's Simon de Montfort's envoy," Katelina said. "They want Pèire for that filthy invasion. It's my worst fear."

Pèire embraced Hugues like a Catalan shepherd greeting his long-lost brother. They clasped hands in the way Isabella had seen old crusaders do when they journeyed to visit Pèire. As he finally released his visitor's hand, Pèire said, "I never dreamed they'd send you to fetch me."

"I'm not sent. I chose to come." Hugues pulled a sealed packet from the pouch on his belt and gave it to Pèire, who tucked it inside his own tunic without a word.

"Pèire is too old for another crusade," Katelina whispered.

When Pèire led the marquis to the ladies' table, the famous crusader knight took Katelina's hand and kissed it, in the French style. He had reversed the proper order by honoring Katelina first, but then he took Isabella's hand.

"Ma dòmna, I am honored." Hughes bowed again. "Your old friend Pare Abát of Fontcours speaks highly of your talents."

Abashed, she murmured thank you. She'd just been complimented by one of the greatest knights in Christendom. Even as an old man, Hugues incarnated *cortezia*, the spirit of grace and courtly honor in troubadours' songs.

When the men left to sit at Pèire's table, Katelina leaned back. "Just when life seems to be especially fine."

She held a palm-date in her fingers, pushing out the seed with her thumbnail before biting into it. If Isabella hadn't known her better, she'd have thought Katelina fought tears.

.

When Chrétien dug a sharp elbow into his side, Tomás tore his eyes away from the marauding senhóra of Valerós.

"*Ai*, Tomásino! Did that senhóra's knee in your nuts dislocate your vow of celibacy?"

"Me, tempted by a backcountry widow? A woman whose son is next in line to steal Montcava from our family?"

"I laid a significant wager that your vow will expire within fifty days of Easter."

"Who took that bet?"

"Me. Myself. I bet I'm about to collect a pile of silver from myself. And she's the only candidate in the castle."

"No more women. I made my vow because the devil's own adulterous wife nearly got me killed on Cyprus. A plain-as-wool Montcava widow cannot tempt me."

"Yet you can't stop looking."

"I'm curious about the kind of woman our enemies used to get heirs. And what kind of woman marries a thief and a bastard."

"*Aiieee*. Maybe ask her brother-in-law." Another sharp elbow in Tomás's ribs.

Renoud, the current usurping seigneur of Montcava, stood in the archway of the great room. The man Tomás hated most in the world. The sight of him sent searing pain streaking through scar tissue. Tomás clenched his hands, ready to fight. But at that moment, it was impossible.

Rather than saluting the baron of Valerós first, Renoud crossed to the women's table.

"Ma dòmna."

He seized Senhóra Isabella's hand and bowed deeply. The object of his attention seemed even paler than when she tackled Tomás in the alley. Most women's faces warmed and became lovely in torchlight, but she turned ashen. Renoud ignored the other woman at the table and then advanced to fawn over Pèire Leteric.

Tomás had learned in Toulouse that ladies considered the *baquelar* Renoud to be a lion among southern seigneurs, but he was a boil on the hind-side of mankind, as far as Tomás was concerned. After Renoud was seated at the baron's table, he frequently leaned back in his seat to smile at Senhóra Isabella whenever Pèire strained forward to speak with Hugues.

Tomás poked Chrétien, and they drifted together to the table where the minstrels feasted, close enough to the seigneur's table to hear what was said, if one listened closely.

"Senhór Renoud and I married sisters," Hugues said, "though his poor wife now rests with God."

Renoud wore a mournful mask, which Tomás knew to be utter hypocrisy; in Toulouse, the gossips claimed Renoud's marriage had been a travesty of mutual infidelities. Tomás made it his business in the past year to learn everything he could about the man, while letting the seigneur have no glimpse of who'd placed a request for judgment in the bishops' court.

Hugues said, "I didn't want to come south again, after what happened in Béziers last summer. But Senhór Renoud invited us to bivouac at your child's Fontcours estates. To help keep the peace."

"We stand for the Church," Renoud said. "But we need to protect our holdings from any French crusader who mistakes our land for booty."

Tomás rubbed at his scarred cheek, hating the man. You'd think Renoud was a champion of virtue. If you didn't know. The air in the room became difficult to breathe: too smoky, reeking of knights and squires who had ridden horses all day. *Our holdings, our land.* Chrétien, too, whistled a note of disgust and then rested his arm on Tomás's shoulder, as a subtle reminder not to leap over the table and slit Renoud's throat.

"How thoughtful." Pèire wrinkled his nose as if pondering it. "It's nice of you to ride all this way to tell us, Senhór Renoud."

"But I don't want to trespass on your grandson's hospitality," Hugues said. "That is, unless you are joining us, Pèire."

Renoud interrupted. "We seigneurs have to protect our households. I mean to declare the House of Montcavas for the Church."

"*Ai*," Pèire said. "There's not many who'd be so brave."

Renoud looked confused by Pèire's compliment, which made Tomás laugh aloud. Chrétien whispered in Tomás's ear. "Hugues is rich as Croesus, yet he treats the baron of Valerós as his equal."

Tomás reached for his wine cup. Chrétien whispered again.

"So entertaining, sitting at dinner with our enemies. Renoud, for example, has no idea what we plan for him."

Servants brought a new round of supper. While Renoud persisted in asking after his nephew Sebastián, Pèire Leteric ignored his queries and dished food onto Renoud's plate.

"A host shouldn't serve garden rocket when his domus hasn't got a free woman to offer his guests later," Pèire said. His transparent contempt for Renoud piqued Tomás's interest. *The enemy of my enemy is my friend.* Did his father say that? Or his swordmaster in Cairo?

"I'm too old to care." Hugues's handsome face twisted in a wry smile. "In the old days, you and Miquel were the real cocksmen."

Chrétien shivered beside him. The cold that gripped Tomás could have been the hand of his father's ghost, back to urge him onward. These two old men bantered, flinging his father's name as if he were one of them.

"How about you, Senhór Renoud?" Pèire asked. "Best leave off the spicy stuff when you got nothing to stick your sword in later."

"I'm only here to greet my nephew and sister-in-law," Renoud said. "I don't have any other interests."

Senhóra Isabella pushed her plate aside with a clatter, staring down at the table with hooded eyes. The darker woman beside her seemed rapt in watching Pèire Leteric and Hugues de Beaurain.

"With all respect, senhór, ladies are present." Renoud's voice grated on Tomás more than his sore tooth.

"These women?" Pèire said. "They're as comfortable in a camp as in their own beds. They've seen bodies laid out after battle and everything else laid bare, too. There's no Fainting Fleurettes here about to die if they hear about the size of your *punxor.*"

Senhóra Isabella rose from her seat and strode out of the room without a word to anyone, looking to neither side.

When she left, Tomás whispered to Chrétien, "How could you mistake that for a man?"

"*Ai*, brother, you are interested. If you marry her, then her son becomes your son. And *flic floc*, just like that, Fontcours and Montcava return to our family."

"It's Fontcours that matters most. The old count gave it to our father, to pass to his eldest son."

"That would be you, if we can prove it."

The hideous Father Clémence, whose pocket Tomás longed to pick for the letters inside it, rose ponderously from his seat to follow Senhóra Isabella. A few moments later, Renoud of Montcava made a traveler's excuse of fatigue and wandered out, with a brace of servants behind him.

Pèire Leteric didn't seem to pay attention to the departures, busy paring his nails with his dinner knife, a practice that Tomás's mother abhorred. "Tell me, Hugues. Why are you riding with priests and a city-bred seigneur? Who's guarding your flank?"

"Senhór Renoud was popular with his men in Constantinople." Hugues spoke loudly enough for Tomás to hear. "Other seigneurs in Toulouse respect him. This crusade needs diplomats, not warriors. Men like him will help us get better cooperation in the Languedoc."

"All the dancing angels pray that I can be as sure as you," the old man Pèire said.

Chrétien whispered in Tomás's ear. "So, we deal with that wretched priest first, to get the papers you need?"

"That's the plan. Though Renoud here is a gift of fate." Tomás mused on what to make of his enemy's presence. "I've been stalking both Father Clémence and the remaining bastard son of Montcava."

"We've saved some time since we don't have to next track down the marquis. While you stalk Renoud, I'll pursue the famous crusader," Chrétien said. "Though we could just slit everyone's throats and take what we're seeking."

"Except our father wouldn't consider it sporting or fair," Tomás said. "Besides, I want Seigneur Renoud to witness every moment of his own destruction."

"Well, we've come to an interesting castle." Chrétien stretched out his legs. "Good food. I don't know when I've had better entertainment. Do you suppose we can find games of chance later?"

"I hope so, after I had to spend weeks with a pack of priests," Tomás said. "We retrieve the letter from that priest tonight, and then we're back on the road tomorrow. We need to be in Toulouse by Pentecost."

13

God's Own Agent

Isabella at Valerós
30 days before Pentecost

ISABELLA DRESSED IN TRAVELING leathers, buckled a baldric across her shoulder to hold her dagger, and prepared to take the only logical action: fetch Sebastián from the bachelor-knights' barracks, beg Master Benito to serve as a companion, saddle horses, and then ride to the small castle at Arracheuse.

But when Isabella entered the courtyard, she met Katelina, as if the woman waited for her. "You can't run away in the dead of night."

"Our horses see better in the dark than we do."

"You're safe here, Isabella. Don't leave."

"I'm not leaving because I'm afraid. I have to act. If I stay, I might kill him. I don't want to upset Pèire's household."

"Let Pèire keep you safe," Katelina pleaded. In the dark, Isabella heard so much pity in her friend's voice that it almost broke her resolve. "I should call the marshal to stop you."

"You know what Renoud did to me, Katelina."

Katelina squeezed Isabella's hand, her many rings grating against her knuckles. "I love you like a sister," she said. "Do what you must." Then Katelina kissed her and left her alone.

Isabella went through the courtyard, avoiding the marshal's men or anyone else who might interfere. Outside the barracks, Father Clémence appeared, standing so close she felt his hot breath, reeking of garlic. He laid his huge, damp hand on her shoulder.

"God wants to forgive you. You can't run away from Him."

"How dare you!"

"As God's agent, I must warn you. For the sake of your soul."

She backed away from the priest, not out of fear but in retreat from her own fury. In mid-step, she felt arms close around her. "The senhóra is with me now. I'll guard her soul." Renoud's voice close by her ear sounded like the trumpet of doom.

"Òc, senhór. You can serve as God's hand."

As the priest's hulking form retreated into the dark, Renoud touched her face. The edge of his sleeve brushed her neck. She fought her instinct to recoil, since she'd learned long ago to resist reacting to the scorpion sewn on his cuff or the ridiculous tattoo on his hand.

"What a surprise to see you here." She moved away from his embrace, but he held her arms. She couldn't reach her knife. "How long will you be staying?"

"Only tonight," Renoud said. "We're joining other knights at the Lagrasse abbey to dedicate ourselves for this new crusade."

"The abbot of St-Féliz must be happy to hear of your dedication to the Church."

Renoud laughed. "Ai, you and Pare Abát are old friends. But in these times, we must appear as Catholic as possible. Don't we?"

"Pare Abát taught me that how it appears to God is what matters most." She recalled the tiny abbot as one of the few friends she had in those bad years in Toulouse.

"Sweet sister, you were always a philosopher." He traced her jaw. Repelled, she bristled at the rasp of his fingers across soft hairs on her neck when he slipped his hand under her head cloth. The light from the watchmen's torches showed how he'd aged; lines marked his face and streaks of silver snaked through his russet-gold mane. But then, he was twenty years older than she was.

"Why did you come here, Renoud?"

"I miss you. And I worry for Sebastián. You can't keep him in swaddling clothes forever."

"He trains with the best fight-masters in Aragón. And he's safer up here than down among the marauding French."

"Hugues de Beaurain's knights will keep our estates safe. Sebastián needs to be with his family."

"Sebastián belongs here in Valerós," she said.

"Let's not quarrel. Our time together is too short. Take me to see the boy. I brought a pony and other gifts for him."

"He's confined to his barracks, for breaking the marshal's rules. You can't see him tonight."

Renoud studied her in the way he used to before a battle to gain what he wanted: total submission. In his sweetest voice, he said, "Because my new wife didn't want you with us, I believed it was for the best when Pèire took you away. But when my wife died at Twelfth Night, I longed for you again."

He crushed her hands in his. She froze, certain the poison in him would seep through his scorpion claw and pass inside her.

"And neither my wife nor any mistress ever had children." He spoke as if they were friends catching up on old times. "That curse you put on the House of Montcava seems to have worked."

"What curse?" In her mind, she'd cursed him every moment of life in Toulouse, but she didn't believe in hexes and wouldn't have recklessly cursed him aloud.

"What you said the day you left: 'If God answers prayer, no child will ever again be born to this house.'"

"*Ai.*" That day in Toulouse, she'd merely described a curse, not pronounced one. And she still wanted to take her knife to him, but the idea of all the blood caused her to hesitate.

"Because of you, Sebastián remains the only son of our household. You and the boy must come home." He ran his finger over her chin and down her throat, resting it where Nicolau had cut her on their miserable wedding night. "I'd marry you, if only the Church allowed a man to take his brother's wife."

She shuddered.

"You're trembling, *xiqueta.*" He pulled her closer. "Don't worry. My cousin Louis will oblige us by marrying you."

"How thoughtful. A sixth-degree cousin to keep our holdings under your control. That's what you really want, isn't it, Renoud?"

"*Xiqueta,* I mean to protect you along with everything else that belongs to the Montcavas. To keep you safe, I need you beside me." He crushed her hand again. "By Pentecost."

"Are you threatening me?"

"Bring Sebastián, too. I love you, Isabella." He put his hand on her, the way he used to when he groped her behind Nicolau's back. "Otherwise, I'll find another way."

"What will you do? Storm Castell-de-Valerós with your six ill-trained house-knights?"

He laughed, the way he always treated her challenges as jests. "*Ai*, my dear sister, I could simply condemn you as a heretic."

"*Bon Dèu!*" She adopted her most reasonable voice. "Your mother is a goodwoman. Pare Abát has been trying to reclaim her soul for years. Do you want to see her in the bishops' court, too?"

"Or perhaps I reveal your past sins with other men. Remember the donzel Jaume?" He fingered the leather thong that held the purse around her neck, as if he knew it held her sole memento from Jaume. "The bishop won't leave Sebastián with a Magdalen."

Rage choked her. "Why do that?"

"To make you come home to me."

"No one in Christendom will believe you."

"My entire domus will swear to it if I ask them. Father Clémence heard your confession."

That priest had condemned her when she spoke in confession about Nicolau's cruelties and Renoud's perpetual pestering. She'd confessed sins that never matched the enormity of how she'd been sinned against.

"Why do you want to hurt me?"

"I don't." He stroked her jaw again. "I'm merely desperate to have you both home again, where I can protect you. Every invading French knight is anxious to take our land and our women." He pinned her arms to her sides. She still couldn't reach her knife, though she imagined being brave enough to try. "You like to tease me, Isabella. If you want to protect Sebastián and our domus as much as I do, stop teasing me."

"As you wish." She spoke one lie, and then she chose the next most convenient falsehood. "I will marry by Pentecost."

Then, as if a heavenly saint intervened, Benito called her name.

"I'm here, Master Benito," she answered.

When Benito clattered down the steps to the portico, Renoud disappeared in the night. "I stepped out for some air," she said, although she stood there in her riding clothes.

"Let me walk with you, ma dòmna. It's been a trying day." Benito dropped his voice. "Pèire Leteric hasn't given me permission to take off that *baquelar's* balls. Though I intend to ask later."

14
Cain and the Seigneur

Jean-Luc at Valerós
30 days before Pentecost

"HERE HE IS, SENHÓR."

The voice outside the barracks door was his brother Yves, with his wretched accent when speaking the southerners' tongue. Jean-Luc stirred. He wanted to tell his brother about—

But Yves was dead. Jean-Luc must be dreaming again.

A flurry of motion and voices in the doorway roused Jean-Luc, but it wasn't sentries coming off duty. It was the seigneur Pèire Leteric and his marshal causing the commotion. The marshal held the door as Jean-Luc's angel departed.

Pèire surveyed the discarded heap of blood-soaked linen and then examined Jean-Luc, who lay helpless on his cot, hoping Pèire wouldn't recognize him. Fifteen years before, he'd fought alongside Pèire briefly in the Outremer, but Jean-Luc didn't believe Pèire could discern any trace of that very young squire in a vagrant smith.

"Had a tussle and got a scratch, did you?" Pèire asked.

"It's of small consequence, senhór," Jean-Luc said.

"The lad didn't tell a clear story." It was the marshal's voice that had wakened Jean-Luc. "We hope to hear what happened from you."

Jean-Luc described what he'd seen in the gathering darkness. "He wasn't your common brigand. The man had been trained at arms in the way Frankish soldiers are. Yet his knife was Greek, and he wore a leather corselet. I didn't see any insignia."

"Greek, eh?" Pèire mused. "A big man? A match for you?"

"He was the same size as—" Jean-Luc started to say *my brother.* "Your marshal."

63

"Could you tell from his speech where he was from?" The marshal had long hair and long, silver-streaked moustaches, not at all like Yves; but the marshal had the same erect, knightly bearing and a collection of manners one learned while training under a Norman lord. Jean-Luc shook his head, more to toss off the image of Yves than to answer the marshal.

"He said one word in a strange tongue. But he looked Frankish," Jean-Luc said.

"Or the devil's own Norman." Pèire uttered an invective. "Marshal Guillem says you couldn't much account for yourself when he found you."

"He was dead to the world, senhór." The marshal argued Jean-Luc's case for him.

"I often go to the garden for a bit of comfrey," Jean-Luc said. "An old wound troubles me."

Pèire grasped Jean-Luc's hand and examined the forearm, which was scarred by Greek fire from palm to elbow. The marshal looked down, too, and then caught Jean-Luc's gaze, and tugged at his moustache, a habit Yves had. Except if it were Yves, at this point, he'd say, *"Why tell a lie when the truth will do as well?"*

"You must be a clumsy smith," Pèire said. "Who did you say you served last?"

"A master smith in Limoges." Jean-Luc fought off wooziness.

"One of our bordoniers says he saw you in Constantinople," Pèire said. "Did you take up the Cross at one time?"

Jean-Luc, who'd carried all of Constantinople on his shoulders like a cross every single day, hoped he looked like any man unfortunate enough to be caught in that debacle. He nodded his assent.

"Too bad they sent you young men on such a piss-ant crusade," Pèire growled. "Are you taking up the Cross again now that the pope is preaching crusade again?"

"The abbot of Vaux refused to go to Constantinople," Jean-Luc said. "He tried to break up the army and then left us in Zara, saying God didn't mean for Christians to crusade against Christians. Now in this new crusade, the same man comes as the pope's prelate…"

He stopped, revealing too much.

"Lofty thoughts for a smith." Pèire was laughing at him. Then he grew sober. "They say these days a man's craft is his first loyalty, and he moves from town to town until he finds his fortune."

"As I have, senhór," Jean-Luc said.

"In my house, a man is either for me or he's against me. You did a service to my family, so maybe you stand for me. If that's so, you're welcome here. If you can't give me your oath by Sunday fortnight, you'll be on your way."

"Òc, senhór." Jean-Luc could remain uncommitted, free to stay here, until that Sunday, which was three weeks before Pentecost. But he could finish his work for Viscount Gerard by then, and therefore be gone.

They left him. Jean-Luc settled into his cot, his leg throbbing in pain. Perhaps he'd learned the answer to one question for his lord. Pèire seemed to have all his wits and retained the perception and agility of a much younger man. However, Pèire Leteric hadn't recognized him. Otherwise, the old man would never have asked for his oath, because throughout Christendom the knight that Jean-Luc had been was known as a Cain, a man who killed his own brother.

15

A Packet of Parchment

WHEN ISABELLA WAS TEN, she found a warren of cells that had stored provisions generations before, when the castle defended against invading Moors. She and her sisters played Knights Templar in their monks' cells. When she returned from Toulouse, she found her sisters had commandeered the cells as private sleeping spaces, except in the dead of winter when it was too cold to sleep alone. The chill stone cells offered the only solitude in Valerós.

Unable to sleep, Isabella fingered the leather pouch that contained a pathetic collection of mementos: three of Sebastián's baby teeth, reminding her how it felt to cradle her only child and smell milk on his breath; a worthless ring her husband Nicolau had given her, in the old tradition, to bind her child to her, but now the ring was only a token of a cruel, selfish man; a tiny silver cross from her mother, which once helped her remember her mother's face but hadn't worked well for years; and a scrap of vellum where Jaume (her lover for a fortnight, long ago) had penned the only words he learned to write: *eu vos amor*.

She felt stupid clutching childish treasures for comfort, especially a badly scrawled declaration of love.

In the dark, anger seared her spleen. She'd learned to forget Renoud, and then as soon as he appeared, she was twelve again and stalked by him. And the vicious Father Clémence had come here, to her own safe home, the man who'd called her a sinning whore who led men astray. Her sins had been so tiny, not even as much as a speck in God's eye; once more she questioned God: He was supposed to forgive and forget. And protect the innocent.

Disgusted with fretting, she threw back her quilt. Time to move forward. No fear. No use tackling the bone-headed, muddled evil Renoud carried in his head. But she could confront Father Clémence. She was no longer a young girl to be cowed by his false religiosity.

Near the mews, a row of cells that usually held winter stores now housed visiting pilgrims. She could guess where the priest slept, because he'd have bullied everyone until he possessed the best option. The heavy wooden door that kept vermin out of their food stores now stood ajar. Inside, a rush light burned, casting a weak shadow onto the cobbles. She knocked and then pushed open the door, calling Clémence's name, as imperious as the Queen of Jerusalem. The empty room smelled of garlic and sour man, the odor that smothered her when she knelt in confession in Toulouse. The priest's satchel lay beside a bedroll.

After a night meditating on the enormous punishments dealt for her slight sins, she was not inclined to restrain herself. If the priest carried bad news to Pèire, she had every right under God's heaven to know. She tossed the bedroll, seeking anything that had been folded into it. Then she snatched up the satchel and examined its contents: filthy breeches; a wooden cross on a leather lanyard; a dried chunk of bread; woolen leggings. A packet of parchment.

Unashamed, because the priest had polluted her peace of mind for years in the malodorous city of Toulouse, she stole the packet, because it most likely contained a summons for Pèire to join the crusade and any other bad news spawned by Renoud. She walked the battlements, intending to stay there until it was light enough to read. However, in the watchman's torchlight, she found she wasn't alone.

·

Pèire and Hugues walked on the battlements in conversation. Before she could retreat, Pèire pulled her to him while talking with Hugues. She felt an unholy pleasure in being admitted to their private talk.

She'd hear firsthand whether the Marquis de Beaurain could persuade Pèire to ride with him during crusading season.

"Last summer, Pedro asked if I'd help protect the peace, but I couldn't see my way to leave home," Pèire said. "Share some of this?"

Hugues murmured thanks for the portion of bread and cheese Pèire handed him. They traded portions as she'd seen knights do when they ate in the saddle to make fast time.

"This year?" Hugues said. "Has Pedro called you to arms?"

"I'm too old and too poor to do squat for Pedro," Pèire said. "I need to do my duty, to protect my domus."

Hugues said, "When I met with Simon de Montfort last—"

"Simon's a Norman, isn't he?" Pèire sounded merely curious, his prejudice restrained.

"Simon's lands are in England and near Paris," Hugues said. "On the last crusade, Simon left for the Holy Land when the mercenaries rioted at Zara. He proved to be an adequate leader."

"But came home broke, I hear tell." Pèire slipped a little knife from his tunic belt to pare cheese, handing a portion to Hugues.

"Many French crusaders are opportunists," Hugues said. "But Simon believes God gave him a duty to wipe out heresy."

"Too bad for him the seigneurs won't lie down and let the French ride over them," Pèire said.

"Hear me out, Pèire," Hugues finished a bite of bread before continuing. "Last winter, after most of the French army went home, many seigneurs turned rebel."

Pèire wrenched apart a loaf of last night's brioix. "It's our land. Our people. We're true to our honor. It's paratge, not rebellion."

"And yet," Hugues said, "one seigneur near Fontcours captured some French knights crossing his land at Candlemas."

"Near my boy Sebastián's land?" Pèire asked.

Hugues nodded, then glanced at Isabella, as if unsure what to say in front of her. "Instead of asking ransom, as is the custom, the seigneur cut off the nose and upper lip of one knight and then sent them all back to Simon without their armor."

"A mal punt," Pèire muttered. A bad state.

"The result? Simon asked for more support from Philippe and the pope."

"You know I have no sympathy for popes' peeves," Pèire said. "They cried the Peace of God for a hundred years, forbidding our seigneurs their traditional battles." He passed another portion of bread and cheese to Hugues.

"Our grand-sires were known to battle each other for the pure joy of it," Hugues said.

Pèire said, "But now that spit-licker Simon and this pope want to forget peace and burn our cities, saying the Christian goodmen in Béziers and Carcassonne got what they deserved."

"Seven thousand people massacred in one day at Béziers," Isabella said, though it wasn't her place to speak. "Goodmen and Roman Christians together."

"Tragedies happen in war," Hugues said. "It hurts your soft woman's heart, but soldiers must think of other things."

Isabella didn't believe she had a soft heart. "With all respect, senhór, it offends any decent person's honor." She felt Pèire's hand rest on her shoulder as a mild restraint. "Is this crusade an excuse for murdering innocent people?"

"Béziers." Hugues clenched one fist at his side, "was just baggage boys and poorly trained soldiers running amok."

"That's not what we heard," Pèire said. Isabella relaxed, knowing she'd expressed what he thought.

"I was there," Hugues said. "We'd just arrived, thinking it'd take weeks to wear the city down in siege. So, you know what the real soldiers were doing?"

"Òc," Pèire said. "Building barricades, felling trees, setting up the kitchens and their lords' pavilions, caring for the horses. A thousand chores." Isabella could imagine all of that, since Pèire's stories were about provisioning more often than recounting actual battles.

Hugues said, "While our soldiers were doing real work, a raft of baggage boys floated down the river outside the city, trading insults with men on the city walls. Some of our younger knights joined in, riding onto the bridge to call taunts at the defenders. Inside Béziers, a score of youths couldn't abide the heckling and threw open the gates to attack the fools on the bridge."

"And then your noble lords of France saw the opportunity to attack," Pèire said.

"No. The so-called king of the baggage rabble led his lads in with clubs. The half-naked, barefoot thieves and ruffians who glean what's dropped behind the real army. When the bullies pressed through the gates, the city's defenders left their posts to fight them. That's when Simon's army entered the town."

"To burn women and children and the Church's own priests," Isabella said. "These excuses won't quell the anger and fear everywhere in the south."

Hugues lifted his palms toward heaven, as if in surrender. "I'm riding this summer for the sake of the Peace of God. I'm not here to steal booty from Christians." His voice dropped low. "Which way are you going, Pèire? With the crusaders or the rebel armies?"

Pèire snorted. "There's no rebel army. Our seigneurs don't trust each other enough to build an army. And they're too selfish to buy one."

"So, you'll help keep the peace?" Hugues asked.

"Pedro d'Aragón is my suzerain lord, not the king of France," Pèire said. "He hasn't joined this crusade, one way or the other."

Isabella listened for the note in Pèire's voice that meant he'd declared that he'd refuse to ride, so she could tell Katelina to stop worrying about whether Pèire might be pulled into this filthy crusade. She didn't hear it yet.

"But Pedro d'Aragón supports the Church more than any other king in Christendom," Hugues said.

"If Pedro works to unite the south, I'll do what he asks." The bread and cheese gone, Pèire fiddled with his little knife. "Pedro hasn't yet accepted Simon's oath as viscount, so I don't have to do what Simon asks. I shall only preserve my honor by protecting my own people."

"Pedro's efforts to unite the seigneurs and viscounts will sprout jealousies everywhere," Hugues said.

"Yet I'm betting on Pedro," Pèire said. "Until he asks, this so-called crusade is none of my business."

Then Pèire would not ride. But why continue with his deplorable battle strategy to marry Isabella to an ancient French lord?

"I promise, my friend, that Simon will make it your business," Hugues said.

"How can you be sure?"

"My brother is a priest. He says Simon is the pope's hammer and anvil who'll force the seigneurs to hand over every heretic goodman."

"Every family in the Languedoc has goodmen for half their relatives. Will Simon say, 'Hand over your mothers, daughters, and aunties?'" Pèire shook his head in great doubt.

Hugues said, "My other brother held land near Carcassonne for many years. When Simon took the city last year, the Church threatened to excommunicate him and seize his land."

"Because his wife is a goodwoman? We heard of such things."

"Yes. When forced to choose, my brother said the Creed. And then annulled his marriage."

Had Pèire made his battle strategy knowing Gerard might easily let her go, as Hugues's brother had done?

"I'm not riding out on crusade just because the pope wants people to say their prayers all the same way. Please, Hugues," Pèire had his hand on Hugues's wrist, "don't call on my oath as your brother in arms. This isn't the right fight for that."

"I'm not asking that," Hugues said. "You could help me keep soldiers from running wild. And, God knows, I'd be honored to ride with you again."

Pèire shook his head—but it was a different motion than earlier. Was he seriously considering Hugues's request?

"Simon sent that gold-bug priest Clémence up here to sniff for gold in my manure pile, or wherever he thinks we bury our wealth. Meanwhile, I can't pay Simon's demands for new taxes. And I have no heretics to surrender."

She hadn't discussed all that with Pèire earlier. She'd have to ask him more when they were alone.

"Most towns in the south are hereticated," Hugues said. "That's why the pope cried for crusade."

"People here all name Jesus as Savior. May golden singing angels remind those French devils that crusaders don't kill Christians."

"I understand your thinking," Hugues said. "I'm grateful that you still feel free to share with me what's in your heart."

Maybe Hugues understood from the conversation what was in Pèire's heart, but Isabella didn't know. Was he riding into this crusade as a peacekeeper with Hugues de Beaurain if Pedro d'Aragón asked? Or was Pèire adamantly staying home—and forcing her to marry and go away as part of his strategy to protect Valerós?

The two old crusaders wandered down the battlements. Isabella lingered behind them. Hugues said, "Did you raise an Amazon?"

"My Isabella could lead an army better than Eleanor ever did."

"Could she?"

"My girl knows to worry about her horses and her men. Old Eleanor only thought about herself. At least, that's how she was when I knew her in Antioch."

"Pèire, you liar." Hugues slapped him on the back. "You were sixteen when Eleanor was in Antioch. You didn't know her even as well as I did."

"You rascal. You got to her, too? And I thought you went the other way. You never did care for ladies."

"*Ai*, Pèire, enough! Point me to where your knights are dicing. I need to gamble against fate as a rest after sparring with you."

"There's a warm spot in the armory. I'll join you in a bit. It'd be a pleasure to take a pile of silver off you, to help with our taxes."

After they departed, Isabella intended to go to her room to read the letters she'd stolen from Clémence. Beyond the attacks in the daylight, the night brought too many visitors with secrets and demands. People wanting things from Pèire. Renoud relentlessly seeking her surrender. If Pèire was headed for the knights' dice game, she couldn't speak to him again until morning. But she needed to know: had the pleas from his good friend Hugues changed Pèire's mind about peacekeeping?

Most important, had any other visitors—or perhaps Katelina—caused Pèire to reconsider his battle strategy for her safety?

She headed for the stairs that led off the parapets. Below, that deceitful scribe crossed the courtyard, creeping into an alley. One more question she had for Pèire.

16
Dice

TOMÁS DE MORELLA Y CYPRUS skulked through the alleys of the Valerós castle-village, the linsey-woolsey scribe's robe he'd stolen in Toulouse scratching through his linen undershirt. He'd gone looking for Clémence but found only the man's doss-kit. And no letters. More than itchy wool was getting under his skin.

He'd been in the mood for a good street fight ever since he and Chrétien left Toulouse, wanting more chances to test whether he'd recovered his speed and agility. Up here in the back of nowhere, people attack you for no reason, and you can't fight back. Your mortal enemy appears at dinner, and—

"You have to sit and swallow watered-down wine and tall tales." Miquel joined him, chuckling, looking sprightly and joyous. Young. Dressed in the studded black-leather cuirass of an old-fashioned Aragón mercenary, a warrior with more honor than coin.

"It was a mistake to come here." Tomás didn't turn his head to look. It was no surprise. His dead father appeared often in the past year, telling him how to think, how to move, how to plot and plan. As if he were twelve again, a young *fadrin* in need of guidance.

"This is the most interesting place for your hunt." Miquel stretched and yawned. "And there's dicing in the armory."

"I know. I heard at dinner."

"You'll let Chrétien get there first? And then you spend tonight playing foolish gambler, like I taught you?"

"Go away. You have nothing more to teach me. You're dead."

"Not so dead that I don't enjoy watching people deceive themselves. It brings back such good times. *Ai,* I know.

"Go away!"

It wasn't healthy that he let his mind toy with him, even believed sometimes that his father was there. But in truth, they'd hit his head too hard when he took that beating on Cyprus.

Tomás bolted ahead through the alleys and then backtracked toward the armory. Before going in, he stopped at the midden heap behind the stable to relieve himself, looking around to see if Miquel had left him alone, startled when the Marquis de Beaurain came up, as silent as Miquel in his approach, stopping at the manure pile for the same purpose.

"Pèire is as crazy as ever, isn't he?" Hugues said.

Tomás was at a loss for an answer, but then saw that Hugues addressed Father Anselm, the chaplain of Valerós. Lamplight from the armory shone on their faces, while Tomás stood in the shadows.

The chaplain said, "Crazy as a fox. It's reassuring, don't you think, that certain people never change?"

"But you, Anselm? You in a cassock?" Hugues said. "How did that happen?"

"You know I took up the Cross for more than the joy of battling Saracens. I left the Outremer believing I had a vocation."

"There's no man better to help the dying and the battle-sore than you, Anselm."

"Thank you for saying it, though all my gifts come from God."

"But what of Yasmin?"

"I lost her in childbed," the chaplain said.

"*Ai,* my friend, I am sorry. Words won't do. I know what she meant to you."

"She's with God, where I try to be every day."

"Is it enough for you up here, playing confessor to sheepherders? If you came to me, I'd find you a good place, perhaps in one of the knights' orders."

"I don't require your simony, Hugues. There's enough work for me here. I don't need a gift so grand."

When the men walked to the armory, Father Anselm said, "Is that priest Clémence in your entourage, Hugues?"

Tomás listened more keenly. Clémence carried the letter Tomás needed to save his inheritance from Renard.

"No," Hugues said. "Why do you ask?"

"Don't you remember him in the old days?" Anselm said. "Pèire never trusted him as far as we could fling him with a mangonel. I pray God has indeed saved his soul."

"You can't know what's in another man's heart, Anselm. But I shouldn't be the one preaching forgiveness. The pope's prelate, Arnau Amalric, is using Clémence as a gold douser."

"That old mountebank? Powers to sniff for gold? Is he using a witch-hazel fork or that great snout of his?" The chaplain spat in disgust. "In the Holy Land, when Clémence tried that gold-dousing swindle, Richard threatened to have him whipped in the streets and stripped from his order."

"I'm staying out of Arnau's way," Hugues said. "They are doing everything to find the wealth that seigneurs and heretics in the south have been withholding from the Church. The pope's people haven't asked my advice, and I don't offer."

"And what of your companion, Senhór Renoud of Montcava? Pèire doesn't trust him," Anselm said.

"He made that obvious at dinner."

"Pèire's granddaughter Isabella lived an unhappy life in the Montcava household."

"But she must like what Renoud has done for her son," Hugues said. "He's made the Fontcours estate wealthier than his brother ever managed."

"I didn't know that," Anselm said. Tomás did know, from his searches in Toulouse, and it made him hate Renoud more and long to snatch Clémence's letter, then to run to the bishops' court. "And I shouldn't judge, since tonight is the first time I've seen the man."

"In mixed company, Renoud plays the overbred city-lord," Hugues said. "But in action, he's a fierce business man. He did well after his brother was killed, when he took command of the brigade in Constantinople. I'm betting on Renoud this summer."

"You always knew how to temper your bets," Anselm said. "It is to be hoped that you've retained that skill."

When Father Anselm entered the armory, voices greeted him casually. But when Hugues entered, everyone stood, disrupting the game underway. He motioned the men back to their dice; he wanted to join. The players shuffled positions, because only the knights presumed to play with the marquis. Backed into a corner, Chrétien glanced around and then stayed in the game. Tomás admired his brother's boldness.

Father Anselm seemed to play only for the camaraderie, gambling casually, like a man who makes love for relaxation. Hugues, however, cherished the game. He smiled when he lost, but you could see him recalculating the odds. When he won, the marquis threw everything right back into the game.

Tomás leaned forward, eager to be in a game with this man, but he was supposed to be a lowly scribe. He stayed in the shadows, pulled up the cowl of his robe, and tugged the leather wrapping around his wrist.

■

Tomás felt that tooth, loose ever since the beating on Cyprus; in the last fortnight it had begun to ache. Tired and affected by wine, he listened to the series of stories told while they gambled. Pèire Leteric wandered in to watch. While tossing the gamers' bones, Hugues de Beaurain described the new war machines Simon de Montfort had brought south with him. Tomás let his attention drift, trying to judge how well-trained the bordoniers and house-knights here might be.

"Thinking about French mangonels reminds me of a time with Don Miquel," Pèire said. "That mestitz rascal."

Tomás jerked, knocking into the man next to him. Chrétien dropped his dice, as if clumsy.

Pèire settled back to recite a story. "It was when we were young lads baking in a stinking wasteland outside of Edessa. Miquel and our captain sneaked into a Greek camp to spy on their siege engines. After that, Miquel made a little one to show our engineers how to build it. That baby mangonel had a kick to it, though it was only about so big." Pèire flexed his arm in a gesture, the ropey knots of muscle more like the arm of a fifty-year-old soldier than a man of eighty. "Miquel brought it out at supper to fire beans and hard biscuits at squires in the next camp over. He'd send cobbles flying as far as where the Knights Templar bivouacked just east of us."

Hugues looked up with a smile and murmured to Pèire. Tomás barely caught the phrase, "Hadn't thought of that in years."

"Those Templars' black surcoats and red crosses caused a lust for glory to seize some fellows in our camp. Of course, those boys lacked a few Templar essentials. Like discipline and virtue."

The old man chortled at his own joke; Hugues de Beaurain was the only other person laughing. Pèire said, "One evening a couple of those lads were in their tent with a few Joans and Marias from the baggage train. You could hear them clear over to where we sat. All of a sudden, ol' Miquel bet me he'd win a horse-race."

"To my memory," Hugues said, "you always sat a horse better than Miquel."

"I won't deny it," Pèire said. "I took his bet, but I lost sight of Miquel in just two shakes after the race started. Sweet dancing angels, I had the finest pony then. But when I came to the finish line, everyone was with Miquel at the other end of camp."

Pèire quivered, trying to keep back his own laughter.

"What happened?" another knight called out.

"When Miquel rode by where the baggage girls were visiting, he had an accident that pulled the tent down. Which drew a crowd."

"Did your Templar neighbors see?" someone called.

"By my saintly balls, they surely did," Pèire said. "And that was the end of Templar dreams for those boys with their breeches around their knees."

Hugues, still laughing, said. "My brothers were in that tent, you know. They were mad as the devil. But I thank God Miquel saved them from the Templars."

"*Bon Dèu!*" Pèire exclaimed. "Those Templars think they're holier than a whole race of priests."

A man called out to Pèire, "Did you ride with Miquel or Hugues after that, senhór?"

Pèire said, "Those two stuck together for years, and I rode with them many a time. If you needed a well-trained general," he tipped a finger to point to his visitor, "Hugues was your man. But if you wanted pure guts, you went with Miquel, because he'd save your sorry hind end. Miquel was the best fighter God ever made."

While the story was being told, Chrétien wiggled his way to stand beside Tomás so he could whisper, "These old *peccadors* aren't the same as the others we hunted."

Pèire Leteric offered a toast to riding with Don Miquel de Morella, passing a stone jar among the men. A dozen knights and bordoniers in the room raised their botas and cups. None raised a cup higher than Hugues de Beaurain.

"*Qui s'ho creu?*" Chrétien whispered. *Who'd believe it?*

Tomás still didn't. He treasured the small comfort that no one here knew them, so this scene hadn't been played to seduce him into thinking these people might be friends.

.

The marquis left, which removed the interest for Tomás, since it wasn't his night to gamble. He departed when Chrétien proposed to teach the gullible gamblers a card game he'd learned in Cairo. In the dark, Tomás couldn't find a decent passage through the maze of alleys. Outside what must be the kitchens from the smell of banked-down fires, roasted meats, and garlic, he heard a man's loud whisper echo against the stone walls.

"Hey you! Bastard boy! I'll whip you till your arse bleeds."

Then Tomás heard a stick cracking on flesh. He stepped toward the bully and stuck out his right foot to sweep him down. The man fell but rose up again in a flash. Tomás heard the whisk and clang of a sword being drawn.

"Run, boy!" Tomás called. "Go home now!"

He pulled his dagger from his boot and freed the cord of the cursed scribe's robe, swinging it like a lasso. He whipped at the bully's sword hand, deflecting the thrust of the blade. Then he leaped to attack the brute. When they both fell to the cobbles, Tomás pressed his knife at the man's throat.

Renoud of Montcava cursed him.

Surprised at who he had at knifepoint, Tomás made sure Renoud felt the prick of his blade. Fear—Tomás hoped it was fear—twitched across Renoud's face, puckering a scar in his cheek. Tomás fought a desire to sheathe his dagger in Renoud's throat. Too much yet to be learned from the man.

"Here now. What's this?" a man growled.

Tomás faced Pèire Leteric and his marshal, leaving Renoud on the cobbles, denying himself the pleasure of killing the man who stole his legacy. Before Tomás could answer, Renoud rose, swearing. He kicked Tomás's hand. The knife clattered across the alley.

"This bastard Moor jumped me," Renoud shouted. "Why do you allow mestitz trash in your house, senhór? He needs whipping."

"I didn't know you in the dark either," the marshal said.

"He's just a vagrant bastard."

"No, this man is my scribe," Pèire said. Tomás stepped away from Renoud, astonished. "He's a member of my house."

"You allow your men to attack their betters in the dark?"

"I allow my men to exercise their good judgment. In the dark as well as the full light of day."

Strangely, the old man had declared Tomás his ally. Because he too distrusted Renoud?

"My sword will be the judge if that mestitz *baquelar* ever crosses me again," Renoud said.

Ai, just you wait until your time comes, senhór. Tomás stood, head bent, as the humble scribe he was supposed to be—and to make sure Renoud never had a good view of his face.

"Marshal, help Senhór Renoud find his quarters. I'll go with Tomás the scribe to remind him of the way."

Ten steps beyond, when Marshal Guillem and Renoud were gone, Pèire said, "Never did like that *punxor*. How did you end up with a knife at his gullet?"

"He was beating a child."

"Maybe it was his child to beat."

"I didn't think to ask," Tomás said. "And I lost my best knife."

"Isabella always said Renoud is the devil's own. Yet I can never catch him at it. Hunt for your knife in the morning. Then come talk with me. I'd like to hire your services, Master Scribe."

"Whatever for?"

But Pèire disappeared into the darkness without answering, whistling through his teeth. Worried that the old baron toyed with him, Tomás walked through the twisting alleys, seeking the bachelor-knights' barracks where he'd been given a cot for the night.

"*Qui s'ho creu?*" Tomás muttered. *Who'd believe it?*

"I told you, didn't I?" Miquel hung his arm around Tomás's shoulders, leaning on him as they traversed the cobbled alleyway. "But you boys never listen."

"Make yourself useful. Find the knife that bastard lost for me."

17

Indulgences

ALONE IN HER ROOM finally, Isabella struck a spark to light a candle and read the scrap she'd stolen from the dead priest's satchel.

> I wish you loved me. I would give my life for you, without regard for my immortal soul. Now you have gone away. "To go with God," you said.
>
> If only you could understand how I ache, beyond all knowing, hoping you will turn to me.
> At least do not abandon our sons. They are our gift from Heaven. I wish that I could cry it from the housetops: these are my two sons, not the children of the devil you married.
>
> I remain your own, dove of my heart. I beg you to find a corner for me in your own heart. Now I say to you:
> *Go with God*

At first, Isabella believed it was from Renoud, repeating the ridiculous conceit that he loved her, because it was signed with the same crescent cross as his silly tattoo. But Renoud was barely literate, and the author talked of having two sons with his lover. It wasn't Renoud, then. And Father Clémence couldn't have penned such lyrical words of loveliness.

Reading it again, the sense of aching loss in the letter touched her. That scrap of the letter—and Renoud's abrupt appearance in her home—set loose memories she kept buried. But why not let those memories roam free? She'd formed a battle strategy for herself once, to fight her way out of hell. She must have learned something from those evil times that she could use now.

.

Isabella in Toulouse
August 1204

Isabella, dressed in leathers, burst through the covert passage into the Montcava villa, elated from her secret shopping expedition: a horse, packed and provisioned for traveling; the services of a guide to take Isabella and Sebastián through the Languedoc, up through the Corbières hills to the edge of the Pyrenees; a morsel of St-John's Gospel in Greek purchased from her friend Avraham ben Yitzchak after they haggled over the price for Nicolau's armor, which she sold to finance the horse and a guide to take her home.

"Isabella!" Renoud shouted. Her brother-in-law's voice echoed through the stone hallways. "The abbot of St-Féliz is here. He's asking for you!"

Hurried and harassed—her normal state inside the Montcava household—Isabella wrapped a robe around the stolen falconer's leathers she'd worn to the market. She sprinted through the hallways for the inner courtyard, arriving breathless.

The diminutive abbot from St-Féliz-de-Fontcours waited for her in the cool shade by the fountain in the Montcava inner courtyard.

"It is good to see you, Pare Abát." She sank to her knees and kissed the ring that weighed down the abbot's small, delicate hands.

"Senhóra Isabella! It's always a blessing to meet with you." He bade her rise and then peered up at her, since she stood half a head taller and he was short-sighted. "You seem tired. Poor child, widowed so young."

"It is as God wills," she said. *In my favor, this one time.*

Nicolau had played with his knife when he first took her to bed, but he managed only a single cut before she wrested the knife away and held it to his throat. A girl half his size and a third his age. Yet the cruelty continued from that night until he was called to crusade.

The abbot's warm brown eyes showed how he worried for her. He stroked her hand, enveloping it in warmth. No one else touched her gently, except Sebastián. "But you have a strong faith to help you bear the pain."

She whispered, "I worry about whether Nicolau is with God."

"Ma dòmna?" He strained to see her face.

"How much indulgence did the pope grant these crusaders? I wonder if his soul is still in torment." She hated the tremor in her voice, fearing that she betrayed a wish.

"*Ai*, ma dòmna, it's time for you to look to the future. It's your duty to help Sebastián grow to be like his father." The abbot still held her fingertips, rubbing his hands over her nails and knuckles. What felt warm and comforting a moment before now felt irritating.

"Pare Abát, pray for me."

She knelt in submission, the ridges of the courtyard bruising her knees through the leather leggings under her robe. The abbot's hands rest on her head as he muttered prayers of absolution.

"For your penance, Senhóra Isabella, do your duty to your son. Come to St-Sernin every day to pray for your husband's soul."

That's more than God should dare ask.

After the amens, she asked, "You helped me to buy indulgences before, Pare Abát. Can you do that again? For Sebastián's father?"

"Of course, my child. Ask your brother Renoud for the money. He is now steward of all your son's lands and your own wealth."

She hoped the near-sighted abbot could not see her dismay.

"I will do my duty, Pare Abát." Isabella believed her sole duty was to take Sebastián home to Valerós.

The Montcava villa and estates didn't matter; like most of the south, three dozen cousins owned slices of the properties. But Sebastián inherited Fontcours, given to Nicolau's father by the Count of Toulouse to be handed from oldest son to oldest son. No Montcava cousins could claim a share. Yet taking Fontcours back from Renoud would have to come later.

When the abbot departed, Miró the footman closed the gate. A stooped old man who Sebastián called *fada d'atri*, the fairy of the courtyard, he blessed her.

"May the Mother of our Lord and Savior rain blessings down on you, ma dòmna."

As she stepped into the cool of the house, Senhóra Eloïse blocked her way, her wraith of a mother-in-law who lurked in the shadows whenever they had visitors.

"I do not wish you a good end." She offered the opposite of a goodwoman's greeting.

"Not now, Mother." Renoud stepped between them.

Isabella stood helpless, a despicable sensation, as he tilted her face up to his, the embroidered scorpion on his sleeve scratching her face. He traced her throat, her collarbone, and then rested on her breast, where Nicolau had cut her. He tugged open her robe and fingered the leather jerkin she wore underneath.

"*Ai*, Isabella," he chided.

"You mustn't touch her," Senhóra Eloïse said. "She's filthy with sin. That's why she never had another child."

"Sebastián is the only child because this house is cursed." Bitterness flooding Isabella's veins. "If God answers prayer, no child will ever be born to this house."

She slipped away from Renoud and returned to her room. She barred the door and held Sebastián close until he fidgeted and broke loose to play on the floor, singing a nursery song she'd sung to him in his cradle, though she didn't know where she'd learned it.

> I saw the wolf before the wolf saw me.
> I'll kill the wolf before the wolf kills me.
> God take the wolf and God save me.

▪

In her room in Valerós, Isabella folded the scrap of a letter and tucked it into the little pouch with her mementos. The missive reminded her of the years when she too had mourned lost love. But those thoughts brought her back to musing on the sins Renoud threatened to tell Pèire. When she was fifteen, she'd loved an orphaned donzel who lived in the Montcava household. Her husband Nicolau still lived then, so it counted as both adultery, even though they never got as far as fornication. The donzel Jaume declared undying love for her, and Isabella felt lonely beyond all telling.

Then a horse trampled Jaume in the streets of Toulouse.

For a year, she wept daily and spent every silver penny she could steal to purchase indulgences for his soul. The boy was surely in heaven. He was far too innocent for God to assign him elsewhere.

Then, three years after Isabella returned to Valerós, she'd dallied with Pèire's seneschal. It lasted for a fortnight. She and Etienne had been left in charge of the early harvest while Pèire and the family visited the king at Narbonne. She'd lost her head in the August heat. That counted only as fornication, she believed, because neither of them was married. Etienne tried to convince her to approach Pèire about their marrying, despite his lack of land and family.

But one day, Etienne told Isabella not to give his men direct orders when he was present.

"*Ask me to do it for you. It's not a woman's place to order my men.*"

The affair ended. However angry she felt, she'd remained enamored of Etienne and had been crushed with grief when he died a month later while in Toulouse on family business. She confessed and purchased indulgences from the priest at Valerós, where the same money bought much more Divine atonement than it did in Toulouse.

Father Anselm said God had forgiven that sin also, although it still nagged at her in the heat of summer.

Isabella tried to determine, based on Renoud's threats, what he knew. She'd confessed to Father Clémence about Jaume. And perhaps they'd been seen—and every manservant and maid in the Montcava villa would sell their souls for an extra helping of beans and sheep's cheese. Yet Renoud couldn't know about Etienne, because she'd spent only that fortnight alone with him in Valerós.

Katelina claimed that you're supposed to learn from your sins; that's all God cares about. After all her soul-searing regrets, Isabella learned one thing: *Loneliness is easier to bear than searing grief.* Among the many reasons why she could never marry again.

Whenever her thoughts strayed to Jaume, she wanted to read the letters she'd written to him. They contained only fragments from *cançós d'amor* and passages of scripture she'd copied in Master Avraham's workshop. But she read them sometimes for comfort, to be reminded of the one boy who treated her kindly long ago. But when she dug through the chest in her room, the packet of old letters was missing. She tossed through the rest of her possessions before concluding that she must have left the letters in the scriptorium.

She folded the letter she stole from Clémence and placed it in the pouch of mementos she wore on a cord around her neck. The letter had plunged her into a funk of sad remembrances, but it helped her in no way. She needed to sleep. She needed to rise in the morning and pursue a way to avoid the hell on earth that this new crusade promised for her. The next steps forward must begin in the morning, to act without fear.

Find her misplaced letters in the scriptorium.

Get all the malicious visitors out of the castle.

Learn from Master Guillem what must be done to prepare Valerós for siege.

Spend every possible moment creating aged Gospels to sell in Narbonne, so there was silver for taxes.

Ask Benito to supervise Sebastián more closely.

Carry more than her penknife, all the time.

Find a way to persuade Pèire that his battle strategy for her future was wrong-headed. And doomed.

All before Pentecost. Isabella counted that out. Pentecost was fifty days after Easter. Therefore, how many days in the future? Twenty-nine days, since it must be close to dawn.

Before she blew out the candle, she read that sad letter again.

> If only you could understand how I ache, beyond all
> knowing, hoping you will turn to me.

A foreign emotion. People here needed her to take care of Valerós and Arracheuse. But no one ever begged her to turn to them for help. And there was no one that she might turn to in the way that the letter-writer mourned, except perhaps her friend Katelina. Most definitely, the help of an aged French viscount was not needed. She had to stop that idea come morning.

Lubos in Camp

IN THE COOL OF the night, high in these hills, Lubos laid a fire in the heathen way the folk of that Dalmatian village did, laying the main sticks so they aligned with the North Star, and then creating an eight-pointed cross around the anchoring sticks, praying all the while. He liked it best in the odd language that his woman Aykuna spoke, because those sounds summoned her to mind. The language of the prayer didn't matter, except Latin didn't sound right.

He no longer prayed to Our Father in Heaven because his needs were better served when he did as Aykuna taught: conjuring the lower spirits who inhabit the stones, waterfalls, and the wind. Père-Izsák agreed that only a fool believes there is but one God, and it takes another kind of fool to believe that God has only two natures, as if simple "good" and "evil" described the many gods. If you pray to only one God, you can't harvest the powers of all those other spirits, those now maligned or forgotten by most men in Christendom.

Lubos didn't even need to know the spirits' names to call on them: they swirled around him everywhere, especially here in the woods where the abiding silence made it easy to discern their voices. They never left him alone.

His camp smelled of juniper, which rankled the nose like cat piss. The tinder he fed into the nascent fire was last season's lavender, which he hated because it reminded him of the pampered soulless creatures he formerly bedded. And he smelled of too-tired horse and his own blood.

If he didn't think it would be importuning beyond his merit, he'd ask the spirits to deliver him from his sense of smell. The lavender-fueled memory reminded him how much he disliked the smell of a woman after coupling. Aykuna was wise enough to remove herself so he didn't feel defiled afterward.

Once the fire flared enough to warm him, Lubos slung the blanket from his bedroll over his shoulders, stripped his breeches, and opened his soldier's kit, grateful that he knew how to pack properly:

he had once been a crusader-knight. But he was short on thread and had to unravel a portion of his other shirt for sufficient strands.

As he sewed up his wounded arm, he pretended it was Aykuna who chanted the prayers to the spirits and guided the needle. It hardly hurt when she touched him. And she could do it faster than he could: he needed to fly with the spirits before dawn, to return to the task Père-Izsák asked him to do.

PART TWO
Whispers

...My world was ended by a too bonny magpie
Who made such of fool of me, that I want her to burn.
And I should hang, which I very much earned
Because I did not guard against such mean work;
And I will tell you the whole foolery so you can laugh.

— Friar Raymond de Corned
"A San Marsel d'Albeges, prop de Salas"

In Part Two

18
Donzel

Tomás at Valerós
29 days before Pentecost

PAIN SHOT THROUGH BROKEN bones. Tomás's mouth and tongue were so swollen that he choked instead of screaming when one thug held him down and the other began violating him with his staff. One thug jerked Tomás upright and raised a fist. The cross tattooed across the back of his hand had a crimson crescent at each point. Tomás strangled on a cry as the hand mashed his ruined face.

When Tomás opened his eyes, blood trickled in his throat. He spat, then shouted for help.

"No fear, *fadrin*. Your brother will come."

"Father, are you here?" It sounded like a voice in a dream. Yet only Miquel called him "lad."

"Be patient. When Chrétien sets you free, I'll ride with you. We'll take back what's yours."

A creature scurried nearby. Tomás looked around, but it was beyond dark where he lay.

Black.

Not even shadows flickered. Something crawled across his bare legs. His hands and feet were tied, so he couldn't brush it away. The rope cut into his wrists, and broken bones screeched in unendurable pain when he tried to wiggle free.

Chrétien didn't know where Tomás was. Tomás didn't know either. That meant his brother would never come.

Tomás shrieked in the dark, until his throat burned as raw as the rest of his flesh, begging his father to help.

"Father, help me!"

Once again, he woke screaming.

Outside the barracks door, dawn malingered on the horizon. Tomás stared at the ceiling of the barracks, wishing he was back on warm, sweet Cyprus instead of lying on a cold, lumpy straw pallet in a barracks on a ratty hill in Aragón, where the stone floor and thick limestone walls here would never get warm, no matter how hot summer might be, if it ever came. He needed to get up and finish his business—to get that letter from that priest they called Clémence. But last year's broken bones still ached, slowing him down.

He felt with his tongue for the tooth that grieved him, but it had quieted down, perhaps numbed by the stony chill of this backwoods castle. The men from this barracks had gone, probably to practice. He'd observed them the previous evening with bows and staves. They were good fighters. But then again, everyone in Castell-de-Valerós went about armed to the teeth.

Or the knees.

The pain in his lower back from that woman's attack led him to guess that he'd be pissing red again, although the ache in his kidneys and balls did take his mind off that sore tooth. Waiting for his father Miquel to appear and chastise him, Tomás reached to check the damage the grey senhóra had done to him, just as he saw he had living company: Pèire Leteric's great-grandson perched on the cot opposite him, sitting cross-legged and serious as a young lord, waiting for Tomás to awaken.

"I want you to teach me all you know." The boy didn't wait for Tomás to speak but instead rushed to plead his case. "Benito, our master at arms, says a real knight goes to work early. So here I am, ready to learn."

Tomás licked the roof of his mouth, hoping to clear away the film of last night's wine, masking his embarrassment. The boy had surely heard him cry out in nightmares. "I'm not a teacher. I'm just a scribe."

Sebastián gazed at him as if to say, *You're lying.*

"What do you think you can learn from me, donzel?"

Of all the ridiculous moments since he'd come to this castle, this beat all. The son of his enemy, the wrongful inheritor of his father's legacy, begged to be his student. Was this what Pèire meant, that he wanted to hire Tomás's services?

"I saw you fight Renoud in the street last night. I want to be a warrior, like Pèire Leteric and my grandfathers, who are warriors."

"People say Pèire is a great warrior. Who are your grandfathers?"

Go ahead, name my enemies.

"My mother's father died on crusade in Constantinople. My other grandfather is a great crusader who's vassal to the Count of Toulouse and the king of Aragón. They tell stories about him late at night when I'm supposed to be in bed. He still lives in the Outremer, so I've never met him." He dropped his tone. "Have you heard of him? He's Don Miquel of Morella."

"*Bon Dèu!*" Who had lied to this boy? Or sent him to tease the legitimate son of Don Miquel in this outrageous way?

"You know him?" Sebastián became even more excited

"I've heard of him. If that's the kind of warrior you want to be, donzel, you'll have to work very hard indeed. And you must always do what Don Miquel would do. No stealing. No running away. And never put others in jeopardy."

Sebastián sat still, struggling inwardly. Tomás remembered how he stood before his Nizari swordmaster a dozen years ago, hungry for the master's knowledge but worried about the pain required to gain that knowledge. He learned later that his master was a dissolute renegade, not a real Nizari. Sooner rather than later, the boy would learn that Tomás was no better.

Sebastián brightened. "If you make all the rules for my training, I would never disobey."

The boy's eager desire was intriguing, because it wasn't a request to play games. However, the lad's family had stolen Fontcours from Miquel. "Why me?"

"Because you are the best fighter I've ever seen. I need the best swordmaster. I want to be a knight at the same age as Pèire was when he first went to the Outremer."

"But I'm a scribe. I can't help a donzel who wants to be a knight." He repressed a smile at the ludicrous notion of taking on any child as a student, much less the false heir of Montcava. "I can teach you how to write your name."

"I can read and write Latin and Greek." The boy drew his thin body up ramrod straight. "And I speak Catalan and the common tongue of the Languedoc. Father Anselm says I speak French better than my mother, and—"

"Then no swordmaster should start your training with a pen-knife. I could teach you Arabic." That language might be the only subject at which Tomás outpaced this would-be pupil.

"Thank you, senhór. I have enough problems with Greek. I'm not ready for another tongue."

"If you want to start your studies now—"

"Yes, senhór, if you please!"

"I haven't agreed, donzel. And I can't. I'm leaving Valerós today."

"*Ai.*" A cloud flitted over the boy's face, but then he grabbed onto another idea. "Then today only. I'll have this chance to learn everything I can in a day."

"If you want a day's work, then begin with my friend Chrétien."

"A jongleur?" The boy sounded puzzled rather than offended.

"He won't teach you to sing. But he can teach you how to move with a sword. He had the same masters as I did."

Another storm passed over the boy's face.

"What's troubling you?" Tomás asked.

"If I saw that you are a fighter, then Pèire must know you are a knight, too. He knows everything. Why are you in disguise?"

Mustering supreme sternness, Tomás said, "You must give me your oath, donzel. You won't speak of this to anyone, on the honor of your grandfathers."

"I swear it. I, Sebastián of Fontcours, son of Isabella of Valerós and grandson of Miquel of Morella, swear it as a man of paratge." The boy offered a solemn oath on his honor.

Why trust me, you fool? Any way Tomás considered it, Sebastián was the false heir to the stolen Fontcours estate. Yet the boy looked up at him with all the seriousness of a warrior, or a little brother.

"Now you swear," Sebastián said. "If you receive a man's oath, you have to swear to honor it. On your father's honor."

Did Pèire put the boy up to this? Tomás felt compelled to tell at least a kind of the truth. "A hidden enemy tried to kill me. I remain in disguise until I discover who it is. And I cannot swear another oath until I kill him."

"Perhaps it's the man who grabbed me in the garden." Sebastián's excitement bloomed. "Maybe we have the same enemies."

"Then you must learn now how to protect yourself."

"Yes, senhór."

"We need to be at morning mass." Tomás yanked the miserable, itchy brown robe over his linen shirt.

The boy leaped up. "What do I call you?"

"When we're with others, you call me Master Tomás. When we're alone, you call me Don Tomás."

"Don Tomás of where?"

"Of wherever I am at any moment."

He pulled on his boots and followed the boy to the chapel. Then he slipped in among the warmth of the archers and bordoniers at the back, where he observed the seigneur and his family. While Tomás surveyed the strength of Pèire's men and the character of the man's family, Pèire caught Tomás's wandering eyes. His white bushy brows waggled, though Tomás couldn't tell whether the old man was worried or laughing at him. Standing behind Pèire and the angry dòmna of Valerós, Renoud tried to look holier than an entire pack of priests.

Tomás lifted his hands with others in prayer. He came here to find his enemies, where the young donzel was the third generation of that breed. Instead, the donzel wanted Tomás to play stern uncle. Well, he hadn't promised anything. He'd made it clear that he and Chrétien would be on the road before night fell.

As he pretended to pray, Tomás recalled Sebastián's claim. "*My other grandfather is vassal to the Count of Toulouse and the king of Aragón.*" The pale, red-headed donzel had no Moor from Aragón for a grandfather.

To keep from laughing, Tomás prayed sincerely, asking to find his best knife when he searched the alleys. He felt the ghostly breath of his earth-bound father, whispering at the back of his neck.

"So, my son. You're here to stalk our Montcava enemies, not the other way around. Buy or steal your letter from the disgusting priest, and then get back to Toulouse."

19
A Troublesome Priest

Isabella at Valerós
29 days before Pentecost

AFTER MORNING CHAPEL, ISABELLA paced along the parapets. A booted eagle drifted upward on the morning breeze. Isabella wished that she too could soar over this side of the Pyrenees and float over the Corbières hills. The eagle circled the upper garden in search of vermin, its claws out to strike; then it swooped to attack, missed, and rose to dive again. This time it caught its prey. A sharp *aiieee* echoed up from the garden. A viper in the bird's claws writhed, trying to bite its captor. The eagle soared up to a perch beyond the castle.

She descended to join the others when Pèire freed Sebastián from his punishment to accept the horse his uncle Renoud brought. Sensing Renoud nearby every moment, like a viper in the bushes, and so never letting her son out of sight, Isabella stood in the lower courtyard while Sebastián inspected his new mount.

Finally, Marshal Guillem came to the courtyard, asking Sebastián to put his horse in the stable and finish his chores. Before Isabella could leave the now-empty courtyard, a silk-clad arm reached around her waist.

"Did Hugues convince your grandfather to join us on crusade?" Renoud's voice grated on her ears, making her even more jittery.

"I don't know what Pèire thinks," she said, although she'd heard exactly what he thought. *I'd forgotten how easy it is to lie.*

"The smart seigneurs are declaring for the French." Renoud, self-satisfied, counted himself in that lot. "When it gets too hot and the French go home again, we'll let the rebels cut apart the army left behind. After another season, the French will stay home."

96

"You are such a crafty warrior. Hugues de Beaurain must admire your insights."

"Hugues doesn't know. Isabella, persuade Pèire to ride with us." He rested his hand on the nape of her neck, which in the old days meant she was to do what he wanted, *at that very moment.*

"Pèire doesn't take advice from women." *Or vipers in the weeds.*

"Yet, you don't want Simon de Montfort to think Pèire shelters heretics." He waggled her head. She wiggled out of his grasp. "If that happens, though, I shall happily serve as the master of Valerós when Pèire's is condemned."

"Stop! Leave me alone."

"You are such a tease," Renoud whispered, his breath stinking of breakfast ale. "First luring me, then setting me afire, then pretending you hate it."

She wrenched away, colliding at the corner of an alley with the Celt jongleur.

"Oofff!" Chrétien wrapped his arms around her to keep them both from falling. "It's the Pyrenees trout, caught again."

"Excuse me, Master Jongleur. I must join my grandfather."

"He's down at the gate with the marquis."

"You'll never get what you want in that quarter, *xiqueta,*" Renoud called. His hands closed into fists. "You'd have better luck with Pedro *el Rei* or Pèire's Moorish sodomite."

Renoud stalked off toward the gate and, mercifully, was gone.

Chrétien became serious as soon as Renoud disappeared. "Are you all right, ma dòmna? Can I help?"

"I'm fine," she snapped. "Do I look like a fainting fool?"

"Never in this life."

"Then step out of my way so I can pass."

At the gate, Hugues's men-at-arms had packed the horses and waited to depart. Hugues called to Renoud that it was time to resume their journey. Pèire stood at Hugues's side, saying farewell. When Isabella joined Pèire, he rested his arm on her shoulder.

"I wish I could stay more than one night," Hugues said.

"Simon will be at Carcassonne when we pass through next week," Renoud said to Pèire. "I can give him your answer then, senhór."

Pèire said, "Tell Simon de Montfort that I always give every-thing possible when my king and pope call. Any man who says other-wise is a liar."

"I'm happy you'll stand with us," Renoud said. "If we clear up the claims of heresy quickly, we can send the French army home at the end of summer." He whispered to Isabella, "I'll see you at Pente-cost, sister."

"Where's your friend Father Clémence?" Hugues asked Renoud. "Didn't he ask to travel with us?"

·

That innocent question launched a series of calls across the battle-ments and a cacophony of shouts as men searched for the priest in every Valerós alley. Then silence fell when men found the priest's body in the family's garderobe.

To avoid Renoud, Isabella stayed close by Pèire, who dragged her deep into the scene with him. She had no choice but to look.

Still seated on the privy, Father Clémence bent in a meditative pose, his face turned to heaven with a look of sad beseeching, his hands twisted together and stiffening in prayer. A trickle of blood had dried at the corners of his mouth. Despite the blood, relief flooded through Isabella's veins: now no living person knew her worst sins. But then she prayed for the priest's untidy soul.

Men laid the body on the plank floor. A dagger had been jammed at the collarbone into the body cavity. Isabella stepped back, not wanting to see the blood.

Pèire studied the blood-black stain around the top of the priest's linen undershirt. "It wasn't a trained soldier who did this. It takes time for the man to bleed so much and die." He picked up the dead man's arm so the hands came untwined; the sleeve of the robe fell away to reveal an odd cross tattooed above the wrist.

"What's this?" Hugues toed a scrap of parchment on the planks. Isabella struggled to appear as inscrutable as Pèire. She knew what the parchment contained, because she had written it; but she didn't know how Father Clémence came to possess it.

"It looks like magical writing," Renoud said.

"Don't be a—don't be foolish," she said. She'd copied that text out in her teacher's workshop in Toulouse, because it was the most beautiful of all the scrolls her master possessed. Now it had a despoiling footprint on it. "It's the Creation story in Hebrew."

"How do you know Hebrew?" Hugues asked, openly curious.

"Then it's devil magic!" Renoud said at the same time.

"I've just seen it before," she said, ignoring Renoud, "in a friend's library in Toulouse."

"But Jews use magical writings to harm Christians." Renoud persisted, though Isabella sensed he wasn't concerned about either the Hebrew script or the dead priest; rather, he enjoyed harassing her.

"The Hebrew people believe in One God and the same creation we do." She reached to take the fragment from Hugues's hand. "It should be treated with the same respect as a Gospel if you believe Genesis to be the Word of God."

Hugues relinquished the scrap. "What does it say?"

"The same as they teach in church: *In the beginning God created heaven*—"

Renoud interrupted. "Clémence had other letters he was carrying to our host. Perhaps he still has those." He bent over the corpse, as if intending to search the priest's pockets. But he rose, holding the knife at hand's length, showing it to Pèire. "This belongs to that filthy Moor who attacked me in your alley."

"The scribe was with me all night until morning mass," Pèire said. Isabella stiffened, hearing what Pèire said, but she couldn't take her eyes off the steel blade, even though she hated blood. "If you want to accuse the scribe, then call me a liar."

As Pèire spoke, Tomás the scribe stepped out of the crowd to stand by Pèire, arms crossed. The hood of his robe shadowed his face, but Isabella imagined the same ugly glare as when she first met him.

Hugues commanded Renoud to cease his accusations. Then he said, "Pèire, I want your word as bond. Promise to appear with this scribe before the bishop to answer questions. This priest was working for the prelate, so this murder is serious to the Church."

"I swear by my sword."

"And I shall go with you to Toulouse to do so," the scribe said.

"Narbonne," Pèire said. "I'm sworn to Pedro d'Aragón. His bishop is at Narbonne."

"Fine," Hugues said. "But do it by Pentecost. Otherwise, your scribe must forfeit his person to the king of Aragón, since this is his knife. And Pèire—"

"I'll forfeit this castle." Pèire saved Hugues from asking it. For Isabella, it was a heart-stopping declaration. Forfeit Valerós?

"So swear," Hugues said.

"As a man of paratge." Pèire swore his most powerful oath: as a man of honor, that honor stretching back through generations.

His vow outdid all the horrors that morning—the dead man, blood everywhere, Renoud haranguing her. Pèire just pledged his castle for the life of that deceitful scribe. Everyone seemed calm, satisfied by Pèire's outrageous pledge. Her heart beat so hard, others must hear.

Then Hugues pointed to some men standing about, including Chrétien the jongleur. "Take care of this poor priest. Father Anselm will tell you where to bear his body. The rest of you, those who came with me, finish preparing to ride."

Everyone moved at Hugues's command, proving what Pèire said about the marquis' ability to command men. The moving mass of men jostled Isabella, repeatedly saying, "Excuse us, ma dòmna." The turmoil separated her from Pèire. She turned around, looking for where he'd gone—and faced Renoud again, as if the devil woke up that day with a desire to pester her every five heartbeats.

"You had every reason to want Clémence dead." Renoud said. "He knew all your sins. Did he also sniff out heretic gold here?"

"We have no heretics and no gold."

"Clémence brought messages," Renoud drawled, "that ensure Pèire Leteric will send you to me by Pentecost."

"*Bon Dèu!* What did you tell my grandfather?" Isabella strove for years to keep Pèire from knowing what happened in Toulouse.

"That he's done a great job teaching the boy Sebastián. That as Sebastián's uncle, I'm ready to do my duty to make him a warrior in the southern tradition."

Pèire would never believe a word of such flattering tripe.

"And I told him you promised to come to Toulouse by Pentecost, to marry my cousin Louis and bring Sebastián back to the House of Montcava," Renoud said.

"*Bon Dèu!* What did he say?"

"He seemed stern, but then he slapped my arm and called me a warrior to rival Richard Lionheart."

The sole consolation of the morning: that Pèire was laughing at Renoud.

"Renoud!" Hugues called. "We need to be on the road. It's far too late in the morning."

■

Isabella leaned against a wall, holding her breath to keep from being sick. Though the sight of Renoud riding away eased her anger and the chaos in her thoughts, her stomach churned from the sight of the priest's blood and his boot-heel on that scrap of writing. *Darkness was upon the face of the deep.* The letter she'd stolen from the priest's satchel was still tucked inside her pouch. As the next task for the morning, she needed to find her letters in the scriptorium.

On her way there, she met Katelina. Anxious to find her missing letters, Isabella didn't want to chat. But Katelina seized her hand, her many rings cutting into Isabella's fingers.

"I've never told Pèire, *xiqueta*. No one knows but me."

"What?"

"Of anyone in the castle, you had excellent reasons to wish that priest Clémence dead."

"Katelina, you don't think—"

"*Òc*, I don't. And I won't speak of it, either. You always resist old memories."

"I don't have time to remember. There's too much to do. I need to go forward. If you tell Pèire anything, tell him it's a mistake to make any man marry me."

Beatriz called to Katelina just then, so Isabella turned up an alley, needing to be alone. But Pèire hailed her.

"*Xiqueta*, tell Benito to find the scribe and send him to wait for me in your scriptorium." Pèire still waved as Hugues de Beaurain led his party down the trail, away from Valerós. "Make sure your son apologizes to the smith. Then make the scribe welcome until I come. No knee in his privates this time."

"Grandfather, you lied for that scribe. You went to your room alone last night." Isabella could barely hold her question until the Beaurain and Montcava knights rode out of sight.

"I'm not about to quibble with Renoud." He started across the courtyard, waving across the way for Guillem's attention.

"But you pledged the castle for a stranger's life."

"It won't come to anything, *xiqueta*. We'll go to Pedro and the bishop as I promised. The king is a reasonable man."

"But how can you ride with the French? You said before that this crusade has nothing to do with us."

"I didn't say I'd ride with the French."

"Everyone heard you promise as much just now."

"Hugues and all those priests and pilgrims in the courtyard heard me call Renoud a liar if he tells Simon we aren't supporting the Church. That's what the bastard plans to do, isn't it?"

"I expect so," she said.

Pèire spat. "And I bet Renoud also says the best tactic is to suck on the French like eels all summer and then murder them in their beds when winter comes. What a shining example of southern manhood. A tribute to paratge."

"Then you won't ride with Hugues de Beaurain?"

"Talking with Hugues made me think I might. But then I got to thinking about the bleached bones of my son Vidal laid to waste in the desert," Pèire said. "And I'll be damned if I ever send boys from this valley to crusade again, be it Jerusalem or Toulouse. Now, go make sure your boy apologizes."

20

It's Nothing

Jean-Luc at Valerós
29 days before Pentecost

GREY LIGHT LEAKED UNDER the archway of the barracks. At one point during the night, Jean-Luc prayed for his heart to stop beating, because each pulse sent shards of pain from his belly to his knee. Still wracked by pain in the morning, Jean-Luc tried to choke down the porridge a bordonier brought him. His stomach resisted, but he needed to restore his strength after losing half his life's blood.

Felicia came with Senhóra Isabella and Sebastián, who proved to be older than Jean-Luc had guessed in the garden.

The boy said, "I've come to beg pardon for placing you in jeopardy. And to thank you for the service you did me." Instead of an arrogant little donzel addressing a servant, Sebastián spoke respectfully, man to man.

"You fought bravely yourself." Jean-Luc shook Sebastián's hand, though the effort taxed his strength.

"Do you say so truly?" The boy brightened at the compliment. "I think the man who attacked us was a brigand. Or a spy. What do you think?"

His mother spoke sharply. "Master Smith thinks you caused a great deal of trouble."

When Senhóra Isabella spoke, it sounded as if her throat had been burned raw. He studied the woman that his lord was supposed to marry. She was tall, with wisps of copper hair escaping her head covering, the same color as the boy's red mop. Her worried expression made Jean-Luc think of his own mother, who had cared too much about the family business and her foolish boys. Although this

103

senhóra was still young, worry had spoiled her looks, and she bit her nails. When had a man last removed her head covering, untied her robe, and made her forget her cares?

"I thank you for my son's safety."

She took Jean-Luc's hand in the Catalan greeting. Like Pèire and the boy, she treated him as an equal.

When mother and son left, Felicia stayed to tend his wound. He'd been raised in a world of chivalry, so he argued the imprudence of her remaining unchaperoned with a man.

She laughed at him.

"Everyone knows you can't chase a mouse under the bed at present," she said. "I'm certainly safe with you."

"You are the best nurse I've ever had."

"*Merci beaucoup, maître forgeron.*"

"*Il n'y a pas de quoi.*" His reflexive reply spilled out in French. *It's nothing.*

His angel laughed again. "I thought so. Your accent wasn't learned at the knee of any Breton we've ever known."

Jean-Luc felt his face burn with embarrassment. He couldn't look her in the eye—not because his deception had been found out so easily, but because his angel caught him in a lie. He bit his tongue to keep from confessing that he spied for Viscount Gerard.

"I learned French from a priest, but I think you learned it from your mother," Felicia said.

"She married a Breton smith. I learned French from her and smithing from my father."

She pursed her lips and concentrated on her work, seeming to forget his deception. While she replaced the dressing and then convinced Jean-Luc to take more broth, he pondered how soon he could resume the work that Gerard asked of him. By the time his angel had finished, he was exhausted physically and couldn't force his mind to do the work that was his duty, to pry with questions about Pèire Leteric and Valerós.

The girl seemed to have nothing better to do than sit with him, chatting about life in the castle. Comfortable with her sitting so near, Jean-Luc drifted away, lost in sleep. But even with an angel at his side, he couldn't defend against his nightmares.

.

At dawn, the signal passed for the ships to slip anchor. Galleys towed the transport ships toward the mammoth walls of Constantinople, rising straight up from the sea. Towering clouds scudded across the sky, and then a gust passed through, pushing the fleet against the city walls. Sailors labored to keep the ships from crashing into the walls while soldiers like Yves and Jean-Luc scrambled up the scaling ladders.

As they burst through to the city towers, Yves screamed like a berserker, slashing at the city's defenders. Jean-Luc too felt a cry surging from his throat as he settled into his work, thrusting an armored elbow into the throat of any enemy who came up behind him.

By vespers, the battle fever died out. The eastern emperor, whom the Venetians called a usurper, fled and his army retreated in disarray. Inside Constantinople, the conquering crusaders found mostly women, children, and old men, all of whom sought to flee rather than fight.

As they patrolled the city, Yves threatened their own band with loss of manhood if they joined the pillagers, while Jean-Luc threatened merely the loss of their immortal souls and thieving right hands. When the crusader-lords sent word to prepare for a night's rest near the captured towers, Jean-Luc and Yves urged their weary men to the walls with the promise of food and sleep. On the way, they skirted an enormous vaulted church dedicated to St-Mary.

A grey-haired nun, her veil torn away, screamed in the street.

"In the name of our Lord Jesus, mercy!"

She cried out in Greek as a Frankish soldier hurled her down onto the steps of the church. He tore her robe and forced himself on her. Jean-Luc and Yves ran across the square and pulled the soldier off the woman. In a fury, Yves ran the man through.

The nun stood frozen, looking down at the bleeding man. Jean-Luc began shouting at her in battlefield Greek.

"Run! Hide! Go now!"

She shook her head and instead returned to the church, wavering as she walked. "I must care for the others."

Jean-Luc and Yves ran past her into pandemonium. Inside the church, a swarm of crusader-mercenaries crawled up make-shift ladders to strip the gold-leafed icons and sculptures. Women screamed in Greek nearby. Scrambling in the dim light, Jean-Luc stumbled across the bodies of Orthodox priests and nuns heaped in the nave. Bile burned in his throat. Yves shouted for order in the name of God.

A man ran past with a golden, dolorous Madonna figure in his arms.

"Stop!" Jean-Luc yelled. It was a crusader-captain from Toulouse, a large man with shaggy red hair like a northern pirate, blood to his elbows from the day's battle. Jean-Luc bellowed in the man's face, "In the name of God, I command you to stop."

The Languedoc captain laughed like a madman and ran down the steps. Jean-Luc thrust his boot to trip him. The man slashed up at Jean-Luc. Outraged, Jean-Luc kicked him in the head. Yet the man's sword found the gap between Jean-Luc's mail chausses and hauberk. He felt the sword pierce his thigh.

"Sancta Maria!"

Jean-Luc knocked the man's sword away with his mailed fist as a host of men wearing the thieving captain's colors came at him. Half-blind in the smoky torchlight, he thrust his sword at one man after another as the rioting soldiers attacked him. An array of swords and pikes crowded around him, and he hacked and parried as bodies fell at his feet. He shoved a man off his blade and turned and slashed again.

Yves stood there, surprise frozen on his scarred face.

Jean-Luc's sword had sliced into his brother's middle and now blood spilled over them. Jean-Luc sank to the stone steps, catching his brother in his arms. He cradled Yves, rocking them both and tasting grief. A hole opened where his heart used to be, while his brother's soul bled out.

Beside them lay the dead Languedoc captain who had wanted that golden Madonna so badly. Another crusader-soldier rushed past, and the statue tipped and fell into Jean-Luc's lap alongside Yves, as if the sad-eyed Madonna also needed comfort.

21
Poulain

LINGERING AMONG CURIOUS MEN, Tomás watched Renoud pack up the dead priest's bedroll and then command his men to load it onto a pack pony. Renoud and the marquis rode out, carrying the last hope for seizing Clémence's letters.

So, Tomás went to find Chrétien. They needed to be on their way.

He muttered curses that could only be learned at the knee of Miquel of Morella, condemning this loss. Yet he'd been wrong to let his hopes be raised in pursuit of that rumored letter. They needed a new strategy now, to bring proof to the bishops' court.

"Forgery?" Miquel suggested, walking beside him. "Bribe false witnesses? That's what the Montcavas used to steal Fontcours."

"You'd never recommend such deceit when you lived. You taught us to be honorable men."

"Yes, but when you're dead, you get a different perspective."

"*Bon Dèu!*" Tomás wanted to cry for mercy, having just lost his last best hope.

"Master Scribe!" A man hailed Tomás. The master at arms, Benito, seemed a good fellow from what Tomás had observed, including at the previous night's dicing in the armory. "Senhór Pèire asks that you wait on him in the scriptorium."

Benito led the way to what proved to be the fanciful name for a small room with a writing table and cupboards filled with scrolls. The room's only special attribute was a modest-sized window that allowed in daylight, its covering made of sheep's horn split into sheets, polished and braced in a wooden frame.

Miquel bent over the table, studying a manuscript. Smooth stones held down corners of the scroll, and another piece of vellum was being scribed with a copy. "It's fragment of the Gospel of St-John. This copy is as fine as the original."

"Given the catastrophe with the dead priest, Chrétien and I need to be gone from here." Tomás regretted speaking aloud. Treating Miquel as if he still lived only encouraged the ghost to return.

"You've only been in Valerós one night," Miquel drawled in the backcountry accent he used when teasing children. "Stay a while."

"We need to follow Hugues and Renoud. To see what more I can learn from the last of the Montcava bastards."

"Without hope for that dead priest's letter, the best idea is to stay here and learn what you can from Pèire," Miquel said.

A woman's voice echoed in the hallway. "Sancta Maria! Go away. I don't need a guard. I'm perfectly safe in my own home."

Senhóra Isabella flew into the room like an irate merlin, her hawk's eyes flashing as they had when she mashed his face into the cobbles. She placed her hands on the back of the chair where Miquel sat. Milky pale, save for a slight sunburn across her hawk-like nose, she was exactly Tomás's height. And she was so angry that he felt the heat from her body, closer than any woman had been since—

He stepped back and made the sign his master taught. He gave up women after that attack on Cyprus, determined to never again let a woman near enough to do him harm, especially a Montcava widow.

She spoke brusquely. "Pèire is delayed. I'm to stay with you until he comes."

He prepared to defend against her assault. "You don't mind sitting with the fellow accused of dispatching a holy man?"

"He wasn't holy, and Pèire claims you didn't do it."

"But you seem upset, ma dòmna. Was the deceased priest a friend of yours?"

"*Bon Dèu*, no!"

Tomás had a bad tendency to want to control passion in a woman. But he again returned to his vow. He took another step back.

"Will you please move away from the scrolls?" she said. "This work needs to remain clean while the pigments cure."

"Is this your writing?" He indicated the copy of the Gospel on the table, ignoring that she implied he wasn't clean.

"Yes." Golden flecks in her eyes glittered in the light. She was proud of this work. She rummaged in the shelves, seeking something.

"You'd make a fortune in Barcelona with such grand talents, ma dòmna."

"Perhaps."

"How did you obtain this Gospel?" he asked. "It's quite old."

"A Jewish collector in Toulouse knew what I like. One of those scholars who moved to Toulouse from Toledo."

"You must have had a broadminded husband."

"No, I didn't. He simply wasn't aware," she said. "Please stop staring at me."

"Was I?"

"You are. And you do it to distract me. Let's say it worked for you—though it didn't—and so now you can stop."

"Whatever you command, ma dòmna." Chrétien had described the Montcava widow as amusingly innocent. Yet she'd enjoyed jamming Tomás's balls into his aching wisdom teeth the night before. "I'm just curious. This work is unusual."

"Because I can write Greek? Or because I can write at all? We're not ignorant here, Master Scribe."

"I'm impressed." Indeed, he'd met women who could read, but few who bothered to do so.

"Our tutor was Greek and—Sancta Maria, please stop that."

"What?"

"That rude sign you make with your hand."

"This?" He made his master's sign for focusing his attention.

"Yes. Stop, if you please."

"Apologies, ma dòmna. It helps novices concentrate."

"Catalan sheepherders use that sign to ward off evil," she said.

"I didn't know."

"Everyone from Barcelona to Narbonne knows that sign."

He repressed the absurd impulse to tell her the truth. "I was isolated from Catalan shepherds in Barcelona."

"Or perhaps isolated from all civilizing influences of society. Do they regard prevarication as a sin in your quarter of Barcelona?"

She called him a liar, but he pretended she meant something else. "I didn't kill that priest, ma dòmna."

"Perhaps God cares who killed him, but I don't." She spoke casually. Then she brightened, seeming to find what she sought, because she slipped something into the folds of her robe.

This lesser Montcava tribe, mother and son, threw him off his bearings. Time to find Chrétien and clear out. Find a new strategy to attack his enemy in Toulouse.

But then Pèire came to the scriptorium. Tomás greeted him in the Catalan manner, managing to get one gesture right. At the slightest wave of Pèire's hand, Isabella left without a word, destroying Tomás's belief that she'd never obey any man's command.

"Now, let's talk about how you can help me, Master Scribe."

.

"My girl wasn't squeamish about sitting with a priest-killer?"

Pèire sat in the chair Miquel had abandoned and fished in his jerkin for a small knife, the kind a woman might carry. Rummaging around the table, Pèire found a whetstone, spit on it, and began sharpening the blade.

"Senhór, I appreciate you speaking for me, but I didn't do it."

"Even the lesser weeping angels know that. Isabella could do a better job with her penknife." Pèire glanced down at his work rather than at Tomás. "Though my girl is as good with a javelin as a pen."

"She has a few surprising gifts," Tomás said.

"How about you, *fadrin?*" Pèire called him "lad," the way old crusaders addressed Tomás on Cyprus. The knife and stone snick-snicked for several heartbeats. "What are your gifts? Were you lucky enough to get Miquel's genius, or only your daddy's good looks?"

Both humiliation and relief flooded Tomás's senses, knowing he'd been discovered. He bowed his head and brought his hand to his breast. Even as he did it, Tomás knew it was an Outremer gesture of servitude. His toothache pounded.

"I regret I didn't announce myself properly."

Pèire dismissed that with a wave of his hand. "As if your face isn't an introduction. Though you didn't take good care of what Miquel gave you."

Tomás pictured his father's thin, ash-grey face with a permanent rictus of pain around his mouth and the canyon-deep creases in his brow, though Miquel's ghost was a handsome young man. Like Tomás had once been.

Pèire said, "I saw you in the alley yesterday, chasing my boy. I bet Miquel sent you to Cairo to learn to fight. He always said Latins didn't know a sword from a bludgeon. He called us all 'Latins' like the Saracens do."

"He sent both of us to Cairo." Why had he revealed even more? Yet, despite unmasking Tomás, Pèire seemed friendly. Jocular.

"You and your tall friend?"

"Yes, we were raised together. Chrétien was abandoned in our camp as an infant."

"Ah, yes. After Saladin took Tiberias. The women in camp found him wrapped in a crusader's tabard. We never did find the mother, much less his father. Miquel kept the boy when he left for Cyprus."

"That's the family story." Tomás shifted, uneasy that Pèire Leteric knew more about his father's life than any other men he and Chrétien had tracked down.

"Knowing ol' Miquel, I'm sure he worked your tail off. Never let you rest from the moment he put a sword in your hand, eh?"

"He knew every fight master between Barcelona and Antioch. He said—" Tomás stopped, mystified by how Pèire got him to talk.

"You can't know how good it was to see that face again." Pèire tugged away the leather wrapping around Tomás's wrist and touched the bonfraires brand. "If my men saw this, it'd be like a herald's shout announcing you."

Tomás rubbed the place where his father had burned him with a hot crossbow bolt. A perfect square, white and indelible, alongside the vein running from his palm. Chrétien had one like it, as did all of Miquel's aging knights on Cyprus.

Pèire rolled back the linsey-woolsey sleeve of his tunic, showing an identical brand. "And this says we're brothers, *fadrin*. But why do you *poulains* wear costumes instead of chainmail?"

He said *poulains*—*you colts*. In the Outremer, men used the word to deride the mixed-blood children of Arab or Kurd mothers. But Pèire made it sound like a pet name instead of a pejorative.

"*Ai, fadrin.* I worried when you didn't say hello. Then Hugues and the damnable Renoud come visiting. Too much coincidence."

"Renoud of Montcava is my enemy. His family stole my father's rightful legacy." Tomás rubbed his cheekbone, where that scar itched. "I came to learn whether you are joined with my enemy."

"Sweet Savior dancing in the golden heaven with all the sobbing angels," Pèire cried. "Did Miquel not say you can trust me?"

"I trust no one." Tomás stuck with his challenge, despite the warm welcome he'd just endured.

"I led the bonfraires with your father. Who more can you trust on God's green earth?"

"You married your child to our enemy."

"Isabella? Her father arranged that marriage. He was a sixth-degree Montcava cousin and half-Norman himself, the useless *punxor.* I tried to take her back when I heard it, but she was already carrying a babe." Pèire held his blade up to the light, peering at its edge. "The bishop in Toulouse called me out for breaking the Peace of God when I threatened the cur she married."

"Did you reveal how Eloïse of Montcava betrayed my father by marrying him and then hatching another man's sons?" There, he'd said it.

"No, on my honor as a knight of the bonfraires," Pèire said. "My own family believes Don Miquel is the boy's grandfather." He responded to the doubt on Tomás's face. "You're thinking Sebastián is too pale, so only a fool might believe it. But after forty years, no one in Toulouse remembers Miquel. And I don't tell tales."

"You tell great stories, like you did last night."

"Not secrets." Pèire thumped the table. "I don't tell my best comrade's secrets."

"So that your family can take my father's land?" Tomás made the boldest challenge, despite the old man's charm. He couldn't let go of a lifetime of caution.

"After I got Isabella away from those scorpions, we stayed free of Montcavas until yesterday." Pèire set down the knife and stone, looking grim. Or even hurt. "Why did you or your papa never come before now? We could go after those *baquelars* together."

"He made me swear not to go after Eloïse while she lived."

"Yes, that's Miquel," Pèire said. "He was God's own chivalrous knight. We were big heroes back then. We had fiefs from King Amalric in Jerusalem and booty from crusading. And we had the two most beautiful women in Toulouse thinking the sun rose and set on our bum rear-ends. Anglesa, the sweet one I married, didn't have much of a dowry, but what did I care? I was a booty-rich crusader."

"And Eloïse?"

"Her cousin Eloïse got the lion's share of Montcava when her daddy died. That made Miquel a grand seigneur. He already had Fontcours, which he got for saving the old Count of Toulouse in a raid near Jerusalem."

"So my father told us." Tomás gritted his teeth and paced, unnerved by the old man's friendly words. "But my father never had that woman, as a man has his wife, I mean. After he married Eloïse, she acted afraid of him, and he said—"

"I know. I heard him say it a hundred times: 'There's not a woman born that I have to force.'" Pèire glanced about as though he didn't see Tomás pacing. "He returned to Jerusalem after he learned his new wife carried another man's child when he married her."

"Did you return to the Outremer then, too?"

"My Anglesa died when our girl Melisinda was born. Without my wife, I lost interest in cutting trees and draining swamps in Valerós, so I went back to the Holy Land, to wander again."

"You joined Miquel?"

"Of course. My old uncle Sanç took care of getting Melisinda married. That's Isabella's mother. When my boy Vidal was ten, I came to fetch him, so he could ride with me. Vidal was like your papa. They both found the Outremer better than here. The food, the heat, the women."

"What happened to Senhóra Eloïse after my father left?"

Pèire picked up the thread of his tale and at the same time returned to grinding his little knife. "After a few years, she swore Miquel cheated on the marriage articles and then deserted her, so the Church gave her an annulment. Neat piece of work that was."

"Nicolau and Renoud got Montcava." Bitterness once more corroded Tomás's veins.

"Then Miquel was caught in a raid near Aleppo. His men got stuck through with arrows, and Miquel was sold in a Saracen slave market. If that fierce little Kurd woman hadn't sneaked him out of the city, he'd have rotted there, stacking stones for a Saracen citadel."

Pèire coughed and set the knife down. He rubbed his temples as if his head hurt, then resumed his story.

"Three years," Tomás said. "He was enslaved for three years."

"Yes. Three years after we found his men's pecked bones, Miquel rode into camp with that woman, her belly swelling up with a baby. Why, that must have been you. They say she's related to Saladin himself. She was more beautiful than any queen I ever met. Did she stick by him, your mother, I mean? She was hell on fire for Miquel."

"Yes, to the end," Tomás said.

"The end?"

"My father died last year. You didn't know?"

The blade rasped on stone. Pèire breathed in rumbling gasps. Tomás feared the old man was ill, but then saw tears flooding from Pèire's eyes.

Wherever had he come to? Did he know anything about his own father?

22

On Your Mother's Honor

Jean-Luc at Valerós
29 days before Pentecost

WHEN JEAN-LUC AWOKE NEXT, it was afternoon. A tiny old woman peered down at him, wearing the cap of a kitchen worker and carrying a tray of broth and ointment. She grinned broadly upon seeing him awake, which softened her old face so that she seemed girlish.

"I brought your bone-mend, Master Smith." She handed over his packet of comfrey leaves. "It fell from your clothes when the girls did your washing. So here you are, a man after my own mind for what heals and what consoles."

She undid Felicia's bandaging and clucked over the black gash that ran alongside the older, longer white scar. She washed his leg again and applied a smelly, burning yellow salve before tying a new bandage in place.

"That's a good bit of stitching on your poor leg," she said as she worked. She managed the conversation without Jean-Luc's help. "Senhóreta Katelina taught those girls well. She came when Senhóreta Beatriz was a new-hatched mewling thing, whose mother we laid in the grave just days after the little girl was born."

The old woman wrapped the discarded linen bandage into a tidy package and laid it on her tray, where she placed the broth bowl after Jean-Luc had eaten enough.

"Any person can tell Senhóreta Katelina was more than a nurse and tutor once upon a time. Listen to her talk and you hear she's a fine lady, although no one knows where she came from. East of Venice, they say. Greece or one of those wild places. Who can tell the names of them all? She's taught those girls to be excellent nurses for child or soldier." The woman paused to consider. "Except for Senhóra Isabella. She watches Master Benito train Pèire's men instead of learning how to fix busted up warriors."

Jean-Luc learned more about Pèire's family from her in three moments of chatter than in his three weeks of piss-poor spying.

After she tended to his bedding, the woman handed him a small packet from her tray of medicines. "Let's just tuck this little bit of salt under your blanket to draw off sickness. It's too bad Marshal Guillem can't lay his hands on the knife that cut you. You'd be rubbing it with this same ointment in the name of Jesus and the Holy Ghost. Then there'd be no fear of your leg going bad."

"Do you believe in old wives' magic?" Jean-Luc enjoyed the idea of this herb woman tending him.

"Being an old wife myself, I say it's best to do what my mother taught, to uphold my mother's honor. And you carry the good luck your own mother wished on you." She pointed to the silver boar's-tooth amulet around his neck.

"Yes." He touched it.

"You look like a man who needs all the luck mothering can give. Is that good woman still with us?"

"No, she's gone to God," he said.

"Pray God granted her a good end and that she's now rid of this evil world."

"Thank you." Jean-Luc didn't know how else to reply to a heretic's prayer.

"Now you're a sight to break a mother's heart. I'm of a mind to give you a brushing and a trim. If you will allow it."

She didn't wait for Jean-Luc to agree before she attacked him with a tortoise-shell comb and a razor, talking all the while. "It's a wonder you didn't scare that boy to death instead of saving him."

"The lad doesn't frighten easily," Jean-Luc said.

She patted his shoulder, laughing. "That's as true a thing as ever was said. No, Master Sebastián is much the same as his mother was then. Poor little girl, sent away to be a wife so young. That fearlessness, it's in their blood. Or is it foolishness? I recollect the old seigneur was that way, or worse, when he was a child."

Jean-Luc said, "You're much too young to remember. That's a story from your grandmother, surely."

"Aren't you the smooth one!" She knocked him on the skull playfully, as his own grandmother used to. "With a face as bad as yours, you need a sweet tongue for the ladies."

"I think it's a good enough face." He tugged at his beard.

She pushed Jean-Luc's hand away. "In a better world, you'd of kept your nose out of trouble. After you break it a time or two, it tells against your beauty."

By the time she finished with the comb, she had jollied him up. "Madam, tell me your name and let's be friends," he said.

"Ermessen. Just Ermessen. I don't have a husband now, so there's no other name to tell you. You can find me in the kitchen. I'm too old for more than keeping the serving girls out of trouble."

"Good day, Ermessen. God bless you for your healing." Then he had to ask. "How long have I been here?"

"Just since last night. Tomorrow's Sunday, when I'll be back with your breakfast. A man your size needs meat on his bones." Ermessen was still talking as she left the room. "It's a shame no woman is taking proper care of you."

∎

"So, your papa Miquel sent you hunting." When Pèire spoke after learning Miquel had died, it was a statement, not a question.

"The Church declared Miquel's new wife—my mother—wasn't a Christian—though she is. So Nicolau of Montcava got Fontcours, too," Tomás said. "My father asked me to take revenge against our hidden enemy. Therefore, I intend to kill Renoud and his sire as soon as I find out who that is."

"It couldn't be Renoud who hurt your papa. Was it the priest in the garderobe?"

"No. The priest wasn't on my father's list. I believe he carried letters proving Miquel's claim on Fontcours. But that hope is lost now. Renoud carried away Clémence's satchel."

"I just wish that *punxor* priest hadn't got the wild idea to get himself killed in my house." Pèire handed Tomás a worn, creased piece of vellum. "Look, *fadrin*."

The quill used to write the message must have been sharpened to a needle point, because the script was tiny. Tomás mouthed the Latin without speaking it aloud, translating as he read:

> I saw the wolf before the wolf saw me. I'll kill the wolf before the wolf kills me. God take the wolf and God save me. I'll hunt you to your lair. I'll take your mate and cubs. The other wolf is already destroyed.

Instead of a signature, the note ended with a lunate cross.

"I found that in my house the day I buried my son Vidal," Pèire said. "He died in the raid where your father was hurt so bad near Damascus."

"*Ai Dèu.*" The note was bone-chilling, yet Tomás felt an odd sense of relief. Pèire was his ally.

"That's why I returned to Valerós," Pèire said, "to be far away from whoever wanted to hurt what I love. For fifteen years, I've kept them safe. But now my children are being attacked, even with my men close by. And that dead priest and Eloïse's bastard son both bring me threats the same day."

"How did that priest threaten you?"

With a frown, Pèire pulled a sheaf of parchment from inside his jerkin. "He brought testaments from seigneurs that I've never met, saying I consort with schismatics. That my family is hereticated. That I refuse to pay my taxes because I'm a cheese-eating heretic."

"But you pay taxes to the viscount at Narbonne and to Aragón," Tomás said.

"Simon claims Arracheuse owes taxes to him, since he's now Viscount of Carcassonne. He demands my taxes, and says I'd best send my knights to support the crusade. By Pentecost."

"Pentecost? My agent placed a charge against Renoud in the bishops' court. I have until Pentecost to bring proof that Renoud is a bastard. That Fontcours legally belongs to me. But I don't have Clémence's letter. So, I don't have proof or know where to find it." Tomás handed back the scraps of parchment. "What will you do?"

"Those threats might be just noise in the wind." Pèire made a gesture of disgust that was becoming familiar. "That priest also wanted to tell me how my girl Isabella's a wanton heretic who'll bring Frankish crusaders to my doorstep."

Tomás considered that notion, rejected it. "I'm a stranger here, but it doesn't seem likely."

Pèire snorted. "I told that priest, 'Good for her. She deserves it.' He about choked on his own bile. Sweet dancing angels, does she look like a woman who's had a moment's happiness in bed? The fool was just Renoud's barking dog, who doubled his foolishness by getting his own self killed in my privy."

Pèire grabbed Tomás's wrist again, rubbing the bonfraires brand. "Do you think it's the same hellhound after us both, *fadrin*?"

"Yes." Tomás shivered with the thrill of finding an ally.

"I swear on my sword we are brothers." From inside his jerkin, Pèire retrieved Tomás's ill-used dagger and handed it over. "Help me protect my cubs. And I'll help you get Fontcours back."

"They say you have the best knights in Christendom. How can I help you, senhór?"

"Use what Miquel taught you to protect my children." Pèire put the whetstone away and wiped the blade, ready to end their talk. "Just until I get my girls moved to safe places. Keep Sebastián with you, until I can get Gerard to take him somewhere safe."

"Gerard?"

"The Viscount de Chartrain. Another friend of Miquel's. He's promised to protect Sebastián's land from this crusade."

"Sebastián..." Tomás paused. Did he possess a secret he shouldn't reveal? He decided not. "The boy asked me to be his fight master. He has an ambitious plan for how soon he becomes a knight. I promised him that Chrétien would share his sword skills."

"Good. Then your brother has a reason to carry a sword every-where. I'm calling for your help, on your oath as a bonfraire. I don't want another event like last night in the garden."

"How long? I have to go see the bishop in Toulouse."

"Say, a week from next Monday? Then you and I will go to the bishop at Narbonne."

When Tomás didn't answer, Pèire clawed at Tomás's wrist.

"You are going with me to Narbonne, aren't you?"

Until that moment, Tomás had intended to leave with Chrétien before sunset. "If I can still get to Toulouse by Pentecost." He had the distinct sensation of losing his rational judgment. "Is Narbonne nice in the spring?"

"When does weather matter to a vagabond like you?" Pèire said. "Meanwhile, make yourself useful." He gestured to the little scriptorium. "I kept lists of the knights in every company I ever rode with. Find more men who need hunting." He brightened. "You could be the scribe writing my history."

"Crusader legends?"

Pèire grinned. "I hear tell vain *punxors* in Narbonne and Toulouse pay to have their boasts and lies saved on parchment."

"I would be honored."

"But keep this between us. My men shouldn't see this." He tapped the brand on Tomás's wrist. He started for the door and then came back to fetch the little knife he'd sharpened. "Your friend Chrétien—he's teaching my men that Egyptian card game."

"Is he?"

"You know he is. Those that haven't seen the Outremer don't know how that sort of gambling works. If you rob my men, I'll be unhappy."

"Why do you think I'd do that?"

"Because I saw your papa do it a hundred times. I'd lay odds at a thousand to one that you colts learned the scam in your cradle."

"Those are steep odds."

"Too steep to gamble." Pèire found this immensely funny and, laughing, nearly walked into a wall. He groped for the doorway. "Tomorrow, I want to hear your hunting stories. Meanwhile, start poking through the lists in the cupboard. Here's a key."

Left alone in the scriptorium, Tomás opened the cabinet and examined the well-organized stacks and rolls of vellum and parchment. Where to begin?

"Start here." Miquel pointed to a packet wrapped in leather and tied with a thong. "I remember those."

"*Per l'amor de Dèu*, I don't need your help," Tomás said.

"I'd never interfere." Miquel seemed to turn his back.

"You always do."

"*Quiquid*," Miquel said. *Whatever*. "What else should I do while sitting outside Paradise? You can only spend so much time choking your chicken."

"I have to explain to Chrétien that we changed our mission."

"It's just a slight detour."

"A detour? I'm responsible for a donzel that I believed was our enemy. I can't pursue Renoud until Pentecost. I promised to protect a mob of women, at least one of whom wants to stab me with her penknife. And I'm supposed to wear this damnable scribe's robe, which scratches beyond anything you'd find in hell itself."

"*Ai*, you don't know that," Miquel said. "Also, you just now promised to go to Narbonne, to throw yourself on the mercy of the king of Aragón. And a bonfraire always keeps his oath."

∙

While Tomás worked, Miquel left him in peace, merely reading by his side but not speaking as Tomás studied Pèire's lists and letters. It must have been midafternoon when Tomás replaced the first of Pèire's lists in the cabinet and attempted to further sort which scrolls belonged together.

"Did you come here to kill that priest and me?" Sebastián manifested like a phantom, though Tomás refused to be startled anymore by this family's movements.

"No, I'm not here to kill you. And I didn't kill that priest. Aren't you supposed to be at lessons?"

"But you hate Montcavas and want them all to die." Sebastián ignored Tomás's question. "And I heard the story Pèire just told. Don Miquel isn't my grandfather."

Tomás groaned at the pain in the boy's voice.

"My mother hated my father," the boy said, "and she hates my uncle Renoud because he always used to make her cry. And you hate the whole Montcava family."

"I have no reason to hate you. In fact, I like you."

Sebastián sat by Tomás, staring at him for a long moment. Then he shivered, comprehending. "My uncle Renoud tried to kill you, didn't he? That's who you are hunting."

"Yes. He's one"

"They lied that Don Miquel was my grandfather. But you are so lucky. He truly was your father." Longing lurked in the boy's eyes. "I don't want to be a Montcava."

"You're born who you are."

"But you should have told me they lied. You're my master now. I have to trust you."

How had he ended up with Montcava spawn lecturing him about deceit? *I'm hunting Montcavas, not the other way around.* "I'm your teacher for now. I'm even your friend. But I'm not your master."

"Since people think Don Miquel was my grandfather, they'll think you're my uncle," Sebastián said earnestly. "It's only natural that my uncle is the master who teaches me how to fight."

"I'm no one's master. And Pèire hasn't announced my father's name to anyone. You and I, like everyone else, will do only as Pèire commands. Swear it."

"Of course I swear it. On my mother's honor." Sebastián beamed, his whole face lit like a rush lamp. "But that's what Pèire commanded. You are supposed to keep me with you. And he said to use your sword. This is the best thing that ever happened to me."

"The best thing right now, donzel, is for you to return to your lessons and your chores. You can't train to be a knight if you're confined to the barracks."

.

When Jean-Luc heard the knights' dinner bell, the boy Sebastián appeared with a bowl of lentil potage, a mug of broth, and little black sausages with a mustard paste. But Jean-Luc only managed the broth.

"Do you want the rest, donzel?"

He shook his head. "I'm to be your companion while others are at dinner."

"Am I your punishment, then?"

"I've had worse. Once, when we let pups loose from the kennel and they got into the kitchen, I had an uncomfortable fortnight," he said. "Going without my supper isn't so bad. But I want to be training with my master instead of polishing chainmail with the stable boys and talking to you."

"Your master?"

"Yes." The boy's voice picked up. "I'll be a warrior like my grandfather. I know the riding styles of both Turk and Aragón cavalry."

"In full armor?" Jean-Luc tried to recall the cuirasses and plating of Aragón men he knew in the Outremer.

"Not yet. My past master Benito gave more timid lessons than my new swordmaster. Still, I know how to ride with a javelin and a spear. The lance will be easy to learn."

"Will you ride with Pèire Leteric when he joins the crusade?" Jean-Luc asked what he'd been sent to Valerós to learn.

"The Valerós knights are staying home." The boy stood by the bed, gazing down at Jean-Luc on the cot, serious as a pope's prelate, though his eyes darted now and then to the platter of sausages.

"Won't you share my supper?" Jean-Luc nudged the bowl of lentil stew toward him. "I have no appetite."

"No, thank you. I am to forego food today." The boy turned his head from the food and broadened his stance.

"So Pèire Leteric is not for Philippe." Jean-Luc said.

"We only care for Pedro and the free seigneurs of the south. Philippe is just another greedy king like Richard Lionheart, whom we despise. Though he's dead now and gone to hell for his sins in the Holy Land."

"But the Count of Toulouse is Philippe's vassal."

"Don't you see? The French knights will once more get too hot and go home before summer ends." Sebastián crossed his arms, imitating Pèire. Jean-Luc wanted to warn the boy about saying too much to strangers. "Pedro is the king we pay tribute to. And Grandfather says Pedro won't fight his own people. And that you can't trust most Languedoc seigneurs."

"But your uncle is a trusted seigneur in Toulouse." Jean-Luc considered the seigneur Renoud, who had helped him escape from Constantinople.

"Pèire doesn't trust Renoud," Sebastián said. "My mother says he's responsible for the brigand in the garden. And for the murdered priest too."

"Murdered priest?" Attending to the boy taxed his strength. Which of them did Pèire intended to punish by sending the boy here?

"My uncle Renoud accused my new fight master of murdering a priest found dead in our garderobe. Pèire says that priest should not have been so bold to have used our privy to piss in, much less die."

"That's bad for your grandfather."

"No. Pèire pledged to clear his name with Pedro *el Rei*."

The barracks door crashed open. A rag-tag Celt stood in the door, his hair bound up in a knot like long-haired northerners do before battle. He held a short-sword in either hand.

"Donzel, the sun is down." The man spoke Catalan with the accent of a *poulain* raised in the Holy Land. "Now that you're free, your master orders you to the practice yard with me."

The donzel leaped up. "The bosc practice blades are in the squire's cupboard."

"We use steel," the white-haired *poulain* said. "Not wood."

"Sweet angels! What luck for me!" At the door, Sebastián had one parting word to Jean-Luc. "You are wrong about Renoud. My mother says he is profaning Pèire's reputation, telling lies."

"It's not profane unless it involves the Lord's name," Jean-Luc said as the door closed.

You know better than that. Your honor has been profaned.

He once more heard Yves speaking, and then accepted that it was his conscience, not Yves's voice.

He should sleep, but he had to ponder the spy's trove of details he'd learned while lying in his sick bed.

·

After dinner, Tomás slipped out of the great hall when the men settled into storytelling, gambling, and attempts upon the kitchen girls. For him, the women were no temptation, but he missed the sound of dice and the joy in taking others' coin. Chrétien had discovered, however, that there wasn't much coin to be had in Valerós.

In the scriptorium, Tomás began once more to read Pèire's letters by the light of a tallow candle filched from the great hall. Searching through that crusader's history thrilled him, the thrill amplified by the urgent need to find proof to take to the bishops' court.

The Greek duenna knocked on the door and entered when Tomás greeted her. While Isabella of Valerós was a perpetual tumult of ice and fire, Senhóreta Katelina was the opposite: imperturbable, as calm as a placid sea. The bangles and bracelets she wore rang as she took his hand in the bonfraires greeting.

"I'm Katelina of Naxos. Though you didn't tell us your name, I insist on telling you mine. You don't remember me from the old days, but I was once your mother's friend."

"Ma dòmna, you aren't the first to humiliate me over my deceit." His face burned in embarrassment.

"No matter. I call on Numa's name to trust you with a secret."

"Jesus and the sobbing angels, is this a conspiracy?" He inadvertently used language he shouldn't.

"You speak just like your father. I hope you are capable of the same kinds of action."

He bowed and motioned for her to sit. He had no choice but to listen, since she called on both his mother's and father's honor. "I'd hate to encounter you in combat, ma dòmna. You have already won."

"In our world, there isn't time for chivalry. You have all suffered horribly, but there's more you must do." She held out a note. "I found this in Pèire's bed this morning. When everyone was looking for Clémence."

She pressed the note into his hand. It was a fresh piece of parchment, with a message in the same miniscule handwriting as on the Wolf letter Pèire showed him earlier. And signed with the same lunate cross.

> We'll take your cubs from your den.
> Your Rock can't help you.
> My Wolf topples that one next.
> God won't come to Aragón, when Aragón is Gomorrah.

"*Ai Dèu!* You have to show this to Pèire."

She shook her head. "Please don't tell him about this."

"Why?"

"He carries too great a burden for his age. He's too worried about the children being in peril. He's so excited that you agreed to protect our girls. Please just add this to what you promised him."

Tomás hadn't felt so far beyond his depth since Miquel taught him to swim by throwing him in the mill-pond behind the sugar refinery. Who knew the water was so deep?

"'The cubs' must mean Pèire's grandchildren."

"Obviously, *fadrin*," Katelina said. "You must protect them."

"But what does it mean by 'the Rock'?"

"It can only mean Pèire. His name, you see? 'Pèire' is the rock, the same as St-Peter, his namesake."

"Unless it means Castell-de-Valerós," Tomás said. "But why is Aragón the same as Gomorrah? Aragón is just sailors, soldiers, and sheepherders. Hardly a civilization of sinners."

"Renoud wants Isabella in Toulouse." She plunged ahead without answering his question. She touched his hand again. "You can't let that happen, Tomásino. Don't let him near our Isabella again. Kill him if you have to."

"You don't have to beg me. I intend to do that as soon as I've learned what I need from him."

Katelina grasped his hand again. She was a serene woman, yet she expressed utmost urgency. "On your mother's honor. Swear you'll protect Pèire's children."

His life hadn't been worth much for the last year, and he'd already promised Pèire, but she squeezed one more oath out of him as she held his hand.

"Yes. On my mother's honor."

She nodded, seeming sure that their business was done. "Burn that vile garbage." She pointed to the new note. "Pèire shouldn't find it. There's no use piling new grief on old."

The woman's imperious manner nearly covered any other feeling, but he saw her hand tremble as she pointed to the note. His wits had slowed along with his broken bones, so it took him a moment to realize why it upset her so deeply.

"*Bon Dèu*. This monster was in your house, ma dòmna. He was in your bedroom."

"Whoever this is, he is coming closer each day."

"I swear I'll kill Renoud. He's the root of all—"

"Tomásino, I think you're missing something."

The pet name brought him up short. "What?"

"Renoud wants Isabella and Sebastián. But he insists he wants to protect them. And Father Clémence was his companion. Whoever wrote this killed the priest and intends to take Pèire's children."

"I can't see that."

"Surely you can, Tomásino. Our enemies are at war with each other. Please keep those children out of their battle."

"*Sodalitas, fidelitas, virtus,*" he said. Then he added another portion of the old oath. "I'll do what best pleases God."

"*Renrén.*" She called him a fool. "We haven't time to trust in God right now. Use your sword."

"*Òc,* ma dòmna, I shall. As a man of paratge."

As she left, Katelina said, "On your mother's honor," her voice echoing as footsteps clattered on the stone steps.

Miquel clapped his hands together, rubbing them with relish. "The Montcava woman and her boy. My bonfraire and his children. *La donna* Katelina—what a woman! You're protecting them all now, *fadrin.* What's next?"

"*Ai, Dèu!*" Tomás said. "You sent me into this. Give me a hint what to do."

But of course Miquel was gone, his whistle in the stone hallways echoing into the night.

23
Staying or Going

IT TOOK THREE FULL days and nights after Jean-Luc fought the brigand in the garden before his mind cleared and his leg throbbed less. He calculated how much time he'd lost, and how much time he had left to do what his lord asked of him, to finish and be gone before Pentecost. But he also had to worry about the day when he must give his oath to Pèire Leteric or be gone. Only a week until then.

When he conquered fretting about that, he next worried about the courier, the man who was to carry his reports to Gerard. If the man came to the castle, they'd feed him like any pilgrim or vagabond, but how could the courier learn that Jean-Luc lay in the bachelor-knights' barracks, treated like a captive, presided over by women? Jean-Luc needed to return to work.

Whenever Ermessen came, she brought a bowl of potage with warm bread and watered wine on a wooden tray, the spoon turned down to keep out the devil, as Jean-Luc's nurse had always done when he was a child.

"Madam, you are force-feeding me like a goose. I'll grow fat lying idle all the blessed day and eating the feasts you bring."

"Don't I know what a man your size needs to get you steady on your legs? My last husband was nearly the size of you. And don't I miss bringing a man like that his breakfast?" Ermessen spoke with a thick backcountry accent. "And you'd best eat up and heal. The marshal wants you back at the forge."

"What for?"

"*Ai*, he hasn't confided in me."

Whenever Ermessen visited, he found it as easy as stoking a blaze at the forge to get her to talk, allowing him to learn a great deal of what he'd been sent by his lord to discover. And Felicia spent several long moments each day beside him, stitching on her handwork, talking about everything under the sun. He asked after Felicia's family, since Gerard had sent him here for just that purpose.

"They were poor seigneurs with a candle-making fief in Béziers," she said. "They called themselves goodmen and so left for Narbonne before the crusaders came. When the French took the city, my sister and I lost the house our mother left us."

"Does your family here pray without the intercession of priests?" People here greeted each other as goodmen as often as anywhere in the south. What he wanted to know was whether Pèire's family included heretics that the Viscount de Chartrain would be called on to protect.

"Pèire says people live in all sorts of different ways, as they learn with their mothers' milk. You can't just eat others' food or say their prayers and instantly see God in a better way. So, we eat meat and cheese and eggs. Food from the congress of beasts."

"Are your sisters good Catholics?"

"We pray to the Holy Virgin and listen to what Father Anselm tells us about salvation."

"You have an old crusader as your confessor?" He meant to tease, but she took it seriously

"Pèire says we must make do with what we have."

That's what he heard in every conversation. *Pèire says, Pèire says...*

She continued. "We take our faith the same as we take our bread and salt. Pèire says we'll do fine with St-Jordi and *sodalitas, fidelitas, virtus.*

Jean-Luc clutched the coverlet, startled to hear that oath from a young woman's lips. Especially a woman he'd come to see as too attractive, too kind. He needed to be on his feet. And then on his way. Time to go.

∎

Isabella sat with Katelina, Beatriz, and Felicia as they stitched in the solar, the women's work room. Isabella, who couldn't sew, usually rolled skeins of thread while being scolded for lack of care. Now, however, she rolled linen for bandages, one of the tasks on Marshal Guillem's list of tasks to prepare the castle for siege.

Katelina was a needlepoint and fine embroidery artist. Beatriz, attempting to imitate her, concentrated in silence, but finally said, "I'm shy of the idea of marrying Senhór Dolcet, if that's what Pèire truly plans for me."

"Maybe that's because he's older than limestone," Felicia said.

"An older man can mean a kinder, richer man," Katelina said.

Isabella said, "If I were the queen of Jerusalem, I'd choose my own husband. That is, if I wanted to marry, which I don't."

"Pèire says the queens of Jerusalem weren't nice people," Felicia said. "You don't want to be like them, Isabella."

"But they were free to do as they wished with their sons and their armies."

"That was the source of their problems, if you listened to our grandfather's stories," Beatriz said.

"Other widows in Aragón and the Languedoc serve as guardians for their sons and manage their land without a husband." Isabella regretted the querulous sound of her own voice. She'd pleaded that case with Pèire the night before. She was a widow, free to make decisions for herself and her child. Pèire had only shaken his head and changed the subject.

Beatriz said, "Grandfather lets you manage the estates however you want. And help with the siege plans. Why aren't you satisfied?"

"He insists," Isabella governed her voice, "I take a husband because of the new crusade."

"The husbands Pèire chose will keep us safe," Beatriz said.

"I'd prefer passion to safety," Felicia said.

"Beatriz prefers sanctimony to passion." Isabella teased as she ripped a length of linen and rolled it into a ball the size of two fists.

Katelina said, "You all deserve to know what it's like to lie in the arms of an adoring lover."

"Katelina!" Beatriz quivered in shock.

"I wasn't cloistered before I came here. Life is short. Certain experiences must not be missed."

"Passion isn't important." Beatriz's clenched jaw testified against any idea that a man would ever pry open her lips for a kiss.

"I disagree." Felicia stretched from the strain of sewing. "I long to satisfy my curiosity about passion."

"You'd contemplate adultery out of curiosity?" Beatriz asked.

"It's not adultery if you aren't married," Katelina said.

"It's just plain fornication," Beatriz said. "And no man in all this country would dare to sin with you, Felicia, because of Pèire."

"Perhaps I'll practice passion with the man I intend to marry. It would be delicious to know before the priest comes, wouldn't it?" Felicia said.

That stopped Beatriz's sermon for several moments. Isabella silently ripped linen into strips, wrapping each into a tight roll.

"You owe chastity as part of your dowry," Beatriz said. "And what if you get a child too soon before you marry?"

"Katelina taught us how to avoid that. And, unlike you, I have no dowry." Felicia tied a knot with her needle and then bit off the last length of thread, which Katelina always decried as uncivilized. "Isabella, don't you want passion before you die?"

"I don't know," Isabella said. "Though Pèire commanded that we always do what Katelina tells us."

"Felicia is teasing." Beatriz seemed disturbed by their talk.

"No, I'm exploring a platonic ideal, as Katelina taught us to," Felicia said. "Isabella, tell the truth. Wouldn't it be exciting to be with a man who wanted you?"

"My imagination doesn't stretch so far," Isabella said.

But it did; she'd chided herself for thinking too much about what she felt under that scribe's robe when she jumped from the wall. What she imagined from how he walked across the courtyard. Siege tasks like rolling bandages filled only half the empty space in one's thinking. While working on copying old texts, her mind had too much room to roam, whether it was pondering the impossible attractions of that scribe or seeking a plan to defeat Pèire's battle strategy for her.

Katelina caught Isabella's eye, most likely reading her mind. "The rational question is whether it's a virtue to avoid knowing a man passionately in this life, in hopes of a reward in an afterlife."

"The spiritual question," Beatriz sat up very straight, "is what you lose in God's eyes by foregoing purity for passion."

Felicia said, "The practical question is whether you'll have anything interesting to contemplate while you wait to get into heaven."

"The philosophical question is whether carnal knowledge without marriage destroys our hope for salvation," Isabella said. "Since we are taught that God is merciful, the answer must be no."

"I'm confident that God wants me to know why He created both man and woman." Felicia closed one eye to thread her needle, biting her lip in concentration.

"What weak examples of thesis and antithesis! It makes me think you girls dozed when we discussed Aristotle," Katelina said. "If you're in love, the only questions are about opportunity and fidelity. Not chastity. Fidelity. You won't care what God thinks."

Beatriz began to weep, the tears falling on her embroidery.

"*Ai*, sister!" Felicia cried. "Don't cry for our souls. God will forgive such petty sins if we dare to commit them. Especially when I only wish for honest passion."

"I wish I were someone else," Beatriz said.

I wish I were leading knights into Toulouse to defeat my enemy.

Three sisters so different. Isabella guessed that she might be the only one absolutely determined to get what she wanted. But how to have knights under her command, much less ride to Toulouse to confront Renoud?

·

Tomás at Valerós
24 days before Pentecost

Tomás was ready to work immediately after breakfast, but Chrétien wanted to nag him.

"Your new friendship has its benefits, dear brother, besides keeping your neck out of a noose." Chrétien lounged on a bench. "Sugar for our porridge. Which I haven't seen since Cyprus. What's next? Will you swear a knight's oath to serve a backcountry seigneur?"

"You know my aversion to any oath, except the one we gave our father. And our bonfraires oath. That's all I'm doing here. And you—shouldn't you be out working with the young donzel?"

"If Father were here, he'd chase our asses back on the road."

"He wants us to be here, Chrétien. It's the best place to learn how to hunt the man we want."

"Sweet dancing angels! Ever since Cyprus, you've claimed divine knowledge of what Miquel wants. He's dead."

"Pèire is an ally."

Chrétien said, "You're in love, Tomásino. That old *peccador* stole your heart."

"We need Pèire as an ally if we're going to find justice." Tomás regretted that Chrétien didn't perceive the deeper value of his new friendship.

"If an old man and a donzel can make you hot for new alliances, perhaps you can also be enticed to forget your pathetic vow of chastity. Give that up and marry your way into Fontcours."

"I'd rather eat dirt than marry." Tomás spoke with more warmth than he intended. "I especially won't let another Montcava woman near me for any purpose on earth."

Benito called beyond the doorway.

"*Bon día*, ma dòmna."

It was the fire-breathing senhóra of Valerós, who sought to annihilate him with that hawk-like stare of hers.

She must have overheard his last words, since she seemed once more to be in a white heat. He started to prevaricate his way out of any consequences for what he'd said. However, when she glared at him, angry as a cat on fire, he wanted her to see him as an honest man.

"*Bon día*, ma dòmna."

Isabella pushed past him without a word. She opened the cupboard and began searching through it.

Chrétien brightened in the way he did when he could amuse himself at Tomás's expense.

"Welcome to the Grail Castle, *Reyna de Valerós*. Parzival was just speaking of you." Chrétien bowed and left, although Tomás was certain his brother would listen outside the door.

133

"They say Pèire persuaded you to abandon your hopes for the Church," she said, instead of hello. "What will you lose next, Tomás the Scribe who-wears-a-sword?"

She stared at him so intently that he rubbed the wretched scar across his cheek. He often forgot his face had been ruined, but when women and children looked at him that way—

"Is it my face that bothers you?" he asked.

"Your face doesn't matter to me." She picked up a pen-knife and whacked at a discarded quill on the desk. "I've had enough of handsome, deceitful rogues for all this life. I want to know who you are. Why did Pèire stake our domus on your life?"

"I'm Tomás of Barcelona." He paused, it taking a moment to hear that she called him handsome; the rogue part he expected. "The famous crusader Pèire Leteric has asked me to help write his history."

"And I'm the Queen of Jerusalem."

"You are a bit like her," he said. Jesus in heaven might know why, but he wished she didn't hate him. "You should have your own knights, instead of only sheepherders and bordoniers to call you ma dòmna."

Her eyes flashed. "I mark conceit and cunning against your character."

"It's been said of me before. But maybe, as with you, what they say isn't true."

Her expression proved that he'd succeeded in unsettling her, which offered a petty consolation for how much she unnerved him. But before she could answer, Pèire entered. When Tomás greeted him in the Catalan manner, Pèire took his hand as an equal. Tomás judged that the gesture wasn't lost on Isabella.

"We have a week to work together here," Pèire said. "Then I'm riding to join Hugues de Beaurain. We'll stop in Narbonne on the way, to get the bishop off our tails for that dead priest."

"But you said you wouldn't send young men on crusade again." Isabella sounded agitated, but Tomás couldn't tell whether it was distress or joy.

"Only old buzzards like me will go." Pèire chuckled at his own good idea. "I've been thinking on it. We don't want those *francimand* crusaders to come here looking for heretics. Half the grannies and aunties in our villages are goodwomen. And Senhóreta Katelina never quit her Greek church. She couldn't confess falsely to save her own self."

"Let me come with you," Isabella said. "Let me help defend Sebastián's land." She stammered: "*Ai*, I know what you'll say. 'Wait for Gerard de Chartrain to take care of that.' But please..."

"You can travel with us," Pèire said. "I sent Gerard a message today, to meet us at Fontcours with Hugues. There's no use hauling his knights up into these hills and back down again."

Her face brightened. The golden bits in her eyes flickered with excitement Tomás hadn't seen before.

"And then you can go home with Gerard when the crusading season is over." Pèire nodded his head, satisfied with his plan.

Isabella's eyes clouded over, as if doors quietly closed on her soul. Angels counting stars wouldn't begin to understand why, but he nearly reached out to comfort her. While Pèire drummed his fingers on the table, not seeing her anguish, Tomás tried to read her face, to understand that passion. Then she caught him studying her.

She made a sign with her hand—to ward off evil.

"And," Pèire said, "I need to make sure this gaggle of girls gets married before I leave Valerós."

It was painful to watch her as Pèire spoke.

"You better go, *xiqueta*." Pèire gently shook her shoulder. "Marshal Guillem needs you to tell him how to pack his bags."

Isabella bowed, not acknowledging Tomás as she rushed from the scriptorium.

"You are riding with Simon's crusaders, senhór?"

"I had been willing to let the French take whatever land they conquer in Toulouse," Pèire said. "Sebastián has Valerós and Arracheuse. That's enough for a man. But after you and I talked, well, the infernal angels can damn my soul before I'll let any Montcava bastard steal Miquel's land."

"May I ride with you? Or am I too young?" What an impetuous request, especially since Chrétien begged daily to return to their planned hunt.

The old man grinned. "It's your land. We'll stop in Narbonne on the way, because of that infernal dead priest. We'll see if Pedro wants to hang our sorry asses."

"I hope not, senhór."

"Me either. I enjoy your conversation so much, Don Tomás. I'd miss it if you ran off now."

"I'm not inconstant, senhór."

"Of course not. Damn me as a dark devil if Miquel ever was."

24
Vulcan Rises

Jean-Luc at Valerós
24 days before Pentecost

AFTER A WEEK BEING coddled, Jean-Luc could no longer tolerate lying still. Seven days of depending on Felicia and Ermessen to help him to sit up when he ate. Of waiting for one of the marshal's men to come by to help him with his other bodily needs, both laughing to forget the humiliation.

He needed to move. He needed to be eating in the common rooms, to be able to meet Gerard's courier when he came. He needed to be doing his job, to prove his worth to his lord.

Testing, he learned how to shift around without tearing the stitches and then managed to roll off the narrow cot onto the cold flagstones, where he stretched his shoulders. He turned over without wreaking havoc on his bad leg, and then he lifted his entire body using his hands and his healthy leg as leverage. On the cold floor, it felt so good that he continued the exercise until his lungs worked properly again. A healthy sweat drenched his shirt. His pulse pound down his stitched-together leg.

Jean-Luc pondered how to rise and return to bed. His thigh pounded with pain in protest, so he just pulled the coverlet and pillow down and stayed on the floor.

"Fall out of bed, did you?"

The odd accent tricked his ear and his mind: it sounded like Yves, but it was the Norman knight, Guillem. That accent was born in Sicily, not the Pays de France. Guillem stood in the doorway, looking amused, with no mercy in his expression.

"A man can't lie in bed all day like a puling child. I need to move."

"You look like a kicked dog down there," Guillem said.

"Please be so kind as to help me up, marshal."

"Is that what you want? I'll call my men."

"No, please. I've been humiliated enough in the past days. Just give me your arm."

Jean-Luc tried to do most of the work, but in the end the marshal had to help him onto the bed.

"That's the most graceful dance I've ever seen by a one-legged bear," the marshal said.

"You can chain me in the courtyard. I'll do tricks for meals."

"Ermessen says one more day before she's sure the stitches took."

"Can you just slice my gullet like you would a hurt horse?"

"And get in a pickle with Ermessen? She's adopted you for a house pet."

"I don't keep well indoors. I'm like a Great Pyr. You only want me inside long enough to clean up the bones under the table."

Guillem said, "Dogs don't eat under our tables. Senhóreta Katelina has never tolerated it. She says it makes the fleas worse."

"The ladies' duenna sets the castle rules?" Jean-Luc needed to learn still more about life in Valerós, which added to his frustration that he couldn't do what he came for while lying in bed.

"Senhóreta Katelina merely lets her preference be known. In our fighting days, she…" Guillem stopped. "Anyway, I came to tell you what my men found. That brigand left a trail of blood to where a horse waited for him. You gave him a hurt as good as you got."

"God forgive my joy in knowing that." Jean-Luc groaned as he shifted his leg to be comfortable.

"We had hounds follow the blood. But he must have ridden into a stream. We lost the trail." The marshal hesitated, and then he changed the subject. "We need you at the forge, Master Smith. Our seigneur wants us to prepare to ride this season. So, don't cock it up by rolling on the floor again."

"He's joining the French crusaders?"

"*Si.*" With that Sicilian accent, he sneezed the Catalan word *yes.* "That's today's news. Though I don't know if riding with the Marquis de Beaurain is the same as riding with Simon's army. No matter, though. We go where Pèire tells us."

"What an unusual choice for a seigneur of Aragón." To ride with the marquis? How close was Pèire with Gerard's old friend?

"Pèire says when we resisted at Jaffa, it was a miserable position. Isn't it better to defend from the outside?"

"I wouldn't know." Jean-Luc had to tell a lie. He'd fought in that resistance at Jaffa. And he resisted any revelation that might cause Pèire to recognize him. He still needed to leave as soon as he could travel.

.

At midday, Jean-Luc felt well enough to hobble out to the courtyard. Ermessen waved him over to a trestle table and brought him bread, black sausages, and a stew of wizened apples for his breakfast.

While he was offering thanks to the Virgin Mary for his health and to his Heavenly Father for his victuals, a pilgrim sat by him on the bench and folded his hands in prayer like Jean-Luc did.

"*Hé, connard.*" The pilgrim cursed him. "I thought you'd never show up, prick-head. I froze my balls in the god-damned chapel here for three blasted days." It was Gerard de Chartrain's courier, unhappy that Jean-Luc has missed the planned rendezvous. "I've run out of excuses for why I don't take my sorry pilgrim ass back down the road."

"I was injured a week ago." That's all Jean-Luc shared. He refused to apologize for spending seven days on a sick bed. The courier, however, remained irritated that Jean-Luc had wasted time.

"*Je n'en ai rien a foutre.* Just give me whatever load of horseshit I'm supposed to carry back to his lordship, so I can get back to civilization. Tell me why the viscount is marrying into this indigent pigsty. He better not expect us to garrison here."

"Care to share my breakfast?"

"*Non, troud'cul.* How can you eat that swill?"

Father Anselm walked on the other side of the courtyard, and the pilgrim-courier crossed himself.

While he ate breakfast, Jean-Luc reported (almost) everything he'd learned.

There were no heretics among Pèire Leteric's family.

Pèire's famous intelligence remained wholly intact.

Viscount Gerard's bride wasn't excited about her coming marriage. (Felicia described the senhóra's feelings as rage and despair, but Jean-Luc didn't add that to his report.)

Pèire's marshal was arming the castle as if expecting a siege.

"That's true everywhere. What else?" the courier said.

"They want me back at the forge, but the real armorers are working at Arracheuse, making mail, swords, and crossbow bolts." Jean-Luc recounted what he'd learned gossiping with Ermessen, questioning Felicia, and eavesdropping on the other residents of the barracks. "Small boys spend half their days rolling barrels of oily sand around the courtyards to clean the chainmail packed inside."

"Like every dog-crap excuse for a castle in these lands."

"Pèire pledged to forfeit his castle if he doesn't appear before the bishop in Narbonne. It's about a priest found murdered here."

"I heard that," the courier said. "The rumor is spreading so fast, it's likely Viscount Gerard knows. He's in Toulouse now, so he's heard all the gossip. *Bon Dieu*, I forgot to tell you about Toulouse."

"What is there to say? I dislike that city as much as you dislike this fine country castle."

"Do you remember Thibault, the bastard from Troyes who was with you in Constantinople?"

"Of course, I do. He was a good soldier."

"He's bearing Viscount Gerard's standard now. At a tourney in Toulouse, Thibault left us to go to confession."

"Do Thibaut's sins matter to us?"

"His own sins aren't even interesting. But in the church, Thibault overheard another man moaning that he'd accepted silver for telling lies to ruin a knight in Constantinople."

"*Bon Dieu*." Jean-Luc felt blood rush to his head. He pushed his breakfast away.

"Thibault followed the *charogne* and begged to hear his story. But the rogue refused, saying God will never forgive him, so why would any man."

"Where is that man now?"

"He claimed he had a job as a cook with the Marquis de Beaurain's army. But then he gave Thibault the slip. The rogue had lost an eye, so you figure Thibault might keep track of him. But hell no."

Jean-Luc played with his spoon, unable to speak. He had to find that man. In Toulouse still? On his way to join Hugues's army?

Oh my brother, ever the hopeful heart.

He hadn't heard Yves's voice for days, but it came back the moment he felt hope surging through his veins, as if he needed to be cautioned to expect only disappointment.

The courier said, "The viscount thought you'd want to come to Toulouse when you heard this story. To clear your name."

"I can't go now." Jean-Luc's heart thundered because he wanted to rise and run to Toulouse without even finishing his breakfast.

"Why stay on this shit-farm?"

"I can scarcely walk. And I must finish this work for our lord." Yet Jean-Luc's fancy flew to the streets of Toulouse. "The most important message for Gerard is that Pèire Leteric will rendezvous with him at Fontcours, near Toulouse."

"I hadn't heard as much, but I'll carry the word," the courier said. "*Baise-toi, fif.* Did I come all the way to this hellhole and that's all you have? Is there no more to report?"

"No, " Jean-Luc said, "nothing else. "

He didn't report that Felicia's touch felt as gentle as the angel he first mistook her to be. That she was kinder to him than anyone in the world. And he most certainly did not report that Felicia's almond eyes and flawless features would grow into great beauty, like Queen Eleanor had possessed, lighting a room like a thousand candles.

He had no other news, except his immortal soul was in deeper peril than before. He added a plea with this courier that the next man to visit him should bring a second horse, so he could depart.

■

Jean-Luc at Valerós
23 days before Pentecost

The first morning Jean-Luc returned to the forge, he considered what to do next to find the one-eyed soldier who'd betrayed a man in

Constantinople. But then Guillem and Father Anselm came to the smithy to chat while on their way to another chore.

Guillem was the best kind of leader, meticulous in his work and his person. When other soldiers told the boys tales about sporting with girls in the baggage train, Guillem turned his back, muttering that he preferred respectable widows. Alone with Jean-Luc, Guillem said he avoided marriage because he didn't want to leave a woman lonely; to his way of thinking, a soldier's widow was the soul and symbol of loneliness.

With a dry humor now becoming familiar, Marshal Guillem said, "In the old days a lord crippled his smith to keep him at the forge."

Father Anselm spoke in his good-natured way. "Our seigneur Pèire just takes advantage of this man's bad luck. You're stuck with us now, Master Smith. It'll be summer before you can resume you vagabond ways."

Summer? No. A week and no longer. But Jean-Luc didn't have time to dwell on that thought.

That morning the smithy became the favorite place for folks to chat while putting off chores. Jehan the heroic smith had become popular. So Jean-Luc spent every moment talking with the men-at-arms and kitchen girls, having learned that if his visitors talked and laughed loudly enough, he'd make it through a whole day without missing Felicia's voice, her laughter, her touch.

Ermessen came late in the morning. With her young-girl's smile, she produced a kerchief containing small barley loaves and cheese. He received the package gratefully; it had been a long stretch since breaking fast at dawn.

She held up a badly dented copper pan. "This sad old thing has forgotten it's supposed to be a pot. Will you trade this copper for a few old broken blades you might have?"

"Whatever for?"

"It's good to slip a bit of iron under the pillow of them that can't sleep at night. And for those that worry about evil spirits, I give them a charm to feel safe. I bet you like a bit of iron under your bed, too."

He'd slept with a knife under his pillow for twenty years, but it wasn't to ward off spirits.

"Ermessen, do you sell charms?"

"No, but I'll trade good luck for a bit of whatever another body might want to be rid of."

"Does Father Anselm know?"

"*Ai Dèu, òc.* Doesn't he join us when we light the new fires on Easter morning? He blesses the binding charms I make for girls' wedding nights."

Later, a young boy brought him a new wool-and-down pallet. "My grandmother Ermessen says straw won't help you heal."

The next day at work, men riding with Pèire needed repairs to their arms and armor. Late afternoon, though, Jean-Luc tallied his visitors: all grey-bearded bachelors who'd spent decades in the saddle. Guillem seemed to be the youngest, though the marshal must be close to fifty.

Father Anselm and Guillem wandered in, locked in conversation. The priest was saying, "If the king and counts of Jerusalem didn't have professional soldiers, where would they be?"

"You mean to say mercenaries," Guillem said.

"Indeed," Father Anselm said, "the need for professionals, men like us, became fundamental. The lords in the Outremer can't find enough true-to-the-cross crusaders."

"That's because the pilgrim knights tend to die of a bloody flux. Or they sail home after a few sword slashes go putrid," Guillem said. "Since we left, those Outremer lords turned to the Orders like the Ransomers and the Knights Templar."

Without thinking, Jean-Luc said, "And the Outremer barons can't harvest their own crops or hatch their own heirs. Meanwhile, the Saracens teach themselves new strategies while our armies use the same maneuvers time after time."

Father Anselm and Guillem stared.

"Or so I've heard," Jean-Luc said awkwardly.

"The Christian armies are the best in the world. Do you claim the Saracens can defeat us?" Father Anselm said.

Guillem said, "How can you say we're the best, Anselm? A good army is disciplined. The best army in the world didn't rape its way through Constantinople or burn Béziers."

"When it was us, we were the best," Father Anselm said. "And the army didn't burn Béziers. It was just baggage-boys gone mad."

"Admit, then, that Simon de Montfort isn't a proven strategist," Guillem said. "He just turns rabble into pillagers."

"I can't agree."

"Master Jehan," Guillem said, "is Simon a good general?"

"Me, senhór? I don't know." Jean-Luc hesitated. He hadn't seen Simon in action to judge him. "From his recent handiwork, he must be as ruthless as King Richard was outside of Jerusalem."

"See!" Guillem crowed to the priest. "As ruthless as Richard! And Richard pissed off the Saracens so much they gleefully whipped our asses as soon as the treaty ended."

"What are you arguing?" Father Anselm spoke coolly.

"Simon's undisciplined knights will cock it up for him," Guillem said. "The Franks can't hold on here any better than in the Outremer."

"By your logic," Father Anselm said, "the seigneurs need professional armies as disciplined as the Saracens."

"What do you think, Master Smith?" Guillem called.

"Discipline has a better chance against ruthlessness than any other strategy." In fact, he was thinking how arguing with intelligent men felt as satisfying as Ermessen's extra meals.

Later, after the crowd disappeared into their afternoon tasks, Benito, the master at arms, came to sharpen a sword and asked Jean-Luc to repair a hardened leather cuirass. While Benito honed his sword on the big whet stone, Jean-Luc hunted up the basket of studs and worked at repairing the cuirass. Then Guillem dropped by the smithy again, seeking Benito's agreement on a list of instructions for the Valerós defenders in their absence.

"It looks right to me," Benito said. "But this castle hasn't been armed for a siege in a hundred years."

Guillem stroked his drooping moustaches. "The past generations of kings cried the Peace of God on the seigneurs to stop their fights. We'll just hope we've thought of everything."

Jean-Luc paused from his work and stood by Guillem to study the list. "You need a great deal more water. That's all that's missing."

Guillem's eyes widened as his moustache twitched. "Who knew they teach Breton smiths to read?"

Jean-Luc had to be on the road. It seemed that each day, he did a worse job of hiding who he was.

25

An Unpracticed Widow

Isabella at Valerós
23 days before Pentecost

PÈIRE HAD PROVISIONED THOUSANDS of men on hundreds of journeys, but this time he left all the tasks to Isabella. She couldn't tell if Pèire was merely indulging her; his sole order had been: "Don't bring any of the really good horses."

Isabella didn't deceive herself. Marshal Guillem and his men, eager for adventure, politely pretended she was in charge; the Valerós soldiers didn't need a woman half their age to supervise. She stuck to calculating amounts of lentils, salt, and hard biscuits to bring.

While the provisioning work with Guillem brought her a bit of peace, each time she went to work in the scriptorium she found the scribe had already captured the space. He claimed to be writing a memorial for Pèire, but she seldom saw him write anything. If he was absent, the cupboard was locked, so she couldn't retrieve all her copying tools to work on that Gospel. It galled her that Pèire entrusted the cupboard's key to a charlatan. For the fifth time in two days when she went hoping to work, she found Sebastián hanging about. This time, Benito stood over him.

"Donzel, you have chores elsewhere," Benito said.

Tomás was unloading the entire cupboard, but he nodded to Sebastián, who then said, "As you say, Master Benito."

When Benito and Sebastián had gone away, she greeted the scribe, feeling uneasy seeing all the scraps of parchments, sheaves of vellum, and old scrolls stacked on the table.

"*Bon día*," she said. "I hoped to work on my manuscript."

145

"Perhaps later." He seemed distracted by what he sorted on the table. "I haven't soiled your text. Senhóreta Katelina wrapped it and stored it away this morning."

Curious, she lingered.

"What kind of catnip do you keep to attract my son, Master Tomás? He's been truant ever since you arrived." The lightness she forced in her voice did not sound normal to her.

Tomás thumped his dagger on the table. The violence of the gesture made her jump. "The boy wants to learn to jump from walls and use a sword. You've seen us in the practice yard every evening."

Isabella sat at the table. She pulled her knife from the sheath at her waist, picked a goose quill from the cup on the table, and began whittling a point. The knife steadied her nerves, but she quickly ruined the quill.

"You've lured my son from his Latin and numbers," she said.

"He has no peers here. He can't learn to be a knight while running around with village boys in the mews and kennels."

"He's too young," she said, though it wasn't true. That quill ruined, she pulled another from the cup and trimmed its point.

"Rubbish. Sebastián should be living away from his family so he can concentrate without coddling."

"Mendicant scribes are expert at raising children?"

"You asked me a question. Sebastián wants to be with men. He's too old to be sneaking out of bed at night to listen to those old crusaders telling tales."

She didn't know Sebastián did that. And she didn't like this stranger knowing more about her son than she did.

He picked up his dagger from the table and slipped it into his tall leather boot in a way that seemed deliberately provocative; the odor of oiled leather and spice disturbed her.

Tomás studied two pages side by side for a long time. He fingered his beard, tracing one of the white streaks. She spied one of her personal letters lying amid the stack of texts beside him. She must have missed it the night she rescued the batch of them. Alarmed, she reached to take it back, but he deftly tucked two pages he was reading under it. Then she longed to see what he hid. She sheathed her penknife and moved closer, reaching out to take the pages.

When he glanced down, it drew her eyes also, and she saw the belt of her robe entangled in the hilt of the dagger at his waist. She stepped back, but her belt remained caught by his knife, and when she reached to free her belt, her hand grazed down his leather jerkin.

Honestly, she didn't mean to touch him.

•

Despite his sworn intention not to engage with a woman, Tomás stirred. She stood so close, forcing him to guess what game she wanted to play. Choosing a defensive position, he began as he did with every woman he'd met since leaving Cyprus.

"We both know I was never going to be a priest," he said. "Yet I abstain to be a better warrior. So please stop that."

"What do you mean?"

"Don't pretend it's an accident when you touch me."

"You have a fanciful sense of your person."

Instead of being outraged as usually happened when he used this tactic, she seemed amused.

He persevered. "Don't involve me in your impulses or fantasies."

"Why would you be an object for my impulses—if I had any?"

She'd reverted to her usual haughty air.

"Neither of us is innocent to the world," he said. "A widow like you finds it easy to take a lover. And you repeat goodwomen's superstitions to justify taking pleasure wherever you find it. But you won't be taking a tumble with me."

"As I told you before, I'm not a goodwoman," she said, indignant. "And I don't believe in just taking pleasure."

"I see. You need to believe you are in love first, like in a troubadour's song. But you shouldn't think about me in that way either."

Senhóra Isabella grew angry, which was just what he wanted, to keep her away from him. But then her face went blank and cold, so neither his gambler's instinct nor his swordsman's knowledge helped him to know how she might attack.

"Your *bon amics* told me how much he abhors the company of women." She called Chrétien his *boyfriend*. "Hence your so-called abstinence?"

"I like women fine, but I don't trust them. And Chrétien isn't my friend, he's my brother."

"How can that be?" she asked, blinking in surprise.

"We have different mothers."

"Both of whom must be bitterly disappointed." Her anger subsiding into her usual disdainful manner.

"You are changing the subject. I am merely cautioning you that I'm not interested."

"You seduce Pèire and my son with who-knows-what lies. But I don't trust you, and you accuse me of designs on your person?"

"Tell the truth. Don't you wonder what it might be like with me?" Tomás, standing taller, wanted to make her angry enough to leave him alone. Each time she touched him, he spent a day regaining self-control.

"I hadn't wondered." She offered a strange smile. "Show me."

She had one hand under his jerkin as she pressed him against the table and kissed him ardently, if not lasciviously, while she groped ineptly in the folds of his linen undershirt. He reacted despite his resolve, wrapping his arms around her. His tongue wanted to press into her mouth, but her lips resisted as he prodded for entrance. Each bit of tissue in his body responded to her touch. Even the tiny bumps around the hairs on his arms stood, aroused.

Isabella pulled away, seemingly unaffected by what had just happened, and said in Greek, "Shall I bow in awe of your superior knowledge of women, or hang my head in dismay over your unearned arrogance?"

Used to wild accusations from women, although not in Greek, he was unaccustomed to being kissed for the sake of humiliation. To save face, he prepared to concede a misunderstanding, but just then his overly eager apprentice rushed upon them.

"It's back from the tanner!" Sebastián's voice echoed off the stone walls. He waved a disgusting animal skin.

Isabella seemed instantly to forget their conversation, for she took the pelt from the boy to admire it. Then she gave it back. "I'll leave now so you can practice being great warriors together."

He believed the humorless senhóra laughed at him when she left.

"What is that animal?" he asked Sebastián.

"It's the wolf my mother killed when she saved the marshal's life. I'm going to ask Felicia to make it into a collar for a cloak. Do you think my mother will be pleased with such a wedding present?"

"I'm not the best person to give such advice."

While Sebastián chattered, Tomás matched the image of a woman who killed wolves with the one who aroused him despite his vows. A woman who was about to marry an ancient French viscount.

When Sebastián ran off again with his wolf pelt, Miquel stood beside Tomás, laughing.

"That must be the most unpracticed widow in Christendom," Miquel teased.

"Perhaps."

"A blind man can see that she kisses like a virgin."

"It's not your business." Tomás bit his tongue, knowing better than to speak to ghosts.

"Right you are, my son. I'll step away while you wrap your hands around your monastic resolve."

■

After that day's adventures, Isabella rejoiced at having retrieved her letter. However, judging from how the so-called scribe stared at her throughout dinner (which, of course, Katelina commented on), there'd be a steep price for distracting his attention. And she couldn't confess that silly sin to Father Anselm, especially since she'd also have to confess to discovering that the man's belly under his leather jerkin felt like a chamois pelt stretched over steel.

"Isabella." Pèire called her to where he sat at dinner. At his gesture, she took the chair beside him. "Katelina says I'm working you too hard. Is that true?"

"You know I choose to work hard. Both the planning for a siege and the provisioning work are mere *mathematica* practice, not hard labor. I do wish," she took a chance, "that my scriptorium was free so that I can work."

"Three, four more days and we'll be on the road. You can't play with your quills and inks while we're riding."

"No." She'd started a bold course, so she continued. "Grandfather, I want to come home—here—at the end of the crusading season. To continue my work for Valerós."

"Still chicken-hearted about marrying? I tell you girl, Gerard will be dancing with the angels as soon as me. Then you'll live for fifty years as the dowager viscountess, and you can do as you please, anywhere in Christendom."

"But for your battle strategy, to protect Sebastián's future, there's no reason for me to live in a foreign country. You said he's not seeking children or a wife as chattel. There's no use in my trekking to the Pays de France."

"*Ai, xiqueta.* If every soul in the Languedoc doesn't believe you're a real wife, then ol' Gerard will spend all his waking hours begging bishops and petitioning kings to disprove Renard's lies. The angels will bless you for doing your duty."

She lost that skirmish. Worse, when she bid Pèire good night and turned to leave, that infernal scribe still watched her, and had likely heard every word. She went to her room in search of sanctuary.

Burning a rush lamp for light in her narrow cell, Isabella examined the page she'd stolen from the scribe in the scriptorium, where she pondered the wages of that sin. This new stolen page proved disappointing. Spidery writing crawled across the page, beginning with a child's rhyme:

> I saw the wolf before the wolf saw me.
> I'll kill the wolf before the wolf kills me.
> God take the wolf and God save me.

Then it shifted to another message:

> I'll hunt you to your lair.
> I'll take your mate and cubs.
> The other wolf is already destroyed.

All that effort, boldly assaulting the scribe to steal a nursery song.

She couldn't waste more time teasing the so-called scribe. She needed to claim the scriptorium before he arrived in the morning, so she could finish enough texts to sell when Pèire made that side-trip to Narbonne. Her plan for earning silver was falling behind.

Most of her plans remained inadequate. Katelina had done nothing to plead with him about changing his so-called battle strategy. She needed a new tactic.

To plan for a siege that would likely never occur.

To provision a journey that would deliver her to a husband she didn't want.

To tussle with Pèire effectively.

To create a plan where she could picture herself still alive when the crusading season ended and winter came.

If only she had what she wanted most of all: a dozen loyal knights to ride with her to Toulouse, to confront Renoud in the family villa, and then frighten him into proper behavior. What would be proper? Renoud should crawl to the bishops' court, beg her forgiveness, and surrender all his holdings to Sebastián. She hated blood, so she couldn't imagine actively advancing a worse fate for the current seigneur of Montcava. But she could pray for it.

Disappointed with having gained so little from that day's theft, Isabella padded barefoot down to the scriptorium, where she tucked that stolen page under the corner of a quill-box. A small leather pouch lay on the table, left by the scribe. As she tugged at its clasp, the smell burned her nose.

Cloves. That's what had scorched on her lips half the day and into the night.

Jhezu del tron! She had to fight with Pèire to avoid being forced back into the hell of marriage. Now she also had to fight unwanted attraction to this wretched man that the dark angels had thrown in her way.

26
A Hawk on the Wind

Jean-Luc at Valerós
23 days before Pentecost

TO KEEP HIS HEALING angel out of his thoughts, Jean-Luc spent the day devising a plan to leave as soon as possible, rather than wait for the next courier. At vespers, Senhóra Isabella appeared, but not the Senhóretas Beatriz or Felicia. As he skidded across the wet cobbles to the smithy, he conceded the deficiencies in his plan for leaving immediately: no horse, poor weather, a bad leg.

He prepared the smithy for the next day's work and checked the pack he'd stashed for his escape, exchanging that night's bread for the older rations stuffed within it. After eating the day-old bread and brushing away the crumbs to deter the mice, he'd exhausted all possible diversions, so he hauled his body and his worries up the ladder to bed.

Where Felicia waited.

"Senhóreta!" he whispered.

"I want to ask a favor," she said.

"How did you get here?" he asked.

"There are passageways all around the castle. I can come here more easily than you can yourself."

"Can others come here using that passage?" He'd never been in greater jeopardy off the battlefield.

"No one comes into my room except by its front door, which is barred. That particular passageway isn't used by the men at arms." She pointed to the small hatch he'd never been able to open.

"What can I do for you?" He felt hell's doors gaping wide.

"Will you leave at Pentecost?"

He couldn't lie but didn't tell her how soon he'd be gone. "I'll travel north before the summer turns hot."

"Let's be truthful," she said. "I think we understand each other in a special way."

"I think you're a young girl who'd better go home now."

"I'm sixteen, and I don't have a home." She fingered the silver cross that hung from a cord around her neck. "I'm an orphan."

"You have a family that cares. You shouldn't be here."

"Do they care?" she asked. "I'm just another woman here who's either convenient or in the way at any moment. Right now, the convenient thing is to marry me off to one of Pèire's old cronies."

"That's what young girls do. They marry."

"Most likely I'll be married before Pèire departs on this God-forsaken crusade." She looked at him while she freed the cross from the folds of her robe and lifted it with its cord over her head. "When will you leave?"

"Very soon, though please don't repeat that." He fingered the boar's tooth on a leather string around his own neck. "Ma dòmna, I won't enter into the business of debauching young girls, as I believe you are about to propose."

He perched on the small bench across from the pallet where she sat, as far away as possible in the tiny loft. He crossed his arms in a gesture meant to indicate finality.

She didn't pout, unlike most girls when thwarted. However, she dismissed his argument. "It's not debauchery if I have no prior duty to forsake."

She chose the old meaning of debauch, the way Pèire had used the word, to describe a knight going astray.

"You have a duty to keep your virtue for your husband," he said.

"My guardian has chosen a husband for me who is too old to discern virtue in a darkened room."

"Felicia, this isn't like you. You're a sensible girl."

"I'm a woman who," she took a breath, the cross dangling from her fingers, "who touched a man last week and believed he cared. Who talked to a man and believed he listened."

Jean-Luc couldn't hear what she said. *Maiden, this is a young and innocent maiden.*

"I won't cuckold another man," he said.

"I'm not betrothed to anyone. I too couldn't betray a man if my oath were given. After that, it's too late."

Felicia cast the cross onto the bench and moved from the pallet to kneel before him, taking his hand in supplication. "If you want me to beg, I will."

He felt her breath on his hand, and he smelled lavender and mint in her hair. He meant to take his hand away, but instead covered her small one with his own. She kissed it softly and then tilted her head up to kiss his lips, although he hadn't meant to be so near her.

She said, "Just show me what it's like. Then you'll go away and I'll marry, and it will be a secret that's never told."

He risked one kiss and then tried to pull away from her. But she whispered, "Just this once in my life, I don't want to be alone." Then he was lost, tasting her, feeling the silk of her hair in his hands, stroking the soft curve of her neck. Then he showed her how to gracefully trade off with their tongues and how to bite a lip in just the right way. He discovered that the tip of his tongue on her earlobe caused her to squirm against him in a way he'd never felt before.

Through the night, they strove together to find a way past the awkwardness, to kiss and touch each other, and to be comfortable lying in each other's arms. But then she pressed her slender, bared thigh against his and sighed. "Show me how."

Jean-Luc came back to his wits for a moment and attempted to turn them in the general direction of the path of righteousness.

She said, "I know it will hurt, but I'm not afraid."

"No, I won't hurt you." He had to stop it, feeling how small she was. His hands enclosed her waist. He couldn't say the word *innocent* again. Instead, as she continued to hold him, he concentrated on her fragility and resolved to leave her intact: she didn't know what to expect. He barely eased inside her as she moaned; he felt what a strain it was for her to accommodate even that much. He silently recited a series of *cançós de guerra*, lying still, and then he counted backward from one thousand in Greek while murmuring small reassurances to her.

But she thrust her tongue in his mouth and pushed against him, and he was unexpectedly deep inside her.

She cried out, and he covered her mouth with his, softly moaning *chérie*, shushing her and calming them both. After endless moments, she relaxed again and nestled her head on his shoulder.

"So that's it?" She brushed his neck with little kisses, which started a shiver that made him want to buck wildly. "Will it hurt the next time? It was over so quickly."

"*Chérie.*" He couldn't speak for a moment, even in French. "That's just how you start."

"*Ai,*" she said. "Then show me what to do next."

•

Felicia stirred beside him. "Will you tell me something?" She still spoke French.

"What's that, *chérie*?" Jean-Luc stroked her shoulder. The comfort of not being alone and the after-love warmth worked like a drug. The sound of French, after all the years he'd spent speaking other people's languages, was yet another comfort. She brushed the scarred flesh on his arm, which sent shivers through his whole body.

"Whose spy are you?"

His heart stopped.

"If you tell me," she murmured, "I'll say which of the things they made me tell you were true."

"Viscount de Chartrain is my lord." His voice cracked.

She sighed as if relieved and rubbed her hand down his arm, the burned one.

"My lord doesn't mean ill for your household." He rushed to explain. "He wants to know about certain rumors."

Felicia didn't speak, and he couldn't see her face in the dark to guess what she was thinking.

"Did you tell me anything that's true?" he asked, feeling reckless with relief now that this one secret was in the open.

"Everything." She sounded smug. "I've been honest about our household. Just like Pèire told me to be."

"And me the bigger fool, thinking those afternoons were private between us," Jean-Luc said.

"But don't you report every word I say to your lord?" Felicia said. "You're a spy and I spied on you. We're a matched pair."

"What *is* private between us?" He heard a plea in his voice. *Did she make him feel weak or strong?*

Felicia put her leg over his and drew closer. "The part that isn't your lord's business or my lord's," she said.

·

Jehan the smith spent the next day at the smithy, banging away at Valerós kitchen pots, wagon fittings, and ancient crusader armor that hadn't seen battle in years.

That afternoon, Guillem, the marshal of Valerós, sent Jean-Luc up on the battlements to fix the hinges on a door, an exhilarating assignment, because on such a clear day it was possible to see half-way to Cyprus. A hawk wheeled on the wind, sending the smaller birds into an angry fit. The crows launched combat, flying above the hawk to dive down on it and then circling again until they had chivvied it off to another part of the valley.

While he worked, the seigneur's family came out to the courtyard below, so Jean-Luc spied on Pèire with his granddaughters. He despised the role now. But Pèire clasped Felicia in an embrace as if she were his own and whispered something in her ear. Jean-Luc felt pleased seeing her treated equally with the other women. When Pèire let go of Felicia, he scanned the battlements and caught Jean-Luc watching. He saluted and then turned back to his family, putting his arm around Felicia and Beatriz as they crossed the courtyard to the family quarters.

Felicia, the orphan of Valerós and Jean-Luc's healing angel, spent the night in his loft. They spoke French as another way their tongues took pleasure from each other; they talked because sleep would steal time. After Felicia came to him, Jean-Luc began laughing. Once he started, he couldn't stop until his ribs ached, which felt like yet another comfort enveloping him in Valerós.

He ceased to hear Yves's ghost speaking amid the people talking in the smithy each day and Felicia murmuring in the night.

But it was Friday. On Monday, Pèire's fortnight would expire, and the seigneur would demand that the smith make up his mind. Meanwhile. Gerard was traveling to Fontcours to meet Pèire. Jean-Luc might not have another chance to send a message to his lord.

Time to be rational again. Felicia was safe here, and what he felt for her was a distraction to what he had to do next. It was past time to go hunting for the one-eyed soldier with a bad conscience that Thibaut heard confess in Toulouse. Then Jean-Luc could come back here and tell his new friends his real name.

▪

However, Felicia appeared again soon after dark. She curled up beside Jean-Luc and ran her hand through the hairs on his chest until he shivered.

"How did you end up a spy?" she asked. "Are you a younger son without enough land to stay home?"

"I can't go home." Jean-Luc always spoke truth now.

"Did you quarrel with your father? Was he cruel?" She tickled his ear, teasing him. He grasped her hand to stop it.

"My father is the best man in the world, but I can't go home."

"Why is that?"

"Because of Constantinople."

After he told the story, Felicia moved closer, not away. She stroked his temples with more tenderness than he'd ever felt.

"Every day, every night, I look up to see Yves so surprised to find my sword in him." He sat with his head in his hands, trying not to see it yet again. "I'm not a murderer. I loved my brother. But we quarreled earlier, so they say—"

"Who says?" Felicia entangled her small fingers with his.

"The men who lied to condemn me. God sent me to hell that night, but He forgot to let me die. God stole Yves to heaven. I couldn't even find his body to bury him properly." Jean-Luc told the rest as quickly as possible. "Men I never met swore I murdered my brother in anger when he tried to stop me from looting. Under the rules of the Church legates and the generals, looting meant death by hanging."

"You ran?"

"I rode across the eastern empire, and then north," Jean-Luc said. "I traveled through Mantua and Lyon to get home. It took months. I worked for a smith while I recovered from my wounds, and then I ran again, working for food or stealing when I had to. I wanted to tell my father myself."

"Anyone would," she murmured.

"But by the time I returned, he'd already heard the news from a priest who'd been in Constantinople. I was excommunicated for stealing the Church's booty and banished from Christendom for deserting."

"*Bon Dèu!*"

"*Ai, chérie.* My father is so good. He begged to hide me from the world. But that made no sense. Every time he looks at me, he's reminded that he'll never see Yves again."

"Where did you go?"

"Back to the Outremer. For a year, I fought in Antioch as a mercenary. Then I worked fighting the Seljuk Turks. But I couldn't stand any more: the food, the weather, the way the Frankish vermin lords cosset you one day and betray you the next. I came back to the Pays de France, because even though I can't be a knight, I need to be of service. So, I became someone else. Now I—"

"Spy," Felicia said.

"I find out things for my lord. The Viscount de Chartrain is a good man. I've never known him to do evil."

"What was your name before?"

Jean-Luc brushed a finger over her lips. "God sent that man to hell. It can't do you any good to know."

She held him in her arms, as when she'd first ministered to his other wound, offering more tenderness than he deserved. She kissed him so softly that he groaned, but she went on, touching him and kissing him the way they had learned to share. They moved together slowly, and she kissed him until he shuddered in release.

"I'll stay with you," Felicia whispered. "As long as you let me."

"No, this is impossible."

"But, *cheri*, consider how much you've already done that would be impossible for other men." Her touch while she spoke made him shiver. "All this goodness we have here, that seemed impossible. But now? We'll find a way."

It wasn't a time to argue. It was time for Jean-Luc to get on the road and regain his own name. He'd leave the next time he met Gerard's courier, who'd have a horse for him and money for travel provisions. He'd stop living in this dream.

27

Crux Lunata

Tomás at Valerós
22 days before Pentecost

WHILE HIS MILK-BROTHER CHRÉTIEN played at being a jongleur, singing at supper, Tomás's aching tooth nagged at him. In his stolen scribe's robes, Tomás managed the role of innocent through a long evening of dicing with Chrétien and the Valerós squires, house-knights, and stablemen. He disliked that role.

With the work Pèire gave him on his mind, sleep proved impos sible. Tomás went to the scriptorium to read Pèire's old lists of knights and bordoniers by candlelight. Miquel, his dead father, never appeared to offer advice, such as which names belonged to possible enemies. If he followed Pèire's plan to ride to Narbonne and Tou-louse, then he had only three more days to learn as much as he could from these records. And from Pèire's stories. He wasn't succceding yet at what Pèire asked of him, much less finding one step forward on what he'd promised his father.

Three more days. Then a different kind of action would be required if he was to appear in the bishops' court at Pentecost.

When dawn gave way to sunlight, a kennel boy appeared at the door of the scriptorium.

"Senhór Pèire begs you to attend him."

In the stable yard, Tomás did honor to Pèire in the Catalan way, having imitated the gesture enough that it felt natural.

"Come riding with us, *fadrin*. I want to show you boys the castle defenses," Pèire said.

Behind him, Chrétien led three horses from the stable, handing one lead to Pèire and another to Tomás.

Chrétien linked fingers to give Pèire a boost into his saddle. The old man groaned. "I'm not hearing the golden angels in Paradise sing our Lord's name when I get on a horse these days."

As Chrétien mounted, Pèire frowned. "That's Benito's pony."

"Not any longer." Chrétien's blond hair gleamed white against a Valerós surcoat. He'd replaced that ragged crimson silk coat he'd won in Marseilles.

"Got a new coat, too? Any of my men walking shirtless?" Pèire seemed amused. "Are you leaving my men with anything?"

"My second-best Cairo cards," Chrétien said. "And stiff lessons on skill versus chance."

"I feared as much. It's good I'm not a gambler. Else you lads would have the castle out from under my feet."

They followed the meandering path down and around the castle. Pèire showed Chrétien and Tomás the castle's defensive tunnels: where the hidden escapes lay, how they could be used to get behind siege lines.

"If you ever need to leave without notice," he said.

They rode where early-morning dew wet the white oaks and gorse among the granite outcroppings. Then Pèire led them to a hummock overlooking the valley. Jays squawked from the oaks, and swallows dipped and glided over the fields. At the foot of the hill, frogs croaked in a pond and a heron tiptoed in the reeds. Startled by the horses, the bird rose up in flight, its huge wings wider than the full span of a man's arms.

"Magnificent!" Chrétien spread his arms in imitation.

"It bothers me that Miquel made you boys into his assassins," Pèire said. "Didn't he give you *poulains* more to do? It's a shame to waste your life on revenge."

"We swore to find his enemy," Tomás said. "It's enough."

Chrétien agreed. "We haven't suffered."

"The angels know Miquel deserves it," Pèire said. "From the time Miquel first lifted a sword, boys were so loyal they'd die for him. Who but a Saracen would want to destroy him?"

"We hadn't heard the story you told about the horse race," Chrétien said. "But that band of boys you didn't get along with in Edessa? The ones camped near the Knights Templar?"

Pèire sat quietly for many long moments, stroking his horse. Then he began reciting men's names. Chrétien and Tomás described which of those men were dead and which they'd discounted as innocent. After a dozen names, Pèire stopped. "That's all, I think."

"Except Hugues de Beaurain," Tomás said. "Our father's old comrade and yours."

"No, *fadrin*." Pèire spoke with kindness, but firmly.

"Hugues was in Edessa with his younger brothers when you and Miquel were there," Tomás said.

"His brothers were very much younger," Pèire said. "They fell ill and didn't stay the whole campaign."

Tomás repeated a litany of all the times Hugues had been nearby when catastrophe struck Miquel. "That raid at Aleppo when our father ended up enslaved among the Saracens. And Hugues was visiting the king on Cyprus when our sugar fief was burned and I was attacked." He omitted the details.

"That's two coincidences. You can't judge based on that." Pèire wiped the blade on his tunic, studying it.

"You can see the answer to the mystery in Hugues's face," Chrétien said. "Tall, tawny. The Montcavas sons who stole Fontcours both look like him. Renoud and his dead brother Nicolau."

"All Normans look the same," Pèire said. "Hugues is the one man who's better than his ancestors and cousins."

"Hugues's family once held Fontcours," Tomás said. "The old Count of Toulouse forced Hugues's grandfather to forfeit it."

Pèire shook his head. "Hugues was happy when Miquel received Fontcours. As if his own brother got it."

"When you and Vidal and Miquel were attacked near Damascus, Hugues was out on raid nearby." Tomás didn't need to say more: Pèire's son Vidal died that day.

"We noticed you and Hugues trading looks over the tattoo on that dead priest. The mark is on Hugues's arm, too," Chrétian said. "I saw it when he gambled with your men that night."

"And the same mark was on the scoundrels who did this." Tomás traced the worst of the scars across his face. "Crux Lunata. It was signed on your Wolf letter."

"Those knights are the stuff of child's tales, *fadrin*," Pèire said.

"I suffered from hands carrying that mark, senhór."

Pèire shifted in his saddle, grinding his teeth in what seemed to be anger. "Hugues, Miquel, and me, the three of us tried to break into that bunch, thinking the Knights of the Lunate Cross was a real Order. We were—what? Maybe twenty-five years old, ten years in the Outremer each of us, hearing stories about their magic. Hugues and his brother Colomb made it through their initiation."

"Ha!" Tomás said.

Pèire ignored the outburst. "But they were a gang of thieves, not a real Order. When they saw we didn't believe their magic tripe, they left Miquel and me to walk home through the baking desert in the Saracens' country. They're only playing at brotherhood. Our own bonfraires, that's real."

"But my father says—" Tomás began.

"Said," Chrétien interrupted, emphasizing the word. "Our father *said* those Knights suck blood and steal souls."

"He meant it as a parable," Pèire said.

"Hugues wears the mark of the Lunate Cross," Tomás said.

"They booted Hugues from their society, *fadrin*. He did not bring Miquel to grief. If it were Hugues, I'd no longer care to have God save my soul." Pèire rose in his saddle, looking out over the valley. "Here's what else I wanted to show you. See how Sebastián can handle a horse."

·

In the valley below, Tomás spied a band of squires lined up on horseback at intervals along the cart path around the grain fields. Sebastián, clad in leggings and a shirt, shortened his stirrups, and buckled on a cuirass before mounting the new pony, the present from his uncle Renoud. Beside him, Isabella in leather huntsman clothes mounted her Arabian pony. Together, they started down the track.

At first, Sebastián and Isabella rode neck-and-neck at race speeds. Then they began a relay. When Sebastián rode ahead, Isabella dropped to the side of her saddle and raced up to snag the scarf at his saddle pommel. Sebastián came from behind, using his javelin to lift the scarf from Isabella. From there, each exchange grew more dangerous.

"I learned that game while spying on Seljuk Turks doing their training, back when Miquel led me out on look-see trips," Pèire said. "I taught Vidal when he was a boy, and then Isabella when I came back home. My other little girls don't care to learn."

The next ride around the track included a javelin-throwing game Tomás knew: he'd learned it from his father's knights on Cyprus. Sebastián was good, his mother perhaps better. Tomás had climbed up to Valerós a week earlier, and now lived with people who were beyond his former experiences. And he'd seen a lot of the world.

"What man will you serve when you finish Miquel's business?" Pèire looked at Chrétien.

"I go where my brother goes," Chrétien said.

"We haven't decided," Tomás said. He still went to sleep each night thinking they'd leave the next day, and each morning it became more impossible, and his oath to Pèire crucial to his sense of honor. Pèire could provoke as much worry as Miquel, keeping Tomás perpetually checking that he was living as an honorable man. "Our father left behind parcels of land from the kings of Aragón and Cyprus. We only know the king of Cyprus."

"I don't trust that king," Chrétien said. "We won't serve him."

"We also don't trust either Philippe of France or the Count of Toulouse," Tomás said, "since they let the Church take Fontcours from our father."

"That leaves Pedro d'Aragón, who's the smartest of the whole lot nowadays," Pèire said. "Give Pedro your oath."

"I don't know," Tomás said. "Except for the promise to my father—and to you—I'm adverse to oaths."

"Miquel made you both capable of big things," Pèire said. "We need men like you to keep our world in order. Stay here. Join my home and my knights. Make a family."

"My brother is my family," Chrétien said.

Pèire nodded. "I see that in you. But the road doesn't have to be your home."

Isabella raced in their direction on the trail below.

Jolted by the sight of her, Tomás listened to Pèire admonish them like the Tempter on the mountaintop, while Tomás had stumbled nowhere near the path of righteousness. Here in Valerós, he'd expected to find another Montcava she-wolf, but Isabella possessed a subtle mind, her passions aroused by riding a horse too fast and forging old gospels.

She spotted them on the hill and waved the banner she'd captured. To Pèire; she waved to her grandfather; she still hated Tomás.

"Has Isabella asked what you're doing for me?" Pèire asked. "She can be pretty damned nosy."

"I haven't told her, senhór. You must tell her."

Pèire turned his hand over in a Catalan gesture of refusal. "No. My girls need to be protected. How do you two get along?"

"My brother fared slightly better than that wolf in the upper hills." Chrétien answered for him.

"She must like you, *fadrin*."

"To be honest, senhór, I think not." Tomás tried to achieve the same levity as Chrétien.

"Don't take that to heart." Pèire laughed at him. "I keep putting men in her way, but it never comes to anything."

"*Bon Dèu!* Is that what you intended for me?"

"Well, I didn't intend her for your singing brother." Pèire's words were partially lost in the noise of their horses' shuffling stamp. Their beasts were eager to join the pair racing below.

"What kind of a man are you with women, *fadrin*?" Pèire asked, now speaking quite clearly. "Like the devil Miquel was when he was a lad? Or like Miquel when he had a wife?"

"After this," Tomás touched the gouges in his own face, "I took the same vow a priest does."

Behind Pèire, Chrétien silently laughed at him.

"*Ai, fadrin*," Pèire said. "A woman who takes your hand won't care what happened to your face."

"I let my guard down because of women," Tomás said. "A waste of time on the way to what we promised my father."

Pèire held his hands up in that Catalan gesture, imploring the heavens. "Didn't Miquel arrange a wife for you? Don't you want a family and a home?"

Chrétien said, "My brother will tell you he'd rather eat dust."

"Then, as the shepherds say, let all be as it pleases God" Pèire laughed. "I fooled with a notion that Miquel's son might take my girl as wife and keep her safe."

Isabella and Sebastián rounded the track again and their horses pounded toward the hill where the men observed the riders. Tomás heart leaped at Pèire's words. *Take my girl as wife.*

"Senhóra Isabella says she doesn't like marriage." Chrétien shook Tomás out of his daydream, grinning, likely reading his mind. *Give up your vow and marry your way into Fontcours.*

"The Montcava bastard she married tried to break the poor girl," Pèire said. "Lucky he didn't wake up dead in his own bed. Renoud can't get what he wants by threatening to condemn her to the Church."

"Dire indeed, if priests are forced to argue faith with Senhóra Isabella," Chrétien said. "We'd best condemn Renoud for plotting to destroy the Church."

Pèire slapped Chrétien's knee, laughing. "She's getting used to the idea of marrying ol' Gerard. I made a good choice there."

At the next bend, Isabella rode two horse-lengths ahead of Sebastián, who failed to snatch a scarf from her saddle with his javelin.

"But I worry about my little Beatriz," Pèire said. "However, I won't ask you to take her, *fadrin*, since you've sworn to say no."

Tomás's mind remained caught on the idea of Renoud's threats, not of marrying Pèire's infant granddaughter. Because Tomás wasn't on the mountain with the Tempter; he was Moses looking across the Jordan River at a Promised Land he'd never enter.

"God help me, I will destroy Renoud before summer is out."

"You *poulains* can't just murder him." Pèire motioned with his head, like a captain leading a patrol, taking them back up to the castle. "You need proof. All this started when Miquel married Eloïse. But he made me swear to leave her alone."

"Did you know she's a goodwoman?" Chrétien asked. "We worry Simon de Montfort might take her lands as forfeit for heresy."

"Gerard will protect Fontcours. That's why I asked him to take Isabella. He's loyal to the Church, so if any land is forfeited because you prove Eloïse cheated Miquel, then…" Pèire stopped.

"You see, now, senhór? If I prove Eloïse betrayed our father—"

"Then you prove Sebastián's father is a bastard," Pèire said. "Fontcours will be forfeited. To you."

"It's only Fontcours that's to pass whole, undivided, to Miquel's oldest son. By your southern customs, Sebastián will share a slice of Montcava among all the other Montcava bastards," Tomás said.

"Any that aren't condemned by their own cousins as heretics," Chrétien said.

"I'll explain to the boy that his portion of Valerós and Arracheuse are enough. Fontcours belongs to Miquel's true son."

"It won't be necessary for you to speak, senhór," Tomás said.

"No?" Pèire said.

"Sebastián heard us the first time you and I talked."

"*Bon Dèu.*"

"But, senhór, I'm deeply troubled now that I know Sebastián as a friend and a comrade. How can I destroy what he believes is his inheritance?" They'd arrived back at the castle mews and were surrendering their borrowed horses to the stable boys.

"This valley is enough for Sebastián," Pèire said. "He has Arracheuse. He can take my name and make it in this world on his own."

"Your deeply troubled concerns, dear brother?" Chrétien scoffed. "I must remind you that we can't prove squat in the bishops' court. The best we've achieved so far is to keep enemies from attacking the boy and his mother."

·

"Poor Parzival," Chrétien drawled, speaking the marketplace Arabic they'd learned in Cairo.

While Chrétien nattered at him over dinner that night, Tomás endeavored not to watch Senhóreta Katelina and Isabella.

Chrétien persisted with his torture. "But not Parzival as in the *cançós d'Arturo.* We have before us an abstinent man without a dram of chastity. You're an aberration of nature. Maybe you can bite the heads off chickens at village fairs." He held up his portion of the evening meal: chicken with a sauce of fennel and almonds.

"Go soak your lice-infested head, you leprous beggar." Tomás concentrated on the food.

"Give it up, Parzival. You were born knowing how to get a woman to surrender."

"This is different."

"Indeed. You've had far more beautiful women. But didn't you say that beautiful women usually aren't good in bed?"

"Can you find it deep in your flea-bitten soul to forget what you think you know about me? *Per l'amor de Déu.*"

"She snared you with her seductive manner. An amorous hedgehog might learn from the way she tries to please you."

"Chrétien, this is the same behavior that led a Brabançon mercenary in Burgundy to try to slit your throat. What do you taste beside cinnamon in this chicken?"

"Saffron. Senhóreta Katelina's kitchen people know their spices." Chrétien poured more wine. "Listen, dear brother, I can help. I'll tell the senhóra you don't have a heart to break. She'll want you then. She's born contrary."

"Stop. My vow is more important than a moment's desire."

A boy came to Senhóra Isabella's table and whispered in her ear. She stood abruptly, jarring Senhóreta Katelina and spilling her wine. Isabella didn't look back as she ran after the boy.

"Come, noble Don Tomás. I stole a jug of unwatered wine to drink. Let's eat our supper and then go dicing. Better yet, let's do as our father taught us: free a couple of horses and leave."

"Miquel would want us to stay."

"*Aiieee*, the golden Savior with all the dancing angels." Chrétien cried. "Dice, then. I assume we aren't leaving tomorrow morning. It's twenty days until—"

"Twenty-two, counting today." Tomás indulged his tendency to sulk when he was failing.

"Plenty of days to find answers and ride to Toulouse," Chrétien said. "And then after that, we have the entire crusading season to catch our enemies and destroy them."

Lubos and Esau

JESUS WAS A SON, but he seemed to have an uncaring father. Or perhaps, as Lubos thought about it, they didn't teach the correct story about Jesus, like so many things. Perhaps, like Lubos's own father, Jesus's Father in Heaven intervened and saved him, showing Jesus why we must endure pain and suffering in this world.

Lubos pricked another lunate cross on his arm as he contemplated stories about sons. It was his own idea: keeping track of Père-Izsák's list with a new mark for each name he found and killed. He didn't have red ink, so he made do with charcoal from the camp fire that crackled and sang to him as he pricked his arm.

Isaac was another son, although his father Abraham required the intervention of angels to stay in harmony with the world. Lubos had learned from his woman Aykuna that those intervening angels were the same spirits in rocks and streams who speak to him now.

May all beneficent forces of this mired world protect me, Lubos prayed, from ever offering a son as sacrifice. Abraham made a mistake, believing God wanted him to do that to his son. You put your seed into the vessel of a woman so you could reach into the future, not to satisfy a fickle god. That's what Père-Izsák told him.

But Esau was a son, too. Lubos didn't understand how Isaac, who had once been saved by angels, failed to see which son loved him most. Isaac had even been blessed to have two sons living in his home, until he made a blind mistake. Lubos pondered Esau's predicament: loving his father the most and yet losing his blessing.

Right now, though, Lubos needed to eat a meal, repair his gear, and do as Père-Izsák asked. Therefore, he must find the next name on his list and finish his mission: to keep the world in harmony when kings and lords strayed. He laid the fire in the correct way, with the eight-pointed cross and the proper prayers. Then he lifted the rabbit he'd trapped earlier that day and tore its coat away. He enjoyed hearing the rabbit scream as it died. It sang in harmony with the voices of the spirits in stones.

✳✳✳

168

PART THREE
Thrice Broken

Sweet thing, whatever you hear them say,
Don't believe anyone knows greater sadness
Than a lover who parts from his love,
Believe me, I know it myself;
Ai, lord, what a paucity of night is left!
Ai! I can hear the guard crying,
'Go! Now! Because I see the day,
Coming after the dawn.'

— Gaucelm Faidit (attributed)
"Us cavaliers si jazai"

In Part Three

169

28
Scant Silver

"KATELINA, PLEASE REMEMBER. YOU swore not to reveal what I've been doing all this time."

Late in the afternoon, Isabella slipped the bar on the inner solar bar, locking the two of them in where Katelina was wrapping up her needlework.

"When I join the angels, you shall say that I always kept my promises," Katelina said.

Isabella unfolded her leather satchel, the one she'd used in Toulouse to protect her scrolls. The satchel was far too light, so it took only a heartbeat to show Katelina how much silver her texts had earned in the past year. "When Benito was last in Narbonne, selling my manuscripts, too many lords and churchmen pleaded poverty. They're saving their silver because of this French invasion."

It was a pathetic pile of coins, compared to what she'd earned last year, when she'd boasted to Katelina that she'd pay off the Arracheuse mortgage by the year Sebastián came of age. "And with that *scribe*," she heaped contempt on the word, "practically living in my scriptorium, I won't finish new work for Benito to sell in Narbonne."

Katelina hummed but didn't answer.

"So, as a steward for Valerós and Arracheuse, how am I to do my duty to hoard enough silver? What do I do? Sell my horse?"

"Only if you want Pèire to get after you with a stick." Katelina tucked her precious steel needle into its wallet. "Besides, there's no knight here who can afford the price of a horse. And what will you ride when you go with Pèire to Toulouse? That's three days away."

Isabella ignored that painful reminder. "We won't have money from crops until after Michaelmas. There's no way to pay our taxes."

"You're missing the beauty of Pèire's strategy, and his pact with Gerard." Katelina wound a scarlet thread into a neat ball, preparing to store it in her sewing bag. "Gerard has no heirs, and he's rich. You'll be doing what Valerós needs, because Gerard promised to pay the Arracheuse taxes and mortgages. By Pentecost, you'll have done what's needed to free Arracheuse from Simon's threats."

"I have to act. I have to find a way to go forward." Isabella folded the satchel around the miniscule pile of silver. "It's one thing if Pèire is conspiring with his comrade over our taxes. Or to rally a defense against the French invaders. But Pèire's strategy won't protect me from Renoud and how he intends to use this crusade against me."

"That's why," Katelina's many bracelets rattled when she settled her hand on Isabella's, "Pèire wants you to go north with Gerard. At least until the invaders go home and stay home."

Isabella denied this, shaking her head.

"*Ai, xiqueta.* But consider how last week's attacks all ended when Renoud and his henchmen rode away. It proves Pèire's point. That distance will matter for your safety."

"Or maybe it's because Pèire watches that false scribe and the jongleur so closely, they can't hatch any new plots."

"Pèire says those two also consider Renoud as an enemy. And if Tomás is plotting against you, it doesn't involve harm to your person. I'll repeat, he wants you."

"Those two came here lying about who they are." Isabella fingered the leather cord that closed her satchel. "Maybe I should use this silver to pay them to bear false witness against Renoud, the same way he intends to destroy my honor."

"Seriously, Isabella?"

"I wish. But they're nobody. Their oaths would mean nothing in court. It would be a waste of silver."

"Sebastián says they are knights. Chrétien is teaching him the skills of a knight."

"Knights with no sworn lord? With no horses? If they're anything, they're mercenaries who would probably sell themselves for ten silver morabatins and a warm bed."

Katelina had tucked everything into her sewing basket, finished with work for the day. She stood. "I won't argue with you about that. For a handsome set of mismatched twins, it's easier to think they're assassins than heroes of a troubadour's song."

"Assassins?" Isabella stood up rapidly, clutching her too-light satchel. "Would that be the best use of this silver?"

"Isabella, no."

"Of course not." Isabella unbarred the door and walked out of the solar beside Katelina. "It would be a great sin to pay others to do what I'm too cowardly to do myself."

"*Bon Dèu,* Isabella. Pèire's strategy will make you safe. You just need to do whatever it takes to make yourself happy."

"Make myself happy? That means a dozen knights at my command—with horses and lances—riding into Toulouse to defeat Renoud. That would be true joy."

"You'll have that, *xiqueta.* But the knights will be wearing Gerard de Chartrain's colors and carrying his banner."

"*Aiieee!* Katelina, we're friends. Why won't you—"

"*Ma dòmna!*" On the external stairs, the stableman's son hailed Isabella. "My father says you must come now. Your horse is ill."

.

Al-Malik, her horse, lay in the straw, shaking. Isabella knelt and rubbed where Al-Malik liked best, near his ears. The animal's eyes fluttered open, all white and wild for just a heartbeat. Then he lay still again, somewhere between sleep and the nether world.

"We found him sick when we came back after feeding the other animals," Joris the stableman said.

She stayed beside her horse, guessing with the stablemen what brought Al-Malik so low, so fast. Katelina came by with Ermessen from the kitchens, who with Joris were the most knowledgeable physicians of either human or beast. Ermessen said, "This horse has been poisoned."

"I'd think so," Joris said, "except no one in Valerós is so evil."

"But no disease progresses this way. And he has no injury gone foul." Katelina stretched after kneeling so long. "Isabella, you were up before the dawn. Get some rest. I'll watch with Joris for a while."

173

Isabella caught the looks exchanged between Joris and Ermessen. "You want me gone so you can put down my horse," she said. "If you must do it, I need to be with him."

"No, ma dòmna. We won't send him to God," Joris said. "We will make him well."

"*Per l'amor de Dèu*, I hope so," she said. "Yes, I'll leave him in your care."

She climbed the stone stairs to the family rooms, but instead stepped out onto the battlements. As exhausted as she felt, her anger and fear for Al-Malik left her restless. Half-way up the stairs, voices drifted up from the stable.

"Pèire will have my hide for this, won't he, senhóreta?"

"It's not your fault," Katelina said. "Your lord is a fair man."

"I don't know how this happened on my watch," Joris muttered.

Isabella's footsteps crunched along the stone walkway atop the castle walls. Years before she had learned discipline, not to dwell on matters she couldn't control. But a creature she loved was hurting. Or dying. One prays, in such cases, that it might be as it pleases God. But why would it please God to let His creatures suffer? One could only pray to learn to accept the cruelties God allowed to be served up to His creatures.

She circled the battlements six times, fighting the powers of her own imagination. The guards, long familiar with her night wanderings, didn't bother to greet her. Exhausted, she rested her hand on the stone wall to steady herself.

It seemed better to return to the stable and insist on spending the night beside Al-Malik. Perhaps Felicia, who had helped her nurse a foal the previous spring, might join her.

As she retraced her way along the battlements in search of Felicia, she stumbled once more, stupid with sleeplessness.

"You cold, sinning whore."

A voice whispered behind her as a huge hand covered her face. Another hand pawed her breast, the one where Nicolau had cut her.

Everything bad had come home.

29
Lightning

TOMÁS ABANDONED CHRÉTIEN AND the dicing game to find Pèire, whom he discovered sitting in the dim light of the scriptorium. They talked into the night, with Pèire coaxing stories from Tomás about his training in Antioch and Cairo.

Pèire rubbed his temples the entire time they talked. Then he put his head in his hands. The gesture had become familiar, but this time it caught Tomás's attention, and he reached out and waved his hand. Pèire did not follow the motion.

"Are you all right, senhór?"

"I have a bit of a headache now and then, lad."

"And when you do, you can't see."

"I can move around places I know. I can't see your face. But I know it's you when you speak."

"Where does your head ache?"

"I can't tell exactly. It's like when you look up at the sun in the desert. The light seems to fill you. The pain's so fierce at times, I wish someone with a sword would just end it."

"Shall I walk with you to your room?"

Pèire said, "That would be grand, *fadrin*. I know you'll say nothing to anyone."

"You have my word, senhór."

They ambled in the moonlight toward the keep, Pèire's hand on Tomás's shoulder, but nothing else betrayed that Tomás led the way and steadied the old seigneur. As they crossed the cobbles, Tomás asked, "Senhóreta Katelina is more than a duenna, isn't she?"

"Yes," Pèire said.

"I was only eight when you left the Outremer. But there was a woman who lived in your camp then. I was far too young to have any sense, but I believed she was a queen from a far-away country. It was Senhóreta Katelina, wasn't it?"

"Yes. I wanted to let her rest at home this summer, though we always travel together. Now I think I need her with me."

"That might be best."

A moment later Pèire said, "You're a betting man. How likely is it, after all the times I dodged swords and arrows, my luck finally leaves me far up here in the hills with this headache?"

"About as likely as being struck by lightning," Tomás said.

And then the woman fell on him again.

•

Isabella fell on a man, and the blow pushed him to the cobblestones. The man's arms wrapped around her, and he rolled them both over. More in shock than in pain, she stared into Tomás's face as he gazed at her in the moonlight.

"I told you not to fall for me."

Her lungs heaved, trying to work again.

"Who is it?" Pèire called.

"It's Isabella. She's had the wind knocked out of her and can't speak yet." He lifted most of his weight off her but kept his knee between her legs.

She gasped, still trying to breathe. Tomás rolled off her and onto his knees in a single motion.

"That bruise on your cheek will turn nasty," he whispered. "Let's see what you broke, besides your fall at the expense of my shoulder."

Pèire called for the guard while Tomás probed her limbs and ribs, checking for broken bones. When he touched the base of her breastbone, she curled up in agony, trapping his hands under her breasts. She gasped, sucking in another jagged breath, and tried to unfold herself.

Men pounded down the steps from the upper walls.

"Best protect your privates, gentlemen," Tomás called. "She's leaping from the parapets again."

"No," she whispered.

"Can't a man walk down the street without you jumping on him?" Pèire raged.

"I think she fell, senhór," Tomás said.

"No." Isabella panted for breath, desperate to tell them. "A man pushed me over the wall."

.

In a blur of shadows beyond Pèire, Tomás saw a figure dart into a passageway. He sprinted after that shadow, and his own momentum carried him down a dozen steps, where he collided with a wall in the darkness. The force of the collision spun him around a corner, so he fell another dozen steps and then tumbled and sprawled across uneven flagstones.

It was black as the hellhole where he'd been dumped on Cyprus.

Tomás listened for footsteps in the dark. All sensations felt skewed: the floor wasn't flat, the walls weren't straight, the ceiling threatened to descend on him. In the black space, he breathed in fear and exhaled panic. He groped his way to an opening that led into a hall or tunnel, with a pair of stairs leading up.

Something scrambled nearby. He held his breath, listening to dungeon sounds: small creatures of the dark that crawl on you when your hands are tied.

He couldn't breathe. The darkness pressed on his body like a weight, and fear grabbed him like a mailed fist, as if he were back in that dungeon on Cyprus, hoping to die.

"Hey, *poulain*. Draw your sword."

The echo chased itself down the corridor, while Tomás tried to find which way to turn. A whine escaped his throat.

"Crying like a dog, *poulain*? That's what your father did the night the devil finally took him."

"The devil hasn't got me yet!" Miquel shouted.

Tomás snatched at his sword, banging the blade and his hand into a wall as he drew it. He yelped again.

"Over here," the voice said. "This devil is behind you."

"It's all right, *fadrin*!" Miquel cried. "Stay by me. No fear!"

177

Then the voices of Valerós soldiers rattled down from above, and the laughing whisper dissolved in the darkness. By the time the guards arrived with torches, Tomás couldn't hide his terror and ran past them into the open night air, where he vomited in the gutter until his belly heaved empty and dry.

Pèire still leaned against the stone wall where Tomás had left him. Trembling after the purge, Tomás sank onto the cobble pavement beside his father's friend. Isabella seemed to breathe again; but he could not. His stomach still lurched. Sweat dripped from his face, but he couldn't wipe it away because his hands shook so badly he had to sit on them.

■

With Guillem's help, Isabella stood and found her bones were fine, but then she sank to the steps, her back against the wall

Pèire said, "You need a hired sword as much as a husband. Maybe the Moor can do that, to take care of you."

"Take care of me?" Astonished, Isabella only echoed his words.

Shouts echoed from the gallery above, but it was only the guards finding each other. Marshal Guillem sent his men up the towers, waking everyone and accosting anyone found in the shadows. Then Guillem returned to Isabella's side. "Shall I call Senhóreta Katelina to see to your wounds?"

"I'm fine," she said.

In a few heartbeats, Tomás returned and sat by her, breathing hard from whatever he had chased.

Isabella said, "I wanted to talk with Felicia, but didn't find her. So, I went to Katelina's room, looking for Felicia. When I passed the portico, a man grabbed me and tossed me over the edge."

Pèire and Guillem challenged each other over what had happened, while Tomás sat silently.

Guillem said, "It's not the smith. My men keep an eye on the smithy. He can't scratch an itch without me knowing about it."

"And it's not the scribe. He was with me," Pèire said.

"We don't have many strangers inside the walls. I suppose there's the jongleur," Guillem said.

Master Benito joined them. "No," he said. "He's in the armory taking my men's silver in that damn Egyptian card game."

While they debated, Isabella felt Tomás shaking beside her. His lips twitched faintly, and a fine sheen of sweat on his face glistened in the torchlight. He sat staring at the stone steps, not listening to the others. Without meaning to, she touched his hand to offer comfort. He shivered, looking down at her cool, pale fingers on his dark, hot hand. He rubbed his face with his other hand, as if those scars hurt him, then he shook his head and seemed to pull himself together.

Her mind was returning to its natural, skeptical state. What happened in the passageway to alter the man who had boldly pressed his knee between her legs and whispered in her ear moments before?

.

Felicia left his bed when the commotion began in the courtyard. Jean-Luc could let her go only by telling himself he'd hold her again the next night.

He moved over as he always did when she left, to smell where her hair had perfumed the linen cover and to curl up in the soft hollow where she'd lain. He felt under the pallet for the binding charm he kept there, and then he slept again, holding the tiny figure wound around his silver boar's tooth.

.

Isabella called a greeting when Felicia appeared at the top of the stairs. Pèire berated Felicia for being out in the dark.

"I was just in the garderobe," she said.

"From now on, you women will use a chamber pot and stay indoors at night," Pèire growled.

Guillem said, "Let me help you to your room, senhóreta."

After Guillem and Felicia departed, Tomás stood from his seat by the wall, and then staggered arm-in-arm with Pèire toward the keep with Isabella and Benita following. Pèire chatted with his new friend, whose hands still shook from whatever had frightened him. Yet Tomás solicited Pèire's well-being. They whispered in each other's ear in the same conspiring way he conversed with Chrétien the jongleur.

"I've had it with spooks," Pèire said. "Benito, stay by Isabella so this doesn't happen again. You got to take a leak, stick it out an archer's loophole. I'll whack it off if anything happens to her again."

"Yes, senhór." Benito took up a post at the corner of the hall, where no one could pass him.

"The boy better sleep in the barracks with you instead of with the marshal's men," Pèire said to Tomás.

"Yes, senhór, I'll see to it." Tomás's voice was raw, with none of its usual honey-coated tones.

"And the blasted guards who let this happen can sleep in the women's doorways until Twelfth Night." Pèire stopped by his own door, fumbling at the catch. "If that doesn't end up causing even worse trouble," he muttered.

Tomás let go of Pèire's arm and leaned against the wall. "Who's doing this? The attacks started when Renoud came, didn't they?"

"It also started the day you came, but that means nothing," Pèire said. "Where are you off to now? Will you come to me in the morning?"

"I'll come. Right now, I'm joining Chrétien for a bottle of wine and a game of chance," Tomás said.

Pèire nodded. He stepped inside his room and closed the door.

"Though I don't stand any kind of chance at all," Tomás murmured. He turned, seeming surprised to find Isabella still there.

Isabella said, "Thank you, Master Scribe. I didn't know you were such a good friend to my grandfather."

As usual the man avoided her eyes. "I admire your calm, ma dòmna. Chrétien says when he found you in that man-trap in the hills, you were mad instead of scared."

"It's like when the wolf attacked Guillem. You must act. Being afraid doesn't help." She could admit that she felt fear when she fell, but she wasn't about to be afraid with every breath she took.

"Maybe you haven't been afraid enough yet. There is pure evil in the world."

"I believe fear abets evil. What did you see in the tunnel?"

Tomás squirmed beside her. "Nothing. It was dark. I'm not as cold-blooded as you, ma dòmna. I'm just a scribe."

"And I'm the Queen of—"

He put his fingers on her lips to silence her, and then let them linger there, tracing her mouth so tenderly that she almost responded.

"His heart will break if they hurt you," he said. "Don't give them a chance."

"Who?"

"I don't know," he said. "Just stay inside at night until—"

"What? Until when?"

"Until your new husband can watch over you."

"Sancta Maria! I don't need to hear that from you, too."

In her cell, she threw off her clothes and decided against a night-dress. She lay down on her wool-stuffed pallet and let the night air wash over her, drying the last of her damp fear. She thought about poor Al-Malik instead of remembering the mauling and her fall. The single image she allowed, as she said a paternoster over and over, was Pèire and his scribe arm-in-arm, like brothers holding each other up. Yet every time she dozed, her muscles twitched violently and once again huge hands sent her flying through the night.

30
Hawk and Vixen

SWAYING SLIGHTLY, TOMÁS STOOD over the senhóra before dawn, watching her sleep as he'd watched others: her Montcava husband that died, the brother-in-law she hated. He'd hunted those men to see if they wanted killing, but this time he ended up ensnared, filled with desire.

Asleep, all her brittle resistance melted and she looked just like her son, who in sleep became a guileless child. The cruel bruise on her cheekbone had begun to bloom. To his eyes, cat-like in the night, she shimmered as if all light in the room came from her. Another thing of beauty which a Montcava bastard had taken and which Tomás couldn't have.

He longed to touch her bare arm, to know if it was as soft as it seemed. He wanted to put her mouth to its best use.

"Be brave, *fadrin*. Ask the old man for her," Miquel said. Moonlight glittered on the silver buckles of his leather jerkin. He slouched against the doorpost. "Pèire will give my son whatever he asks."

"She'd refuse."

Isabella stirred, but only to turn a bit, her long arm flung across the bed and her wide mouth slightly open as she breathed.

"See how she crooks her arm," Miquel said. "It's an invitation for a husband to be there."

"She hates men."

"No, just Montcavas, *teu peccador pech*." He called Tomás a dumb sinner.

Tomás shook his head. "The senhóra guesses what Pèire knows. You made me into a monster."

"*A mal punt.*" Miquel sighed, the way he did after a bad throw of the dice. "Still, I'd wager a thousand barceloneses you could sneak into her heart easier than you distracted the guard to come here."

"Go away. You don't have even one morabatin to lay as a bet. You're dead."

"Throw the dice for the fair senhóra," Miquel whispered. He tugged at the door to leave. "Though you've won far prettier."

Tomás swayed. The woman stirred again, and Tomás nearly cried aloud from the ache. Those sighs in the night would never fall on his shoulder. As she stirred yet again, her linen coverlet fell away, revealing that she slept unclothed. Tomás looked away, to preserve her modesty.

He didn't know which name of God to call upon for mercy.

■

Tomás in Toulouse
Twelfth Night 1210

Tomás didn't trust anyone to know what those men had done to him. Except for Chrétien, who rescued him. Tomás trusted least the person who watched it happen.

"I don't know why you are so upset." That's how the vixen Hélène de Beaurain answered when Tomás confronted her in Toulouse, when he still needed a stick to walk. "The whole affair on Cyprus was a warning for me. I'm the one in danger."

"Perhaps I'm upset because I was plucked from between your legs and beaten nearly to death," he said.

He set her needlework aside so she'd pay attention. With great effort, he refrained from breaking her neck. He believed the attack had been arranged between Hélène and her cousin Renoud, but he couldn't prove it and she wouldn't confess.

"Someone wanted to scare me." Hélène pouted. She had the dark, limpid eyes common in the Languedoc, but the pouting lips revolted him. It nauseated him that he'd once touched her.

"Did my bleeding in your boudoir scare you as they intended?"

"I was afraid my husband might find out," she said.

"Surely you accommodated such fears years before you met me. I almost died because of you, sweet senhóra. If your enemy is the seigneur of Montcava, tell me why. I will happily kill him for you."

Hélène pursed her lips. "My sister Valencia was Renoud's wife. She learned something he doesn't want people to know. When she died, I profited from her knowledge."

"Tell me. You owe a debt for what happened to me."

"There isn't enough profit to share." She sulked again. "And why should I tell you? I have my own protection."

"You're so well protected that men came into your bedroom to interrupt our fun."

"Those men knew my guards. They were dicing companions. They said my brother-in-law wanted to play a little joke on me."

"I almost died laughing. What do you hold over Renoud?" He fingered her neck, tempted again to break it, but she squirmed away.

"His mother's husband wasn't his father."

"*Qui s'ho creu?*" Tomás said. *Who'd believe it?* Though he did believe it, of course. "How did you learn that?"

"My sister found a letter to his mother. When Valencia died, I threatened to send the letter to the Count of Toulouse. So Renoud has been more generous with me than he was with Valencia."

"Who is the mysterious father?" Tomás asked. He strained not to betray how his heart thumped in anticipation.

"The letter doesn't say. It isn't signed."

He snorted in disbelief.

"Truly, that's all I have. But Renoud doesn't know that. Anyway, it's easy to guess, isn't it?" she said. "Look at Renoud. His brother was the same."

"What do you mean?"

"They don't look like Montcavas, do they? They're surely Beaurains. My dear husband Hugues sowed some wild seed long before I was born. I'm just harvesting what he sowed."

"Your little business with Renoud cost me a great deal. You can pay me back with that letter." He curled his fingers around hers, closing around them too tightly.

"I don't have it," she whimpered. "I gave it to a priest to hold. After that night in Famagusta, I was afraid of being robbed."

After Famagusta, Tomás was afraid of many things that never gave him pause before: the dark, a woman's touch, a lunate cross tattooed on a man's arm.

"Look at my face, senhóra." He tilted her head up. "You saw how this happened, and you owe me for it. Give me your proof about Renoud's father."

"Betray my cousin and husband to a *poulain* like you? Why would I do that?"

"You've undoubtedly betrayed your husband a thousand times before. You'll do it this time to stop me from exposing you to the world for what you are."

She laughed, scorning him. "Who'd listen to a barbarian—worse, an animal—like you?"

He ignored the insult. "You owe me."

She snatched her hand away and picked up the needle from her handwork. He flinched, thinking she meant to attack him with it, but instead she punched at the hot wax in the candle burning on her table. As she punched, she chanted.

"Thrice the candle is broke by me, thrice thy heart shall broken be." She held the needle in the flame, blackening its point. "I owe you nothing. If you threaten me, I will return the pain a thousandfold."

"Even if I believed in your devil magic, it's futile. I have no heart to break, senhóra. My father had it removed when I came of age."

She plunged the needle deep into the melted wax pooling at the top of the candle. "Stay away from me, Tomás. Go back to Cyprus. Or I'll see that a Montcava blade is stuck into your empty chest."

31

Where the Sun Goes Up

Jean-Luc at Valerós
21 days before Pentecost

AT SUNDAY MASS, JEAN-LUC prayed that the courier would return that day, or the next day if God willed it. Pèire would demand his oath on Monday, and he needed to chase his fate in Toulouse. Then he prayed at mass for the protection and health of another person, and the Blessed Virgin (who surely had grown tired of him praying only for his own selfish desires) had granted him a moment of peace.

After mass, Jean-Luc sat outside the smithy with his hand-work, another aged cuirass that needed new brass studs. He surrendered to a sweet lethargy, his hands busy, his mind free. Idly chewing a blade of grass while basking in the sun, he recalled a childish love-chant his cousins sang. Turning his head from east to west, he whispered the chant.

> Where the sun goes up
> Shall my love by me be.
> Where the sun goes down
> There by her I'll be.

Jean-Luc had saved a dozen of her long brown hairs from his bed. Now he braided half of these around the leather thong that formerly held his silver boar's tooth. The other six strands he braided into his own hair as he whispered the binding spell Ermessen had given him. He didn't in fact believe you could bind a person to you by braiding their hair into your own.

And he couldn't carry the weight of another person's life along with his greater burden. But her essence was still on his lips and moustache, and it was so pleasant to taste salt and musk in the full light of day. And to pretend, just for a moment.

Several people stopped to greet him and ask after his wound. Ermessen came by with a bowl of strawberries and a packet of herbs she'd plucked that morning.

"Best thing in the world, herbs picked of a Sunday. I carried them to early Mass and Father Anselm blessed them. Here is a little comfrey especially for you, Master Smith."

After she left, he turned his face to the sun again and closed his eyes to thank his Blessed Protector for leading him to a place where he was nearly human again.

"Now, there's a pretty sight," a Sicilian voice said, "Vulcan saying prayers to the gods in the full light of day."

The marshal stood over him, stroking his long moustaches.

"I don't have your helmet ready." Jean-Luc roused from his fugue to stand and take the marshal's hand in greeting as he'd seen people do in this part of the country. "I swear it will be ready before you ride."

"I'm not here for business, especially on the Sabbath. I just stopped by to enjoy your company."

"Then I'm obliged, I assure you. I was just wondering why I was blessed with these strawberries. Sharing with you must be the answer."

The marshal settled beside him, and they sat with their backs against the wall, taking in the spring sunshine, the bowl of strawberries balanced on Jean-Luc's knee. Across the courtyard, young boys played at quoits while a few other boys, along with Pèire's great-grandson, put the dogs through their hunting commands.

"You heard we had trouble last night?" Guillem asked. "On top of Senhóra Isabella's trouble in the hills? And the murdered priest? And the brigand you fought?"

"The commotion woke me last night."

"I know you like your beauty sleep." The marshal ate a strawberry. "Nothing much rouses you."

Jean-Luc concentrated on selecting a berry from the bowl. He knew he was being watched, however kind they were about it.

"Pèire wants all the knights to wear their hauberks and carry their swords," the marshal said.

"Seems sensible." Jean-Luc didn't like this turn.

"Benito is hunting up a hauberk for you."

"No need. I'm not a soldier. I only sharpen their swords."

A passel of knights came by, hailing Guillem with a salute. Some acknowledged Jean-Luc with a nod.

"Damn it, man!" Guillem exclaimed when those knights passed. "We need you. Why are you hammering pots at a forge?"

"I'm a smith." Jean-Luc's heart beat hard enough to betray him.

"The old man thinks not." Guillem grasped Jean-Luc's arm and again studied the swirl of burn scars. Jean-Luc calmly pulled his hand back. "Pèire knew you the moment you walked in the gate." He pulled his own sleeve back, showing Jean-Luc the scar on his wrist, the square burned by a crossbow bolt. "He called the bonfraires to meet at midnight, and he expects you to be there."

"*Bon Dieu!*" A desire rushed in Jean-Luc's heart, pulling him to that meeting with brothers-in-arms. Except another desire ran wildly in pursuit of Felicia. And a third wanted that one-eyed man in Toulouse. Here, where he sat, Jean-Luc felt grateful to finally be honest with his friend Guillem.

"Me, I've wracked my brain," Guillem said, "and I still can't recall when we met you. How long ago was it? Fifteen years?"

"Seventeen. After Philippe returned to France, we rode with the Marquis de Beaurain as squires when Richard pushed everyone on to Jerusalem."

Guillem chuckled. "Then you were just out of swaddling clothes with scarcely any beard, much less the bird's nest you hide behind now. The old man says you and your brother are the best our bonfraires have ever seen."

Jean-Luc felt his face burn. Guillem's flattery, exposure, and his own shame sent blood racing through his veins.

"It's a long way to travel from great crusader to piss-poor spy," Guillem said.

"A man might fall on hard times," Jean-Luc said.

"And lose his armor and his horse? Can't you just find a new one? Ride under another banner?"

"The Church excommunicated me. Philippe banished me."

"Lords in the Outremer pay for warriors without asking about their pedigree. Pedro hires his mercenary-knights in Aragón."

Jean-Luc wanted to speak truthfully, because he respected the marshal. "I tried that. I want my own horses and banner."

"Will you join your lord when he comes here to marry?"

"No. Philippe warned my lord against keeping a banished man in his court."

"Why don't you stay here, my friend? Pèire owes fealty to Aragón, not the Pays de France. You can slip in among our knights and no one's the wiser. I'd be proud to count you among my men."

Jean-Luc fished in the bowl for another strawberry, not wanting to look at the marshal.

"If the world hadn't gone cock-eyed, I'd beg to ride under you," Guillem continued. "I'm lucky to call you brother, as a bonfraire."

"You are too kind. But it goes against my honor."

"What will you do?"

"Get my own name back. Keep seeking the men who lied to destroy me. There are rumors in Toulouse that one of those men might want to confess. To purge his soul of betrayal."

"I wish you luck. If you succeed, come back to Valerós. You're welcome here, you know."

"Yes, I've been made to feel it."

"Come on, man," Guillem urged him. "Join us in the courtyard to practice. If God ever made a warrior, he made you. Ride with us this summer."

"After Constantinople, I won't join any more crusades."

Guillem set the bowl of berries down. "God knows, I don't need any more crusades, either."

"You don't want to go?"

"No, I want to stay here. Get married. Chase wolves and brigands. I'm more goodman than not. I think of marriage as comfort."

"It's clear Pèire is not really riding out to fight," Jean-Luc said. "Why should you go along?"

"I gave him my oath."

"But I thought goodmen didn't go to battle or give oaths. Doesn't an oath bind you to the material world, or some such?"

"A goodman promises and preserves his honor without worrying about God condemning him. I gave Pèire Leteric my oath years ago. He needs me." Guillem clenched his fists. "We grew up with the faith of our fathers and *cançós de guerra*. That's what our lives were made of, all those years in Jerusalem and Antioch."

"But men learned to crusade for wealth in Constantinople," Jean-Luc said. "Béziers wasn't about the faith of our fathers."

"Yes. I shall never utter a word against my lord in this life. But I don't understand what Pèire is thinking."

A pack of hunting hounds and Great Pyrenees dogs descended on them then, chased by a horde of boys shouting at the dogs to obey. Ermessen followed, scolding the boys for harassing the dogs when God made dogs to be man's companion.

Guillem rose. "Farewell, my friend. Come meet with the bonfraires at midnight."

Jean-Luc kept his hands around the strawberry bowl, not waving farewell. The midnight meeting wouldn't happen. God would grant his prayer, and so Gerard's courier would arrive this afternoon, bringing a horse. Jean-Luc expected be back on the road long before midnight.

.

When night fell the courier had not arrived. When Felicia appeared in his loft again, Jean-Luc knew it was his duty to stop it. But he let them both get wild. Drenched in sweat, they neglected to keep as quiet as they should. Eventually they collapsed, with only their fingers touching as they lay in the warm air that drifted up to the loft from the remains of the forge fire. In the darkness, he had to ask the question lingering on the tip of his tongue for the past days and nights.

"You know medicines and herbs, *chérie*. Do you know how to keep from getting a child?"

Felicia rested her head in the crook of his arm. "It's a bit late to worry about that, isn't it?"

"Just tell me."

"There won't be any bastards here. Pèire says I'm to be married soon." She wiggled away but then faced him again. "Is this the last time for us?"

He couldn't say yes, as he honestly should.

Felicia was unnervingly quiet. Then she said, "I had no idea I'd feel like this. I can never be with another man in this way."

"It burns my soul, *chérie*, but I can't be a husband to you."

"But I'm just saying that in my heart and before God's eyes, I am joined to you for all eternity. Don't you feel the same?"

"*Oui, chérie.*" What bitter folly had he led them into?

"Don't go."

"I've spent every day dreaming about how I might stay. Perhaps Pèire could give me a bordonier's portion. A freeholder who serves Pèire Leteric is respectable."

"A bordonier's portion?"

"Can you go that low with me? Keep a small hut while I raise a vineyard and hammer at a forge?" It was no more possible than anything else he dreamed.

"You're a knight," she said in a small voice.

"No. I'm exiled. I'm excommunicated. If you join with me, you are outside the Church, too. Even if I lie about who I am, you can't sink as low as I must live. I can't take care of you."

After silence echoed for several moments, she said, "I kept you from bleeding to death. I gave you the information you wanted for your lord. I have never told anyone what you tell me. So, it is I who take care of you. Where did you get the notion that you need to take care of me?"

"It is what men do," he said.

"I come from six generations of crusaders. And God knows what our men did before they took up the Cross. And none of those crusaders' wives had men taking care of them." She rolled away from him, although his arm remained around her. "We count on men leaving. That's what they do. That, and dying."

"Don't try to hurt me," he whispered, "because it only takes a little bit." He drew her back to hold her closely.

"I won't let them marry me off until the crusading season ends at Michaelmas. Perhaps you can take your own name again by then." She snuggled against him and then kissed his neck, leaving a bite mark. "I'll spend the summer like any crusader's wife, pretending you're coming back."

"Don't just pretend. Pray for it."

They nestled together until she slept.

When the seneschal called for new guards, it signaled midnight was at hand.

He needed to be on the road. He'd have to walk, since the courier had failed him. He checked his pack again, adding the shirt he'd worn the day before. But instead of picking up the pack to go, he pulled on his shirt, breeches, and boots and went to answer the seneschal's call.

He'd meet the bonfraires of Valerós and say the proper prayers. Then he'd head for Toulouse and the army camp where he'd find the one-eyed man who could tell a tale, the kind of tale that would allow Jean-Luc to reclaim his name. And then come back here to claim love and comfort.

32
Through a Chink, Dimly

Isabella at Valerós
20 days before Pentecost

"COME SEE THIS." KATELINA led Isabella to her room after vespers and then, carrying an oil lamp, led her down a passage to the lower depths of the castle.

"Grandfather doesn't want us in the tunnels," Isabella said.

"No one else can get to this one. Stop here. We'll set the lamp behind us. Look through this chink."

Following Katelina's direction, Isabella stood on a ledge and peer through a crack into an alcove off a cave-like room, where a picture covering most of the far wall showed a naked child carrying a torch and a knife.

"That picture is as old as the castle walls," Katelina said. "We think it was left here by the Romans. Soldiers have probably used this room since before Jesus was born."

"I didn't know this was here," Isabella said.

Katelina shushed her. Men entered the room, laughing and jostling. All the knights came in, plus a handful of others she didn't think of as knights, like Tomás and Chrétien the jongleur. Sebastián stood with the younger knights.

"This is a brotherhood of men who fought on crusade." Katelina whispered in her ear. "They call it the bonfraires. They swear an oath of allegiance to each other when they are initiated, and then give each other challenges."

"Whatever for?"

"Honesty, fortitude, faith. Pèire and his comrades created this brotherhood in the Outremer."

"How do you know this?"

"Pèire told me, of course. He wanted you to see, because it's a special night. No one else knows we're here."

Sebastián was greeted by several of the men. The new smith put his hand on the boy's shoulder and then shook his hand.

"What's Sebastián doing here? That smith isn't a knight."

"Sebastián is being initiated," Katelina said.

Pèire took a seat in the alcove, and the room grew quiet. Katelina whispered to Isabella. "Pèire looks magnificent. I love seeing him like this."

"We're here to swear allegiance as brothers," Pèire said, "and tonight we welcome my own child among us."

Father Anselm, wearing a crusader's old surcoat over his priest's robe, said a long prayer in Latin. Afterward, Pèire said, "As is our tradition, we have a challenge match to start the night."

People nudged each other in anticipation.

"Guillem the marshal has challenged me, and I accepted."

The room fell silent, as if everyone was trying to guess what Pèire was up to. The marshal was middle-aged, although still a sturdy fighter, but Pèire was thirty years older.

"However," Pèire obviously enjoyed that he had everyone's interest, "according to Father Anselm, I owe Pedro d'Aragón my body and can't risk it on a wager. And we don't want to send Marshal Guillem on crusade with his backside hurting. And so, we'll have champions."

People called out their approval.

"For my champion, I have Tomás of Cyprus," Pèire said. Tomás knelt at Pèire's feet and received a sword from him. "He has learned strength and fortitude at the third level, and so he is rising tonight to the fourth level of the bonfraires."

"And my champion," the marshal called over the noise, "is Jehan the smith, who did service protecting our lord's family."

The smith looked startled at the nomination, unlike Tomás who seemed to expect it.

"What does Marshal Guillem get if his champion wins?" someone called out. Guillem, in the act of handing his sword to the smith, seemed to blush.

"The marshal has asked for my ward in marriage." Pèire stood and walked out among the men. "If he can whip me, he deserves to have Senhóreta Felicia as his own. Just tricking her into falling in love with a battered crusader isn't enough to my reckoning." After a general round of whistling and hazing, Pèire raised his finger to get attention. "So, the marshal persuaded Father Anselm to insist on champions. He can't risk losing."

Men huddled to place bets. Chrétien moved among knots of them more quickly than any other man. The two champions stood in the alcove and stripped off their clothes. Isabella stepped back, but Katelina, laughing silently, pulled her forward again.

Stripped, the smith looked like a shaggy beast, with that beard and a mat of black hair on his chest. His shoulders bulged with muscle from his work at the forge, and a mass of scar writhed down his right arm. One muscled thigh was still striped red and raw from his injury.

Beside the smith, Tomás resembled an Arabian palfrey matched against a French destrier, or a greyhound against a Great Pyr. Unlike the smith, Tomás had a sleek, hairless body. The white streaks of hair made him appear older. His angular muscles seemed more like steel plates under a hard-leather cuirass than like the hot, living flesh of the smith. Isabella winced when Tomás turned around; a maze of white scars crossed the dark flesh of his back and arms.

Tomás's eyes sparked in the torchlight and his scarred mouth twitched into a smile of anticipation. Clearly, the coming fight delighted him, while the smith looked like a feral dog trapped by a pack of hounds.

33
Bonfraires

JEAN-LUC HELD A SWORD to fight for the first time in a year.

Fight to win—and lose her to another man.

"I will give you this match." He spoke quietly enough that no one could hear except the swordsman, who was called Tomás. His head pounded so he couldn't think. But it was better that way, easier to focus on the fight ahead.

"Why would you do that, Master Smith?"

Jean-Luc tried to recall what he knew of Cypriot fighters, but only remembered that Angevine knights called them pigeon-hearted thieves years ago, after Richard sold the kingdom of Cyprus to the Knights Templar.

"Pèire wants an oath tonight that I can't give." Jean-Luc's hand tightened on the sword. *And Guillem wants something I can't lose.* "If you win and take their attention away, then I can leave." *I'll find Felicia and she'll come away with me.*

"You assume I won't win unless you forfeit." The haughty swordsman challenged him.

"I didn't mean—"

Tomás said, "*Ai*, but you did. I'm sorry, but I only fight to win."

"This isn't about you and me." *But will she come away with an outlaw and lose everything?*

"*Òc*, my friend. You chose to be Guillem's champion."

"No. This is a surprise to me. I can't shame him by refusing."

"Fight me," Tomás said. "Try to win. Or I'll make sure it hurts enough that you'll wish you were dead."

"Be reasonable, man." Jean-Luc fingered the braid bound with strands of her hair. *But I can't give Guillem what he wants. She loves me.*

"Reasonable? *Jhezu del tron*, I'm fighting a flea-bitten smith to entertain a gang of backcountry greybeards. It defies reason. Get your sword, Master Smith."

Jean-Luc followed the Cypriot into the bright torchlight in the center of the room. Each had a sword, a dagger, and nothing else. Jean-Luc's head pounded again when the knights in the room roared in anticipation.

"Three cuts will win the round, and no one is to die," Pèire called. "Those are the only rules."

Jean-Luc took a swing from a high guard position while Tomás fiddled around, taking his stance. Parrying Jean-Luc's sword with the flat side of his own, Tomás stepped toward him at the same time and then pushed off Jean-Luc's chest with his hand, still not raising his sword to strike.

But he raised Jean-Luc's annoyance several degrees, just by touching him.

"Jehan the smith, is it?" Tomás talked as they circled each other. "And you don't come from anywhere? Don't smiths come straight from hell?"

Tomás whipped his sword in a series of circles and motioned with his dagger for Jean-Luc to come at him. Jean-Luc perceived the ploy: the swordsman created distracting flurries of movement to mask where his attack might come from. As he moved, Tomás talked incessantly.

"Guillem's a fool to trust his sword to your grindstone and his wedded bliss to your skill." Tomás purred. No other word described how the man spoke, as confident and smug as a cat.

"A man who speaks contempt?" Jean-Luc disparaged Tomás's evil tongue. *I can't have her, but I can't lose to this charogne.*

The pounding in his head changed to pure anger. Jean-Luc swung with such force that if the swordsman had still been standing in the same place, his outstretched arm would have gone missing. But Tomás caught the blade just as it lost its principal force and dragged it up with his own sword; then he parried when Jean-Luc lifted his sword again, forcing the blade to scrape along the length of his own forearm.

Jean-Luc caught his breath, having never seen anyone take a cut on purpose.

"*Ai*, the first cut!" Tomás cried.

"Fight like a Christian!" Jean-Luc shouted. "Not a Nizari assassin."

Tomás flicked Jean-Luc's sword up again as they began a serious exchange. Although they'd been given long-swords, Jean-Luc's was much heavier. Tomás wielded the slimmer, lighter sword that Pèire gave him, moving as if born with that sword in his hand.

"*Va te faire foutre.*" Jean-Luc cursed him, falling into French as anger throbbed in his skull.

He lunged, but Tomás was gone before the sword reached where he'd been standing. Once again Tomás parried Jean-Luc's blade up, to cut his own arm.

"Another cut! Say, old man, you're doing quite well with that French bludgeon. I'll have to defend myself better."

Tomás used the whole room, as the men crowded back against the walls. Each time Jean-Luc followed him, the swordsman danced a dozen steps. Jean-Luc defended from the middle in the classic style, struggling with his balance because of his injury.

After Tomás circled the room a few times, he set a pattern: whenever Jean-Luc had his back to the men in the room, Tomás's sword flicked up to his throat or chin or breastbone, but instead of taking the cut he obviously could, Tomás flicked his blade away and engaged Jean-Luc's sword. Six opportunities, and he still had left no mark on Jean-Luc.

"So, you say your father left you nameless, Jean-Foutre? Isn't there a word for French boys whose papas won't claim them?"

Jean-Luc took a murderous swing from high guard, in perfect form, and then carried through the arc and swung again, the kind of brutal sword work taught to the knights in Hugues de Beaurain's court.

But Tomás jumped up along the arch of the alcove and flipped over to land on Jean-Luc's other side, smiling in a way that would gall a saint.

"And you say your mother misplaced you, Juan Zoquette? Or simply discarded you?"

However much Tomás prosecuted his torture, calling him Jehan Chump, two facts were clear: no one in the room saw the humiliating near-touches that Tomás forfeited, and Tomás didn't take advantage of Jean-Luc's injury. That he dealt out humiliation privately infuriated Jean-Luc beyond reason.

Tomás was throwing the fight, so Jean-Luc's victory would mean humiliation coupled with the worst outcome of winning: losing Felicia. But Jean-Luc couldn't let this man beat him—either with a sword or by throwing the fight.

．

"But enough of the old folks." Tomás chattered incessantly. "Let's talk about your sister. That must be where you got the mark on your neck. Or do you Franks prefer to go down on your brothers?"

Tomás flicked his sword while forfeiting another opportunity to make a cut, and Jean-Luc lifted his sword to strike. But before he finished the motion, Tomás dropped the dagger and stopped Jean-Luc's blade with his bare hand at the hilt of the sword, grazing a cut across his left hand. At the same time, Tomás brought his own sword up in a clatter against Jean-Luc's, as if there'd been a real attack.

"*Ai*, a third hit!" Tomás cried. "You win the day, Master Smith."

"Keep fighting, you bastard. We aren't done."

"Can't, Jean-Foutre. You won."

They both leaned against the wall, the acrid smell of their sweating bodies filling the alcove. Both men panted, but Jean-Luc saw that the swordsman breathed with far less effort.

"*Baise-toi*," Jean-Luc said. "I'll make you sorry for this."

"Must I apologize, Master Smith, simply because you are better at sword-play?"

"We didn't finish the fight."

"You won, Master Smith. But only today."

"You, senhór, are a sodding arsewit."

"It's been said before."

As Jean-Luc moved away, Tomás called after him, again so softly that no one else might hear. "Pèire Leteric insisted you win. Next time, we'll do it your way—if you're sure you won't die of it, Jehan the smith who has no name."

"Next time, I'll kill you." Jean-Luc whirled around, the single braid in his hair whipping out like a lash. "I'm called Perseus in this bonfraires, a fifth-level brother. I've been a brother since before you were weaned, if you ever were."

"*Qui s'ho creu?*" Tomás protested. *Who ever knew?*

Tomás stepped away and received a strip of linen from one of the men to wipe away the sweat. The donzel Sebastián and the jongleur came to help their losing champion dress again. Tomás laughed as Sebastián expressed concern while pouring wine over the swordsman's cuts. Tomás gave his dagger to Sebastián, insisting that the boy take it, showing him an inscription on the blade.

The other men were paying off their bets and jostling with the marshal. The jongleur spoke to someone at his side, and one of the bettors tucked coins into the purse at his belt, which seemed to mean that the jongleur had bet against his Moorish friend.

"When's the wedding?" someone called.

"Michaelmas. At the end of crusading season," Pèire said. "Otherwise, there isn't enough time for the marshal to properly warm his wife's bed before we ride to Narbonne tomorrow."

Grinning, Guillem came to Jean-Luc's side and offered a swath of linen. Jean-Luc recoiled when the man touched him to wipe away the sweat. "Thank you for my prize."

"This infernal match was fixed," Jean-Luc said.

"No," Guillem said. "I chose the best fighter in these hills."

"Wagering over a woman is despicable." Jean-Luc walked away before he caused harm.

"Senhór Pèire is waiting for you," Guillem called after him.

Jean-Luc pushed his way to the door but men crowded toward the alcove where Pèire sat, forcing Jean-Luc back, too.

"Our brother Perseus," Pèire addressed him by his bonfraires title. "Will you kneel and swear?"

Trapped, still naked and dripping sweat from the fight, Jean-Luc knelt at Pèire's feet with his sword clasped in his hand. He hardly dared look up at Pèire Leteric.

"You know the oath," Pèire said. "I don't need to lead you."

"*Sodalitas, fidelitas, virtus.* Upon my honor I swear absolute loyalty to my brothers when called to arms. I swear to stand by my lord and king. I swear to stand ever ready to serve as a defender of the poor and of the Holy Catholic Church." *Loyal to every brother. But what happens when a brother takes your beloved?*

"Swear it on the name of Our Savior and on St-Jordi."

"I swear in the names of Christ Jesus, St-Jordi, and the Blessed Virgin Mary." Jean-Luc felt his hands trembling on the sword.

Pèire leaned forward. "Now give me your personal oath."

"I can't do that."

"If you have the courage of our bonfraires, swear on the blood of St-Jordi that you won't break your father's heart any more than you already have."

Stunned, Jean-Luc whispered, "I swear."

As Pèire spoke again, Jean-Luc bent his head closer to Pèire to hear, and the single braid with Felicia's hair fell over his cheek.

"If I was your father, I'd raise all the armies of France to bring you home. Yet all I can give you is pity."

Jean-Luc knelt back on his heels, not able to speak. He rose, snatched his clothes from beside Pèire's chair, and batted away Guillem's arm as he held out a hand to greet him.

34
Corax

WHILE ISABELLA WATCHED BEHIND the wall, Pèire called for the next order of the evening. Then he had a goblet of wine in his hand and Tomás of Cyprus kneeling at his feet.

Tomás solemnly repeated the same oath as the smith, in contrast to the raucous hazing he'd dealt out during the fight.

"Give me your personal oath," Pèire commanded.

"What will it be, my lord?"

"You didn't have to be such a giant *punxor* with the smith," Pèire muttered.

"That's my oath? Not to be a prick?"

"No, *fadrin*, you couldn't keep such an oath. You're too much like your father." Pèire settled back into his chair, laughing. He motioned Tomás to sit by him. "Be my eyes for the night."

Katelina said, "Your Moor has captivated Pèire. Why do you think that is?"

"He's a perverse, conceited knave," Isabella said. "And he's not 'my Moor.' Are you baiting me?"

"*Òc, xiqueta.*"

A dozen knights took turns kneeling before Pèire. As each approached, Tomás murmured the man's name to Pèire, who closed his eyes whenever he wasn't fixing a piercing stare at the man currently on his knees before him.

"Who's left?" Pèire murmured to Tomás. Very little, Isabella hoped. She couldn't take too much more of this ritual.

"Just the initiates," Tomás whispered. "Sebastián is too young. Don't do it tonight."

"My boy will catch on fast enough."

They were pulling her son into this game? Tension rose, from her fingers to her heart. But it didn't feel like fear for the boy. More like...jealousy.

Stripped naked, Sebastián and the other two initiates were brought before Pèire. Though goose-flesh covered him head to toe, Sebastián didn't shake and shiver as the others did. The other two were a decade older than Sebastián.

Pèire said, "You come to us tonight as Corax, the crow, to learn humility and to understand death. The crow guards the battlefield, and it's your charge to understand what the crow knows."

The three initiates lay face down on the stone floor. A cup was brought to Pèire, and as Father Anselm said prayers in both the common tongue and Latin, Pèire flicked droplets on each of them. Isabella guessed it was wine. Then her stomach turned: it was blood.

After all the knights repeated another prayer while the initiates were lifted and blindfolded. Then everyone left the room silently, and only Tomás and Pèire remained. Katelina motioned Isabella away from the wall and back up the tunnel.

"We might as well go to bed," Katelina said. "I'm so chilled. I can't imagine how those boys fared on the cold stone floor."

"Where are they taking Sebastián and the others?"

"They have to endure a night of trial to show their bravery."

"I can't believe Father Anselm participates," Isabella said.

"Don't call it heresy," Katelina said. "Those prayers are all fine."

"No, it's a bunch of grown men acting like boys playing a joke that's gotten out of hand."

"I thought you'd appreciate the ritual."

"Ritual is what you do in church to call on God. Not splashing blood around and pretending you're a mystical order of knights."

At the top of the stairs, Katelina stopped. "Senhóra Isabella, I swear you're as much of a prig as Beatriz."

35
A Man of Paratge

"SEBASTIÁN IS TOO YOUNG," Tomás said again. The other men had left him alone with Pèire in the cellar room.

"I want to see it. Might be my last chance. I'm knighting him in the morning after Guillem burns the mark."

"If the boy makes it through the tests."

"You have any doubt that he will?"

"No. He's brave. He just hasn't learned enough to be ready to act as a knight."

"You can teach him, *fadrin,*" Pèire said. "There isn't another day left for him to be a boy."

"You trust Sebastián with me?"

"Even though you're a *punxor* like your papa, I'd trust you with my own life." Pèire laughed again, and then clutched his chest, his other hand at his head. "God will get me yet for laughing."

"Are you all right, senhór?"

"No, not at all."

"Shall I fetch Senhóreta Katelina or take you to her?"

"Help me to my room. The stairs are right here."

Behind the wall-hanging was a door, and Tomás finally understood how Pèire had managed to make his mysterious appearances.

"I need a light." Tomás took a torch from the grotto's wall.

"I suppose so. I forget that others can see when I can't."

They labored up the stairs together, Tomás's arm around the old man and his legs doing the work for the two of them. At the first landing of the stairs, Pèire begged a rest. Tomás eased him down and then sat on the step below him.

"Did you never swear allegiance to a man?" Pèire asked. "I don't mean what these southern lords swear, promising not to support their lord's enemy. I mean a real oath, fidelity to another man?"

"To my father, of course," Tomás said. "And our bonfraires."

Pèire dismissed that with a wave of his hand. "If you don't swear allegiance to your lord and your own domus," he used the common word for a seigneur's household, "how do you know who you are? How can men trust you if you're just a vagabond and a mercenary?"

Tomás had no answer; Pèire merely pointed out the obvious.

"You had hard masters, *fadrin*," Pèire said. "Pledge a real oath. You'll see life more clearly."

"Shall I pledge my oath to you now?" Tomás felt a surge of excitement, like preparing to jump a chasm.

"By God and all the golden angels, yes!"

"What shall I pledge?"

"Can you stay here to make sure all the children are safe. See that Isabella goes to Gerard and Felicia marries the marshal." He stopped talking, his breathing shallow. "I had an old man's foolish idea once, that Beatriz could be a wife for Miquel's son. But Beatriz is a sweet girl, and a man like you—maybe a man like you never marries."

It was half past the moment at which Tomás could say what he wanted. Instead, he said, "No, I think not."

"Please watch over Katelina. Guillem is sworn to care for her if I can't. If anything happens, you must take on her care."

"Yes, senhór."

"Swear. You know how it goes, even if you never did it before."

Sitting on a step below Pèire, Tomás saw Miquel seated on the stone step behind Pèire, putting his hand on Pèire's shoulder. Tomás took a breath.

"I swear on the name of Jesus, our Holy Father's Son, on my own honor," he touched the scar on his wrist, "and by my father's hand that I will protect you and yours as if we were brothers sharing one heart."

Pèire nodded, thin rivulets of water running from his eyes, and another trickle escaping from his mouth, as if he couldn't swallow.

Tomás continued, "And I swear to deliver your children to their husbands, and all your kin into the safest hands. I swear to guard their safety foremost, above even peril to my life."

"Very sweet," Pèire murmured, his hand on Tomás's head like a benediction, and Miquel reached over to add his own hand.

"And I swear," Tomás said, "to kill the men who mean your children harm, even at peril to my own soul."

"You couldn't leave that out?"

"No, senhór."

As Pèire sighed, his breath rattled in the moisture he couldn't swallow. He fumbled in his jerkin, finally finding what he wanted.

"Here. I had Senhóreta Katelina make this. It gives you a holding called St-Joachim in Barcelona that I have from Pedro's father when he was king. This makes you my seigneur, so we're partners in this."

Tomás knelt before him again, and Pèire touched his head in the modest knighting gesture of an Aragónese lord.

"Thank you, senhór. I promise loyalty to you as long as I walk on God's own earth."

After a few moments, Tomás got Pèire to his feet, and they staggered the rest of the way up the stone stairs, with Miquel behind them. He bit back a wish to ask permission to carry Pèire, since the old man would never allow it.

They emerged from the passageway into Pèire's empty room.

"Help me to her room to wait for her. It's more peaceful there." Katelina's room was as immaculate as a nun's cell, and barely larger. In one corner was a narrow bed, tucked tightly with crisp linen and a woolen coverlet folded at its end. A chair sat before a tidy desk, where sharpened pens lay next to a stack of Castile paper, with an oil lamp and a pile of bound books. The room's sole ornament was a Greek cross resting on a small table, like a personal altar; a cushion lay on the floor below it, showing the marks of someone having knelt there.

"Do you want to lie on the bed, senhór?"

"No, the chair. It might be better to sit up."

"Shall I fetch Senhóreta Katelina, senhór?"

"No, stay with me."

Tomás sat on the stone floor beside him, there not being another chair in the room. He felt Pèire's hand rest on his head. Miquel knelt beside them.

"In this light, I can make out your profile and hear your voice," Pèire said. "*Ai!* And Miquel with me again, eh, my friend? It was always us two trying to decide whether to stick with a lord who can't pay or strike out to find a better one. Those Outremer lords were such snakes and fools."

"My father always said those were—"

"Hard years for good soldiers." Miquel finished the words.

"Men used to think I was this great warrior," Pèire said. "How in God's name did it happen that I'm bunkered up here in the hills, trying to protect my children from a demon I can't name?"

"I can't answer for God, but I'll find that demon." Tomás put his hand on the old man's knee, not knowing how to give comfort.

"Lord, it hurts," Pèire said. "If I could just get my breath."

His hand rested more heavily on Tomás's head as he labored to breathe.

"*Fadrin*," Pèire whispered, "when you go to Pedro, tell him I murdered that blasted priest."

"*Ai, no, peccador*," Miquel cried. "Bad strategy. You'll lose the battle. Say it was me."

"*Baquelar!*" Pèire roused his strength. "Pedro is no man's fool. He knows a dead man can't wield a knife."

"You want your honor shat upon by Montcavas?" Miquel groused. "For a cowardly priest who sold his soul in Jaffa?"

"*Ai*, dear brother. We don't want that Montcava rogue telling everyone it was Isabella. Trust me."

"Fine, then." Miquel turned to Tomás. "Do whatever this fool says, *fadrin*."

The weight of Pèire's hand lightened, but still rested on Tomás. After several moments, he spoke again.

"Miquel stopped trusting me when I wouldn't kill him on the road to Damascus. I've asked myself all these years why I couldn't do it when he begged me."

"Senhór—"

"Me, in forty years of battle I could run a sword through a man, no matter what mercy he might plead. But I couldn't do it when a man who was more than a brother to me asked for mercy. I thought I could save him, after I failed to save Vidal." He reached out to Tomás, but his hand faltered. He pointed to Miquel. "I wish it had been me instead of you."

"Never in this life," Miquel said. "On my mother's honor, I swear—"

"Ha!" Pèire laughed and coughed. "You're dead now, *baquelar.* What's the use in swearing more oaths?"

"Habit." Miquel spread his hands in that Catalan gesture of surrendering his will to Heaven.

Pèire laughed till he choked and coughed. He breathed a dozen ragged breaths before he spoke again. "I dragged Miquel back to camp that evil day. Best I could do was to keep the flies away and leave him the color of death at his wife's door. *Ai,* your mother! Lord in the Glorious Heaven, I haven't asked you about her. She's well?"

"As can be," Tomás said.

"The Devil can take me, for I carried the worst of all nightmares to her door."

Indeed, Pèire had sent a nightmare home to them: pain, bad dreams, anger, and misery inhabited the house for fifteen years while his father waited to die.

"Sebastián looks just like Vidal," Pèire murmured. "You can see the same eyes in Isabella and the same look about the mouth. But the fire, the vitality, as if God shone within. Sebastián has the same fire as my son Vidal did to his dying day."

Miquel put his hand on Pèire's shoulder again. The younger girl, Beatriz, appeared in the shadows by the door. Tomas didn't know how to signal for her to fetch Katelina. The old man tugged at Tomás's hand, wanting to say more so that Tomás, of all people, listened to the last words of an old crusader.

"I'd like to have died myself," Pèire said, "if it hadn't been for Katelina. You can live for love of a woman when God fails you. Or is that what God gives you when He takes away everything else?"

"Why do you think He cares at all?" Miquel asked.

"*Ai ,mon amic!*" Pèire said. "He cares when He remembers to."

36

Crusader at Rest

Isabella at Valerós

20 days before Pentecost

AFTER SPYING ON THE bonfraires and their rituals, Isabella slipped out to pace the battlements, where a handful of young guards stood at their posts. No one had returned from whatever they were doing with the initiates. One of the young men-at-arms followed her.

"Ma dòmna, Senhór Pèire doesn't want you out alone."

"You don't need to stand at my elbow to protect me."

She peered over the walls into the dark, waiting for her eyes to become accustomed to seeing by starlight. But there was no movement among the trees or in the farther fields, except a lone figure came out the castle gate and loped down the path to the valley. She clawed in agitation at the stony edge of the battlements, thinking she faced the lonely prospect of a cold marriage with an ancient crusader. She intended to throw off her childish feelings of helplessness.

She resolved now to refuse to marry. Pèire must still be awake, waiting for his knights to return from their adventures. She walked through the galleries and up the stone stairs to seek him out and declare that she'd rule her own life.

A wail sounded from the family quarters. As Isabella sprinted for their rooms, Beatriz came down the hall shrieking. Isabella couldn't tell if it was terror or anger. Katelina followed close behind her. Beatriz slammed the door of her cell.

"Go to them!" Katelina pleaded, pointing back to her room. She pounded on Beatriz's door. "Let me in, Beatriz."

Isabella came to Katelina's room, where she found Tomás on the floor, holding Pèire across his lap. Tears streamed down his face when he looked up at Isabella. Although Catalan knights weep at anything, she'd never seen a man weep in such an unguarded way.

"He's gone," Tomás said.

She knelt beside Tomás and put her hand on Pèire's head.

"Pèire showed me what a man should be." Tomás choked on the words. "Pain destroyed my father's life, leaving him filled with bitterness. But Pèire made me his friend. I must seem like no more than a child to him, the same as Sebastián—"

He stirred.

"*Bon Dèu,* what am I saying to you? We were only new friends, while he's everything to you. I am so sorry for you that he's gone."

As Tomás's tears ran across Pèire's face, she saw how much Pèire and Sebastián looked alike. But Pèire's spirit no longer resided in that body. She took some of the burden from Tomás's lap. Together they held the old man and cried over him, first rocking him, and then sitting still and just weeping.

Twice Tomás broke the quiet of their private wake to extol Pèire's virtues as a man and a warrior. At the end of the last declamation, he said, "He loved his family with a passion I've never known. It seems as far away from me as heaven itself."

Dawn light crept through the slit of a window above Katelina's desk. Tomás shifted the burden he held. "We have to help Katelina," he said. "Help me lift him to the bed."

Together they laid the old man on Katelina's narrow cot. He tenderly drew the linen coverlet over Pèire's body, folding it down so that it seemed as if Pèire merely slept. "Let's not cover his face," he said. "No one is done looking at him yet."

Isabella wiped at her tears with her sleeve, thinking that Katelina didn't need to tend to two upset children. Together, they sought Katelina and found her outside Beatriz's room, talking softly to the unopened door, trying to coax Beatriz out.

Tomás placed his hand on Katelina's head. "Come, ma dòmna. Isabella can tend to her sister. Let me assist you."

He gave his arm to Katelina, and she leaned heavily against him, turning her face into his jerkin as they walked down the hall to her room.

When they were gone, Isabella cleared her throat. "Come out, Beatriz. Let's find Felicia. There's work to be done, and there's only us to do it now."

37
Fadrins, Branded

KATELINA HELD ONTO TOMÁS'S arm as if she didn't want him to leave. When the bonfraires returned, Sebastián came running through the castle with Guillem behind him, the chainmail of their hauberks ringing in the hallways. But the eager look faded from the boy's face when he found Tomás and Katelina kneeling by the cot.

Sebastián fell to his knees between them and put one hand over Katelina's. A flame lit in the boy's cheeks while the rest of his face turned white as ivory. As they knelt there, Sebastián first shook in silent grief and then gradually drew up, as if he were growing into that ill-fitting hauberk.

"What would he want us to do?" Sebastián said.

Tomás said, "Pèire intended to stay up, because he knew you'd pass the test. He wanted to see it."

"We are enough," Katelina said. "Let's finish exactly the way Pèire intended."

Guillem heated a crossbow bolt on the brazier while Katelina knelt beside Pèire. The marshal applied the brand to the boy's wrist while Tomás said the long prayer in Latin and then spoke the oath for Sebastián to join the bonfraires.

The burnt smell lingered in the room. Tomás said, "Pèire also planned to make you a knight. He made me one of his seigneurs, so perhaps you'll let me do the honor here, as if Pèire could see."

"I'm not ready." Sebastián's voice broke into upper registers.

"But you have the heart and the will," Guillem said.

"Pèire said you have the wisdom to know what it is to be a knight." Tomás put his arm around the boy's shoulder, knowing how much Sebastián longed for praise, because he once had, too.

The knighting was much briefer than the long prayers and initiation oaths of the bonfraires.

"Are you my master now?" Sebastián whispered. "I won't go with anyone else. Not that old man my mother has to marry."

"No one is going anywhere right now," Katelina said. "Except some of the knights need to rendezvous with Gerard and Hugues as Pèire promised."

She looked at Guillem as she spoke, but he shook his head.

"I need to be here," Guillem said. "I promised Pèire to look after you, senhóreta. The castle itself needs defending."

She put her hand over Guillem's. He still held the crossbow bolt. "I'm safe here, my friend," she said. "The others will protect Isabella. You already made plans for our defense. Tomás can work with the constable to carry out your orders here."

With a look sharp enough to pierce armor, Guillem said to Tomás, "I saw you give your oath before the bonfraires. What did you swear? Reassure me that if I leave what I love in your trust, I'll find it whole when I return."

"I swore by my father's hand to protect Pèire's family, as if we were brothers sharing one heart."

"But who is your father? What gives that oath any worth?"

"Don Miquel of Morella in Aragón. Did you know him?"

"Why didn't I see it?" Guillem cried. He grasped Tomás's hand in the Catalan style, the crossbow bolt amid their clasped hands. "What better oath than by Miquel's own hand?"

"Then we'll trust you to join Gerard and Hugues, Marshal Guillem," Katelina said.

"I'll take a dozen knights. We'll leave as soon as we can be ready. Am I also taking Senhóra Isabella to her husband?"

Tomás couldn't swallow. His tooth started to ache again.

"Isabella must stay here," Katelina said. "If Gerard can't come this summer, I'll persuade her to write to the king for a protector. Pedro d'Aragón can find her another husband."

Guillem agreed. Tomás remained quiet, certain Isabella would chafe at decisions being made for her.

"You both need to swear that Renoud will never come within a dozen leagues of Isabella, ever again," Katelina said.

"I swear to crush that scorpion under my heel if he interferes with this family," Guillem said.

"Tomásino?" Katelin looked at him, calling the name only his family used.

"I already intend to crush the man at the earliest opportunity."

"I'll swear, too," Sebastián said. "I'm a bonfraire now."

Lubos Conjures

HE OFFERED A SIMPLE prayer to the tree spirits to conjure courage. The spirits answered his call, as the stone spirits did when he conjured Death, asking for help to draw life out, by letting blood or sucking spirit. Yet Lubos hadn't received help from any of the spirits in gaining his heart's desire. They didn't listen, leaving him to attend to work on Père-Izsák's mission, to set the world right, instead of pursuing his selfish needs. There would be time enough in a healed world to pursue what he longed for—a son.

But when he had to sit in the baking sun and wait for long days and nights, he sometimes felt that Père-Izsák asked too much of him. Too many names, too many leagues to travel, too much waiting. He needed a rest and the chance to take care of his personal needs. But lately, the spirits threw up shields rather than guiding his hand. Because of that, he had to spend more time waiting than he liked. He wanted to hurry and finish his father's business, so he could go home to Aykuna again. The girls would crawl in his lap and beg to be tickled, pretending that his whiskers scratched them if he hadn't shaved that day. But he had dreamed too long of conjuring at least one son to return with him.

His heart had flagged a little. He felt undecided at moments about doing what Père-Izsák asked.

Trying to persevere, he used a crystal to conjure the knowledge of whether God wants a man to live or die. That way, you can tell beforehand whether it's a waste of time to conjure Death. And he remembered what Père-Izsák had taught him, that it isn't enough to kill a man who is an abomination to God. You must wipe out all the spawn from his seed.

With women, it doesn't matter so much what God intends, because thousands upon thousands of spirits are lurking to snatch a woman's life. A woman has no soul, so the simplest thing you can do is to encourage Death to hurry along, the same way you help an injured horse to die.

215

Sometimes, though, it seems that Death won't be hurried. When that happens, you must sit and wait.

The crows start early in those cases, if no one chases them away. He decided that he could be patient; the waiting and resting turned out to be pleasant when he got to watch the crows feasting.

PART FOUR
Scorpions in the Stones

Loves go with the spark
That is mixed in the soot,
Burning the stick and the straw.
(Pay attention!)
And no sap knows which way past
When he's wasted by the fire.

— Marcabru
"Dire vos vuelh ses duptansa"

In Part Four

38

A Murder of Crows

Jean-Luc outside Valerós
20 days before Pentecost

LORD, PLEASE. MAKE SURE *the courier meets me on the road.*

Lord, promise the courier will come.

Jean-Luc fetched his pack and loped down the trail, away from the castle. Rushing along the trail before dawn, he had to focus his vision and his mind to look for stones and ditches that might trip him. He ran to exhaust his passion as quickly as possible.

Moving rapidly, breathing deeply in the clear, cool mountain air, he was well away from the castle when the sun began to light the horizon. As hard as he ran, he heard the last rushed conversation over and again.

Please come with me, chérie.

I can't, Jehan.

But you know I can't stay.

I can't go with you.

If he hurried, he might still encounter the returning courier, who'd provide him with a horse and provisions. Then he'd ride to find his father before going on to Toulouse, as he'd given Pèirc his word to do.

Can't or won't?

Striding on through the heat of the day, Jean-Luc rehearsed what he'd say to his father. As his mind lost the haze from weeks of idleness, he began to devise a plan for action. Darkness came again, so he sought shelter in a grove of tall cypress, kicking over the stones in the clearing to chase away the scorpions before he sat down to eat the oldest of the bread and cheese in his pack.

Did anyone say good-bye?

That thought possessed him while he wrapped up in his cloak. It was a long while before he could quiet his mind to sleep. In the same way he rehearsed what to say to his father, he went over the facts, trying again to understand what had trapped him on the other side of the law and the Church.

■

Jean-Luc in Constantinople
April 1204

His mind numb with grief, Jean-Luc did what was asked by their French masters. He kept his men and Yves's busy for two numbing nights and days of fighting fires and hauling booty to the priest-clerks who tallied the silks, silver, gold, and gems. On the third night, Jean-Luc returned to his bivouac in one of the captured villas, the smell of fire and his own sweat a perpetual stench in his nose, bile burning his mouth. When he arrived at the villa, Hugues de Beaurain came with his men to arrest him for stealing booty.

"You can see for yourself, my lord." The captain who arrested him stood with Hugues, pointing out what they'd found in the room where Jean-Luc slept. "This golden Madonna. A bound Gospel of St-John in Greek. Perhaps one hundred icons."

"What's this?" Hugues toed a rough, bulging sack.

"It's the gold communion service from the church where his brother was killed," the captain said.

As worn as anyone from three days' work in the defeated city, Hugues set his jaw and stood so close that Jean-Luc felt the marquis' hot breath "By the Holy Name of the Blessed Savior's mother, you should hang your head in shame."

Innocent of this sin then and striving to forget how he'd sinned against Hugues in years past, Jean-Luc refused to bow in shame. "It's a lie, my lord. I have spent day and night doing as you ordered."

"A score of men swore to a priest about what they saw," Hugues said. "Here are the goods."

"I did not steal this, my lord."

"How can you—" Hugues seemed to choke on his rage. "Last night we stood in this very room, and I offered you comfort for the loss of your brother. How can you pollute his memory?"

Resisting the sting of those words, Jean-Luc said, "Perhaps the thieves I stopped that night have united against me."

Hugues scrutinized him, and Jean-Luc knew he looked and smelled like the son of a devil and not like the man of honor he aspired to be, especially in the eyes of Hugues de Beaurain.

"They say you killed Yves because he interfered with your looting," Hugues said. "I can't believe that, no matter who swears to it."

"If you deny one lie, why believe the other?" Jean-Luc risked the last of his boldness.

"I have sworn to hang anyone who steals booty. I cannot treat you differently. Do you have witnesses?"

But Jean-Luc's men had deserted him when he was arrested. They fled as if his corpse had lain in the sun for three days.

"I'll send a priest to hear your confession," Hugues said as he departed. "Your father's heart will break."

Before dawn the next day, a hand shook Jean-Luc awake. Renoud of Montcava, another Toulouse seigneur under Hugues de Beaurain, cut the ties binding Jean-Luc's hands and feet.

"Quiet!" he warned. Then he beckoned Jean-Luc to follow.

Groggy with pain and despair, Jean-Luc staggered out, unwashed, unfed, and still bloodied from the past days' battles. He wore the same clothes as when they breached the city walls, although now his sword, shield, and hauberk were gone. His leg throbbed with every heartbeat, because the priest's salve hadn't helped any more than his prayers for consolation. At the city gate, a bearded man who looked Greek held a horse with a pack tied to the saddle. Unsure at first why, Jean-Luc noticed that the bearded man had a *crux lunata* tattoo on his hand.

Renoud unbuckled his own sword and offered it to Jean-Luc. His hand had the same tattoo. Then Jean-Luc knew where he'd seen it before.

"Are you doing this for Hugues de Beaurain?" Jean-Luc asked. "He has that sign too."

"No, I'm doing out of respect for another captain."

"We were never friends." Jean-Luc no longer trusted anyone. "Why take a risk to help me when your command is under Hugues?"

"I lost a brother here, too. I can do no less," Renoud said. "Can you can speak enough Greek to make it through the countryside?"

"What's the use? My brother Yves is dead. The Church will excommunicate me. My land and my good name are forfeited if I desert now. They may as well hang me."

"There's your father to think about," Renoud said. "Ride now so you can tell your story, rather than letting him hear it from strangers."

Jean-Luc, limping badly, led the horse out the gate. He mounted, knowing only to ride north and then west.

.

Jean-Luc started on his way again when light appeared on the horizon.

I can't go with you, Jehan.

Of course not.

By noon that day, he wondered why he'd tortured Felicia by asking her to come with him. He reasoned his way to a semblance of peace. Guillem was the perfect choice, the best man to keep her safe. He continued as rapidly as possible. By late afternoon, he reached the rendezvous, where the courier should be waiting, since Jean-Luc hadn't encountered him on the trail.

Alone, he perched under an oak tree and gnawed the last of the dry loaves and cheese. The rays of the sun cast long shadows, and a murder of crows mobbed the oaks across the ravine, calling their rasping battle cries to each other for several moments, and then darting down to some carrion, quarreling with each other, and returning to the trees. He watched them for a while, annoyed. Crows always reminded him of the aftermath of battle, when they move in for a feast. To fight his annoyance, he scaled the granite outcropping, hoping to see further down the road while he waited.

From the rock, he peered up the empty roadway. And across the ravine, the crows feasted on the body of his courier. Alongside lay more picked-over bones, with a crow standing on the colors of a Valerós knight. Pèire Leteric's messenger.

A bone-sucking bearded vulture swept overhead, annoying the crows. Jean-Luc threw rocks, but the vulture did not heed him.

39
A Slippery Slope

DON TOMÁS OF ST-JOACHIM—the former mercenary without a master, and former scribe without scruples, now knight of Valerós—kept Sebastián at work in the practice yard all day, which proved to be the first baking-hot day of the spring. Tomás remained his swordmaster, though Sebastián now was seigneur of Valerós.

Whenever Sebastián seemed tired, Tomás stopped for water and a discussion of technique, but otherwise kept them both at it. When they rested, the eerie quiet of the castle yards reminded them Pèire was gone. The boys weren't rolling barrels of chainmail. The spring breeze whistled like Miquel breathing down his neck, though the ghost left him alone after Pèire passed. Tomás only knew to keep moving until he found real work to do. He pushed the boy to work hard while enduring his own considerable pain: the cut on his hand from the ridiculous bonfraires duel bothered him in sword work.

Pèire's family and the others at Valerós made it through the first days after their lord's death by spending extra time at mass and then performed mind-numbing chores to fill time: preparing food no one would eat, currying horses no one wanted to ride. The smith had disappeared without so much as a farewell to anyone, even his friend Guillem, so the young knights sharpened their own swords by the cold forge hearth, telling stories about the old days.

The next morning, Tomás breakfasted with Chrétien and Sebastián outside the kitchen. The three of them had practiced in the courtyard since dawn, as miserable as every other person in the castle.

Tomás made it through the porridge but avoided the sausages, because his bad tooth was punishing him.

A guard approached with a message from Senhóra Isabella, the steward of Valerós, who requested Tomás's attendance.

"The first step on the slippery slope of servitude." Chrétien had heard about Tomás's pledge to Pèire.

"Shut up, Chrétien."

Sebastián played with the bandage at his wrist. "If my mother wants more masses for departed souls, tell her we should go hunting instead. That's what Pèire would do, and she knows it."

Tomás crossed the courtyard where a pair of old crusaders sat eating breakfast, a pack of dogs at their feet, hoping to be favored with cast-offs. A guard stood outside the scriptorium, obviously dead with fatigue.

"Go ask Marshal Guillem for relief," Tomás said. "You're no good if you don't rest. I'll be here until another guard comes."

Inside the scriptorium, Senhóra Isabella sat forlorn amid a stack of scrolls and receipts. She was pricking marks on a clean piece of vellum, preparing to rule lines. When he entered, she glanced up, frowning. The tired smudges under her eyes made him think of Lenten ash streaks, and the bruise on her cheek caused him to ache. Several wild strands of her copper hair had managed to escape from her head covering, and the tips of her fingers looked red and raw from where she'd bitten her nails.

She spoke formally. "My family is in danger. I cannot determine whether you are part of that danger. I need to know who you are. Shall we start with your real name?"

"I am Don Tomás of Morella and Cyprus," he said. The tender moments they shared while grieving over Pèire had vanished. Impulsively, he wanted to beg her for mercy. *Take it like a man.*

"Don? You are a lord?" She wore her haughty attitude like armor, and her voice sounded deeper than usual, as if her whole body were overstocked with feeling. "Where in Christendom is Morella, if there is such a place?"

"The Aragón frontier." Tomás braced for the fury he'd predicted when Pèire commanded their secrets be kept from Isabella. "Sometimes the emir at Valencia thinks Morella belongs to him, if he ever thinks of it at all. My father also left me his fief on Cyprus and a few money fiefs in the Outremer."

"You're well educated for a sheepherders' lord."

"As are you, ma dòmna. But in truth, I've never seen Morella. My father never went back after he left on crusade."

"Why did you come here—and in disguise?"

"Your brother-in-law Renoud tried to kill me last year. I came here to learn more about him before I kill him. But Pèire diverted my attention."

"Pèire made you his friend because you hate Renoud?"

"We had a stronger bond than that."

She folded her arms across her chest, not believing his story about how Pèire had become his ally, to fight a common enemy.

"Marshal Guillem insists I ask your help." She shook her head, a decided no. "He wants me to hire you as a mercenary until Gerard de Chartrain arrives. Why should I trust you?"

"The men who fought with my father and Pèire swore fidelity to each other," he said. "Pèire asked me to swear the same oath."

"I know about your boys' club." She spoke with disdain thick enough to spread with a knife on a crust of bread.

"We take our oaths rather more seriously than that," he said.

"Even you?" Her voice dripped with scorn. "That smith swore an oath to Pèire, too. But he left. I'd prefer a mercenary's bond."

"All right, ma dòmna," he said. "Is my payment to be in gold or silver coin?"

"You will probably have to take horses in payment."

He bowed his head in the way he saw Aragón knights do. "You have my sword at your service."

Isabella drummed her fingers on the table, impatient. "Valerós has enough knights. What I need is for you to tell me what Pèire had on his mind." She pointed to the stack of parchment and vellum Pèire had let him study. "Simon de Montfort tripled the tax on Arracheuse when he became Viscount of Carcassonne. And now he wants our knights to join that invasion he calls a crusade." She rested her hand on letters the dead priest had carried to Pèire. "And he wants the Valerós castles rendered to him. Do you know what that means?"

"It means you give him your castles if he wants them for defense. But Valerós is sworn to the king of Aragón. How could Simon dare overstep Pedro?"

"Just help me understand all of this." She pointed to the letters.

He sat beside her, wanting to plead his worth as a man.

"You may sit," she said sharply, after he'd already done so.

"Ma dòmna?"

"I'm the regent and master here until my son is of age. You will treat me with the same respect you gave Pèire."

"I'm truly sorry. Forgive me."

Standing, he tried again to imitate an Aragón bow, and then sat down, swallowing the bitter taste of humiliation.

"Did Pèire show you this letter?" she asked. "I found it in his shirt." She unfolded a piece of vellum that carried Renoud's seal.

Tomás read the last line.

'If you allow me to protect my brother's wife and son, I will help you protect the heretics and schismatics in your house.'

"Pèire told me Renoud threatened you, but I didn't know about this," he said as he reached across the table to take the page she indicated. His arm accidentally brushed her breast.

She turned as cold and hard as the stone walls of Valerós.

He pretended it never happened. Instead, he studied a piece of parchment he hadn't seen before. She pointed with her raw, bitten finger to the Latin text which avowed that a priest had married Pèire Leteric to Katelina of Naxos, who signed her own name and scratched in ink her vows as an Orthodox Christian believer.

"If Simon de Montfort had this, he'd take Valerós from us," she said. "It proves Pèire was married to a schismatic."

"Ma dòmna, do not think Pèire would ever trade you and Sebastián for the safety of Valerós. And Valerós is under Pedro d'Aragón."

"Yet Pèire intended to send us off with an ancient crusader from the Pays de France."

"He wanted badly to protect you. He asked me to tell Pedro that he murdered that priest."

Isabella frowned. "Why would he be so foolish?"

"He didn't want Renoud saying that you were the murderer."

She grasped a penknife beside her, the page of vellum in her other hand shaking.

Distracted, he read the page beside the one she held, where the Latin text described the marriage between Don Miquel of Morella and Numa of Jaffa, a Christian in the Holy Roman Church. He looked away, resisting the desire to take immediate possession of it. Why hadn't Pèire given this to him? Why hadn't he found it? Tomas said, "You and Sebastián are in danger from your enemies."

"I know Renoud wants Sebastián, but he won't hurt him," she said. "All these attacks are to scare me into returning to Toulouse."

"I hope that's all it is, ma dòmna." Tomás didn't believe it, because of the second Wolf letter Katelina had given him. "But we both agree that your domus is in jeopardy. Perhaps Senhóreta Katelina can help you decide what to do."

"She spends all her time trying to comfort Beatriz, but my sister won't speak to her. And Katelina's heart must be broken."

Tomás had an idea of just how heartbroken. Katelina hadn't cried after she finished her prayers over Pèire's cold body. Instead, she comforted the other women. He knew from his own mother how deep an unwept, ravening grief could be. And he saw the same grief burning in Katelina's dry, dark eyes.

His tongue probed his sore tooth as Isabella stared off where the sheep's horn window sash had been rolled aside. *"My girls need to be protected, not dragged into this,"* Pèire had insisted. What a mistake that had been. Aloud Tomás said, "Ask Guillem and Father Anselm for help." Before he could dampen his bitterness, he added, "Since you refuse to trust me."

She stood and paced. Tomás, who still wanted to steal his father's marriage record, stood when she did, trying his best to act like an Aragón knight. As she paced nearby, he breathed the now-familiar smell of her: mint and ink and another sublime odor that was just Isabella's.

"All this grieving is foolish," she said. "Pèire was a very old man who tricked death a thousand times. And when I look at that," she pointed to the letters, her hand trembling, "I'm so angry at Pèire for not trusting me."

Tomás wrapped his arms around her. He whispered, "I am truly sorry."

She relaxed in his arms as if magic had placed another woman there, one who was warm and soft, who molded herself against him. He breathed in her smell and heard the soft rustle of her hair as he nestled his cheek against her linen head covering. Then he felt the other Isabella returned, stiffening. He released her quickly, before she pushed him away.

"Thank you." She'd recovered her composure. "People are kind to offer consolation. It's hard because it came so suddenly."

"Yes, but his headaches were very bad and the blindness coming more frequently."

"Blindness?" She frowned again. "It's nice you were so intimate." She sat at the work table. "What in the name of the Blessed Mother of God am I to do?"

"Follow Pèire's plan," he said. "Send the fewest knights possible to join Hugues de Beaurain."

"I want to take the knights and deal with Renoud. I want to cut his throat." She sat clutching her knees until her grief transmuted into anger, seeming to ripple across her body.

"It's not safe for you to leave Valerós. Marshal Guillem can lead the knights to satisfy Simon's demands and to protect Fontcours. I will help you defend Valerós."

"I can defend Valerós myself," she said. "Then what? Beg the king of Aragón to intercede with Simon de Montfort over our taxes?"

"When Gerard comes," Tomás took a breath to carry out his oath, against his own desires, "he will solve those problems."

She rose, angry with him, not liking his advice any more than he liked giving it. "I thank you for your counsel. But I do not choose that solution. Marriage means terror and pain. I will take care of these matters myself." She left without a farewell.

"You need a champion, ma dòmna," he called after her. "You are not the Queen of Jerusalem."

·

"You're letting women distract you." Miquel manifested again, taking the seat Isabella had abandoned. "You pledged your steel sword to Pèire, not your *punxor*."

"Sweet dancing angels! Leave me be!"

"I'm only trying to help. You need to convince the senhóra to marry as Pèire had intended."

"Where do I start? With Guillem? Father Anselm?"

"Katelina perhaps. But do you remember how you sent your love's bodyguard to take a rest? She's alone."

"*Ai!*"

Tomás snatched the disputed letters from the table and ran after her, doing his duty as he'd promised Pèire. When he turned the corner onto the gallery, he met the guard.

"Where's Marshal Guillem?"

"The marshal's gone," the man said. "He rode away this morning with Senhóreta Katelina and some of his men. The stable boys said Senhóreta Beatriz ordered it."

"Find Senhóra Isabella!" Tomás shouted, already running through the castle. Inside the chapel, he found Felicia weeping. She knew nothing when he asked about Katelina or Isabella. Tomás finally found Beatriz on the upper battlements, staring out over the valley.

"Where's Katelina? Where has the senhóreta gone?"

"She's not a senhóreta." Beatriz's voice sounded hollow.

"If she isn't, no woman is."

"You heard what Pèire's said that night. They lied, day after day."

"It doesn't matter now."

"It changes everything."

"Where is she?" He raised his voice.

"Gone to a nunnery. The marshal carried the Magdalene away."

"You little witch!" He wanted to shake the little ice-hearted queen. "You heard what Pèire said. Katelina saved him when God broke his heart."

"They lied to me."

"And now you want to destroy everything around you?" He hadn't felt so deeply angry for months. Beatriz seemed to want to pull the rafters down on everything good he'd found here, in the warm friendship Pèire freely gave him, and the kind encouragement he had from Katelina. And he'd given Pèire his oath to protect all his children, even this small ball of anger. "You seek to wreak havoc because the world isn't how you want it to be?"

"It's not your concern," Beatriz said dully.

"You have endangered the person who loves you most, you silly girl. Katelina isn't safe if she's gone from here."

"You are a *poulain* beggar with no right to speak to me. Take your dirty hands off me." Unlike Pèire, Beatriz spit the word *poulain* as if it were the filthiest of pejoratives.

"I swore to protect you until you marry. And you damn well will be protected by me!" He raised his voice even further. "Be a woman and stop your tantrums."

"Take Pèire's Magdalene and ride straight to hell together."

"Where did they go?" He ignored her invectives.

"Look at the Abbaye de Fontfroide."

"You are the devil's own wicked sister. Pray God cares to save your soul."

"God doesn't care. I know that in my heart," she said as Tomás ran from the battlements.

40
Scorpions in Surcoats

Isabella at Valeros
18 days before Pentecost

OF ALL THE DAYS not to find Sebastián, this was the worst. After that foolish action, declaring herself master of the castle to Don Tomás-of-wherever-he-lied-about, Isabella seemed unable to get anyone to respond to her commands.

Beatriz stood on the highest wall, having emerged from her room for the first time since the night Pèire died. She stood gazing out an arrow loophole.

"Have you seen Sebastián?" Isabella called as she mounted the stairs to the battlements.

Beatriz made a small wave. "Gone," she said.

"But where?"

"Wherever Don Tomás goes, there goes Sebastián." Beatriz pointed over the wall. "There goes our sworn protector. You can be sure Sebastián follows."

Tomás, armed and dressed in a hauberk, rode at full gallop away from the castle, but the narrow trail curved so Isabella couldn't see Sebastián from the loophole.

"Where is he going?"

"To hell, I suppose. That's where he came from, isn't it?"

Not waiting to hear more of Beatriz's mean-spirited riddles, Isabella bounded down the outer stairs and ran for the stables.

A stableman jumped up from where he knelt beside Al-Malik.

"Ma dòmna, I'm sorry. There was nothing more to do."

She stepped back, seeing that her horse lay still.

"But last night, he was better." A shiver rattled through her.

Joris the stable master said, "God didn't answer our prayers."

"*Jhezu del tron!*"

"Ma dòmna, it's best now, for him."

"Get me a horse. Now!"

At the gate, she shouted at the guards to step out of her way. Gathering up the skirts of her robe, she urged her horse into a gallop by the time they passed the gates.

"You're supposed to be with your guard, ma dòmna!" a voice yelled after her.

The horse they gave her proved less nimble than poor Al-Malik, of course, but she was on the trail across the valley at a rapid pace. She left the path where it curved along the brook and instead followed a straight line through a newly sown flax field, praying it was plowed well enough that her horse wouldn't stumble.

The horse was already lathered, its chest heaving, when she came back to the trail and saw Tomás a few horse-lengths ahead. Her javelin in hand, she kicked the horse. Tomás turned to see who was behind him at the exact moment she caught up and knocked him from his horse with her javelin.

He did a somersault, rolling into a ball as he tumbled, his arms reaching up to protect his head.

"Jove's pissing monkey!" he shouted as he rolled through his fall to stand again. "What are you doing out here?"

"I want Sebastián." Her horse stamped uneasily, having halted too quickly after the exertion.

"Sebastián is back at Valerós, where you should be."

"Beatriz said he left with you. I swear to God, you are not taking Sebastián."

"Jesus and the entire choir of sobbing angels, are all Montcava women lunatics?"

"I'm not a Montcava!" she shouted.

An arrow thunked into the oak behind them.

In the same instant, Tomás pushed her to the ground and covered her with his body, his breath hot in her ear as he whispered invectives. He wrapped his arms around her and rolled them both into the gorse and broom beneath the oaks. Crouching, he whistled to the horses, soothing and leading them deeper into the broom.

"I don't have Sebastián." He spoke while calming his horse. "You don't see him, do you?"

"What are you doing, then?" she demanded.

"I'm following Guillem to bring Senhóreta Katelina back. Your sweet little sister sent Katelina to a nunnery."

"Why ever did she do that?"

Tomás's eyes darkened. "For the same reason you are here with no guard. Because you are both idiots. Or more than that: an entire new race of idiots, unknown in Aristotle's science."

She began to object, when another arrow fell into the brush.

"God's scrofulous pig! We can't stay here. Will we find a sheep track if we go up the hillside?"

"Yes," she said.

"Then we're going to Arracheuse. It's too far to go back."

Darting from bush to bush and tree to tree, leading the horses rather than riding them, they made their way up to a narrow track among the rock outcroppings. They heard no more arrows.

At one point, the track widened enough that she led her horse alongside his.

"Don't talk, ma dòmna. We don't have time for you to harangue me while I determine what in the devil's own hell we're to do."

"It's Renoud's men shooting at us. He doesn't want me dead."

"Even if that's true for you, it isn't true for me. And there's too much chance for accidents and bad shots. I'm trying to see how to protect you."

"I don't need to be protected by you."

"Can't you please just feel terror, ma dòmna? I do."

"I refuse. I'm not a distressed woman in a hero's cançós."

"If there ever was a woman in distress, it's you. You and your idiot sister dragged a host of others into distress along with you."

They walked along uncompanionably. Despite not wanting to, she found herself saying she was sorry.

"Excuse me."

"Blessed Mary and the perpetual virgins, it's too late to be sorry."

"You swear like my grandfather."

"I swear like my own father. It's only a coincidence."

The trail narrowed. She had to walk in front of him. The ride along the twisting trail seemed interminable, although only a few leagues separated Castell-de-Valerós and Arracheuse.

"What's that?" Tomás asked, pointing toward Castell-de-Valerós in the south. A plume of black smoke rose above the hills.

"I don't know. There's nothing that burns near the castle. Everything is stone, slate, or tile. Grandfather says if we ever took Greek fire, we would—"

She stopped, feeling in the marrow of her bones that her entire world was in jeopardy. "It's the wool shed."

The smoke carried off the slim hope that they could pay Simon's new tax. She tried not to bite her lip or tremble or otherwise show Tomás what she felt. He sat on his horse for several moments, and then kicked the beast forward again.

"I'm sorry your first days as Queen of Jerusalem aren't going well," he said.

After riding another league, Tomás stopped and dismounted, looking at the valley floor below them.

"Look there!" He pointed to where four figures rode down the valley trail. The smallest figure among them was Sebastián, red hair flashing bronze in the sunshine. The others around him wore the brilliant carmine surcoats of Montcava knights.

"Sancta Maria!" she whispered, seeing her child caught in a pack of scorpions.

"It's too late for prayer," he said.

He mounted his horse and motioned for her to do the same. They rode toward Arracheuse, letting the horses find their way along the rocky sheep track. Broom and briars scratched her bare legs, which were as badly burned from the hot sun as her face. She'd lost her head covering when they rolled away from the hidden bowman, and her hair fell in loosening braids, protecting neither her ears nor her neck from the sun.

"At least it can't get any worse," Tomás called to her.

∎

Except when they arrived at Arracheuse, men in Montcava surcoats stood along the battlements and fired crossbows at them. Tomás guessed that it must have been Montcava knights shooting at them earlier. He grabbed Isabella's reins and galloped them at an angle away from the castle, out of the range of crossbows.

She snatched back her reins. "Let me ride free!"

He tossed the reins to her, and she caught them as they whipped across her sun-burned legs.

"Ride for that narrow valley!"

He pointed to a passage in the hills, in the opposite direction from where she'd ridden with Guillem to hunt wolves. When she kicked her horse to pass Tomás, he glanced back to see a dust cloud in front of the castle at Arracheuse. Riders pursued them.

Today I battle Montcava knights. But they were too many for him to take on alone. However, he didn't have time to fear them while he struggled to both shepherd and protect Isabella.

After they'd ridden considerably ahead of their pursuers, Tomás caught up and motioned her to move off the narrow trail and into the trees. Again, he found a sheep track. Isabella called to him that she'd ridden this trail before. After a while, though, she reined in her horse.

"I'm not so sure now. I haven't recognized any signs since we came around that last hill."

Yet she easily persuaded him to stay off the main trail. They tried to pace the horses while still moving forward, but finally she called to rest and water the animals.

"They're chasing us with fresh mounts," she said. "We can't get ahead of them if ours are dead."

"We also need to decide where we're going."

.

Tomás drank water. He couldn't think of anything except his need to drink water. Upstream from where the horses drank, Isabella waded into the creek, then sought a place among the rocks where the water might be deep enough to cover more than her feet and ankles. She sat on a flat rock to let a tiny waterfall wash over her legs.

Tomás drank more water while hoping the cold water of the creek soothed her scratched, sun-burnt skin. He came to the brook below where she sat and left his hauberk on a rock. He pulled off his leather vest and the linen undershirt, dipped it in the water, and washed his face, rinsing away the day's sweat and salt. When he pulled his shirt on, the wet linen clung like a shroud. His breeches were stained with horse sweat, his hose snagged from briars.

Then he waded up the creek to see how she fared. Her robe was as wet as his shirt. When he approached, she tugged the skirts of her thin robe down to cover her legs.

"You should wear the hauberk," he said. She'd already lectured him several times about not wanting him to protect her, but an oath was an oath. So, he persisted. "I'm a fool for not thinking of it before. You're the one in danger."

The horses stopped grazing and neighed, flicking their ears. Tomás couldn't get Isabella's attention to see what stirred them. There was no motion or sound, though, except their still-labored breathing.

"If we ride over that ridge to the west," Isabella said, "there's a farm owned by one of Pèire's seigneurs."

"Yes, but we can't get there today."

"Do you have a better plan?"

"That's what you pay me for, ma dòmna. We'll ride over the ridge to the east," he said. "Chrétien and I have a rendezvous site in case we became separated. We'll stay there until Chrétien comes."

"When will that be?"

"The way things are going, we better plan to start a colony, like Franks in the Holy Land." He knew better than to provoke her. And yet. "Perhaps you'll find a new kingdom to rule."

"Tell me, please, when Chrétien will come."

"Tomorrow, probably. Meanwhile, I want to persuade you to do as I ask, though I know it galls you."

"We should agree together on what to do," she said.

"If we'd agreed on what's best, then you'd still be safe at Valerós."

"You work for me."

"I swore an oath to protect you, ma dòmna. I intend to do the best I can, however difficult you make it."

"Why is my life so much worse since you swore that oath?" She managed, as usual, to strike at his soul with a knife.

"It's only a coincidence, ma dòmna."

That was his honest plea. Then an arrow found his arm.

.

Isabella heard its whistle but didn't see the arrow in flight before the sickening thud on flesh.

With no time to judge how dire Tomás's wound might be, she jumped from the brook and ran for the horses, her dripping robe slowing her flight. By the time she got both horses in hand, Tomás had broken off the shaft of the arrow and grabbed his hauberk and jerkin from the rock. They mounted and rode into the trees.

Up the hillside, they found modest shelter, Tomás motioned for her to rein in her horse, while they listened for pursuers. Blood had drenched his linen shirt.

"Your arm!" she gasped. Her stomach wrenched at the sight of the red slick wetting his shirt.

But he seemed to pay no mind to his wound.

"Who was it? It's not who rode out of Arracheuse after us. We'd have heard them." He pulled on his jerkin, easing it over the drenched sleeve of his shirt, and then hefted his hauberk over to Isabella, the chainmail making an ungodly racket, announcing their presence all over the hillside.

"Do you need help putting it on, ma dòmna?"

"I can manage." She awkwardly pulled it over her head. It rattled and rang in her ears while she wiggled to slip her arms into the sleeves. For years she'd wanted to wear a knight's armor. As the garment settled, its weight tugged downward, so she strained to sit more upright in the saddle. The top of her robe didn't rise high enough to shield her neck from the chafe of the iron rings. Even when she pulled down the skirts of her robe to cover her legs, the linen shifted as they rode forward again, and the tail of the hauberk rasped over the sunburn and thorn-scratched wounds on her legs. Exhaustion, hunger, and thirst filled the rest of her thoughts.

They crested the hill and rode a league down the other side. After they drank water and saw to the horses, Tomás struggled to take off his shirt, its sleeve was matted to the elbow with drying blood. She tried to help him.

"I can do it," he said.

"It's easier if I help," she said. "Sancta Maria!"

Stripped of the shirt, his upper arm was sticky with clotted blood, already turning black around the wound. Tomás examined it with no apparent emotion, prodding the edges of it. She struggled not to turn away like a coward.

"If I wash it now, it'll be fine until we find shelter," he said.

"Let me do it." She offered, although her stomach lurched at the idea of touching blood.

"I'd rather take care of it myself." His lips twitched, the same spasm of hatred as when Father Clémence had shoved him, the first day they met.

"I only meant to wash your shirt," she said.

"Just the sleeve. I don't want to take a chill in a wet shirt."

The stream turned red when she dipped the sleeve in to let the water rush away as much of the blood as possible before she touched it. By then, it just felt like linen, although she couldn't wash the pink out of the cloth. More of the shirt got wet than she intended, and her attempts to wring it dry were unsuccessful. She carried the shirt back, feeling ineffective. A failure.

He held his hand tightly over the wound to stop the blood that began flowing again after he washed it. She laid the shirt on the rock beside him.

"Excuse me but—"

"Don't, ma dòmna. Don't be sorry. There's no point in it."

"But I want to—"

"You did what you did. I'm sorry I called you an idiot, but I'm not sorry about calling Beatriz one. I'd be lying if I said otherwise."

"God knows you wouldn't tell a lie." She showed her exasperation with his imperious apology.

"I don't know what it might be that God knows," he said. "Else I'd know why I'm riding through hell on a half-dead horse with an arrogant woman."

"I said I'm sorry only because your shirt is wetter than you wanted. Do you want me to help you put it on again?"

"No, I'll do it myself." His lips twitched again with what seemed to be the same anger. Difficult as it was, he got the shirt on.

She sat down beside him with her arms crossed. "Beatriz behaved stupidly. It wasn't stupid to try to find my son."

"Alone? Outside the castle when we know evil is stalking you?"

"I followed you because Sebastián is always wherever you are."

"But he wasn't with me, and now there's no one at Valerós to help your infuriating sister." He took a deep breath. "Sebastián didn't leave the castle on his own accord."

"Yet we saw him. He must have gone for a ride and been captured by Renoud's men."

"I borrowed his horse to ride. Didn't you notice? I'm not surprised that Beatriz behaved badly about Katelina leaving. Or that you'd be irrational. But Sebastián knows better than to act without thinking. He was carried out of Valerós by force."

"Who?" She ignored the insult.

"Maybe the man who attacked you the other night snatched him. And shot me today, and—" Tomás straightened as if struck again. "*Ai*, forgive me, ma dòmna. Your worries for Sebastián are much greater than my cares."

"Those scarlet surcoats mean that Renoud has him. Because he wants Sebastián at Montcava. At least he'll keep Sebastián safe."

"Pray God that's so," Tomás said. "We'll just fetch him away again. Can you wrap this around my arm, ma dòmna?"

She didn't want to, but couldn't say no. She took the cloth he offered—the scarf tied to Sebastián's saddle, from when they rode relays. Was that a thousand days ago? She did the best possible to wrap his arm, hoping not to hurt him, trying not to see the blood.

"You're shaking, ma dòmna."

"I'm worried."

"Yet you said Sebastián's safe with Renoud. What else is worrying you?"

"The villages around Arracheuse. If Renoud's men are foraging for food, those poor people will lose sheep and food and—"

Tomás held up his hand. "Before we worry about that, we must decide what to do next."

She tied the makeshift bandage, then plucked nearby dandelion leaves to wipe blood from her hands. That left her fingers sticky. She said, "We can't go back to Valerós. I would like nothing better than to rouse the knights there to pursue Renoud and Sebastián. But they need to defend the castle." She'd considered all this while riding, and the answer was what Katelina taught. "We must go forward."

Tomás nodded, accepting that decision without judgment. "I suggest we wait for Chrétien at our rendezvous site. Then we ride to Fontfroide abbey. That's where Katelina is going. Perhaps we'll find Guillem along the trail."

"Yes. Then what?" She could agree, because she'd been thinking the same while they swerved and bounced along the road. She wanted to wipe the stickiness away, but there was only her robe.

"We go to Fontcours," Tomás said. He still watched her, judging. "If we miss Marshal Guillem on the way, he'll be at Fontcours when we arrive. We'll also meet Hugues, like Pèire planned. You shall declare yourself and Valerós for the Church, which will save Fontcours and Montcava."

"Yes, you're right." She surrendered to the only possibility, while also giving up worry for her robe. She wiped her fingers on the back of her skirt, so she wouldn't have to see traces of his blood.

"And then you marry Gerard de Chartrain, so he can deal with the French and resolve all your other problems." He wouldn't let it rest when she didn't answer. "What else on God's own earth can you do, ma dòmna? Your new husband is the only bet you have."

"I don't see it that way." She did, however, dare to inspect her fingers, finding that the dark stains could be anything, from the horse, from the dirty trail, dandelion. Not blood.

"Then let's ride to Narbonne, ma dòmna, and find Pedro el Rei, so your king can find a protector to fight your brother-in-law."

Going to Pedro was just the sort of thing Tomás would say to goad her. She would not argue the question of marrying.

．

Tomás tracked the sun while Isabella chose trails that seemed to wander among steep hills as if made by a thousand generations of sheep. Stunted oak grew among the beech and ash trees, and jays in the oak boughs harassed the riders on every new turn in the trail. The tops of the hills baked in the sun, and buzzards in the trees watched them pick their way among the limestone crags and the narrow, steep-sided valleys that saw little sun.

After they rode in silence for a long while, Tomás said, "I salute you, ma dòmna, for not weeping."

"Weep? About what?"

"All of it. If anyone ever had a reason, you have a dozen."

"I never weep." She lied about all those years in Toulouse and forgot for a moment that he'd seen her weep over Pèire's body.

"My mother weeps on most occasions. All the women I've ever known sobbed for one thing or another."

"I don't see what good it does to weep," she said. "And when we go to Fontcours, I will be leading Valerós knights against my enemy."

"Yes," Tomás said. "If we find them. Look, see down in that valley? That's our rendezvous site."

41
A Woodcutter's Domus

Isabella in the Pyrenees foothills
18 days before Pentecost

ISABELLA WALKED BESIDE TOMÁS because his horse came up lame just before they reached a clearing in a narrow, deep valley. A stone cottage butted up against a rocky outcropping at the far side of the valley, as if it had been there since God separated the firmaments.

"Who lives here?"

"A woodcutter and his wife. This is where we'll meet Chrétien. We hired them to keep our armor and horses. Let's give them a moment to recognize me."

The exhausted horses grazed while Isabella and Tomás waited.

"It's more than that piss-ant Renoud and his men behind all your trouble," he said.

"But they wore Montcava colors. Who else hates me?"

Tomás shrugged, then winced from disturbing his wounded arm. "Renoud doesn't have men as apt as those crossbow-men at Arracheuse. He must have hired mercenaries."

"What do you know about Renoud's house-knights?"

"As I said, we've been following him. Here come our friends."

An old man crossed the clearing to meet them, followed by an aged woman. Both had ancestors among the Moors who crossed the Pyrenees a few generations ago. The old man raised both hands in a Catalan greeting and then bowed as low as one does for a great lord. He was sixty or more, a colossus with hugely muscled arms and a large torso. Beside him, the woman seemed diminutive. With her dowager's hump, she resembled a night heron, her dark eyes shining as Tomás and Isabella approached.

"How are my horses, Master Anfos?" Tomás grasped the man's hands and then embraced Maria.

"Quite well, senhór. Better than these poor beasts you ride now."

"We're pursued by marauders," Tomás said. "I'd like to purchase safety from you. This senhóra is Chrétien's sister and needs the warmth of your hearth."

"What we have is yours. Let's hide these horses."

Before going with the woodcutter to care for the horses, Tomás helped Isabella out of the hauberk. Its weight lifted from her shoulders, Isabella felt filthy and wretched. Inside the cottage, the woman offered her watered wine and a chunk of bread with sheep's cheese, saying a goodman's blessing over the bread.

"Can you sing, ma dòmna? Your brother Chrétien has the voice of an angel. I'd harbor him for the winter just to hear him sing."

Isabella confessed she couldn't sing a note.

Maria sighed. "But he's coming soon, ma dòmna? And then we can hear him again?"

Anfos came in with Tomás, who had changed into a shepherd's smock and coarse, well-worn split hose.

"I don't want to endanger you, especially after all your kindness," Tomás said.

"What would marauders want with an old man and his wife and half-wit children?" Anfos said.

"The men pursuing us are close by," Tomás said. "We saw their dust and heard horses echoing from the hillsides."

"I've faced bandits and marauders all my life," Anfos said.

"My friend, this is more than common bandits. I want you to keep your wife safe. Can you go to your cave without being seen? And stay until you are sure they are long gone?"

Tomás asked for clothes for Isabella, who was soon dressed in an immense sheep shearer's apron so coated in lanolin and animal filth that it had its own stiff shape independent of the body wearing it. Tomás dragged her to the fire pit, calling to Maria for permission to disturb her housekeeping. After Maria and Anfos slipped away, Tomás untied Isabella's frazzled braids and shook her hair loose, then grabbed a handful of cooking fat from the pot near the fire pit and rubbed it into her hair. The smell of mutton was sickening, but

243

before she could protest, he rubbed ashes from the fire pit into her hair and over her face. She winced at the pain from her sunburn.

"Your copper hair was gleaming in the sun all day, ma dòmna. If those men noticed anything, it's your hair. Smile."

He rubbed sheep's fat on her teeth, and then made her bite into a cold piece of charcoal. He untied his own hair and rubbed ash into his long locks and beard, becoming the wild man of the mountain.

Horses pounded into the outer yard.

"Let me talk. If you can't be quiet, don't speak in the common tongue." He opened the door. "I hope you agree this is the best action. I forgot to beg your permission."

"Go to the devil." She spoke Greek, then smiled, nervous that they had to cooperate as comrades in danger.

He grinned. "Been there already today."

·

Tomás the woodcutter stepped into the yard and raised his hands in a Catalan greeting, then bowed. Isabella followed.

The four soldiers remained on their horses, which danced impatiently in the yard. The two taller men were Norman, the largest of whom had numerous wens on his face. A mace swung from his saddle pommel. The other two were Gascons.

"We're seeking two heretics. A man and a woman. They must have ridden through here," the wen-faced Norman demanded.

"That they did," Tomás said in archaic Catalan, sounding like the half-wit son of a woodcutter. "It was about when the sun stood there. No, it was more like over there. Then they rode—" He looked around and back to the sun's position. "They rode directly that way. Going to Quéribus, they were." Tomás smiled like a fool. "Sold them food and fodder, I did. They had good silver. Would you be looking to buy yourself?"

"I'm knackered," one soldier said. "We rode all over hell today."

"Quiet, you!" the leader commanded. Turning back to Tomás, he said, "We're crusaders under the banner of Simon de Montfort's vassal. We have our lord's leave to command all the sustenance we need for God's work."

"You won't be paying then?" Tomás feigned disappointment.

"No, you fool. What have you got that we can eat in the saddle?"

"Some mutton and cheese and bread," Tomás said, distracted when one of the soldiers had dismounted and put his hand on Isabella's chin and tipped her head up.

Tomás said, "You can borrow her, my lord. But take care. I've been dripping and burning since she first came here. No telling where she's been, even her father said so."

The soldier stepped back.

"If that old *peccador* was her father, leaving her here like he did," Tomás continued. "Didn't even speak the same tongue as her. *Ai*, he talked like a Christian, but I don't know what the devil she talks."

Isabella said in Greek, "Are you calling me a whore, you damnable whoreson?"

The soldiers examined her, but clearly none of them understood Greek. Tomás cuffed her, brushing his hand along her greasy hair.

"It beats her nagging. I can't understand a word. Last wife I had about talked me into the grave if she hadn't died first. This one, it's like so many crows on carrion to listen to her."

"The food, you fool. Give us some food."

"Right away, senhór."

Tomás went into the cottage, shoving Isabella in front of him.

"I'll see you in your grave if you strike me again," Isabella said, still in Greek.

"Do you prefer insult or assault?" he whispered. "If you have another idea, tell me. But in goddamn Greek."

The soldiers clanked in behind them. Tomás fetched food out of the larder, chattering the whole time. Isabella chopped round loaves of bread into quarters.

"The woman's got her good points. She don't eat much, even though she's got all her teeth. But then, every time you stick her head between your knees, she tries to bite it off. No matter how I slap her, the very next time she tries to take a chunk out again. Can't teach her a thing."

He piled bread and cheese into the soldiers' arms, making each load as awkward as possible, and still chattering.

"But then, you smell her breath, you don't want that blown on your privates. It's withering, I tell you."

Their leader said, "Meat. You said you had meat."

"Right between my legs like any man." Tomás sounded confused.

"I mean mutton, you fool. You said you had mutton."

"*Ai*, right, my lord. Glad to give my sheep to the pope's crusade. Who did you say was your lord?"

"Renoud of Montcava," one said. The leader shot him a look.

Tomás uncovered a roast mutton leg and whacked at it with the kitchen cleaver.

"You'll want some wine with that, my lords. If you've a silver penny for it, that goes so much better when I have to pay my taxes."

"Not a brass bezant," the leader said.

Tomás pulled down a flagon of wine hanging from the rafter.

"This tastes a bit like sheep's piss," Tomás said. "The woman can't brew any better than she can breed. It may be she spits in the vat and it curdles, like the milk always does since she came here."

Grabbing the flagon from Tomás, one of the men drank deeply and then spat it out.

"You'd best ride along the seaward side of the ridge," Tomás said, "if you hope to see Quéribus by nightfall like those other fellows. Else, you're welcome to sleep with us. We bring the pig and chickens in at night, because of the wolves. The donkey won't mind just standing at the door. So, there's room for you."

The scornful leader turned his horse's head and spurred hard. The others followed.

.

When the riders disappeared over the ridge, Isabella sank onto the bench by the door, laughing.

"We're still alive," Isabella said.

She tugged at the tattered knees of Tomás's hose to pull him down beside her, colliding against his injured arm. He cried out, but he too laughed. She reached out, sorry she'd hurt him.

"You need food," she said. Afternoon shadows had lengthened and filled the valley. The light was fading.

"We need to boil some water," he said.

"To clean your wound?"

"Yes, and we need to wash. Between the mutton fat and horse sweat, we both smell like the devil's own offal."

"Food first." Isabella moved away from him, hoping Maria returned soon so she wouldn't have to touch his wound. "I'll impress you with what I can do in the kitchen."

"You can cook?"

"No, but I can slice bread and cheese. That's all you get until Maria comes back. You gave away all the mutton."

"I'll fetch wood for the fire," Tomás said. "I'm getting cold."

"That'll be a great trick, starting a fire with one good hand. Perhaps you can travel with the minstrels and do magic tricks," she said.

"You'd be surprised what I can do," he said.

As she searched for more food, that's what she pondered. The person she distrusted most in the world, next to Renoud, had saved her life and led them to safety through a hellacious day. While riding, she kept forgetting that she followed the infuriating false scribe, because all she saw was a warrior, powerful and resolute through the day's dangers.

After beginning the day as steward and master of Valerós and ending it as a sham woodcutter's wife, Isabella laid trenchers of bread with olive oil and cheese on the table, and then found a packet of dried fish to add to their supper. The domestic scene made her laugh aloud. Hearing Tomás at the door, she turned with a smile, saying *carpe diem* aloud, but found him with his arms wrapped around a bundle of oak twigs and the four mercenaries close behind.

"Look what the cat brought," she said in Greek, masking fear while her heart wanted to burst her chest.

Tomás set the wood down and cuffed her with a curse, but she'd learned how to pull away at the right moment, pretending he'd struck her, when in fact he was now her only safety.

42

Foragers

Jean-Luc in the Aude valley
Early May

JEAN-LUC WALKED DOWN THE narrow valley toward the plains. He stopped at a farm to trade iron mongering for food and a night's shelter. He had no money to buy a horse, and the farmers here were too poor for him to contemplate thieving. And so, he walked, striving with every step to cease repeating arguments with Felicia.

Please come with me, chérie.

I can't, Jehan.

The failed rendezvous with the courier meant a long walk to Toulouse, where he still hoped to find the man who confessed to ruining a man in Constantinople. If he didn't find him in Toulouse, he'd ask directions to the Marquis de Beaurain's army camp, though going there would put him in jeopardy. But then, if he thought about that, it took attention from putting one foot in front of the other along the trail.

And if he let his attention to the trail waver, he felt slim fingers touching his neck, her tongue at his clavicle, Felicia's soft legs entwined with his, her saltiness on his lips. He recalled a chanting spell to ward off succubae and fox spirits as he fingered the leather braid around his neck, missing the protective charm from his mother. He'd given it to Felicia, for lack of anything else with which to protect her.

Near Termes, where the trail wound through hummocks and hills to join another road, men arrived at the crossroad, some afoot with pikes, some on horseback with crossbows. They spied Jean-Luc on the hill above them. Instinctively, he raised his hand in a greeting any French cavalryman would recognize. Some of the men on horseback were from the Pays de France. The men on foot proved to be Brabançon mercenaries leading mules loaded with the cheeses, chickens, and sacks of grain they'd foraged from local farms. They herded a small flock of sheep destined for crusaders' mutton stew.

"*Bonjour! Comme ça va?*" he called to the foragers in his own language. "I'm happy as hell you found me. I nearly perished amid the heretics' cow-pies."

Sword drawn, their French captain rode to greet him, and Jean-Luc began telling truths and lies.

"I'm a courier for the Viscount de Chartrain. Brigands stole my horse and left me wounded." He slapped his injured thigh. "A crazy old woman in the hills stitched me up and said prayers to St-Gilles and St-Christopher. But I nearly lost my mind, hoping to find countrymen to lead me back to civilization."

The French captain knew the viscount's name and accepted Jean-Luc's story. And though the Brabançon foragers made French sound evil when they spoke it, and despite their savage reputation as soldiers, Jean-Luc found them to be professional and even semi-civilized. They served a lord with minuscule holdings who came south to seek his fortune and joined the larger camp of a distant relative.

Although Jean-Luc was a stranger, they complained freely that this crusade had been a total disappointment. The villages and towns they visited made an elaborate show of submission to Simon de Montfort, so there were no sieges.

"But they're lying ass-biters who won't even admit they hate the sight of the cross," one man said in a thick Low Country accent.

"Each town we're sent to is said to be crawling with heretics," another claimed, "but all we find are old women knitting and chickens pecking in the dust."

"There's no booty. The gold-sniffers haven't found one mark of heretics' gold. It's a shit-eaters' excuse for a crusade," the smallest of the Brabançon foragers complained. He gestured to the food-laden mules. "The only reward so far is all the ancient mutton we can eat."

"We might as well go home, where people live how God intended," another forager said before their captain shut them up.

He camped with them at night. The next day, from the last hill above the plain, Jean-Luc gazed down on a well-ordered French camp. Banners showed the divisions, laid out by the lords according to how the men were ordered in battle, with foot soldiers here, crossbowmen far across the way, squires and knights in their quarters, engineers and sappers within their own enclaves.

The French captain questioned Jean-Luc about his skills and offered him food, and then sent him to the armor-master, who grudgingly accepted him among the smiths. Jean-Luc wandered through the camp, thinking he could find his way blindfolded, since it seemed so familiar: kitchens built to protect from both fire and theft, and their sergeants as fierce as those guarding the armory. The latrines dug on the opposite side from the water supply, where foot soldiers and slingers added a layer of loam and sand every morning. Bawds and baggage boys in their quarters had their own rules and sergeants to enforce them. The foot soldiers drilled with the same discipline as the knights who practiced their conrois formations, every soldier trained to respond at a word or signal from their sergeant or captain.

To Jean-Luc, joining in camp life felt as familiar as stepping into his village church to hear the mass sung again. He couldn't go to his father's house, but he was once more in his second home: the standing camp of the Marquis Hugues de Beaurain.

Only by happenstance, he had an opportunity to search for the one-eyed man before going to Toulouse. If he could keep from being recognized. And hung as a traitor.

43
Housekeeping

THE MERCENARIES DECLARED THE cottage too small for everyone and so sent Tomás and his foreign wife to the fodder crib, then shooed the hens into one end. The smell of wood smoke and mutton fat filled Tomás's nose, the lingering effects of the disguise he'd forced on her. It was too dark to see beyond the shape of her body crushed against his, and his head pounded from fatigue and toothache while his arm throbbed from that arrow wound.

"You invited them. It's your fault they're back." She spoke in Greek as he'd asked.

"No more scolding. I wish I didn't know Greek."

"I'm not a scold."

"That sounds logical in Greek, but not what I experienced today," Tomás whispered. "Damn the luck. I'll have to buy Antos a new pig if the wolves get that one."

The mercenaries left the pig to wander in the yard, however much Tomás protested, giving him the choice of his wife or the pig for the night. Pretending to ponder at length, he'd chosen wife. When the heat of the late April day dissipated, they huddled for warmth under the straw in the crib. The slanted sides of the crib forced them too close.

"There's enough fodder to help keep us warm," he said. "We can burrow into it and share the blanket they gave us."

"My skirts are twisted. I can't turn without hurting your arm." When she wriggled to get her skirts untangled, his reaction was instantaneous, which disconcerted him given the day's danger. About

251

the time they'd composed a comfortable arrangement of their limbs, the two grinning Gascon soldiers returned, having drunk up their host's too-young wine.

One held a fistful of leather thongs. "Our captain says never trust a Moor. Too likely to cut our throats. So, we'd best tie you up." He twined Isabella's arms around Tomás's neck and tied them to the crib slats, then bound Tomás's hands the same way.

"It's not Christian." Tomás resisted crying out at the pain to his arm. "What's a man to do when he has to piss in the night?"

"That's a private affair between you and your wife." One Gascon threw the blanket over the bound captives. Then they staggered back to the cottage, laughing drunkenly.

"We're still alive." Isabella rested her head on Tomás's chest, there being no other option.

"That sounds desperate when you say it in Greek." He spoke calmly, to allay her fears, but he felt more than desperate. The scars on his face itched and burned beyond what a saint could endure.

"Are we safe?"

"Yes. The chickens will keep rats away, and anything bigger will go for the pig."

"Rats?"

"No rats. Only chickens." The pig's snuffling drifted further away. He cursed. "Thanks to those cat-licking Montcava curs, this will be the most expensive doss-house I ever paid good silver for."

"Tomás, will they hurt us in the morning?"

"No. They just wanted a mean joke." He needed to seem calm, since her question veered on panic. She'd been cool as sea air through all their dangers. "We'd rather be here than warm inside with those stinking mercenaries."

"You're jesting, right?" She burrowed her head into his chest, and he wanted badly to comfort her. "Tell me the plan again. Tell me how we're going to get away."

"Chrétien will come tomorrow. He'll bring news from Valerós and Arracheuse. Then we'll go find Marshal Guillem and deliver you to Gerard de Chartrain." He whispered the story and she remained calm until the journey brought them safely to Fontcours.

Then she twisted in his arms, distressed, driving his wounded arm into the crib's slats.

"I can't marry him."

"Why not? It's just a legal contract, intended to help you."

"You don't know what it's like," she whispered. "Your soul is smothered. There's always a man blocking the light, hurting you."

"What nightmare is this?" he asked.

"Marriage. Why force it on children? It never makes anyone happy."

"Ma dòmna, say your prayers and go to sleep. You need to be as stalwart tomorrow as you were today."

He felt her lips moving through the canvas of his jumper. He shifted subtly. Her breath fell on his arm. "A paternoster isn't enough," she said. "Or the Psalms for protection. Do you know strong prayers?"

"Try this one. My father taught it to me."

He repeated in Latin the long bonfraires prayer. Her breathing became deep and regular, and he relaxed, considering possible action. If he was to deliver her from evil, the righteousness path was to find Guillem and Katelina, and then deliver Isabella to her new husband.

"What's your plan?" Miquel squatted, his back leaning against the crib, chewing a straw. A chicken hopped on Miquel's thighs and fell swiftly asleep. "You don't know the roads to Fontfroide abbey. And how can you get to Fontcours with Simon's men roaming the plains?"

"I don't know. I'm figuring how much food to buy from Anfos. And whether I have to buy a pig if the wolves come."

The only sounds in the night came from the pig grazing the oak mast under the trees.

"He's snuffling for acorns," Miquel said. "No sign of wolves. How soon until Chrétien comes?"

"Don't know. I'm still busy calculating whether I have enough silver for a journey to Fontcours."

"Tomásino, have you calculated whether you're fast enough to take on those four in Anfos's cottage?"

"Go away, Father, if you can't be helpful."

He slept before dawn, still without a better plan, but having traveled in his mind every league of the journey to Fontcours.

In the ash-grey dawn, the Gascon hirelings untied Isabella and lifted her out to cook their breakfast, but left Tomás bound in the fodder crib. The hens scrambled out behind her to cackle and scratch in the yard.

Tomás went berserk getting his fetters undone, rubbing his wrists raw to struggle free of the leather thongs. He bashed the crib slats apart with all his strength, including his injured shoulder.

·

"Sancta Maria!" one mercenary screamed.

Tomás grabbed the sword from a startled Gascon and hacked into that man's shoulder.

The other Gascon leaned against Isabella, reaching to grab her skirt. She gripped the handle of the kitchen knife she'd stuck into the man's neck. Blood spurted like a fountain while the man's heart pumped his life out.

Tomás jumped between the other men and Isabella, to fight them away from her, finishing the other Gascon. But the last Norman came at him with a sword and a dagger. Tomás sliced off the man's sword-hand, then stabbed the man while he screamed and stared at his lost hand.

Ghost-white under the ashes smeared over her face, Isabella stepped away from the man who'd grabbed her. He fell forward, surprise frozen on his dead face. She collapsed against Tomás, shuddering as he wrapped his arms around her, although his pounding heart still wanted to find something more to kill. He held her tightly, rocking them both.

"It's all right, *kalila*." He crooned to her the way his mother had when they were hurt. "It's over now. You're safe."

She stared wide-eyed at the dead man until Tomás stepped so she couldn't see.

"Let's go outside, ma dòmna."

His body still pulsed as he coaxed her onto the bench under the arbor. The cat mewled by the door.

"*Aquí, aquí, gat!*" he called softly.

The cat curled up in Isabella's arms and lay still when she began to pet it, which seemed to offer more comfort than he did.

"I have to go to work." He left her and then shouted up the little canyon for Anfos to come home. Back inside, he hauled bodies to the yard and began loading then onto their hobbled horses. His arm throbbed worse than the devil, and the lesser wounds in his hands and wrists opened again, seeping blood. Then Anfos was at his side.

"It's too many to burn or bury." Tomás didn't say hello.

"It's all right, my friend. Let me help."

Anfos heaved the last body onto the horse. By then, Tomás could hardly get his fingers to tie the body upright in the wooden saddle. Anfos freed the hobbled horses and shooed them from the yard.

"Maria and I will walk to the village across the hill," Anfos said. "We'll throw rocks to keep the horses from wandering back, so their friends don't come visiting.

In the cottage, Maria sprinkled sand on the dirt floor and then washed the walls and table, while Tomás sat beside Isabella in the arbor, coaxing her out of shock.

"Here's a robe and soap from Maria. You can wash in the spring."

"You, too. We both need to wash."

At the spring, Tomás helped her out of the pitiful sheep-shearer's apron. She stepped into the water still wearing her own robe and waded part way in, but then ran from the water.

"There's blood on my dress!" she cried, her hands shaking wildly. "It's getting in the water. Get it off me! *Ai Dèu*, quickly!"

He tried to undo the fastenings, but she pulled away, ripping the front of her robe. She let it fall from her without touching it and ran into the spring, immersing herself and frantically soaping her body.

Peeling off his own smock and undershirt, Tomás sat on a boulder, using his dagger to probe the wound in his arm, which had gone too long without being cleaned and tended. It was hot at the edges.

Her face and hands splotchy and ruddy from sunburn and cold water, Isabella dressed in the borrowed robe, which was too short and too full at the bosom. She knotted a length of hemp rope loosely at the middle, like a nun from an ascetic order.

"Go join Maria, ma dòmna. Eat some food. I need to wash, too."

He stripped and stepped into the spring. The cold water ripped like a knife through the torn skin around his wrists and the slices on his hand and arms from that foolish duel before the bonfraires. Rubbing hard with lye-and-ash soap, he ignored the sting and pain as he scrubbed the wound free of filth. He used the tip of his dagger again, to scratch deep into the wound and pry out the last bits. The iron arrowhead was a Greek dart, that kind used with an arrow-guide to let the archer shoot over a long distance.

His probing made the wound bleed freely again, surely a good thing, though he shivered in the cold water. His balls had retracted, and his fingers were wrinkled. He stood up in the water to soap and rinse one more time—and found Isabella staring at him, horror-struck. She covered her mouth and ran toward the hut, stopping to be sick a few yards from the spring.

■

Tomás gave Isabella more of the soporific tea that Maria had left for them, hoping she'd sleep. It didn't work.

The tea and cloves from Maria eased his toothache and the pain in every muscle and bone. He applied more of Maria's medicines on Isabella's sunburn, although it hurt her so badly he could scarcely touch her face. She refused to step into the house, so they spent the morning at the table under the arbor. He laid out a modest meal with food from Maria: figs, dried fish, and bites of ham and bread.

While bees buzzed overhead and the sun baked the stones and dust in the yard, Tomas made Isabella talk, to take her mind away from the morning's catastrophe: how Pèire taught her to ride, how she learned to make beautiful manuscripts, how she'd worked to get Arracheuse out of debt.

Despite the tea, yesterday's wound burned and throbbed. Tomás stripped to his breeches and tugged away the bandage. Blood clotted black around Maria's sulfur salve. Although it didn't feel too hot, the edges were tender. He cleaned it again with water from the three-legged cauldron in the kitchen fire and packed in more of Maria's hell-fire salve, which had to be good, given how badly it burned. Then he wrapped it one-handed, which took several tries before the cloth felt tight enough to stay in place.

The whole time he worked, Isabella petted the cat and gazed out toward the hills. While he was tying up the cloth, she said, "We should go. We need to travel. To find Katelina and Guillem."

"We have to wait for Chrétien. And we have a lame horse. Do you want to come with me to check on them?"

She walked with him to see whether the horses fared well. A light breeze ruffled the trees and the manes of horses grazing in Anfos's pasture. The carpet of thyme and mint near the edge of the pasture spiced the air. For a quick mad moment, he schemed to keep life that way. Forget Renoud and all that represented. Just find Sebastián and take them to Cyprus, where they'd live in a manse like Anfos's.

A lark flickered down from a tree and landed near them, cocking its head and peering at him, waking his wiser angel. Tomás stepped away, leaving more room between them.

"It took me awhile to escape my fetters this morning," he said. "Did that *peccador* hurt you?" It was the first time he'd spoken of it.

"No. He said he would. You came just after he tried to touch me."

"I should have come sooner."

"But you did come." She glanced his way. "You don't fight like Valerós knights."

"I understand my sword better than most Latins."

"If I had your skills, I'd have fought today instead of being a murderer." She shuddered. "Renoud has no right to pursue me, to make my world as dangerous as his house."

"Don't let it prey on your mind, ma dòmna." He lost track of his thoughts each time she mentioned Renoud's name. "The fiend was the devil's own spawn. It wasn't your sin."

"My confessor in Toulouse claimed a man only forces a woman if she is a sinner who beguiles him."

"Curses on the dark angels! That priest was a fool. Though the whole tribe of priests seems ignorant about what women suffer."

"Father Anselm says God forgives those who do what they must to save themselves." She sighed. "I made the bad choices yesterday that put us here, but I'm not sorry about Renoud's men. You see, I was only upset because of all the blood."

He put his own knife in her hand. "When you need to kill a man, thrust up under his ribs and twist." He made the motion to show how to do it. "You won't have to worry about hitting bone, and it won't make such a mess."

"What do we do now?" she asked. "We need to move forward."

"The same as we planned. We wait for Chrétien."

"How do you know he'll come?"

"He always does."

Back at the cottage, Isabella paused before crossing the threshold. But Maria had been thorough, even burning a small fire with herbs before she left with Anfos, so the room was sweet smelling. The ancient trestle table was so worn that no single stain could be distinguished from another.

Tomás sat by the table and peeled back his bandage again.

"This needs attention." He hid his dismay. "Help me open it up again to wash it. Then you can stitch it up."

"No, I can't do it."

"Isabella, please help me. I can't let this wound go bad."

When he revealed what lay under the bandage, she paled and trembled as if in shock, like the day before.

"Come, ma dòmna. I'm rather attached to this arm. I'd hate to have to chew it off like a wolf in a trap."

She bolted from the house, stumbling at the threshold.

Resigned, he washed his arm again with hot water. The knife she'd used on the mercenary had a finer point than his, so he washed it and burned the blade in the fire. He sat down to attack the wound.

After a while she came back, hesitating at the threshold.

"It's the blood." She was still pale as ashes. "When Sebastián was born, there was…so much blood. They thought I'd die. What the physician did…it's why blood makes me ill."

Pity overwhelmed him, but he needed her help. "Can you just turn my arm so I can see?"

"Can't you wait for Chrétien?"

"No, I really can't."

"Can't wait for Chrétien?" a voice called from the yard. "Is there something good going and you didn't save any for me?"

44
Stitching with Silk Thread

Tomás in the Pyrenees foothills
17 days before Pentecost

CHRÉTIEN LAZED IN THE doorway, grinning like a fiend. "It's a family scene, with wounded warrior. Do I sing a dirge or praise anthem?"

Tomás said, "I need your ability with the knife more than your cutting wit, brother. How did you sneak up without our hearing?"

"My horse is hobbled behind the hill. Where are our hosts?"

"Gone to town," Isabella said. "We're happy to see you."

"Isabella is especially happy. Now she can shirk her chores." Tomás tried to join Chrétien's lighter mood.

Chrétien examined Tomás's arm. "Let's go outside, so I can see."

He threw a sheepskin around Tomás's bare shoulders for warmth and led him to the arbor, seeking sufficient light for his task. He asked Isabella for wine, hot water, and linen, and then used half the wine to wash the wound. The other half he poured into Tomás. Then he gave Tomás his belt to bite while he worked.

Chrétien washed away the last of the clotted blood and teased the wound fully open. "I'll do the nasty part, and then you sew him up, ma dòmna. He'll want tidy stitches since it's right where he can see it. Once I botched a seam. I never hear the end of it when a senhóreta complained about the poor quality of my stitchery."

"I don't sew," she said. "I can't do it."

"Don't ladies spent all their time sewing?" Chrétien tied a linen strip below the wound and used it to wipe away blood.

"I can't sew a seam. Or embroider." She looked the other way while Chrétien probed Tomás's wound with a knife.

Tomás moved his mind away from the pain of Chrétien's chore. They'd done this for each other so many times that the piercing sting and ferric smell of blood seemed as familiar as the sun rising.

"Doesn't a man want a woman who can stitch him up after battle?" Chrétien concentrated on the wound. "Didn't your husband complain if you left him bleeding?"

"Only once." She laughed, which seemed odd. Chrétien coaxed her back to life better than Tomás did. "I'm not the sort of woman a man comes home to."

Tomás spat out the leather belt to ask Chrétien what happened in Castell-de-Valerós after they left.

"Let's finish this first, so you'll remember what I tell you," Chrétien said. "This nick isn't so bad. There's only one sliver left inside. A little wine to anoint you." He poured it over the wound. Tomás grimaced at the sting. "And another cup to reward your fortitude."

Chrétien poured more unwatered wine for Tomás before he produced the pouch from inside his jerkin that held waxed silk thread and slender needles. Isabella clutched the table's edge, white-knuckled. When Chrétien pulled the first stitch through, the flesh around her mouth became mottled green.

Chrétien tied off the last stitch, bent to bite the thread, and then washed the wound one more time. "There, *kalila*. It's all better now. Shall I kiss it for you?"

"Another cup of wine will suffice," Tomás said.

"What does *kalila* mean?" Isabella asked.

"Sweetheart. It's what our mother said when she patched us up," Chrétien said.

"She wasted so much thread on us." Tomás slurred his words.

"You are sloshed, brother. Can I talk you into lying down inside by the fire? You need to stay warm for a while."

He slung Tomás's good arm around his neck and hoisted him up.

"I can walk just fine," Tomás said.

"Not after so much wine and pain." Chrétien eased Tomás onto the pallet near the fire. "I have to tend my horse, and then we'll trade stories. Senhóra Isabella, can you find another strip of linen for a bandage and wrap it for our friend?"

When Chrétien left, she knelt to do as instructed. A lock of her hair fell across a fading bruise on her cheek. The sunburn peeled on her nose and cheekbones, and she smelled of Maria's lye soap and the figs they'd shared at lunch.

He wanted to say…no. He shouldn't.

"I'm sorry I was a coward." Her voice crackled like the kitchen fire. "Especially after what you did for me."

"Never think of it again. You are the bravest woman on God's own green earth." The wine fouled his tongue. He wanted to feel her fingertips on his face.

"Teach me like you did Sebastián," she said. "I don't want Renoud to live if he touches me again."

"When it's time, I'll kill Renoud. What I am, what I know, you don't want that pollution on your soul, destroying your peace."

Her finger lingered over the nick on his lip. She snatched it away when Chrétien came in with another bundle of firewood.

"I'll tell my story, if you explain why you deserted me." Chrétien fed wood onto the fire.

Isabella sat back, her hand resting near Tomás's head.

"Senhóreta Beatriz sent Katelina away to a nunnery, so I rode out to bring her back." Tomás had to speak succinctly over the wine. Isabella filled in details while he stumbled through explaining the previous day. "Then some *punxor* managed to get an arrow into my arm. Show him the arrowhead, Isabella. It's by my jerkin."

Chrétien examined the lump of metal. "Do you have enemies among Muslim horse-archers, ma dòmna?"

"No one hates Isabella." Tomás flushed hot. It must be the wine. "It's a Greek arrow."

Isabella finished their tale with brief efficiency. "Four of Renoud's men followed us. We killed them this morning. Now for your story, Chrétien. We know Renoud captured Sebastián, and the wool shed burned. What else happened?" She rested her hand a finger's width from Tomás's bare shoulder, which paralyzed him.

"What started the fire?" He asked at the same time that Isabella said, "Is the wool all burned?"

261

"No one knows how it started," Chrétien said. "Only half burned, but the other half smells scorched. Senhóreta Beatriz has the village women busy washing what's left."

"Beatriz?" Tomás couldn't say her name without scorn.

"Yes. She led the women's brigade with water buckets. Then she organized the cleanup and commanded the search when Sebastián went missing."

"Beatriz told me Sebastián was with Tomás," Isabella said. "That's why I rode out after him."

"Sebastián joined me right after I saw you, ma dòmna," Chrétien said. "We couldn't find Tomás, so we got busy at practice until the fire started. He disappeared while we were fighting the fire."

"That makes no sense." Isabella seemed calm, only puzzled.

"No one at Valerós liked my ideas," Chrétien said. "I believe the same man who pushed Senhóra Isabella over the ledge also set the fire and snatched Sebastián. But I'm merely a jongleur seeking stories to turn into songs."

"It had to be someone inside," Tomás said. "Someone who knows the tunnels under the castle."

"Then who in Valerós doesn't like you, ma dòmna?"

"When we saw Sebastián," Tomás said, "he was with men in Montcava surcoats."

"Perhaps whoever snatched him then passed him on," Chrétien said. "There aren't any strangers in Valerós."

"And Beatriz led the work?" Tomás's lips twitched. He remained angry with the silly girl.

"Including vespers," Chrétien said. With no priest in the castle—"

"Anselm went with Guillem?" Pain shot through Tomás's arm when he sat up.

"Yes. Beatriz led everyone in prayer. Then she spent the night there."

"In the chapel?"

"Banging her head on the stones, as far as I could tell."

"Maybe the silly *mignotta* is at least sorry," Tomás said, "while we're doing penance for her sins."

"Don't malign her. She's my sister," Isabella said.

"Beatriz forced Katelina out of Valerós with the knights."

"People often have a hard time when they lose someone close to them," Chrétien said. "I felt I'd lose my mind when my father died." "Don't blame Pèire for dying," Tomás said. "Beatriz caused all this, Isabella."

"No, I caused this." She touched Tomás's shoulder, startling him enough to take his breath away. "I made wrong choices, so God is punishing me."

Chrétien said, "I defer to your theology. Though God's punishments seem as arbitrary as shooting dice. Perhaps He has a method."

"Finish your story, brother," Tomás said.

"I stayed the night, thinking you'd come back," Chrétien said. "Beatriz said you went with Senhóreta Katelina, which isn't like you. I wish, dear brother, you told me the plan before you rode off."

Isabella's fingers lightly raked his shoulder, sending a shiver of reproof down to his toes. He'd scolded her for leaving on impulse, but he'd done the same thing.

"This morning I packed our gear," Chrétien said. "I called for two horses as a bonfraire in need, and then set out to meet you here. I rode across the valley to Arracheuse first. Sebastián had been there but rode away with Renoud yesterday."

"Renoud's men shot at us!" Isabella exclaimed. "Why did the Arracheuse bordoniers allow that?"

Chrétien said, "Every man in the garrison was sick in the belly since breakfast the day before."

"A poisoner?" Tomás asked.

"Most likely. I hope you had a plan for what's next."

"He does," Isabella said. "We're going to Fontfroide Abbey. We think that's where Katelina went."

"So, we'll find Guillem and the Valerós knights," Tomás said. "Then we'll ride to Fontcours, as Pèire planned. To join his old crusader friends." He didn't look at Isabella, avoiding any quarrel.

"And Sebastián?" Chrétien asked.

"Renoud will take him to Fontcours or Montcava," Isabella said. "I'm sure of it."

"We'll find him. And then call Renoud to law," Tomás said.

"I'll get the horses so we can leave." Isabella rose, ready to leave.

"We're not leaving until morning, ma dòmna." Tomás felt her freeze beside him.

"But the longer we wait, the farther Renoud takes Sebastián."

"Chrétien's horse is tired."

"And our Tomásino needs a night in bed," Chrétien said. "We want him in good repair, with two useable arms."

"All right." She seemed gloomy but didn't argue. "I'll check the horses anyway."

"Chrétien can go with you," Tomás said.

"No, I'm fine. It's close by. Tell Chrétien where the food is. He's probably about to perish from hunger."

∎

"We're taking your senhóra to Fontcours? Just the two of us?"

"Keep her away from me, Chrétien." The wine throbbed in the pulse at his temple.

"If you ask properly, brother," Chrétien said, "she'd do something nicer than knee your balls into your eyeteeth."

Tomás grabbed Chrétien's wrist, rasping his thumb over the square white scar. "On our mother's honor, keep her away from me."

"She's in love with you."

"No, she's just grateful. We had a few rough spots with Renoud's thugs yesterday and this morning."

Chrétien removed Tomás's hand. "Forget your old nightmares, dear brother. Take her to bed and get on with your life."

"I don't want to bed her."

"*Ai, per l'amor de Dèu!* You perverse leper. You want to marry the charming senhóra."

"I just don't want a woman so close to me."

Chrétien teased like he did in the training barracks at Cairo. "You want bambinos and fidelity. You want to forget your vows and *sleep* with her. This is disgusting."

"Keep her away from me, Chrétien."

Isabella's voice called to the cat in the courtyard, startling Tomás. Due to the large dose of medicinal wine, he didn't know how loudly he'd spoken. She called again, trying to charm the cat to her. He feared she'd heard them, while Chrétien sat silently laughing.

She came in, carrying honeycomb in a bed of chestnut leaves.

"You made it back safely." Tomás slurred his words, and felt he sounded too interested.

She nodded. "The horses are fine, except Tomás's is lame and needs longer to recover."

"We'll have to leave it in Anfos's care," Chrétien said, "and then fetch it...later."

"Yes. Look, I found a bee log. Do you want some honey?"

"No, thank you, ma dòmna. I'm going into the bushes to vomit." Chrétien walked across the yard, leaving the door open behind him.

"Is Chrétien ill?" She sat on the bench near the pallet where he lay and broke off a piece of honeycomb, stretching to hand it to him.

The honey dripped onto his fingers. "He's plagued by scrofula of the tongue. I offered to remove it for him."

She licked away the honey drizzling down the back of her wrist, which he found distracting. She bit into the honeycomb, a drop of it escaping from the corner of her mouth. "Shall we save some honeycomb for Chrétien?"

"No." He wanted to catch that drop of honey so badly his chest hurt and the wound on his arm throbbed. "He should have stayed if he wanted some."

·

Isabella went to fetch water. A marbled newt scampered into the reedy marsh at the well. She hauled the heavy oak bucket up from the well, hand over hand, pulling the rope that chafed her palms, which led to picturing the open wound of her recent savior.

"*Keep her away from me, Chrétien.*"

Of course. She'd refused when he begged for help. She'd accepted his comfort but didn't offer her own. Earlier, she'd committed a blood sin, without thinking ahead of the consequences.

Her past days' failures would haunt her long after she found a priest and confessed her sins.

I was foolish. My impulse hurt Valerós.

Tomás took an arrow for me, and I showed nothing but disgust.

I was a coward when my own savior needed help.

Of course he wanted her kept at a distance. The wonder was that he'd still help her find Sebastián and Katelina. But that was only because he'd given his oath to Pèire.

Knights who swore their lives to each other.

She wanted to lead knights, and the first knight she rode out with, she'd nearly gotten him killed.

"Let me help you, ma dòmna." Chrétien met her on the path and relieved her of both buckets. "I found bread and cheese in the kitchen. Is that enough dinner for you? You aren't disappointed?"

"Disappointed? How could I be? Tomorrow we ride horses." She repressed her need to brush away the cinders of humiliation.

"*Ai*, a woman after my own heart." Inside the cottage, Chrétien said, "May I suggest, given how far Tomás wants us to ride across a countryside invaded by the French army—"

"Get to the point, brother."

"You should dress in Tomás's spare clothes, ma dòmna. I also have an extra hauberk in my travel kit, but mine's too large for you."

When the table was set, Tomás rose from that pallet to sit at the table, still looking pale. Chrétien sat beside her, casually placing his long, tall body between her and his brother. She saw the obvious: Chrétien would do as his brother asked. But she already knew to step back whenever she smelled spices and oiled leather or saw the fine hairs on Tomás's forearm if his sleeve fell back. Distance, yes, that was the answer to her disturbed feelings.

"I was pleased to find cheese in a goodman's house," Chrétien said. "And wine. Perhaps a heretic's life isn't as miserable as I've been led to believe."

"Maria makes excellent wine," Tomás said. "And Anfos the woodcutter says if you allow one sin, any other is as bad as the first."

Is that how it worked? Well, in the morning, when they went forward, she'd probably have to allow many sins.

45
Vulcan with the Army

Jean-Luc in the Aude valley
Early May

IT MIGHT HAVE BEEN from being able to speak openly in Jean-Luc's native tongue, or his familiarity with life in a standing camp, or his natural inclination to be useful. But in a few short days he was accepted in the French camp as if he'd been with these men a long time. He'd have felt more comfortable, however, if he weren't looking over his shoulder every moment lest he encounter men who knew him when he last rode with Hugues de Beaurain.

And if he weren't looking in every part of the camp for a one-eyed man with a bad conscience. First it was two thousand men, but more men arrived each day, so Jean-Luc moved from campfire to campfire, hoping to encounter the man who could restore his reputation, return honor to his life. No luck so far, but it remained Jean-Luc's best hope.

He couldn't enter the circles around campfires with men who might know about Gerard de Chartrain. There wasn't anyone he could tell about finding the dead courier, or anyone who might know related rumors, but the other information he needed was when Viscount Gerald might join Hugues de Beaurain's camp.

However, Jean-Luc had work to do, which helped to order his mind. Each day he found it easier to chase away the thoughts that had debilitated him since he left Valerós. The challenges came at night, when he clasped the braid plaited with her hair and imagined her fingers stroking his neck. And he heard Yves's voice in the night again, although he couldn't make out the words.

He worked for Eustache, a master armorer from the Loire Valley who spoke pure French from the Pays de France, which Jean-Luc heard as if it were music. Short, squat, and hairy as the mastiffs guarding the armory, Master Eustache seemed more like a farmer's son than a warrior. From his years at the forge, Eustache had massive shoulders and thighs, and his huge, rough hands looked as if he worked iron without a hammer.

The day after Jean-Luc arrived in the camp, he found Master Eustache at his elbow, examining his handiwork.

"You have the same metal-working skills as the dwarves of Charlemagne's empire." Master Eustache's huge lumpy face was a mask of solemn judgment.

"I can't accept the compliment, Master Eustache." Jean-Luc knew his own deficiencies.

"But I meant the dancing dwarves who clowned in the throne room, not the ones who built the magical swords."

"I don't dance well either," Jean-Luc said. "Yet no one ever faulted me for trying."

Master Eustache conceded that Jean-Luc made up for lack of knowledge with his strength and diligence. They agreed Jean-Luc was a repairman, not a craftsman, and there was plenty of work to be done to maintain the camp's equipment.

Master Eustache liked him enough to take Jean-Luc along as an assistant to inspect the war-engines after the soldiers had spent several days at practice, strewing rocks in a grain field, aiming for the limestone uplift on the far side of the field.

Hugues de Beaurain owned three large magnons and a half-dozen petrarias for flinging smaller boulders. Master Eustache lovingly called the big machines "mangonels," even though they were monstrous modern pieces, powered by counterweight and torsion instead of being sprung by men using their own weight to haul back and release the payload, as with the petrarias. The practicing soldiers slung boulders over a hundred yards with amazing precision.

The master pulled one machine from the practice battery and set to work with Jean-Luc to determine how much repair it needed. A brace of officers paused nearby, speaking loudly to hear each other over the practice.

"You know I want precision as well as obedience," one voice said above the rest.

After days of dreading an encounter, Jean-Luc stood a lance-length from Hugues de Beaurain. He bent his head over the work, keeping his back turned to the marquis. Jean-Luc doubted that Hugues would recognize him after so many years, but he wanted to spare his old commander the embarrassment of discovering that his camp sheltered a man condemned to hang.

The mangonel required a complete rebuild, so Jean-Luc and the master began tearing it down so the main metal parts could be carried back to the forge in camp.

"Hold the bastard-sucking machine," Master Eustache said. "Keep it steady while I put the cross-brace in."

Jean-Luc strained to hold the crossing beam, feeling his muscles stretch to the point of tearing, just as Hugues shouted a warning to a rider galloping in among the battery of machines. Jean-Luc glanced up at the rider whose horse pranced by his side.

Hélène de Beaurain, in her usual self-proclaimed glory. Or Potiphar's wife, as Jean-Luc felt her to be. Her dark hair, shamelessly free of its head-cover, flew around her face in slinky curls as she loved it to do when she was showing off. Before he could bend his head to escape notice, she caught his eye, and then tossed her head, laughing at him.

46

Three Silver Morabatins

Tomás in the Pyrenees foothills
16 days before Pentecost

A MARINE MIST SETTLED on the hill and drizzled cold rain, so the early morning smelled of the sea. The hut had cooled and become moist with Mediterranean air. The previous days' travails caught up with Tomás in the night, and he felt pain with every movement. Wearing just his breeches, he stretched to relieve the stiffness. Every fiber in his body wanted to crawl back under the sheepskin.

"You can't trust a woman," Miquel whispered. Tomás refused to answer. His father shrugged, as he did whenever the boys misbehaved. "Except your mother. But even she is weak."

Tomás breathed smoke from the fire and listened to Miquel as he recounted every mistake Tomás had made because of a woman.

In the arbor after dawn, Chrétien rewrapped Tomás's wound. He looked up as Isabella joined them. She appeared as a squire in leather leggings and jerkin, wearing a linen undershirt and Tomás's second-best boots of soft leather, worn at the heel and toe, laces knotted and reknotted.

Chrétien said, "The length is about right. But you need to work at the quintain if you expect to fill out a jerkin like a man."

"I have low expectations for that. Are you almost ready to ride?"

She'd brought up the horses, who nickered and stamped in the yard, also eager to be off. When Chrétien insisted, she added a quilted gambeson and Tomás's least-best hauberk over her shirt and leggings.

They planned to ride over the eastern ridge to catch the Narbonne market road and then to turn toward the abbey at Lagrasse, because Renoud had said that he and Hugues were headed there. However, after half a day on the road, they learned from shepherds who heard it from some itinerant weavers that Simon de Montfort's men swarmed the lower country roads.

"We bluff our way through," Chrétien said. "By telling the truth. We are on our way to join French forces near Toulouse. Gerard and the Marquis de Beaurain are French, right?"

"We have to be in Toulouse by Pentecost. We have to find Katelina," Isabella said. "And we must avoid any men Renoud might have left behind. He must know we're searching for Sebastián."

"So much can go wrong if we encounter any French forces," Tomás said. "There's only two…three of us. We need to be cautious."

"Are you my headstrong, daring brother," Chrétien said, "or a changeling left in the night? Caution? Fine, we'll do it your way."

They agreed that the best tact was to cross over two more ridges eastward, moving closer to the Great Sea and adding at least two days to their journey.

At their mid-afternoon rest break, Tomás wandered away from them to sit on a rock in the sun alone. And to worry how he was to endure two weeks on the trail with a woman who sat a horse better and showed more courage than any man he knew.

·

"Chrétien, see this knife and this dagger?"

"Òc, senhóra."

"Pèire gave these to me. Teach me to use them."

"You slice bread by—"

"I want to be able to slice a man if I have to."

He called across the meadow to Tomás. "Our mistress wants me to teach close hand work."

"I don't care what you do." Tomás's answer could barely be heard.

Chrétien pulled out his own knife. "A sewing lesson would be easier, but you already refused that."

Then they began the same exercises he'd taught Sebastián.

On the road, wherever they rode, flowering viburnum and terebinth crept onto the narrow rocky trail. A copse of Aleppo pine or a stand of white oak occasionally rose over the gorse. The dense

271

underbrush forced them to stay on the tortuously twisting trail that seemed to double or triple the distance between one hill and the next. The struggle to find the road in the daytime continued into the bad dreams she had at night, full of impotent pursuit and fearful flight, trying to reach Sebastián, frustrated at every turn. They slept in shepherds' rude huts, with Chrétien and Tomás lying across the doorway, barring any intruders who might appear.

Each day, whenever they rested the horses, she practiced with Chrétien, though the drills were the hardest physical work she'd ever done. Baking in the hauberk and gambeson, she felt sweat run in rivulets down her chest and stomach. Tomás's shirt.

■

Tomás in the Aude valley
12 days before Pentecost

Tomás's spirits rose once they left the higher hills. The cicadas and crickets sang out that summer was at hand. His bones felt better in the warmer weather. Maria's cloves soothed his tooth. Shrubby growths of prickly juniper, arbutus, and cork oak kept them on the trail. If a doubt rose in choosing what might be a goat path instead of the main trail, the rockrose and tall rosemary in the undergrowth pushed them back to the correct stony way.

Although they needed to rest the horses more often because of the heat, the roads became easier as they descended from the upper hills. Despite her impatience to find Sebastián and Katelina, Isabella called out for them to halt whenever it grew too warm to push the horses.

On the sixth day they'd traveled, when they had less than two weeks until they had to be in Toulouse, the afternoon turned especially hot. They let the horses rest by a creek while they climbed the next hill on foot to glimpse the trail ahead. In the shaded valley below, they saw meadows flooded with lupine, lilies, and buttercups. Black kites played overhead, and larks sang in the trees.

"This horse the seneschal lent me is skittish," Chrétien said. "It's a constant chore to keep her from dancing off."

"Pèire never had skittish horses," Isabella said.

"Then some stranger sneaked this horse into Pèire's stable."

"You're just making excuses because you don't know how to handle a horse."

"Take my dagger and drive it into my heart, ma dòmna. You couldn't say worse to wound me."

"You two are as bad as children," Tomás said. "You've been squabbling all day."

Chrétien made a face at Isabella. "This beast is skittish. No matter whose horse it was."

"*Bon Dèu*, stop quarrelling." Tomás muttered.

Back on the trail, Tomás eased his mount ahead of them, his neck prickling with the heat. Or with jealousy for Chretien's friendship.

Isabella proved a hard-riding companion, finding ways to help when they camped, staying quiet when they met strangers, and doing whatever they insisted would keep her safe. Her sole rebellion was to refuse to wear a mail coif. It was too hot, she protested, and neither he nor Chrétien would wear one in this weather. Besides, on this trail they encountered only sheepherders and small bands of itinerant weavers and boot makers, every single one of them peaceful goodmen.

Down the hillside, men quarried limestone, the syncopated sound of their hammers echoing up from the pit. When the travelers reached the quarry, Tomás called out a greeting in the common tongue. The stone workers, mummified in lime dust, didn't respond.

Two men had barricaded the trail. Within a ragged corral made of pikes tied together, a swarm of barking, flea-bitten hounds rushed back and forth, baying.

"This be a toll, if it pleases God," said the taller of the two men.

They dressed in the manner of crusaders returned from the Outremer, draped in a motley assortment of Frank and Turcopole hauberks and cuirasses, with the filthiest breeches under heaven and leather bindings crisscrossing their naked calves. The taller one had the concave chest and bulging abdomen of a wine sot, and the shorter man had a face like a battering ram, plus the massive chins and quivering swill-pot belly of a man intemperate with both wine and food. Although the tall man spoke first, only the shorter one seemed to possess at least a small portion of intelligence.

"Please God? I don't know why it should please Him," Tomás said. "Please your own purse is more like it. What lord keeps a toll on this road?"

"Here, now," the squat man said, "we have the concession from these stone-cutters, who need good soldiers to protect them from brigands. What the toll buys is protection on this road."

"I have my own protection." Tomás touched his sword. "And I'm not of a mind to thieve rocks from quarrymen."

"Just pay him," Chrétien muttered at his side, loudly enough that the toll-men could hear. Isabella, mercifully, remained silent.

"*Òc*, that be the wise course," the man said. "It will be three silver morabatins for the likes of you grand knights."

"Three pieces of silver?" Tomás said. "I'd as soon give you three slivers with my steel sword, you scrofulous knave."

"There's no call for that here. We have the concession."

"You are highwaymen, hoping no lord of this valley comes along to stop your thieving." Tomás said.

While he quarreled with the toll-masters, Chrétien dismounted and stood ready to take up his sword. Unfortunately, Isabella also stepped down from her horse. Knowing the toll-men wouldn't let them pass peacefully, Tomás wanted her back on her horse worse than he wanted the mistral to blow these beggars back to the Outremer.

"We're not from this country and don't have God's own reason to pay your spit-licking toll." Tomás flicked the sign to Chrétien to mount his horse, praying that Isabella would follow.

Chrétien had one foot in a stirrup, not yet ready to swing over and mount, when the ugliest of the diseased curs ran out, barking and snarling at the horse's prancing hooves. The horse reared, knocking aside a brace of pikes from the makeshift dog corral. Then it bolted through the opening.

Isabella leaped into her saddle and followed, while Tomás booted the barking mastiff in the head and struck out at it with his javelin. The dog grabbed the javelin in its jaws, and Tomás flung javelin and dog together into the pikes, wrenching his injured arm. Hampered by the pack horse trailing on a lead, he spurred his mount through the narrow gap in the corral.

Chrétien had a strong enough hold and balance that he could grasp his horse's saddle, but couldn't get free of the stirrup or pull up onto the saddle. The horse was too frightened to hear Chrétien's commands.

As Isabella brought her horse apace with Chrétien's, she looped her javelin through the holds in his saddle and then pulled pack on his horse while dipping to the side of her own saddle. She boosted Chrétien up so that in a few more heartbeats he'd gained his seat and then reined in his horse.

Tomás halted a few yards away to give Chrétien's spooked animal room to breathe. Isabella dismounted and took the frightened beast in hand, talking and blowing in its face.

"I wish you'd whisper in my nose," Chrétien said, "to make my heart stop pounding."

"Scared, were you?" Tomás said.

"Only afraid something might happen to my rebec. I should have tied it down better."

"Our friends are about to join us," Tomás said.

"We can take them, brother, unless they set their rabid dogs on us," Chrétien said.

Chrétien slid from his horse, stifling a cry of pain as he stepped to the ground. He cursed under his breath as he drew his sword and dagger to stand with Tomás as the raggedy toll-masters loped down the trail toward them.

"Can that horse be ridden?" Tomás called to Isabella.

"No, but it will follow us," she said.

"Please get on my horse, Chrétien. I'll ride with Isabella."

The peasant toll-masters advanced within a few pikes' length, shouting for their ill-behaved dogs to follow them.

"May you rot in a lepers' house. If it please God!" Tomás called as he sat behind Isabella with as much grace as possible, and they got all four horses started down the trail ahead of their persecutors.

Chrétien's forehead glistened with a waxy sweat, but he spurred his new mount ahead, calling to his own horse to follow. Perhaps for no other reason than that they traveled away from the hell-hounds, the skittish horse came along, and the palfrey loaded with their food and blankets came just as willingly. Moments later they still heard the blaring and trumpeting of the hounds, although the dogs seemed to be raising the devil's own ruckus without actually chasing them.

"You were magnificent!" he said in Isabella's ear.

He felt her shift in the high wooden saddle.

"Sebastián and I practiced that move. Thank God, Chrétien knew what to do."

"But, Isabella, you did it! What a knight you'd make!"

He settled in close behind her, his hands resting on the saddle back, trying to quell his feelings.

The road swung close to the river, where they found shade for a rest. Isabella and Tomás dismounted, but Chrétien stayed in his saddle, letting the horse have enough rein to drink from the stream.

Isabella talked the spooked horse into letting her near. She stroked it and murmured reassurances.

"Are you alright, brother?" Tomás called to Chrétien.

"My leg is broken," Chrétien said. "When I put my weight on it, I felt a too-familiar bit of pain."

Isabella came up beside Tomás. "Lean on us to dismount, Chrétien. This horse needs rest, so you'll have to give up malingering."

The two of them caught Chrétien as he worked free of the saddle. They let him down easily, although he was much taller than either of them.

"We must be close to a village where we can find an inn or a householder who will board us for the night," Tomás said.

"You'll have to spend the three pennies you saved on the toll." Chrétien turned to Isabella. "Ma dòmna, I bet you didn't know our Parzival is a miser."

Lubos and Jacob

IF ONLY YOU COULD *choose a brother like my father chose me to be his son, the world would be a better place.*

Down on the farming plains, it was easy to find food and sleep in warmth. Lubos had plenty of time for contemplation. He spent an afternoon by a stream that fed the Aude, killing fish and thinking.

He worried about being like Esau. People laughed at Esau because Jacob tricked their father into giving away the blessing. And so, wasn't Jacob a thieving liar? How did a bastard like Jacob end up wrestling with an angel and winning? If there were justice in this mired world, then it should have been the angel who triumphed, given Jacob's lies.

It must have been a mistake. The God in the story was just another of the stone spirits. After all, Jacob had a stone for his pillow the night he dreamed of wrestling with an angel. Not all spirits have men's best concerns in their hearts. He learned from Aykuna how some spirits can take a person's will and cause a man to follow like the walking dead, serving that spirit as faithfully as Lubos served Père-Izsák.

He learned from Aykuna how to perform the conjuring to take a person's will, but you shouldn't have to do that with a son. A son wants to come to his father, like a needle seeks the lodestone. That's what Lubos wanted: a son who'd follow selflessly, the way Lubos followed Père-Izsák. What a blessing it would be! A far greater blessing than what Jacob stole from his father Isaac.

Brothers cause discontent. But with a son, you enjoy the same satisfaction in which the gods rejoice—the good gods, not Satan whose fall created all evil.

✱✱✱

277

PART FIVE
Nemesis in Leather

For this, I have less good knowledge,
Since I yearn for what I cannot have;
If what they say proves true,
It is certain
True courage is power
For he who owns his suffering.

— Guilhem IX,
"Pos Vezem de novel florir"

In Part Five

47
Pilgrims, Perfected

Isabella in the Aude valley
12 days before Pentecost

WILD HONEYSUCKLE AND CLEMATIS tangled in the scrubby brush along field edges, and a heat haze rose in the roadway. But their trio made heartening progress once the hills smoothed out and tumbled them onto the plains, where olive groves and cereal fields replaced sheep pastures.

Isabella had ridden hard for six days, believing each day she was that much closer to finding Sebastián, to rescuing the new master of Valerós from Renoud of Montcava. Tomás had finally learned not to mention that infernal marriage Pèire had arranged with Gerard de Chartrain. Rather, she believed that as soon as they caught up with Katelina and Marshal Guillem, her best dream would come true.

She'd ride into Toulouse in command of a dozen knights, prepared to frighten Renoud at the pit of whatever he had for a soul.

That afternoon, when they came upon a scattering of houses, Isabella smelled oven fires with rosemary and roasting garlic. Don Tomás asked a group of children playing near the road if there was an inn, but when they saw Tomás's ruined face, the girls shrieked and ran into the hedges.

Chrétien interceded.

"*Hola, amigas y amigos!* We are pilgrims, taking my brother to be healed at Fontfroide. Can you direct us to an inn?"

"What's wrong with him?" one brave boy ventured to ask.

"A Saracen cast a spell on our mother and turned him into a Moor," Chrétien said. "But it's not painful or dangerous."

Tomás glowered.

After Chrétien dropped a copper penny among them, the whole clattering troop led the travelers to the crossroads.

"We could have found this without spending your penny," Tomás muttered.

The inn had begun as a small stone manse, but a series of rackety sheds had grown around it, some attached, some scattered around the grounds, some of timber, some merely reed-and-wattle huts. As the squire, Isabella held the horses while Tomás negotiated with the innkeeper.

"Are you pilgrims on the way to the great abbeys? Or knights who pay their own way?" the innkeeper asked.

"What's the difference?"

"Pilgrims sleep in the stable in honor of the humble birth of our lord Jesus Christ," the innkeeper said.

"And paying guests can have a room," his wife said, "with clean straw ticking and breakfast in the morning."

"The stable—" Tomás began.

"We'll take clean straw and breakfast." Chrétien produced a silver coin as if by magic.

The wife twitched a mercenary smile and made the coin disappear about as fast as Chrétien had produced it. "And there's supper in the great room now, if you want it."

A boy carried their meager baggage up to the loft, where woven stick-and-reed walls separated a trio of tiny cells. As squire, Isabella had sole possession of the hauberks and other armor, which she wrestled up the ladder-like stairs alone. When she finished and went in search of the "great room," she found a smoky, low hall with rotted rushes covering the packed-earth floor. A maze of trestle tables jumbled against each other, so close that one man's backside scarcely avoided rubbing against the man seated behind him. At one end of the crowded room, a trio of married couples ate in silent respectability amid the raucous noise. At the other end, a dozen male travelers gathered. Chrétien had already found a cup of wine and lodged himself among a quintet focused on a dice game. Tomás talked with a white-haired gentleman wearing the coat of a Narbonnese merchant.

Tomás glanced up as she approached. "Where did you tarry, boy? Get a serving girl to bring me some food. We'll eat over there." He pointed to a table near where Chrétien was lost in the dice game.

Fetching his food seemed less ignominious than hauling his armor. While she tried to get a serving girl's attention, she studied the men with whom Chrétien gambled. Most seemed to be professional travelers who carried arms, and all of them watched Tomás. Even in the dim, smoky light of the hall, he aroused attention because he was a mestitz knight who carried a sword and who clearly hailed from realms more exotic than these farming hills.

When she began guessing what they saw in Tomás, she couldn't stop staring either. After days together, she knew the sound of his breathing when he finally slept, late in the night, and she knew how he controlled a horse (Chrétien was a much better horseman). He ignored pain and was indifferent to whether he ate dry bread and sheep's cheese or a full meal. She also knew what he looked like naked. He claimed to be a mercenary with no personal wealth, yet he had the education and manners (when he chose to use them as he did now) of the Aragónese patricians she'd met in Narbonne.

A tawny-haired Adonis intently watched Chrétien, not Tomás. He wore a foot soldier's long tunic and woolen hose. Although tall and muscular, he moved in the awkward, unsure way of a young man out of his element, and he spoke to the strangers around him with the earnest, unaffected gestures of someone seeking friends with which to spend an evening.

Down the bench from her, a thin, gawky man rocked; his lips moved, in either silent prayer or paralytic spasm. Dark, lank hair fell around his sepulchral face. His moist, red lips seemed shockingly sensual amidst his otherwise ascetic features. His eyes shifted away when he wished her a good end and pressed a goodman's hand-clasp on her. When she lived in Toulouse, where goodwomen were found in every household, she'd learned to return the gesture rather than draw attention by refusing. But because she said *Bon día*, the twitching man scuttled closer to her, human stench wafting from him like the heat from the cooking fires.

"Where are you traveling?" she asked, trying not to breathe.

"I am a weaver and a good Christian," he said. She groaned inwardly, finding herself ensnared in the company of an itinerant goodman who called himself perfected. "I'm walking to the mountains. My friends say the valleys aren't safe this summer. Though I'm not afraid. My heart says God wants me to stay alive to preach."

His strange, wandering eyes made her uncomfortable, although perfected goodmen usually disconcerted her; after enduring certain priests in Toulouse, she disliked sanctimony of all brands, especially the unwashed variety, like the weaver on the bench.

"You have to wonder." He sat entranced for a moment before he continued. "Last summer I left Béziers the day before Simon de Montfort burned the city. Such a coincidence makes you ask, 'Why them and not me?' We don't believe in divine retribution, and yet—"

"It was a horrible thing, done by terrible people." Isabella had no more sophisticated explanation to offer.

He hunched, stork-like; his eyes flitted around the room while he continued inching closer to her. She braced herself, disgusted by the unhealthy smell of body waste. "I must keep preaching because of it." He rocked again. "I have mastered my flesh. I drink only water and live solely on what falls to the ground, like the nuts from trees. By All Souls I will be ready to leave this evil world, having prepared for the Endura."

He spoke of the goodmen's practice of death by fasting, an ascetic suicide, which she considered the stuff of legends, not what people really did. So, she asked ordinary travelers' questions.

"Where will you stop for the summer?"

"Why, Rennes-les-Bains, of course." He seemed surprised at the question. "If you are preparing to depart this material world, where else to go but the very home where Jesus lived when he came here with Mary Magdelene to found his dynasty."

Isabella jerked back, as if moving away from lunacy, but just then the innkeeper clapped a hand on the man's shoulder.

"Here, you. Paying folk want respite from the likes of you." The proprietor got the weaver on his feet with a practiced jerk. "You can preach your cant in the stable yard. The cows may care, but I don't." He launched the weaver toward the door, shaking his head. "Next thing, we'll have a pack of Frankish knights burning our town over cat-sucking sister-fondlers like that. May the saints preserve us."

The landlord motioned to a serving girl across the room and pointed to Isabella. The maid gestured that she was engaged. The innkeeper stalked toward her, had words, and then sent her off, first pointing to Tomás and then to Isabella as his squire, which seemed to instill a greater sense of urgency in the maid.

"What'll it be, boy?"

Isabella ordered food, indicating the three people to be served. The maid tarried nearby with another serving girl, rather than scurrying to fetch food.

"Did you see the dark knight by the fire, Fina?" the first maid asked. "I'd like to show him how to keep warm. You can tell he's seen the world."

"I prefer the innocent type, like this young squire." Fina ran her finger down Isabella's neck. "Your dark knight seems fearsome, Ines. Like he's seen things you don't want to know about."

The maid Ines laughed. "I like a hard ride that's a bit scary."

Ines wandered away, ending up a finger's width from Tomás. She smiled sweetly and offered him a cup of wine. Isabella, having never seen such a brazen seduction, didn't notice the second maid when she sat down on the bench. Wine and onions on her breath, Fina said, "Are you a virgin? Want a good time tonight?" She placed her hand on Isabella's thigh.

Isabella clamped her knees together, accidentally trapping the maid's hand. As the maid inched her hand up, Isabella crossed her legs tightly. She cleared her throat, looking to Tomás for rescue. But he was bent in rapt conversation with Ines, whose lips stayed close to his as she spoke. Fina put her hand on Isabella's neck once more and kissed her lightly on the lips. When Isabella opened her mouth, astonished, Fina thrust in her tongue. As Isabella struggled to move away, Fina's hand trapped her in the kiss.

"You, boy!" Tomás growled. "I asked you to bring my dinner, not serve the serving girls."

■

The maid lazily pulled away, laughing, gazing up at Tomás, who rather unkindly laughed too.

"Later, love," he said to the maid. "We need food first. Please bring it."

He snagged Isabella's jerkin so she knew to rise from the bench. He pointed her to the one near Chrétien.

"See if you can keep from starting a riot."

He greeted Ines, who scattered bowls of food on the table before them and then licked her upper lip as she studied Tomás again. She laughed when the innkeeper hustled her away.

"You should sleep with her," Isabella said. "There's not room enough for three of us upstairs."

"I don't sleep with servants," Tomás said. "Never have done. I'm no more interested in those women than you are." He broke the bread with his hands and gave her half. He seemed absorbed in thought and didn't look at her. "My new friend from Narbonne says Fontfroide is an easy ride from here. You'll be glad when we find Senhóreta Katelina, won't you?"

"I'm praying Guillem and the others are still there also. But it's seven days since they left Valerós."

"We shall see what we find." His eyes followed Fina the maid, his scarred lips twitching as if he might smile.

"It's less than a fortnight until Pentecost." She wanted to drag his attention back.

"Don't despair. Let's just solve the problems placed before us each day." He still watched the maid who had attacked Isabella, his twitch coming even closer to a smile.

"How philosophical," she said.

"Do you want some coins so you can join Chrétien?"

"I don't know how the game is played."

"Eat your supper and observe for a while. You'll see the rules and tricks quickly enough."

Chrétien seized the bowl Tomás handed him. He continued at the dice game while dosing himself liberally with wine. Isabella found the game to be simple and uninteresting. When Tomás joined Chrétien, the tawny Adonis with a flashing smile sat down by her.

"Mind if I sit here?"

Along with his warm smile, he offered her a goodman's hand-clasp. This time she hesitated. He still smiled, seeming not to be offended when she didn't seize his hand.

"The filthy rascal who bothered you a while ago? That's why you don't want to greet me, isn't it?"

"I was trying to be polite."

"Mad men like him give good Christians a bad name," he said. "No wonder the Franks want to torch us, even though all we want is to live a good life and come to a good end, without greedy priests stealing from you."

"I'm Catholic," she said.

"So was my mother. Where are you traveling to?" the young god asked.

"Carcassonne," Isabella lied. "My master wants to find a French lord who pays his mercenaries well."

"Mercenaries, eh? My lord lives in Toulouse."

"I heard Toulouse in your accent," she said. He seemed familiar to her, but perhaps she'd seen him in the city, although he'd have been much younger then. "Which man here is your lord?"

"He's not here. I'm on an errand for him."

"Are you a squire, too?" she asked.

"Me?" He seemed surprised by her question. "I'm just a foot-man. They say, 'Go here,' and I go, or 'Do this,' and I do it. What do squires do?"

"Carry baggage and have our ears boxed."

"I could do that." He made her laugh. "There's not much difference between us. I can't think why they chose me to work for a lord. They want to make me into a soldier, but I don't like to fight."

This Adonis had to be the most guileless person in the world, but as large as he was, it seemed a shame such a man wasn't a warrior.

"Why not? Fighting is what men do."

He shrugged. "Me being bigger than most, some man always wants to pick me out. I tired of it long ago. That's why I like being a goodman. We don't believe in fighting. Nowadays in Toulouse, though, there's street fighting every night, with the White Brotherhood hunting goodmen and Jews. I don't want any part of it."

"Street fighting? I didn't know."

"In Toulouse, Bishop Folquet stirs people up against the heretics." Adonis shrugged again. "But it's the same thugs who always pounded me. Now they're just hunting for a bigger fight."

"What's your name? Where do you live in Toulouse?" Isabella asked. She still felt she knew him.

"I'm Durán. I live near the church of St-Sernin now, but I grew up by the market at the southern gate. What's your name?"

Isabella shivered as he described her old neighborhood. And she needed a name for herself.

"Pèire," she said.

"You don't look like a Pèire."

"I don't?" Everyone in Valerós claimed she did.

"No, every Pèire I know is old. You look more like a Martí or a Ricoldo."

"How do people's faces match with their names?"

"When I look at a man, I try to imagine his everyday life." Durán smiled his disarming, beatific smile. "Then if I learn his name, I try to connect it with his face. Of course, men don't always tell me their real names."

"Why not?"

"Oh, you know." Adonis smiled again and shrugged. "Do you want to get out of here? It's so smoky and noisy. Let's go outside and talk."

"I don't think my master will allow that," she said.

"Why not?" he asked as he put his hand on her thigh.

48
Cavallers Fada

TOMÁS WATCHED THE SMALL boy turn the spit at the open hearth, where a half-dozen fowls dropped fat on the fire, making the room even smokier, adding to the odor of too many bodies crammed together. But then, he smelled his own horse on his clothes.

The change in Isabella since they had been on the road was remarkable. She wasn't happy, of course, but she seemed more vibrant, as if this journey brought her back to life. She'd been fearless when she saved Chrétien from his runaway horse. After the fey females of Toulouse and the lazy, over-pampered ladies on Cyprus, she seemed a goddess. Diana? Was that the one with the arrows?

Chrétien nudged him. "Your squire is trying to beat me out of the friendship I hoped to make later tonight."

Tomás glanced toward Isabella and saw that sweet-faced young footman moving his hand up her leg while she froze under his touch, her sun-scorched face turning even redder.

Like a goddess, yes. Eris. Wasn't she the goddess of Disorder, the one who started the Trojan War?

"Excuse me, senhór." Tomás tucked his head between Isabella and the man, pitching his voice low and trying to sound friendly. "Take your hand off my squire, please. Or I will kill you. Which would be a great misfortune, because you seem to be a reasonable man."

The young man pulled back surprised, but his smile stayed in place. Tomás tried to place the man's face, considering every city they'd passed through in the last year.

"Pardon, *senhór cavaller*. I meant no harm," the man said in the marketplace dialect of Toulouse. "We're just getting to be friends."

"My squire doesn't have friends." Tomás wrapped an arm around Isabella's shoulder, tugging her from the bench. As he feigned dragging a squire out for chastisement, his hand slipped down and rested on her waist, and he automatically pulled her close to him.

"*Cavallers fada*." The flirting maid hissed at them in passing. *Fairy knights.* "No use wasting time with the likes of you."

"Don't say a word," Tomás said in Isabella's ear.

He pushed her up the narrow ladder, seeing that even in breeches and hose she didn't walk anything like a real boy. He needed to keep her covered with a hauberk.

"I didn't ask that to happen."

Through his teeth, he said, "You are an intelligent woman. However, you missed certain basic knowledge in your education."

"But I didn't do anything."

Inside their portion of the loft, he slammed the rattle-trap reed door that formed most of one wall.

"Just go to sleep. Not there—sleep over by the armor where a squire belongs."

"Your arm needs bandaging before we sleep," she said.

"Chrétien can do it later."

"And when will that be? Before dawn, or just after he's taken all the silver from the others tossing dice?"

He had to acquiesce. She did the job efficiently, without showing her previous disgust for his bared body. And his wound had healed enough that Maria's salve didn't sting like holy hell. But he pulled away from Isabella's soothing touch as soon as she finished. He jerked his shirt back over his arms.

"Don't forget to use the stuff Maria gave you," he said. "Your face is burned worse than ever."

"Thank you for reminding me," she said. From the tone of her voice, he sensed no gratitude.

"Go to sleep now."

After making the devil's own racket moving hauberks and other gear out of her way and then preparing the pallet to sleep on, she blew out the lighted rush. Tomás didn't mind the semi-dark.

He'd thrown back the shutters so they had starlight in the room. He tried to quiet his mind, but seeing that tavern maid stick her tongue in Isabella's mouth was too much to bear. And the randy footman was nearly as bad, mistaking her for another kind of boy. He lay on the straw mat and tried to put it from his mind, focusing on how blasted funny it had been. How she could know so much and be so ignorant? But then he'd again see the wench with her tongue thrust down Isabella's throat.

Peace reigned for several moments, except for the jagged sound of her breathing.

"Do you think he's afraid?" Isabella asked.

"No. Sebastián is just like Pèire Leteric." He guessed that she meant her son. "He's never had the sense to be afraid of anything. And he knows how to take care of himself."

"At least Renoud won't hurt him."

Tomás hoped as much but didn't feel as confident. He reached across to touch her shoulder, to comfort her, but doubting his own intentions, he instead wrapped his cloak tighter.

She fell quiet again. But he considered her questions.

"Why are you so sure Renoud won't hurt him?" he asked. "Sebastián is the heir. If he's out of the way, it all goes to Renoud."

"He wants Sebastián to be the donzel of Montcava." She paused, clearly wanting to change the subject. "People think I'm odd, don't they? Why? What do you think they see?"

The first day God separated the light from darkness. He couldn't say it aloud.

Then the woven-reed door rattled open. Tomás leaped up. Isabella moved in a nearly identical way as they both stood with their knives out. But it was just Chrétien, cheery from his dice game, smelling of smoke and burned animal fat, whistling. And thumping. His hurt leg was bound up in a splint.

"Now here's a jolly sight. I get to sleep between the most popular couple at the pilgrims' inn."

"Shut up, Chrétien," Tomás said, as he'd done ten thousand times in this life. He dropped back to his mat, turned his face to the wall, and pulled his cloak over his head, wondering if it was true that God answered prayer.

Chrétien stripped and crawled onto his own straw ticking in blessed silence. The three of them breathed in the darkness for several moments.

"Latins just don't know how to cook goat properly." Chrétien called these people *Latins* like the Saracens did.

Tomás groaned. "Why does wine keep you awake? It puts other people to sleep."

"When Latins prepare goat, the meat is too old when butchered," Chrétien continued. "Then it's cut against the grain and stewed too long. And God forbid a Latin cook ever make a happy union with spices. It's either too much or not enough, or it's the wrong choice altogether."

"Swallow your tongue, Chrétien."

The room was silent for a single breath and a heartbeat.

"Isabella's boyfriend helped me splint my leg. He's very nice. And it's always a pleasure to have a man take off your hose, even in a public room. I'm giving fair warning, ma dòmna: I intend to steal him away from you. At first I thought he wasn't bright, but he's just naïve. And naïveté is as attractive on him as it is on you, ma dòmna."

"Chrétien, go to sleep," Tomás said. "Or go sleep with your new friend. But stop talking."

Again, Chrétien allowed a few heartbeats of silence. "You don't want me to tell you that Sebastián was here?"

Isabella pounced on Chrétien, who pretended to be so drunk he couldn't defend himself.

"All right, I'll tell you," he said, "whether you want me to or not. Our *fadrin* came to the inn yesterday with Renoud and a dozen men-at-arms. They stopped for a midday meal and then left your friend Durán to wait for some missing soldiers."

"Are you sure?" Isabella asked breathlessly.

"Yes," Chrétien said. "And Durán is to tell anyone seeking Renoud that they've gone to meet Simon de Montfort in Carcassonne."

Isabella groaned. "We'd never have thought to go there."

"And we still aren't. Am I right, Chrétien? Where is your new friend to go next?"

"Durán is supposed to wait three days for a handful of Renoud's mercenaries. But I suspect they'll never show."

"And Renoud? He's reached Toulouse or Fontcours by now," Tomás said.

"Durán thinks Renoud is going to Laurac to visit his mother first," Chrétien said. "He has Sebastián with him."

"What's Eloïse doing there?" Isabella said.

"Giving her money away as a good Christian does," Chrétien said. "The senhóra is living among the goodwomen there."

"*Ai Dèu*, no."

Long after Isabella and Chrétien slept, Tomás lay quietly.

"Tomás," Miquel whispered, "did you see how long that maid's tongue was? She licked your senhóra halfway to—"

"Please stop." He pleaded with Miquel. "I want to forget."

"You're a smart boy, Tomásino, not a minnow-brained leper. Have you forgotten what joy is?"

49

Potiphar's Wife

Jean-Luc outside Carcassonne
12 days before Pentecost

"YOU CAN'T BE HERE. It isn't safe," Jean-Luc whispered.

"It's exciting," Hélène said.

"Not to me. I don't want you here."

The woman came to the small tent where he slept at the end of an alley in the armorers' encampment. He didn't ask how she found him, because Hélène managed it every time, no matter how he tried to escape.

"You need to be with me, Jean-Luc."

"Don't call me that. Here, I'm Jehan the smith."

"How deliciously low. I've missed you so much, and I'm lonely here, Jehan the smith."

"Then go be with your husband."

"It isn't the same as with you. He's never interested in playing. The French lords on this crusade are all disgustingly poor, backward asses. And the lords of the south are too distracted by Simon de Montfort to think of love."

"As well they might be." He pushed away her hand where she stroked the burned flesh on his arm. Then he batted her other hand away when she touched the braid in his hair. He rose from his pallet with all the speed and dexterity his wounded leg allowed, groping in the dark tent for his tunic.

"The seigneurs have nothing to fear," she said. "Hugues says the only real soldiers are Simon's knights. Everyone else from the Pays de France is here on a lark. When it gets hot, they'll go home."

"And you'll go home right now, Hélène." He pointed to the path back up through the camp.

"No one will come near your tent while I'm here. I paid good silver for that. And it can't hurt you to talk to me," she pouted.

"Yes, it can. You've been trapping me into 'just talking' for eighteen years, and I never—"

"It can't be eighteen years," she said. "We'd have been children."

"We *were* children when you first trapped me."

"You can't say 'trapped,' darling. You were far too willing and I was too inexperienced. But you were the best. The only one I'm always in love with."

"It didn't mean anything then, and it doesn't now." He lied about his youthful heartache, when he discovered he was neither her first nor only lover.

"I was too young when they married me off," she said. "A man three times my age. Anyone would want a better love life."

"You were seventeen, and Hugues is not some doddering old man." He didn't let his mind wander to the woman he loved in Valerós, who was half his age. "And he has always honored you."

"Please don't preach 'honor' again," she said. "I had to listen to that nonsense the whole time we last spent together. Hugues has his freedom and he gives me mine."

"We weren't 'together.' We were just torturing each other." Jean-Luc wouldn't say it again. He'd said it so many times in Venice and Zara: *I won't sleep with my liege lord's wife.* Instead, he asked the brutal question he'd wondered since then. "Was it you who destroyed me?"

"Whatever do you mean?"

"You threatened me when I left you in Venice. Did you start those lies about me in Constantinople?"

"*Mon amour*, how could you think that? We have always been friends, even when you aren't as friendly as I wish." She grasped his hand, which he pulled back. "Remember what we are for each other. Though you denied me so soundly in Venice, you hurt my feelings."

"All I am for you is a male member transported on two legs."

She laughed, which startled him, because he felt sure the whole camp heard. But then, other women's voices echoed from across the way, where the whores from the baggage train sported with the foot soldiers. He asked the next question.

"Then was it Hugues? Did he learn you and I betrayed him?"

"He would never care." She laughed again. "If he did, he'd be more direct than to accuse you of thievery or murder. In truth, he seemed quite sad about what happened to you. And about your brother, too. It must have been a very bad time."

"It isn't over yet," he said.

"You've changed your mind about deserting me?" she said brightly, touching him.

He moved her hand. "No, I mean, my bad times aren't over. And I haven't changed my mind. You're married to my lord, and my heart is—"

She trilled her irritating, staccato laugh. "Don't tell me you seduced some young thing? And your sense of honor makes you want to marry her? No, wait, I know you. Some sweet thing seduced you. Did you tell her how you gave me your pledge once upon a time?"

"You should go," Jean-Luc said.

"No, I came to fetch you away from here. Come back to our camp. Hugues will kill the fatted calf to welcome you, I swear it. You and Yves were always his favorites."

"Do not tell him I'm here, Hélène. It would put him in a compromising position. I'm sentenced to hang."

"That happened in Constantinople, years ago. No one remembers any more. You're running from phantoms. Look at you. You're a scarecrow. Where's the beautiful boy I love so?"

"Please don't do that." He once more removed her arm from around his neck.

"*Ai Dèu*, how I've missed you. But I won't tease you about being lovers. No one should ever tease you, you're so sensitive."

"I'm sure you stayed far too busy to miss me."

"You are my only true friend." She spoke tenderly in his ear. "Since we were children, no one has spoken to my heart as you have."

She'd never used that method of attack before, so he didn't have an answer ready.

"If I were a man, I'd make the world treat you better," she said. "But I'm a woman, so what can I do, except beg my husband to move the world for you? You need rest. You need to shave that awful beard. Let me order your favorite meal. It's quail and truffles, isn't it? Come and savor it in my pavilion. I'll speak to Hugues tonight."

"I can't let you do that."

"At least let me rub away your headache. We can be friends here for a few moments."

He let her pull him down to lie with his head in her lap, without understanding how she once more got her way. She talked about the days when they'd first met in her uncle's garden in Antioch. Then she reminded him of the little dog he'd taught tricks when they were last together.

"Who's your poor girl?" Her question seemed abrupt.

"There isn't one."

"Yes, there is. You've changed. I can feel it when I touch you."

"It's just from the way I live. I met someone in passing, but nothing will come of it."

"Then I'll promise not to be jealous."

"There's nothing in my life for you to be jealous of. Why do you come after me now, Hélène?"

"Because I've always loved you. And I feel so sorry for you. You belong with your own kind, not hiding out alone with the ribauds and rabble like an outlaw."

"I *am* an outlaw. And this isn't a safe place for you. I can't protect you if anyone sees us." He opened the tent's flap to usher her out.

"*Mon amour*, I always have my guard with me," she said. "He's the sole person I trust, besides you."

Jean-Luc glanced over to where she pointed to her guard. Even in the dark he saw the man who had held the horse when Renoud of Montcava helped him escape from Constantinople. Who had a *crux lunata* tattoo like Hugues and Renoud.

50
Leather and Bone

Isabella in the Aude valley
11 days before Pentecost

ISABELLA COULDN'T RESIST TEMPTATION. Alone in the morning, she picked up Tomás's sword, just to feel its weight. She tried to read the maker's name engraved near the hilt, but it wasn't any alphabet she knew. The grip, bone wrapped in leather laces, had taken on the shape of its owner's hand, sweat having transformed the leather into a substance that felt alive.

Isabella recoiled at the intimacy.

She tossed the pallets into one corner and tied their gear into the proper bundles, then sat on the stack of pallets to roll up her hose, dreading the weight of gambeson and hauberk and the prospect of baking in a metal shell for another day. In the dim morning light, she pulled on her borrowed shirt, which smelled of days on horseback. But then when she grabbed her jerkin and slipped in one arm, the odor of male sweat and cloves flooded her senses with unwanted memories: when she'd tackled him in the Valerós alley, a moment in Anfos's garden, riding the same horse with him. Her deception in the scriptorium, kissing him to steal back her letters.

Impatient with such weakness caused only by snatching up the wrong jerkin, she tossed it aside. A packet fell to the floor.

Suffering the same temptation as with his sword, Isabella undid the catch on the packet and unfolded the contents. She frowned to see the letters she and Tomás had examined just before they left Valerós, including the written vows between Pèire and Katelina, with Katelina's brash notation asserting her schismatic faith.

Another scrap of vellum dropped to the rough plank floor. Isabella unfolded and found the same note she'd read weeks earlier, with the childish wolf rhyme, followed by the crude addition.

I'll hunt you to your lair. I'll take your mate and cubs. The other wolf is already destroyed.

Beneath it lay the letter Renoud had sent Pèire, describing her as a wanton heretic and insisting Sebastián and his sinful mother be sent back to Montcava.

To protect your family and domus from the crusaders.

Which meant Tomás had read that vile letter of lies. Her ears burned with humiliation. Scarcely anyone knew what had happened in Toulouse. Katelina, as a faithful confidante. Father Anselm, who insisted that God saw no sin when a sinner had no choices. The now-dead Father Clémence, who heard her confession in those days. And Renoud, who told lies.

The ungodly racket on the ladder-stairs heralded Chrétien and his splintered leg. In a heartbeat, he and Tomás joined her.

"Don Tomás, please send your guard-dog away," she said. "I want to know why you have my letters."

Tomás motioned him off, and Chrétien closed the woven-reed door as he backed away.

"When you left the scriptorium that morning, I picked these up to preserve them." He sat on the floor beside her and reached for the packet. She pushed away his hand, but he was quicker and took possession.

"Those are my family's private letters," she said.

"Some are mine," he said. "Some we share."

"We don't share anything."

"We share a common enemy, and I gave Pèire my oath to destroy that enemy."

"Who are you? In the name of our Lord and Savior, I ask for truth, if it's possible for you to speak truth."

She couldn't read his expression when he answered.

"My father is Don Miquel. As his only son, I am the seigneur of Fontcours."

She shook her head. "Don Miquel is Sebastián's grandfather."

"Pèire Leteric let that lie stand for Sebastián's sake, and for other reasons," Tomás said. "But I look exactly like my father. A bit cut up, perhaps, but the same face."

"But you said you and Chrétien had different mothers."

"We have different fathers, too. Chrétien is my foster-brother. My father was a Moor. My mother is from a desert people called Kurds. She's not as pale as you, but not dark."

"Then Nicolau and Renoud—"

"Can't possibly be my brothers, can they?" He smiled without humor. "Renoud, for example, was conceived in the Languedoc while Don Miquel was on crusade in the Outremer."

While he spoke, fury bubbled up and boiled inside her as Isabella listened to his long story.

"Let me tell you what our mutual enemy did to Miquel and Pèire," Tomás said. "And to me."

.

Tomás in Famagusta
Summer 1209

After Tomás and Chrétien heard Miquel's wishes and once more made promises to him, Numa sent them away for the night, ordering the servants to bring food. But the koupepia didn't taste as remembered. The dried figs and sultanas, the too-sweet Cyprian wine, tender strips of baked goat, none of it tasted like what they'd dreamed about on the voyage home.

Lingering in the courtyard, Chrétien said, "You swore enough oaths tonight to keep a thousand angels vigilant, waiting for you to fall. So, we go back to searching for mythical assassins who suck blood from their victims?"

Tomás nodded. "Crux Lunata. As our father said. We continue to sell our services to Christian knights, while we search for the Knights of the Lunate Cross."

"So far, we've found only dissolute, aged crusaders with no greater knowledge of evil than most men." Chrétien tried the koupepia again, scowling. "We don't have to join the new crusade against the heretics, do we? It doesn't appeal to me."

"What better place to look for evil than a crusade?" Tomás said. "First, we deal with the Montcavas who cheated our father. Then we find Hugues de Beaurain and the other men our father once knew. The ones we haven't yet visited."

"But Miquel said it's not Hugues de Beaurain." Chrétien was always more obedient than Tomás.

"Where else is there left to look?" Tomás worked to master his feelings. "Damn me for a leper, but our father's pain breaks my heart. Yet I want to be with him through the night, to just—"

He couldn't say it: to hold the old man's hand one more time.

When Chrétien spoke, his voice shook. "Numa doesn't want us here tonight. Come find a dice game at the Raven's Head."

"I'll meet you at midnight. The senhóra who joined our voyage at Nicosia made a point of letting me know she's alone. Her husband remained behind with the king. It might let me forget this for a moment." Tomás gestured across the dilapidated courtyard.

"You're going off with a woman?" Chrétien wrinkled his nose.

"Well-to-do married women are best when you need diversion. They know what they want, and they have no desire to give up their husbands for a poor boy with only a mercenary's sword."

"Tomás, you are such a philosopher. How I yearn to be like you. However, I'm going dicing, and I won't come looking for you. Perhaps I might fall in love while we're home."

"May the bleeding saints cry me mercy, I'm not spending the entire night in a woman's bed. Only a filthy Frank would practice such an unclean act." Tomás shook his head. "I'll find you later. Cyprus has never been a good place for you to fall in love."

"As if you know more than a flea about being in love."

"Blessed dancing angels, I'd rather eat dust."

And by nightfall, Tomás found the silken woman from Toulouse. She offered just the diversion he wanted. She required only obsequious flattery, and Tomás rendered most of that with his fingertips, to which she responded with her quick, hard tongue. The only unpleasantness was the senhóra's little dog, always crawling where he wanted to place his hands. He helped the lady get what she sought, and then he wrapped her legs around his waist, prepared to find his own ecstasy.

But huge hands lifted him from the arms of the silken woman and began to beat him.

The two thugs could have caused all the damage they wanted with their bare hands, but one preferred to use a staff.

"Senhóra Hélène, your Montcava cousin begged us to separate you from this half-breed cur," said a third man. He clutched the woman, forcing her to sit in his lap while they wrecked Tomás's face and then concentrated on softer flesh. The staff man worked with a steady rhythm, breaking a bone at every other blow.

.

Isabella masked any response to the stories Tomás told. "What do you want me to believe?"

"This Wolf letter and the threats that dead priest carried," Tomás said, "prove that we are snared in the same evil."

"I certainly see evil."

"It points to the Montcavas, who stole Fontcours from my father."

"Fontcours belongs to Sebastián." *After what they did to me in Toulouse, Sebastián deserves Fontcours.*

Tomás shook his head, denying it. She continued, insisting. "Nicolau received Fontcours when Eloïse annulled her marriage. Her husband deserted her."

"No," Tomás said. "The Church took away Fontcours when Miquel married my mother. The bishops insisted that my mother is not a true Catholic. They ignored our holdings in Morella and Cyprus, probably because they're worthless."

"How could Eloïse—"

"Perpetuate her lies? The old count of Toulouse died. No one else in Toulouse ever knew Miquel, to notice that Nicolau was too pale to be his son." Tomás laughed ruefully.

He stopped pacing and leafed through the letters in the packet, holding one up for her inspection.

"As you can imagine, I was excited to find this marriage contract."

When she didn't reach for it, Tomás put on his jerkin and tucked it inside. He said, "The man who fathered Renoud and Nicolau is the source of this evil. I'll prove Miquel is not their father, and consequently get revenge for mine."

"You made a pet of Sebastián while plotting to take his inheritance." Furious, guessing what the love letter from Clémence's satchel meant, Isabella wrenched at the sleeves of her shirt. His shirt. Her pouch of treasures contained the proof Tomás was seeking.

"Sebastián knows," Tomás said. "He knows Pèire wanted to join Hugues de Beaurain only to protect Fontcours. For Miquel's sake."

"Pèire would have told me."

"He didn't want you to live in fear as he did."

"Pèire never feared one thing in his life."

"He retreated to the hills with Katelina, because someone wants to kill him and his entire family."

"I don't believe you."

He thumped one fist with such a violent blow, a jolt of fear bumped through her veins.

"Senhóra, someone seeks to ruin your family, the way mine was ruined through perfidy. Read this."

He handed her a note from his clutch of letters, written in the same tiny hand as the Wolf letter.

We'll take your cubs from your den.
Your Rock won't help you.
My Wolf topples that one next.
God won't come to Aragón, when Aragón is Gomorrah.

"Katelina found it in Pèire's room the morning we found Father Clémence murdered. Don't you see?" He rubbed at his scarred face as if it hurt him.

"I can't possibly trust you."

"Ma dòmna, I swear by the holy moment when you and I held Pèire in our arms, my greatest desire is to retrieve Sebastián. Then I will do what Miquel and Pèire asked: find our enemies and destroy them."

The dangerous look he flashed was the same as the day he first came to Valerós. More wolfish than human.

She said, "You're more than a mercenary."

"My masters claimed that they trained with the Nizari assassins. They lied, but they were killed later for betraying secrets of the *hashishiyyin*."

"Assassin. That's the word Pèire used. That's why killing Renoud's men didn't bother you. You kill people all the time."

"My father raised me for that. But I'm Pèire Leteric's vassal now. I'm sworn to protect you."

"I am not your property to protect, senhór. I could protect my family and villages if I knew the truth. What other lies are you hiding?"

He wouldn't look at her.

"We need to ride to Fontfroide to find Katelina." She felt sinfully satisfied that she'd shamed him. "Get the horses, please."

"I'll see to it at once, ma dòmna."

51
Galahad

Jean-Luc outside Carcassonne
11 days before Pentecost

"WE HAD A FELLOW like that in this kitchen. Claimed he saw action in Constantinople. But he drank and started fights. My sergeant put him out of camp, sent him back on the road. I think the sot headed for Toulouse."

"Yesterday? When?" Jean-Luc muffled his excitement.

"I'd say more than a week ago."

This was the closest Jean-Luc had come in his search for the one-eyed man, and he was only a week late. But now he had a firm destination—Toulouse—and a good reason to leave camp as soon as possible, before he was recognized by the marquis.

Jean-Luc was on his way back to his own tent from that kitchen out on the western peripheral, to grab his doss-kit and then find the road to Toulouse.

But his luck fell back from that temporary peak into the put where it usually lurked. He ran into his master from the forges.

"The Marquesa de Beaurain complains that her tent has so many broken rings, it's falling down around her ears," Master Eustache said. "Her servant begged for a smith to make it right."

"I'm not the man to work for lords," Jean-Luc said. After stumbling into Hélène, he felt ever more anxious about encountering Hugues. "Send a better man."

"You know I need all the real ironworkers to stay at the forge. This task is what you do best, Master Smith. Though I exaggerate by saying 'master.'"

With no hope for arguing his way out of perdition, Jean-Luc hoisted a pack of tools and made his way to the marquesa's pavilion, dreading what lay ahead. He trudged along, contemplating sin. He didn't mind confessing fornication, but adultery was a churlish, tawdry sin. And betraying his lord was worse. Yet Hugues and Hélène each held oaths from him before Jean-Luc discovered she was to become the Marquesa de Beaurain.

He managed to get sent with his brother Yves as far across Christendom as possible. Yet whenever he ended up in the same city or camp with Hugues, Hélène arrived, eager to entice him again, like a cat that enjoyed teasing a mouse.

Jean-Luc unloaded the sumpter mule where Hugues's servants indicated he was to work, and a camp boy led the beast to the corral. After the steward showed him the problem with the tent rings, Jean-Luc set to the task, expecting the marquesa to appear at any moment to harass him. Or to get him hung.

As he disassembled the north wall of the tent, he heard an animal growling. He called, "Come, Galahad," thinking it couldn't possibly be the same dog. But there was Galahad, sniffing Jean-Luc's ankles and wagging its tail, which in turn wagged its hindquarters. Jean-Luc knelt to let Galahad jump up and lick his face. The dog nuzzled at the leather braid around his neck.

"Say, old boy! A little grey around the whiskers, aren't you?"

Eight years before, Jean-Luc broke his collarbone while training young knights who wanted to join the crusade. Hugues and Yves marched off with the men; Jean-Luc was to join them when he could sit a horse. Hugues's parting gift to his wife was an eager puppy and a nearly immobile Jean-Luc to care for. Hélène, of course, was a terrible nurse and had no ability to teach a dog to behave itself. Jean-Luc filled the tedium of those weeks in Arles by tutoring Galahad.

And now Hélène had once again brought him to heel. He succumbed to her insistence that Hugues intended them to be together: the same reasoning she used whenever they were alone with her husband gone. He went for years strictly faithful to his oath and his own honor, but then Hélène arrived again and, if she had enough time to work him over, he'd be crawling into her lap like Galahad.

He put the dog down and set to work. While sweating over the portable forge in the heat of early May, he kept expecting the wraith of his persistent sin to whisper in his ear. After reforging the tent's rings, he began reassembling them in their grommets. When he stopped hammering, voices penetrated the tent wall.

"Good heavens, man!" Hugues spoke with as much anger as one ever heard from him. "The Count of Toulouse wants to make peace with the Church. Raymond agreed to be scourged in public, so the beggars of St-Gilles got to see the birch rod taken to his naked flesh. He swore obedience on St-Gilles' own bones."

"The Church needs to see action, not just words." Whoever Hugues quarreled with, the voice was learned and dispassionate, but so soft-spoken as to be barely audible.

Hugues said, "Since Raymond returned from Rome, he's been all over the south, doing what he promised. He's paid enormous reparations to the monasteries, though every seigneur knows the monastery claims are priestly lies. Raymond's men are pulling down those castles the pope deplores." His voice strained with passion.

"Our cousin Thedisius says the Church wants Raymond to confess to murdering the pope's legate," the soft voice answered.

"Half of Christendom wanted Pierre de Castelnau dead," Hugues said. "He was an arrogant, venomous monster."

"A Languedoc knight ran Pierre through on the banks of the Rhône. They say the assassin was Count Raymond's man."

"Raymond isn't that stupid. A murder right outside his own home? No. What more does the Church want from Raymond? His testicles in an ironmonger's pinchers?"

"That's about it, I believe."

"Philippe sent us to crusade against heretics," Hugues said. "We can't just steal people's land. How does the king of France get cooperation in Normandy and Maine, or stay friends with the Duke of Burgundy, if he shows no regard for his vassals' rights?"

"That will be Philippe's problem, not the pope's."

"And what do you believe, in your heart of hearts, brother? Do you support the Church?" Hugues's voice sounded like a plea.

"Hugues, I gave my oath."

"No one has to live up to a bad oath. Especially if there's bad faith on the other side."

"What will you do?"

"I'll do what I promised Philippe, to help keep the Peace of God," Hugues said. "But the whole affair stinks. From Rome, from Arnau Amalric, and from Bishop Folquet. And our cousin Thedisius is as bad as the rest of them. A bastard and the father of bastards. He's a good example of why these heretics want to throw off the yoke of their priests."

The voices drifted off, just as a cool finger ran a feathery line along the leather braid around Jean-Luc's neck, sending shivers down his spine.

.

"Why is Hugues on this crusade?" Jean-Luc asked, without turning to see her. "He's never been a true-believer, and he's never been greedy for booty."

"I asked him to come," Hélène said. "I have a stake in the Mont-cava estates. It's bad enough that Nicolau's bastards keep claiming shares. I won't get my portion if Simon's crusade takes it."

"Can't your cousin Renoud protect it?"

"He's no knight, even if he has spurs and a sword."

She sat on her bed and patted her knee for Galahad to come to her. The dog tried twice to jump up before succeeding.

"You're feeding the animal too much," he said. She, however, was as carefully pale and beautiful as ever. "Galahad jumps when you call, but Hugues de Beaurain didn't march down the Rhône because his perpetually faithless wife asked him to. He could send mercenaries to protect Montcava."

"Philippe asked Hugues to come, and of course he wanted to. He hasn't been in battle since Constantinople."

"But why worry about losing your land? Renoud declared for the French and the Church, didn't he?"

"Renoud has problems beyond his abilities. His mother is a heretic, and that Catalan witch Nicolau married is as bad."

"I don't think so. She's as Catholic as the day is long." Jean-Luc regretted his words as they left his mouth.

"*Ai,* you know her?" Hélène cooed, holding Galahad close and petting him. "Renoud said Senhóra Isabella put a great set of cuckold's horns on Nicolau. Is that how you know her, darling?"

"I met her family on my travels."

"Please tell me she's not as awful as I remember, because Renoud talked my brother Louis into marrying her, to keep her from dragging Montcava into something horrible."

"Renoud is mistaken. She's not marrying Louis." Jean-Luc considered how she always got more out of him than he should say. This time, though, it seemed he ought to speak. "Pèire Leteric chose another husband for her. Most likely, she's already married."

"What titillating gossip you know. And you're only a smith living with mercenaries. Louis will be pleased, but Renoud won't like it so much." Hélène pursed her lips in a familiar pout. "But Renoud might be lying. He's caused trouble for me before."

He wanted to learn more about Hélène's bodyguard and Renoud. "I still owe your cousin Renoud a debt myself. He gave me a horse and helped me escape Constantinople."

"Why, that mongrel liar!" Hélène leapt to her feet, forgetting Galahad, who jumped when she did and then waddled over to lie down by Jean-Luc. "Hugues sent you the horse and armor, and three gold marks. He also paid off the guards to let you through the gate. Hugues was heartbroken about your little drama."

"Hugues sent the horse?" Jean-Luc repeated, like an idiot beggar. He'd been seeking one man that might help him, while hiding from the man who had in fact helped him. At the moment, he needed peace to rebalance how he understood the world, but Hélène rattled on.

"Renoud is a little sneak. I swear I'll have those three marks off him and give them to you myself."

"If you can get them, you can keep them," Jean-Luc said. "I'm sure I'll be gone before then. I can't remain in Hugues's camp."

"But you can, *mon amour.*" She offered an infuriating smile. "I talked with Hugues about you this morning."

"You didn't!" Jean-Luc was so appalled that he sat down in her camp chair, where a smith had no right to be. Galahad jumped into his lap.

"I merely wondered if he remembered you. I didn't say that you are here."

"After I asked you not to speak to him."

"Hugues hasn't forgotten you. He went with your father twice to beg Philippe to intercede. Did you know that?"

"No." *Hugues intercede for me?*

"Your father came to our house at Easter. That's when Hugues last asked the king to help you."

"You saw my father? Is he well? How did he look?"

"*Ai*, my turn to have the good gossip. You haven't seen your father after all this time?"

"Please tell me."

"He seemed well, but Hugues declared him the ghost of his usual self. I didn't know he was so much older than Hugues."

"He isn't. My father is younger."

She ignored his response and instead returned to her earlier theme. "We'll claim you're one of those lordless fait-dits knights who turned Catholic, so Hugues can accept you into his army. Then you could see your father when the crusader army goes home."

"Hélène, do you live in dreams all the time?"

"Then I could tell my priest I'd saved a soul for the Church."

"You can't tell lies at confession."

"Why not? I do it all the time. It's just a charade. Whatever you tell a priest, it always costs half the rents to keep him quiet, and they call it a penance."

"Stop teasing." He growled. Galahad barked, jumped down, and then leaped onto the couch by her.

"Stop breaking my heart." She moved closer to the dog, caressing it. "In the troubadours' songs, you're supposed to pursue me, and I'm supposed to hold your heart in my hands."

"I'm not sure you have a heart, Hélène. You wouldn't treat Hugues or me as you do if you loved either of us."

"What don't I give you? I'm not an unattractive woman, even if I'm not the girl I was. What more do you want?"

"Fidelity."

"*Ai*, so much to ask, Jean-Luc?"

A shout rang from the end of the camp. The captains were beginning inspection.

"I have to go, before you're compromised," Jean-Luc said. Outside, he quenched the forge fire and found the boy to fetch the sumpter mule while he packed his tools.

Hélène stood, Galahad in her arms, both wearing the pleading expression that always used to lure him back.

"I'll tell my master you were disappointed in my work. He'll send a better smith," Jean-Luc said.

"But I want you," she said.

Anyone passing would hear.

"Hélène, this is foolish and dangerous. Please leave me alone. I won't sleep with my lord's wife."

"You always say that. But then you come anyway. You make it very hard for me to forget what a beautiful lover you can be."

52
Rain at Fontfroide

Tomás outside Fontfroide
11 days before Pentecost

TOMÁS FOUND CHRÉTIEN AT a table in the inn with a bowl of porridge and a jug of hot milk before him. And a smiling Durán close by his side.

"Durán, please beg the mistress for more strawberries," Chrétien said. "Jingle two of my pennies if it helps."

The young man jumped to do Chrétien's bidding, leaving Tomás alone with Chrétien.

"He's beautiful," Tomás said.

"And as innocent as a midsummer's day. I think he's also a Montcava bastard but doesn't know it."

"I was trying to place him last night. Renoud or Nicolau, do you think? He looks a great deal like Hugues de Beaurain."

"As Hugues probably looked fifty years ago. Durán was a streethawker's apprentice until a priest came with Renoud to his mother's house a few months ago and recruited him to serve as a footman at the Montcava villa."

"And his new master hasn't trusted him with any family secrets?" Tomás asked.

"Durán only knows the kind of secrets you keep from your mother. What about you, dear brother? What's troubling you?"

"The senhóra is eager to be on the way, Chrétien. Stay here while we ride to Fontfroide. We'll be back tomorrow."

"You're leaving me in lovely company," Chrétien said. "But can you do it alone?"

"I trust my sword."

"That's not what I mean. I want to know how you are."

Tomás couldn't give an honest answer.

"If I knew you were so far gone," Chrétien said, "I wouldn't torment you. You don't have any experience with being in love. Perhaps it's best if I go with Isabella to Fontfroide. I can bear a day's ride for your sake. Why don't you look for Sebastián?"

"No, I'll stay with the senhóra," Tomás said. "If we don't return by tomorrow, then you better join a party headed for Toulouse and find Sebastián."

"You're in danger. And your sword can't defend you. Bring Isabella to her people quickly. Then leave. We'll go back to Cyprus."

"I mean to keep my oath. I'll put her in a protector's hands." Tomás rubbed his head. He hadn't slept enough and his tooth hurt. "Chrétien, do you think—"

He stopped before he gave into an idiot's impulse to ask whether Chrétien still believed Isabella was in love with him.

"What, brother?"

"Do you think it's Hugues we're hunting?" Tomás said.

Durán stood in the doorway, charming the mistress into pouring strawberries into the bowl, the pennies never leaving his hand.

"I confess I don't care right now about the sins of the fathers being visited unto the fifth generation," Chrétien said. "'Comfort me with apples,' that's what I'm thinking. Or strawberries."

•

Tomás ordered a packet of provisions from the mistress, including more cloves for his aching tooth, which she begrudged him.

"I've only a handful left since Easter," she said, "and who knows when a trader from the Outremer will come this way again, what with the French crusaders ruining everyone's business."

He added another penny to what he'd already given her, desperate to stop his toothache. After he saddled his own horse, he began to saddle Isabella's, but then stopped. Begging for trouble. Instead he sat on a bench and waited, pressing a clove against that tooth with his tongue. He closed his eyes, wanting to dream a way out of the quagmire he'd ridden into, at full gallop.

The bench heaved as someone sat beside him. A foul odor of human waste, fetid garlic, and over-tired horse yanked him from his dreams.

"We lost our concession because of you, senhór. And ye crippled my best dog yesterday."

The wretched keeper of the toll booth sat next to him, a morning beer in his hand, half of it spilled across his filthy leather jerkin and linsey-woolsey undershirt.

"Then you won't have to chase him when you want to cuddle. I'm happy to oblige," Tomás said.

"That dog is my best comrade, as true-hearted as any crusader I've known. And I fought with Richard., the king of England and ruler of the Angevines," the man said.

"I've seen your other mutt, so I'm sure that's true," Tomás said. "At least you still have him to fornicate with."

"You've a cruel mouth to match your black heart. What had we done to you, except to make our way in the world like honest men?"

"Honest men do a good day's work for an honest lord. They don't rob pilgrims. You give shame to the name 'crusader.'"

"I'm sure I know my betters, but wasn't I a knight in the Outremer since before you cut your milk teeth? A whelp like you ought not to call out those that fought for the Cross at Acre and Jaffa."

"I was at Jaffa when Richard saved it," Tomás said. "What a pity Guy de Lusignan ever had to beg help from robbers like you."

The man drank from his beer and belched mightily. "If you knew my great lord, you wouldn't treat me so low," the degenerate crusader said.

"And if my grandmother had balls, she'd be my grandfather."

"Aren't I vassal to the famous Pèire Leteric? He promised to keep me in horse and armor for as long as I fought in the Outremer. If it be not true, may God strike me here." He thumped his chest with his mug of beer, sloshing it on his shirt again.

"I know Pèire Leteric, and he never had a scab off the devil's scrotum in his service."

"The devil gave you a hot tongue," the man said. "I got my license and promise from Pèire Leteric, right here in my purse. And I'm traveling to see him now, to be sure I'm paid in full."

"If you're headed to Pèire Leteric's home, you're going the wrong way from where we saw you yesterday," Tomás said. "Castell-de-Valerós is west of here."

The man scowled. "Because of what you did to the stonecutter's dogs at the toll-booth yesterday, they laid into us. You, senhór, owe me a debt for the damage and pain you caused me."

"I didn't owe you three morabatins for the toll, and damned if I owe you for losing your robber's concession."

"But my dog, senhór? You've crippled my companion and given me nothing in return but jibe and jest."

"Then here are two bezants for your dog. He can use them to pay the ferryman when it's time for his ride into the Elysian Fields."

He dropped the coins in the man's beer, thinking the entertainment was worth the cost, amused at the idea of what Beatriz would do to this blackguard if he managed to find Valerós. He crossed the yard to where Isabella appeared, carrying his armor. She stood on a block of wood to act the part of a squire in helping him into his gambeson and hauberk.

"What did he want?" she asked.

"He wanted me to pay for his damn dog. He says it's crippled after I kept it from gnawing on my leg. He'd make me pay for crippling my own horse if he could find a way."

"Why be angry with him? He's just a fool."

"Because men like that gall me," he said. "Pretending to be crusaders. Excusing sins of sloth because they just happened to be in Acre or Jaffa for a single battle."

"Then why did you pay him?"

"I only gave him two coins."

"For a crippled dog?" Chrétien called from the doorway of the inn. "You got my leg broken to save three pennies."

"Two bezants," Tomás said. "They're worthless. The only possible use would be to put them on a dead man's eyes."

"And you just happen to have plenty of experience with dead men," Isabella said as she saddled her horse.

.

315

The wind moved devilish black clouds overhead dumping a significant portion of the Mediterranean Sea on them. Tomás felt rain running under his shirt and across his belly by the time they came to Fontfroide Abbey, where the half-completed tower stood like a broken rock above the cloister buildings.

Tomás pounded at the gate for many moments before a watchman's hatch opened and a voice asked who knocked.

"I'm Tomás of Valerós. A woman, Katelina of Valerós, came here to take the veil. I need to speak with her."

The voice inside said, "You are mistaken. We have no sister house. We don't allow women inside these gates. Women seeking shelter go to the abbey at Lagrasse. Or Peyriac-de-Mer. Or St-Gilles."

Tomás silently wished for the devil's dark angels to take Beatriz away for all the evil her pique had wrought. But he said, "Can you give us shelter until this storm passes?"

The porter, part Moor and part Gallic southerner, opened the gate to them. He wasn't as dark as Tomás, but a flicker in the man's eye and the way he took Tomás's hand in greeting acknowledged their basic alliance. The two men were the same size, and the brother seemed quite robust; but then, a lay brother would grow strong from tending the fields and livestock.

"I'm Brother Andreu. You can rest your animals and take refreshment with us. But we don't have room for guests."

They followed the lay brother through the courtyard. Tomás said, "When I last passed here, Fontfroide was in lively construction. Now your workshops seem deserted."

Brother Andreu said, "Work stopped when the pope's prelate was murdered. Pierre de Castelnau called this home, and the Cistercians here don't have the wealth to build and to help the crusade at the same time. When that work is done, we'll go back to stacking stones to God's glory."

"Is everyone out on crusade?" Tomás ventured to ask more.

"The lucky ones. I may have a chance to join them." Excitement crept into Brother Andreu's voice. "I'm a water-witcher. The pope's men think water-witchers can douse for gold, too. When our abbot returns, I'll beg to help search for the heretics' gold."

The lay-brother let them make a temporary stable for their horses in an abandoned masons' workshop and helped bring fodder from the abbey's stables, which seemed full of horses for how empty the abbey was. Then he led them to a nearby carpenters' shed to wait for the rain to pass.

"Where is everyone?" Tomás asked Brother Andreu.

"The lay brothers are in the fields, probably waiting out the rain. The choir brothers are gone with Simon de Montfort."

"All of them?"

"All those young enough to travel. They sing during sieges to raise the crusaders' spirit."

The lay brother left them with coarse white wool robes, like his own, so they could hang their own clothes to dry. Isabella helped Tomás out of his hauberk first. He hated the sound of wet metal in his ears.

"We need to get the hauberks dried and oiled in the next few days," he said. "I can't abide riding in rust."

"Where will we do that?" she asked as he helped her out of hers. He didn't have an answer and, as she undid the strings of her wet gambeson, he worried that nothing protected her under the borrowed wool robe.

"Tie the robe this way," he whispered, showing her how, "so no one can see you're a woman. And wear the cap Chrétien gave you."

•

"St-Gilles and Peyriac-de-Mer are both too far away," Tomás said. They sat in the courtyard, waiting under the workshop's tile thatching for the storm to pass. "I'm betting Katelina went to Lagrasse."

She didn't concur or deny his guesses about where to ride next, but then, she'd been silent all day.

"It's a day's travel to Lagrasse. If the rain stops, we can ride part way tonight," he said. She still didn't answer; she just stared off toward the choir brothers' portion of the abbey buildings. "We'll fetch Chrétien and be there tomorrow, ma dòmna. Then we'll find Sebastián and determine how to deal with Simon de Montfort."

"I have a new plan," she said. "Only divine providence will get us to Fontcours by Pentecost, for either your purposes or mine. We do need to find Katelina and Sebastián, so there isn't time to go to Carcassonne to plead with Simon. I'll write to him in Pèire's name and send the same letter to Pedro d'Aragón, promising that we will join the crusade and send our taxes for Arracheuse. The last part is a lie, but it might buy us time."

"What about Simon's demand to render Valerós castles to him?" he asked, excited to see again the fierce, hawk-like woman he knew at Valerós.

She made a Catalan gesture of dismissal. "We promise to uphold our oaths to Pedro *El Católico*. Valerós has never rendered castles to Aragón. Simon is too new to ruling Carcassonne to know that."

"We need the help of angels to succeed. How will you get the letters to them?"

"We'll make several copies, and you can hire messengers to deliver them. The pens and parchment I need are over there." She gestured toward the cloister near the half-finished tower. "You can see the elderly choir brothers working inside. After vespers, we'll find the abbot and purchase what I need."

.

Brother Andreu invited them to sup with the lay brothers.

"The storm isn't passing," he said. "You can't go out while the devil is throwing forks of fire. Sleep tonight in the carpenters' shed, where you won't disturb anyone."

Tomás and Isabella followed him across the yard to the refectory. He showed them where to wash in a lavatorium that must have been built by the Romans. They genuflected and prayed with everyone, and then received dark bread and a vegetable stew served in rough pottery dishes. They shared the homely fare in the most common way and drank water served in pitchers, under the abbey's rule of silence.

Tomás caught the furtive glances of the dozen lay brothers at the table, the back of his neck tingling with unease. They didn't like the presence of strangers, but they also didn't like Brother Andreu. The abbey vows of silence didn't prevent them from expressing it: how they passed the bread to each other but set the bowl down instead of passing it to Brother Andreu; how they failed to acknowledge the bowls he passed to them, as if he were invisible. They weren't the first to hate a Moor for no reason than for being too brown, so Tomás felt himself to be an ally with Brother Andreu.

After Tomás and Isabella were left alone to make their beds on the carpenters' benches, he said, "The people we've met, save Brother Andreu, don't act with kindness. This is not a safe place."

"I saw that. I'm going to take what I need from the scriptorium, never mind buying it from the abbot."

"I'll follow and stand guard."

"Who's going to hurt me in a monastery? If I'm caught, I'll claim to be lost," she said.

"Humor me," he said. "Pretend I'm afraid to be left behind."

"Fine. We'll practice thievery together. Let me tend your wound before the light is gone."

They agreed to wait until just before dawn to steal the parchment she needed and then depart immediately. Isabella demanded the first watch. When Tomás woke, he found her seated close by him, dressed and ready for their chore. He dressed too, though the linen hadn't fully dried.

He said, "I'll check our horses. Then we'll do our thieving."

Across the yard where the tethered horses stamped in the straw under a lean-to, Miquel whispered in the beasts' noses.

"They've had an excellent rest," he said as Tomás approached. "And you and your senhóra?"

"We're fine." He saddled the horses in silence.

"Tie your hauberks onto the bed rolls, so you can ride away silently," Miquel said.

"I know how to do it." Tomás made sure their gear didn't rattle.

When he returned to the carpenters' shed, Isabella was gone.

53

Paternosters

Isabella inside Fontfroide
10 days before Pentecost

ISABELLA CREPT ACROSS THE service yard, the sodden linen gambeson clinging like a shroud. As she slipped into the court of honor, lightning illuminated the maze of stone blocks waiting to be hoisted into place. Rain splattered in puddles. Following the partially built walls, she found an opening into the choir brothers' cloister. She stood breathing in the shadows for long moments, repenting.

She regretted that she hadn't conquered her wild impatience, hadn't waited for Tomás. Every ripple in the shadows and every sound in the night made her heart lurch, despite her resolve to cast off fear. After all, tiptoeing through a monastery wasn't as dangerous as confronting a wolf or being hurled from the battlements. She was brave enough to cross the hall to the scriptorium.

Inside, with the smell of pigments and fresh-scraped vellum, she relaxed. This space felt like home. She muttered a dozen paternosters under her breath as she searched, finding a scraper, an awl, ink, quills, and ten pieces of parchment. Perhaps as a divine reward for all the paternosters, she also found a waxed linen bag to carry it all. With the bag over her shoulder, she began to retrace her way to the service yard.

A movement flickered in the shadows at the end of the hall. For a heartbeat, she believed it was Tomás, having expected him to follow her, but another motion—this time with sound—proved to be a man who moved ponderously, not at all like Tomás. Too tall.

She stepped close to the wall when another shadow passed through the opening to the cloisters.

Caution carried her across deep shadows into the half-built church. The walls were mostly intact and the roof fended off the rain, but it felt like standing inside the stone skeleton of a giant. Wind whistled through the openings where windows should be. She passed from column to column, listening for pursuers. After long moments, she tiptoed past the choir brothers' dormitory and navigated around the cloisters to the service yard, dead-ending only once in the maze. Rain pelted her face as she crept among the boulders in the stonemasons' yard. She paused under the eaves of a workers' shed to wipe the rain from her face, shivering in the wind.

A sword cut across the path before her, and a figure stepped beside her in the dark.

"Valerós?" A too-familiar voice challenged. Chain-mailed hands grabbed her, pulling her cap away.

Her hair fell free and the wind whipped strands across her eyes. As she blinked, arms enfolded her and a voice whispered in her ear.

"My sister, my love."

"Renoud." She held her breath, hoping he didn't sense how he frightened her.

"You came in search of me," he murmured. "I never expected so much divine grace. You *are* looking for me, aren't you?"

"Yes. And Sebastián. Is he with you?"

"He's far from here, my love. I'm doing my best to keep him safe. And now I can protect you, too. But how did you know where to find me?"

"It's where you said you were going next. On your pilgrimage." How quickly she remembered the art of lying.

He held her against his chest, so she saw only the scorpion embroidered on his sleeve.

Tomás will come in a moment.

"You are in so much danger that I longed to take you with me." He stroked her hair, which always meant he'd touch tender places next. "But Pèire is so stubborn, I'm surprised he let you go."

She puzzled this for a heartbeat. Why hadn't Sebastián told Renoud that Pèire had died? "I came on my own." She was determined to keep him ignorant.

"*Ai*, how exciting." He nipped her ear as he spoke. "You and I will keep Sebastián safe together."

She choked on the words she wanted to say. *Where is Tomás?*

"Yes, Renoud, just you and me." In her mind, she stepped through the motions Chrétien had taught her.

"Shall we tell your mestitz guard-dog that you don't need him?"

She struggled in his arms, which would never lead to anything but pain.

"*Ai, xiqueta*, I like it when you tease," he murmured in her ear. He pushed her around the last boulder outside the carpenters' shed. There, Tomás lay sprawled face down in a rain puddle, the borrowed Cistercian robe dark with blood.

"*Ai Dèu!* You killed him."

"Not I, dear one. But I can't say I'm sad." Renoud's hand grasped hers, just a finger's width from the baldric holding her dagger. "It's us together against the world once again. My sister, my love."

She stepped back, treading on his foot while drawing one elbow up into his solar plexus. He gasped. When his grip on her loosened, she pulled her dagger and stood as Chrétien taught her. But just as she prepared to thrust up with her knife, intending to drive it under Renoud's ribs, another figure ran at them, shoving at Renoud. Her knife instead slit open the newcomer's surcoat, the blade shrieking as it skittered across chainmail.

The man yelped in anger and turned on Isabella. Renoud struck the man's hands away with his metal-studded gauntlets.

"Traitor!" the intruder shouted at Renoud. He raised a long dagger. The light of the fire showed dark streaks of Tomás's blood on the blade.

"Your father bids you be still." Renoud's voice sounded unnaturally calm.

Like a mangy, kicked dog, the stranger dropped his hand to his side and loped off into the darkness.

Renoud settled a hand on her shoulder again, but she clutched two fingers and wrenched them away, hearing bones break as he screamed and bent in pain. The shadowed figure appeared again, first striking Renoud down with the pommel of his sword, then covering her mouth with a clove-scented hand.

Her pulse pounded in her ears as she was dragged amongst the stones to the gate.

When Tomás released her, she hugged him tightly.

"*Ai Dèu*, I thought you were dead."

"We need to go now." Behind him, the horses stamped and muttered as if impatient.

"I want Renoud to die."

"Not now, ma dòmna. Come away."

They rode out at a gallop. A league away, he reined in his horse and dismounted. She leaped down, too.

"I'm so glad it wasn't you." Still excited, she had her arms around him and came so close that her lips brushed his face as she spoke.

"It was Brother Andreu. He came to check on us. Or to warn us."

"Why didn't you let me kill Renoud?"

"The other man created a ruckus, the one who killed Brother Andreu. He woke everyone in the dormitories with his noise." He untangled her arms and moved away. "Put on your hauberk, ma dòmna. If we're pursued, it won't do you any good packed away."

He helped her tie the bag of stolen pens and parchment securely onto her saddle, and then he held the hauberk while she climbed in. The metal rings clanged in her ear as its weight settled on her still-damp gambeson.

Tomás asked, "What did Renoud say?"

"He imagines he's in love with me. It's a sickness in his mind."

"*Ai.* The spit-licker will wake with such a headache, perhaps he'll reconsider."

She burst out, saying what she needed to tell him. "You told Chrétien to keep me away because I was so cowardly at Anfos's cottage. But I conquered that. I could have killed Renoud myself."

"You are brave, ma dòmna. And I'm glad you're done hating me from yesterday." He prepared to mount his horse. "The rain has ended. We need to ride while we can."

She felt him move away from her, putting distance between them. She had not yet redeemed herself.

54

Nemesis

Tomás in the Aude valley
10 days before Pentecost

TOMÁS JERKED THE SADDLE from his horse, grabbed rags in the stable, and began to rub down his horse.

"You thought the maid at the inn was funny," Miquel said. "You laughed at the naïve Durán. Now you're as lathered as your pony."

"That bastard Renoud touched her," Tomás muttered.

"Too bad we didn't have one spare moment to kill him." His father thrust his gloved hand as if he held a dagger.

"Next time," Tomás said.

"What did that scrofulous *peccador* mean?" Miquel asked. "Ask her what he meant."

"I didn't hear."

"I said, let me do that, senhór."

Tomás looked up, startled. The stable boy held out his hand to take over care of the horse. Tomás gave over the rags and headed across the inn's courtyard, his formerly broken bones stiff and sore from the rain and the ride.

It's us together against the world once again. My sister, my love.

He didn't hear it once. Rather, he heard it ring in his ears a thousand times as they rode through the morning mists.

Tomás asked the inn's mistress to bring Isabella food and a flagon of wine, since her bones needed warming. Then he went to find Chrétien. As he approached the archway of the inner courtyard, a young man's voice carried across the garden.

"I don't want to meet him. He promised that he'd kill me over that squire of his."

"Tomás always says that." Chrétien sounded cheery. "But he hardly ever kills anyone. He just worries about our safety."

"But how was I supposed to know?"

In a tiny garden shaded by a scrubby Aleppo pine, Chrétien sat on a bench with his splintered leg propped on a half-sawn log, a carved cane at his side. His new friend Durán sat beside him, scowling as Tomás approached.

"Tomás, *hola*! All done?" Chrétien's eyes and mouth had the soft look he got when he was either dead drunk or in love. Tomás hadn't seen his brother in love since Zara, when a Venetian lord had crushed his unguarded heart. But it was midday, so it must be love.

"There's no convent at Fontfroide," Tomás said. "However, we met the current steward of my Languedoc estates."

Chrétien understood, but he made no motion to send Durán away, and the beautiful boy put on a close approximation of a jealous pout. He avoided Tomás's eye and folded his well-muscled arms across his broad chest.

"Tomás, meet my good friend Durán of Toulouse." Chrétien called him *bon amic* in the common tongue, which might also mean *boyfriend*. Startled, Durán glanced up from his pout in a way Tomás found touching.

"*Bon día*, donzel." Tomás made the Catalan gesture of submissive greeting, since this footman had enamored his brother.

"I'm not a lord," Durán said. "As you know, senhór."

His marketplace accent confirmed as much, but in the broad sunlight, it was obvious that only a quirk of fate—having one mother rather than another—had separated Durán from being a hawker-turned-footman rather than a donzel with a promising inheritance.

"We met before," Tomás said.

"Yes, I remember." Durán's eyes flitted to Chrétien, who yawned and stretched. Perhaps Durán didn't know how to read the signs: Chrétien wanted more than a single afternoon in the courtyard.

"I hope you'll forget my hasty words and forgive me." Tomás tried to be friendly. "I spoke in error."

Chrétien finished his stretch and dropped his arm loosely over the back of the bench, resting his hand on Durán's shoulder. At his touch, Durán relaxed. He unfolded his arms, one hand grasping the thumb of another in his lap. The hopeful expression on Durán's face would break the heart of a bishop.

"It is forgotten," Durán said.

"It's rude of me to interrupt, Master Durán, but Chrétien and I have business to discuss. Tell my squire I'll join him in a few moments, please. Perhaps we can all eat our supper together?"

Durán didn't like it, but he moved to do as Tomás asked.

As soon as Durán stepped through the archway into the inn, Chrétien said. "Did Renoud recognize either of you?"

"I'm not sure. The man with him killed a lay brother, thinking it was me—the mestitz scribe from Valerós. But likely he didn't recognize Tomás, Miquel's heir. However, he did know Isabella."

"What about Sebastián?"

"Renoud has him somewhere else. Though Durán says the boy is in Laurac, I'm guessing he's in Toulouse by now."

"Then what's next, brother?"

"We're going to Lagrasse to find Katelina. Then Laurac to find Eloïse of Montcava."

"She's your last hope for proof?"

"Perhaps. Can you sit a horse? You'd better go to Toulouse now, to find Sebastián."

"I can ride. But did you know Hugues de Beaurain has a camp west of here? Durán is to ride there tomorrow if Renoud's men don't show. Perhaps Renoud left Sebastián with Hugues."

"I'll poke around Hugues's camp tonight." His aching bones complained at the idea of another jostling ride. "Can you take care of my squire while I'm gone?"

"You have to ask?"

"Chrétien, make sure Durán understands I'm your brother, not competition. And tell him who we think his father is before you sleep with him."

"Why should I?"

"Because he'll find out sooner or later. And then he'll feel you've made a fool of him."

"He's the bastard son of a faithless seigneur. As much as anyone in the world, I know how useless such knowledge is."

"Toulouse isn't a Frankish kingdom like the Pays de France. And it isn't Cyprus or Jerusalem, where they throw bastards to the wolves. Durán can make a claim if he knows who he is. Tell him."

"And how do you know I haven't already slept with him?"

"He's still holding his breath in hope. You must be blinded by beauty to miss seeing how jealous he is."

"Durán is more than just beautiful." Chrétien turned earnest. "He's funny. He's smart. He taught himself to read when he worked as a laborer for the St-Sernin abbey, scraping ruined vellum clean. He learned to sing harmony from hearing the monks sing plainsong. He can carve as neatly as the artisans creating gargoyles for the cathedral in Narbonne." Chrétien fingered the fantastical beast's head on his home-made cane: Durán's handiwork.

"*Ai*, you mongrel mooncalf. It's too late to warn you about anything," Tomás said.

"You don't have a great deal of wisdom to offer about how two people get on together, my dear brother. Go see if Sebastián is in Hugues's camp. I'll take care of your squire."

55

Restoration

ISABELLA CLOSED THE REED gate to her cell in the inn's loft, grateful to be alone at last. She sprawled across the straw bed-pallet and spread parchment on the floor. Methodically, she sharpened pens with the little knife Pèire had given her, and then prepared the first piece of parchment by pricking rules with a needle-pointed awl. But the work failed to still her mind.

In the past eight days she'd become a fugitive who depended on a mercenary to keep her alive. By chance, she'd severed a man's soul from his body and sent it to final judgment. And before dawn she'd also tried to kill Renoud. This many years later, would God still consider it self-preservation?

Pausing, she fingered scraps from her pouch. First, Jaume's childish scrawl: *eu vos amor*. And then her own elegant copy of the script from Master Avraham's workshop in Toulouse that began *"Darkness lay upon the face of the deep."* Two pieces of comfort from an old life, when the rigors of philosophy kept her alive. She needed a conversation with Master Avraham or Father Anselm now, to guide the logical arguments that always saved her from raging against a merciless, arbitrary God.

A timid knock on the door broke her meditations. A rail-thin boy not much older than Sebastián pushed a platter of food and a stone jug of wine at her.

"Thank you," she said.

He nodded, looking stricken with fear as he backed away. What had Tomás said to the poor boy?

The food he'd brought was simple: bread still warm from the village oven and a hen's-egg omelet. She ate slowly, tasting dried sage in the light folds of omelet. And cinnamon.

Katelina gave her an omelet with cinnamon when Pèire brought Isabella home from Toulouse. The cinnamon burned away the taste of murderous hatred and homesickness she'd choked on daily in the Montcava villa. Now she was again in peril and homesick for Valerós. This time, she didn't have Sebastián nearby. And only a satchel of stolen parchment with which to beg for the safety of Valerós.

Pushing aside the crockery from her repast, she determined to find peace in work, answering Simon's demand that Valerós pay enormous taxes, send armed knights, and render castles. She spent the afternoon writing, a pen-knife in her left hand to hold the parchment still and the quill in her right hand to scratch several copies of the letter intended to protect the well-being of ten villages, two castles, and the six thousand people who lived there. Half of whom could be coaxed to say the Creed or swear an oath before a priest.

As the sun shifted, she moved the pallet and her parchment to catch the last light, and then she stretched her hands and sipped from the watered wine the boy had left for her. While resting, she studied the other letters from Tomás's pocket. He'd turned over everything to her: the Wolf letters, the marriage vows, and the clutch of foul missives the priest had carried to Pèire. She wasn't insensitive to what he intended: he wanted her to trust him.

But he also wanted to take her son's inheritance.

She read and reread the Wolf letters, filled with coded threats spanning forty years, seeking the defeat of two families represented by twin vows:

Miquel's marriage to a Christian, which the Church rejected as illegal.

Pèire's marriage to a schismatic, which the Church would also reject, if it knew.

The mark signing the Wolf letters matched Renoud's tattoo, though he was too young to have written the first letter and not learned enough to have authored the newest threat.

We'll take your cubs from your den.
Your Rock can't help you.

My Wolf topples that one next.

God won't come to Aragón, when Aragón is Gomorrah.

Yet Renoud had stolen Sebastián.

We'll take your cubs from your den.

Pèire, named for St-Peter, the Church's Rock Foundation, was gone from this earth and could no longer protect them.

Your Rock won't help you.

Perhaps the Rock meant Castell-de-Valerós.

My Wolf topples that one next.

Pèire died from illness. Had he cheated a would-be murderer? But she was the one who was attacked at Valerós.

God won't come to Aragón, when Aragón is Gomorrah.

Renoud was too ignorant of scripture to write about Gomorrah.

Chrétien and his new friend chatted and laughed on the narrow landing outside. She swatted open the reed gate of her cell, the Wolf letter in her hand.

"Chrétien, what is this?" she demanded, pointing to the lunate cross at the bottom of the letter.

"A coat of arms, perhaps?" He glanced over at his new friend and then moved to block Durán's view.

"Or maybe the mark on my enemy's hand? If you please, Chrétien, no lies."

"It's the sign of an order of knights, Crux Lunata. The Knights of the Lunate Cross."

"Like the Templars or the Ransomers?"

"Hardly. Our father claimed they suck blood and work black magic, though I doubt he meant it as certain truth."

"Who are they? Where are they?"

Chrétien shook his head. "We've found a few doddering old men who didn't know anything. And your brother-in-law. In truth, I think it's just a bad joke."

Durán was impatient, and Chrétien returned to his friend.

"Tell me when it's time to laugh," she said.

As she read each letter again, they began to fit the story Tomás told, except for the Rock and Gomorrah. She pulled the priest's letter from her own leather pouch—the missive of love and longing she'd stolen from Father Clémence's satchel—and laid it alongside the Wolf letters.

> At least do not abandon our sons.
> They are our gift from Heaven.

The two were written by the same hand.

So Nicolau of Montcava was a bastard. Fontcours didn't belong to Sebastián.

She stared until the writing ceased to form words. Chrétien and Durán murmured next door in the loft.

"The Rock"—*Petrus*—translated from Latin to half a dozen names like St-Peter's. Or Pietro, the Sicilian merchant who kept a shop by Master Avraham in the Toulouse marketplace. Or Pierre de Castelnau, the pope's prelate. Or Pèire, the name of thousands of Catalan shepherds and seigneurs, including the baron of Valerós. Or Pedro, about whom it was said—

"Gomorrah" was the story Father Clémence used to preach against friendships like Chrétien's. Which meant that danger threatened more than her family and Valerós.

She shoved aside the parchment filled with falsehoods intended for Simon de Montfort and began a simple message in Latin to the king of Aragón and signed it from the Master of Valerós.

> You are in grave danger. Beware Crux Lunata.

56
Bon Nuoit

THE PREVIOUS SUMMER, THE former viscount of Carcassonne ordered the countryside to hide or destroy food, to make the invasion as difficult as possible for the French army. The viscount's men disabled windmills to stop the grinding of grain, so a hungry French army would have no choice but to go home. Yet despite all those efforts, the crusaders advanced on Carcassonne, the viscount perished in his own dungeons, and Simon de Montfort stole his city and his title.

From atop a crippled windmill, Tomás surveyed Hugues de Beaurain's camp. He identified pennants of French lords who had been on crusade as far as Zara, but the Montcava pennant was missing. In the fading light, men scurried to erect another pavilion alongside Hugues's own tents.

The busy disorder in the second pavilion made it easy to stride into the camp. A knight from the new campsite had conveniently left his traveling surcoat hanging where Tomás could borrow it. And Hugues kept a well-ordered camp, so it was child's play to find and enter the tent he sought.

Hélène sat alone, staring into a silver mirror on her camp table. Seeing her made his toothache rage again, and his bones throbbed where they'd been broken.

"*Bon nuoit*, Hélène. You're still beautiful, if you're wondering."

"You!"

Tomás smiled, pretending sincerity. From the arch of her brows and the set of her shoulders, she was prepared for a fight. Her hand settled around the dagger on her table.

Uninvited, he sat on her camp bed in a provocative position and let his surcoat and hauberk fall between his thighs, remembering that Hélène had said she liked his legs. He motioned with two fingers for her to come to him.

"What do you want?" She sat beside him, although her hackles were still up. Her lap-dog raised its head to see who had roused him and then burrowed deeper into the pillow and slept again. "Are you still mad at me because of the beating my cousin Renoud gave you?"

"I regret we didn't part friends last time. Since I was in the neighborhood, I wanted to apologize."

She eyed his surcoat. "That lord doesn't travel with mercenaries. Did you steal it?"

"I'm offended you'd think so."

"Why did you come here?" She still bristled, but he put one hand on her back, gently moving up to rub her neck.

"I worried when you said Renoud threatened you. Why are you here, Hélène?"

"*Bon Dèu*, why does everyone ask me that? Hugues takes me everywhere he goes. He's leaving me out in the country at the Fontcours estates for the summer."

"You seem distracted, ma dòmna."

As he spoke, he turned her head to kiss her, knowing he kissed a viper. He felt her respond, but she tried to move away, only to come back for more. Then she pulled away again.

"Don't break my heart by telling me there's someone else." He stroked her cheek.

"You can't possibly care. Stop pretending you like me. You treated me badly the last time we met." She threw off his hand.

"Are you sheltering Sebastián of Montcava for your cousin?"

"Of course not. The boy lives with his witch of a mother in the wild woods."

"Interesting," Tomás said. He had no reason to search this camp for Sebastián then. "Do you know why Renoud is trying to kill Isabella of Valerós?"

"He isn't. Who told you that?" Hélène said. "Renoud wants her to marry my brother Louis. But if she does, I swear I won't stay at Montcava again. She pretends to be holier than a saint's mother."

"Who has the letter you told me about? Your sister's letter about Renoud's true father?"

"I'm not telling you. I hope the letter is lost."

"Why? I need that information, too."

"Look around you, *pech*." She called him an idiot, but she'd called him worse the last time he saw her. "There's a crusader army out there. If the legitimacy of Montcava is questioned, the Church will take the estate. Why do you think Hugues came here? We need to keep my portion of Montcava from ending up as crusader booty. So, stay out of it. Go back to Cyprus. Or go to hell."

"But if you and I prove Renoud doesn't deserve to inherit, it means more of the estate belongs to you, Hélène."

It didn't mean that, but he hoped to mollify her. She hesitated, thinking about it. "I can't get the letter back. The priest I gave it to is dead."

"Where did he live? I'll search there."

"He was just a parish priest in Toulouse. They said he was killed by a wild Moor in—"

She whirled on him, but Tomás caught her hands, pretending she intended an embrace.

"No," he said. "It wasn't me. Most likely Renoud killed him. You and I are both in danger."

"Get away from me. You're a monster. I'll call my guard."

He rose. "When Renoud tries to harm you again, please think of me as a friend and ask for my help."

"You've never had a friend in your life. Go away."

He lifted the flap of her tent, seeking signs of anyone other than the guard she trusted so much—who failed to see Tomás enter. He noted the guard's failure with wry pleasure, but he stayed in the shadows, moving through the narrow alley separating her pavilion from the next.

"*Ai,* senhór." A voice came from over his head, and a hand rested on the arm Tomás would use to grab his sword, if he dared. "That surcoat never looked so good on any knight of mine."

Cold steel at his throat, Tomás froze, not daring to swallow.

57

A New Surcoat

Tomás outside Carcassonne
10 days before Pentecost

THE MAN GROWLED IN his ear, speaking Catalan with the same accent as Miquel. "I don't recognize the face. It's been rather ruined, hasn't it?"

"I used to be vain, but others helped me conquer such a paltry sin, Monsenyor." Tomás hoped that was how Aragón seigneurs addressed a king. The blade was far enough from his Adam's apple to allow him to speak.

"What happened to the men who destroyed your face?"

"I killed them. I'm still hunting their master." Steel brushed his throat with every other word.

"Might I have recognized you before that happened?"

"No. But I am your vassal, Monsenyor. For the villa St-Joachim in Barcelona and—"

"St-Joachim belongs to Pèire Leteric of Valerós. My father gave it to him." The king's voice rumbled, still warning of danger.

"Pèire gave it to me when I became his knight." Tomás still felt the blade and fought his fear of the dark in the passageway.

"He discarded our gift without telling me?"

"Pèire died." No one seemed to observe them.

"I wasn't told about that, either." The king's blade scratched Tomás's throat.

"In truth, I don't think he planned it. It only happened last week." Did this man not have personal guards?

"Did you kill him?" The knife still pressed at the tender part of Tomás's throat.

"No. In fact, I feel as much loss as when my own father died."

"They say Pèire Leteric is inciting the rebels in the Corbières hills. They say he and his family are heretics."

"Whoever says so is the devil's own liar." Tomás ignored the tickle of the blade.

"I saw his name on Simon's list of rebels."

"Then Simon listens to liars and fools. Pèire Leteric would never betray his oath to you." Tomás felt excited now instead of intimidated. "You didn't believe those lies, did you?"

"Of course not. Come to my tent so I can see your ruined face."

The king lifted the canvas flap and made a gallant motioned for Tomás to enter, remaining close by Tomás. The red-and-yellow striped tent glowed ruby-red from a lamp hung from a hook.

What Tomás saw in the soft light revealed exquisite taste, intelligence, and athletic grace. The man dressed in silk and silver, but moved like a warrior, and he filled the tent with his presence in a way Tomás had never experienced. His strong, full mouth was framed by a small beard and he wore a single ruby earring. Although several shades lighter than Tomás, his skin was dark enough that his blue eyes flashed their own light. All that marred his perfect looks was a knot of tension between dark brows. The tent itself was the tidy, Spartan camp home of a general, its only comfort a silken coverlet on the narrow cot.

"And you are—?"

"Tomás of Morella, Cyprus, and St-Joachim."

Pedro d'Aragón still held the knife in one hand, but he smoothly poured wine into two goblets. He sat astride a camp stool and, with minimal motion, indicated that Tomás should stand before him.

"So, you're the new lord of Morella? I had your letter submitting yourself to me when your father died last year. Very smartly written for the seigneur of a little sheep-fief uphill from nowhere. Or did you hire a good clerk?"

"I've never seen the place. I grew up and trained in the Outremer and Cyprus. And yes, I can write."

"My father spoke highly of yours." Pedro set the cups of wine down and tapped the tabletop, piercing Tomás with a sharp stare.

"Thank you. It's gratifying that people thought well of him."
Understanding Pedro's command, Tomás removed his sword and
placed it on the table.

"You live on Cyprus now?" Pedro grasped his arm and turned
it over to study the bonfraires mark on Tomás's wrist.

"Not often. My father's holdings don't earn much. I work as a
mercenary. I live everywhere."

"Who have you worked for?" Pedro leaned back, folding his
arms like a man interested in hearing a story.

"The Count of Antioch. The Duke of Burgundy. The Venetians,
but I will never work for those lying cheats again."

"Who is paying you now?"

"I am under oath to complete certain work for Pèire Leteric."

"You aren't very comfortable here, are you?" Pedro's smile
seemed lopsided.

"We encountered each other in circumstances rather unbe-
coming to me." Tomás kept still, not wanting to betray more of his
unease, since he also felt excited by this conversation.

"Are you used to kings?"

"I know the king of Cyprus."

"Does he have your allegiance?"

"I won't betray him to his enemies." Tomás made an instant
decision that this meeting required pure truth. "However, the king
of Cyprus is dissolute, deceptive, and greedy, undeserving of true
allegiance."

"Not a nice way to speak of your liege lord." Pedro sounded
amused rather than offended. "Your father had fiefs everywhere.
What do you hold from other kings? Philippe? Alfonso?"

"I am trying to reclaim holdings my father had from the old
Count of Toulouse."

"That would make you beholden to Philippe."

"I'm not beholden to anyone for those lands, since the Church
falsely deprived my father of them."

"Are you Catholic?"

"Yes, Monsenyor. As much as any man who isn't a fool."

"But do you believe your Creed?" Pedro asked casually, as if he were asking *Do you prefer this saddle style?* Yet Pedro was called *El Católico*. This was the king's most important question.

"I'm not a philosopher. I do my duty and keep oaths I've made."

"Will you kneel and swear allegiance? I need to know how my seigneurs stand with me. A man like you might be useful, if he's loyal."

Pedro's words made Tomás's blood run hot. *A man like you.* And a command to allegiance, like Pèire had admonished him.

"Come, senhór." Pedro moved closer to him. Tomás smelled horse and oiled leather and wine. "Don't hesitate. Are you a maiden waiting for a better offer?"

·

"I gave an oath to Pèire Leteric," Tomás said. "I can't swear another oath until I finish his business."

"Do you know how the lords in Toulouse and Aragón swear to their counts and kings?" Pedro thumped the table with the butt of his knife, impatient. "These lords say, 'We swear to you, our king, who is no better than we are.' And then they only promise not to join their lord's enemies. You can't bring yourself to swear an oath like that?"

"Why bother?" Tomás said. "It's only a promise not to stab you in the back. It's not worth calling on God's name for that."

"What will you swear?"

"Monsenyor, I can't swear more until—"

"Suppose I back your other oath? I won't call on you while you work for Pèire Leteric's family. I'll count it as part of your oath to me."

"Why would you do that?"

"Because I admired Pèire Leteric. If he trusted you, then I should too. It is I who wonder why you'd swear for any reason other than because I had my knife at your throat."

Pedro laid down the knife and drank his wine.

"I know what you tried to do for the Viscount of Carcassonne last year," Tomás said. "If he'd listened to you, he might be alive now. And I know you refused the homage of the despicable Simon de Montfort. I've heard how well you treat your lords in the heart of Aragón. Your brother, as Count of Provence, has his lords' loyalty because his policies are well liked. They say he's instructed by you."

"Is this obsequious flattery? Have I misjudged you?"

Tomás continued, relying on truth. "Pèire Leteric said you were the best of all men in the south, that you will be a great king. If the lords of the Languedoc don't stab you in the back."

Pedro covered his eyes so Tomás couldn't see his face.

"What's your oath?" Pedro spoke from behind his hand.

"I'm mostly averse to oaths, but I'll swear the same one I gave to Pèire Leteric."

"Then kneel and swear."

Tomás, on his knees, closed his eyes, feeling Pedro's hand on his head. How had he come here, to what might be the most important moment in his life? Miquel taught him how knights of Aragón swear allegiance, so he spoke like a man who knew what he was doing.

"I, Tomás of Morella, guardian of Fontcours and St-Joachim and knight of Pèire Leteric of Valerós and Miquel of Cyprus, son of Numa—"

Tomás paused at his mother's name. A knight in this part of the world always swore on his mother's name. But he needed to do more.

"—a true Christian daughter of the Holy Roman Church, will be faithful to you, Pedro *El Católico*, king by Grace of God of Aragón, son of Sanchia Castile, Count of Barcelona and Roussillon, vassal to Innocent the Third of the Holy Roman Church—"

"You can forgo my pedigree," Pedro said.

"I swear on the name of Jesus the Son of God, and on my own honor that I will protect you and yours…" Tomás paused, considering the intimate vow he'd made to Pèire.

"Is there more?"

"As if we were brothers sharing one heart." Tomás plunged recklessly into it. "The rest of my oath to Pèire was specific to his children."

"Then, amen. Rise, senhór."

He handed Tomás a cup of wine. After Tomás drank from it, Pedro passed his knife to Tomás. "I don't have other arms at hand to bestow on you. Take this as a symbol."

"Thank you, Monsenyor."

"Are you married? Do I have to send your wife a present?"

"No, Monsenyor. As Pèire said, I'm not the kind of man who marries."

"However that might be, I need my knights to secure the lands of women in the Languedoc."

"Is this another kind of mercenary work?"

"If Simon maintains a foothold for Philippe in the south, then I can tell you what the pope will do—since I now have a great deal of practice in second-guessing him. He will decree that Toulouse and Carcassonne ladies can't marry Languedoc lords. He'll say it's to forestall breeding heretics. I don't want Philippe taking the south through the bedroom."

"Is this a command, Monsenyor?"

"It's a strong suggestion to knights who want to advance in this world. But perhaps you prefer other men's wives to your own?"

"Pardon, Monsenyor?"

"I saw the tent you came from. Though I can't say you stayed long enough for any decent sort of fornication."

"I abstain from women."

"And the other way?" Pedro regarded him over the edge of his cup, but Tomás wasn't sure the king had drunk much wine.

"Pardon?"

"You understand me."

"I abstain from men also."

"But you haven't always abstained from either."

"No."

"Did you like it?"

"Yes. But only with someone who's equal to or better than me." It came out of his mouth like a thinly veiled challenge. As he stared into Pedro's piercing eyes, he saw they both heard the echo of what he'd said earlier: *The best of all men...* "Anyway, I prefer to do other things with men."

"Tell me what that is."

"Nothing beats fighting an enemy, aligned with a man I trust at my back. Or training together to the point of exhaustion. To share a bottle of wine and a pair of dice."

"Which do you prefer?"

"The dice."

"That's not what I meant, as you know. Do you prefer women?"

"I prefer to abstain."

"You don't look like an abstemious man."

"I have personal reasons, Monsenyor."

"An unattainable love?"

Tomás turned his head away without intending to. Pedro traced one of the rude scars on Tomás's face.

"They hurt much more than your face, didn't they?"

.

Pedro touched him gently. Tomás drew a breath, nearly choking, desperate to understand how this man managed to extract the essence of his life within moments of their meeting.

"I'm whole, if that's what you are asking, Monsenyor. Do you want me to kneel for you in other ways?"

"No. But if I answered yes, would it change your oath?"

"Not at all. It is not a service I owe as part of my oath."

"So, you visited the wife of our host on a mere social call?"

Pedro leaned back, uncrossing his arms, as relaxed and warm as an actual friend. He nudged a wine cup closer to Tomás.

"I'm seeking an enemy, Tomás said. "One who has threatened and harmed Pèire Leteric's family and mine. The woman in the tent has knowledge that might help me."

"Who is your enemy?"

"I don't know, Monsenyor. Evil has come to Pèire's family and mine. It seems to arise from the House of Montcavas in Toulouse."

"Should I be involved? Pèire swore fealty to me. His enemies are my enemies."

"I'm not sure what I can ask, my lord. Some of my business must be done in the bishops' court in Toulouse. Some is personal."

"Toulouse owes fealty to Philippe. If you need help against his vassals, you'll have to come to me."

"Yes, Monsenyor."

"You will ask me?"

"I don't know."

"Why are you hesitating? Asking for aid won't make you any more beholden to me than you are already."

Tomás forged ahead. "I was accused of murdering a priest at Valerós. Pèire promised Hugues de Beaurain to forfeit my life and his castle if we don't appear before the bishop at Narbonne for judgment. But I haven't yet surrendered in Narbonne."

Pedro frowned, the knot of worry in his brow tightening. "I heard a rumor that a gold-dousing priest was murdered up in these hills."

"That's the murder for which we're required to come to you. For judgment."

"If you have a habit of murdering priests, I long to find the man who murdered Pierre de Castelnau, the pope's legate. That murder irritated the pope enough to call this crusade. He thinks my cousin Raymond is responsible. It would help me a great deal if it had been you who murdered the legate."

"Sorry, Monseynor. No priests or legates died by my hand. And many people saw me with the Duke of Burgundy's army the whole season when the legate was killed."

"Are you forfeiting your life to me now, Tomás of Morella?"

"I don't have a choice. I have no proof, only Pèire Leteric swearing I didn't do it. And now he's dead."

"Do I get to hang you?"

"Not until I fulfill my oath to Pèire Leteric. That is, I hope you'll wait, Monsenyor."

"How bad is the story of your enemies?"

"They are using Simon de Montfort against Pèire's family. Simon claims enormous taxes against some of Pèire's lands."

"Valerós is under my protection."

"Simon claims a portion is under the viscount of Carcassonne's protection. He wants taxes, knights, and castles rendered to him."

Pedro drummed the table in seeming irritation.

A solution occurred to Tomás. "Perhaps, Monsenyor, you could put all of Pèire's land under your protection until we can sort it out."

"Done. But I require the rendering of Valerós castles. Will Pèire Leteric's heir accept that?"

Pedro wanted the castles to be available to him if he needed them for defense.

"I'm sure Sebastián will agree." Tomás had to reveal more of their problems. "However, he has gone missing."

"Sancta Maria!"

"It seems to be only a feud with his uncle, the Montcava steward. But if you encounter the boy, will you keep him until his mother or the Valerós knights can fetch him?"

The king studied Tomás, tapping his lower lip with a long, aristocratic finger. "Do you have other problems you want to tell me about?"

"Not any that you can help me with, Monsenyor. May I keep this surcoat? It's a nice color."

Pedro had a deep, musical laugh that showed perfect teeth. "Of course. It looks good on you. Just promise not to murder any priests while wearing it. Now, get out of here. I have work to do."

Tomás picked up his sword and the knife Pedro had given him. "*Bon nuoit*, Monseynor."

"Remember, I own your life," Pedro said. "Come back when you can be useful, Tomás of Morella."

Outside the tent, Miquel rubbed his gloved hands in glee.

"Don't say it," Tomás muttered. "Not one word."

58
Courtesans' Lessons

BACK IN THE IRONWORKERS' quarter, Jean-Luc unpacked the sumpter mule and carefully replaced the portable forge and tools among the camp's equipment. In his tent, he searched his own pack to ensure that every article in it was his own, as he did every night, to be certain that no one could accuse him of thievery.

Then he ate his supper in the mess of another division, so he didn't have to see Eustache, the master armorer who had made the mistake of befriending Jehan the smith. After supper, before the light had completely faded, Jean-Luc returned to his tent to sleep while waiting for the dead of night, when he'd make his escape and go to Toulouse. The braid in his hair slapped across his face when he dropped onto his pallet.

Galahad licked his ear. A warm, soft body slipped in beside him.

"Shh!" Hélène pressed her fingers over his lips. "My guard is making sure we aren't disturbed. We can be together again."

She kept her fingers or her mouth over his lips, so he couldn't speak. Galahad settled against Jean-Luc's backside. "Remember our sweet first year in Antioch?" she said. "Or when we were stranded together in Arles for a month?"

While she whispered, she touched him as they had years before, and his hands wanted to respond. Her skin was as soft and smooth as before; if not when they were young in Antioch, at least as it was when they lost track of time in Arles. She still smelled of almonds and roses, and her dark hair tumbled over them when he pulled a comb free, the long tresses falling in a heavy tangle across his face and chest.

Her breath in his ear sent a frisson of tension and anticipation down his spine. "Or that cold winter in Paris when you and Yves brought horses from the Outremer to Philippe's stables. I had no one to keep me company while Hugues was in Poitiers, and you let me read to you in the thin white light of winter."

"I taught you to read in Paris," he murmured, returning her kisses. He didn't need to recall the past as much as he needed to forget the present.

"Or my favorite time," she whispered. "When we last had long days and nights to ourselves. That beautiful spring when you taught Galahad to fetch. And you taught me what you'd learned from the courtesans in Antioch and Iconium."

His mind wrestled with right and wrong, but his body chose to turn her onto her back, pinion her arms above her head, and pull her smooth, slim legs up to wrap around his hips. She arched toward him, provoking him to dominate her once more, and he pushed into her before she was ready, the way she liked it.

Just before she fell asleep, she murmured, "Come back to our world, Jean-Luc. Come back where you belong." Her words caused Galahad to wake and trot in a circle until he sat down and cuddled against the marquesa again. She whispered endearments to her dog.

Then she said, "You must tell me you love me at least as much as whatever sweet young thing you've been playing with."

.

While thoughtful men told stories around the fires, and happy men cuddled with the baggage ladies, and healthy men slept, Jean-Luc shouldered his pack and moved through the shadows, past the guards who prevented anyone from moving in the other direction, and past the pickets serving sentry duty around the camp's perimeter. He felt sure he'd find his way to Carcassonne in the dark, and then he'd find the main road to Toulouse.

He didn't know how he lived through thirty-two years with so little knowledge of his own mind, or how he could spend so much time determining how to purge his sins, yet never noticed that he always capitulated to the temptations of a small, warm woman who professed pity for him but belonged to another man. This new awareness was more corrosive than any other bitter tonic he'd swallowed lately.

Away from the camp sentries, he slipped down to the river to wash funk from his hands, beard, and body. He stepped from stone to stone in the dark, wishing the water could wash away the stains on his soul. Was every other self-righteous bastard as pathetic a hypocrite as he proved to be?

A rough voice called to him in the common tongue of the Languedoc.

"Halt. You're a spy for the demon of Montfort."

59

Perseus and Parzival

TOMÁS HAD HOBBLED HIS horse across the stream from Hugues's camp. In the moonlight, he removed the particularly fine Aragón surcoat and prepared to ride.

"We always wore whatever colors our paymasters assigned," Miquel said. "I didn't raise you to care about finery."

"I like this surcoat." Pedro's insignia was woven into the silk, with his arms in a deep, rich crimson stitching on the reverse side.

"Tuck it between the blanket and saddle, to keep it clean."

"I thought when you died, I'd no longer be plagued daily with your advice."

"And I thought I was done with counseling ignorant children."

"Father, what did you do that kept you from heaven?"

"What didn't I do, *fadrin*? But I've told you, there's no heaven. There's no hell."

"You can't prove it to me, though."

The narrow track by the stream forced Tomás to walk alongside his horse in the dark as he headed back to the main road, leaving no room for Miquel to walk beside him. Voices wafted over the chuckling of the river rapids.

"We saw you come out of the French camp," a rough voice said. If there was a reply, Tomás didn't hear it.

"You're a spy for the demon of Montfort."

"I'm a journeyman smith," a voice replied in the common tongue, but with a bastard accent. Tomás knew that voice. "I have no weapon. I mean you no harm."

"You're as French as that bastard Simon. I hear it in your speech."
Tomás approached with his sword and long dagger ready. Near
the river's edge, he encountered three ill-dressed men surrounding
a hulking figure.

"This seems dishonorable," Tomás said. "Three to one unarmed?"

"And who might you be?" one voice challenged.

"A sworn knight of the king of Aragón," he said. While he admired the way those words sounded, the victim of the three bullies
used the distraction to knock over one of his attackers with a sweep-
ing kick of his left leg. A massive swing of his right arm knocked a
second man off balance. The third man charged toward Tomás with
his sword out, although he had too much ground to cover for a
charge to be worth the effort.

"*Hola!* Can you fight?" Tomás cried to the besieged man, who
was now his partner by default.

"Yes!"

"Then catch!" Tomás flung his sword to him, the blade flick-
ering in the moonlight. The man caught it neatly, and they both took
the offensive against the attackers.

"Three on one?" Tomás called to the first man who came at him.
"Do you need three with the whores, too? One to hold up your
punxor and the other to stick it in?"

His attacker was ill-trained, and Tomás disarmed him immediately with a hard kick that sent the weapon into the stream. Most
likely, it also broke the man's wrist, given the way he howled.

"Your stench is overpowering," Tomás said. "Perhaps you need
your friends to catch the whores and hold them still for you."

Tomás kicked him in the sternum, so the man followed his
sword into the stream. Then Tomás called to the others: "Any more
whore-catchers who need a beating and a bath?"

His new partner did indeed know how to fight. One of his attackers had a bleeding gash in his arm and couldn't grip his sword.
The other was backing away, clutching his side. The figure rising
from the stream shouted, "Retreat! Retreat!" His friends responded
by running down the trail.

Tomás felt a smug satisfaction that his first engagement as Pedro
d'Aragón's personal knight had resulted in a complete rout of the

enemy. And his timing, speed, and strength seemed satisfactory. He also recognized the sword work of his impromptu partner: it was Jehan the smith. He placed the point of his new dagger at the man's throat in the same way Pedro had confronted him.

"Master Perseus, you left us in the dead of night without saying good-bye. And now you're leaving a French camp like a thief. What stories you must have to tell."

"Sancta Maria! The bastard swordsman is now the arsewit knight of Pedro *le roi.*" He batted away Tomás's blade. "I left because Pèire Leteric told me to. I have private business to attend to."

"Tell me about it." Tomás kicked at the haft of the borrowed sword the man held. Even standing at ease, the man had a strong grip, but a second kick loosened the sword. When it fell at their feet, Tomás booted it out of reach. "I swore an oath to protect Pèire's family. And every day they are deeper in peril."

"Pèire Leteric has a whole cadre of men to protect his family."

"He died the night you left, Perseus." Tomás was forced to call the man by his title in the bonfraires, for lack of his real name. "I need to know you aren't among those who imperil his grandchildren."

"His grandchildren? Which of them?"

"Senhóra Isabella. Senhóreta Beatriz. Sebastián."

"And Senhóreta Felicia? Is she safe?"

"I don't know what's happening at Valerós." Tomás marked the man's question to consider later. For now, he told the story of their adventures on the road. "What did Pèire send you to do?"

"It's my own business."

"If I call on you as bonfraire," Tomás said, "will you tell me?"

"What if I say no?"

"We'll stand here and I'll play arsewit, as you call me, to your stoic through the whole night, until I know."

"You're a better practiced arsewit than I am a stoic."

Tomás bowed. "I'm humbled by the compliment. What is your story, Perseus?"

"I was there when the crusaders entered Constantinople. Someone told lies that put me under sentence of death for stealing booty. Others bore false witness, saying I murdered my brother. Hugues de Beaurain helped me escape, so I'm only excommunicated and exiled. Pèire sent me back to my family."

"What family? Who is your father, Jean-Foutre? Why did Pèire care about you?"

"Pèire and my father were on crusade together years ago."

"Jove's pissing monkey!" Tomás felt he should have seen this. A bonfraire pretending to be a smith? Pèire must have guessed but didn't have time to tell him. "They're after you, too. Why didn't Pèire Leteric tell me about you, Perseus?"

"I prefer to keep my problems to myself."

"Damn it, man, don't you see? Your father is part of this." Tomás explained all of it, from Miquel's losses to the more current evils for Pèire's family. "I've been chasing men all over Christendom, trying to find our enemy. So, tell me."

"Tell you what?"

"Who is your father? That's who our enemy wants to destroy."

"My father hasn't an enemy in the world. He's too good."

"I swear by my own father's hand, someone seeks to destroy you just to hurt your father."

The man considered. Then he said, "My father is the Viscount de Chartrain."

"But Gerard's sons were killed in Constantinople."

"True. But they haven't buried me yet. I am Jean-Luc de Chartrain. And I'm on my way to Toulouse to find a man who might clear my name."

"Sweet dancing angels!" Tomás swore, excited. "Let's go. We must join Senhóra Isabella. I'll wager that Renoud of Montcava is your enemy too, though not as much as mine. We'll help you find your truthteller when we get to Toulouse."

While they decided how best to ride together, Tomás swore again. "I'll have to buy another horse. This is the most expensive tour of Aragón and the Languedoc any knight ever made. At least I didn't have to pay for Anfos's pig."

"What pig?"

"*Ai*, that's a story. We have a long ride if you want to hear it."

.

The swordsman had an intriguing story, but a tension lay under his words that Jean-Luc wanted to understand.

"Are you her lover?" Jean-Luc interrupted the story abruptly.

"No, only her protector," Tomás said.

"Why choose you as protector, instead of Marshal Guillem?"

"She didn't choose me. I gave an oath to Pèire to protect all of them. And Guillem carried Senhóreta Katelina away to a nunnery."

Jean-Luc, behind him on the horse, laughed.

"What's funny? I can feel you shaking."

"Because when I was sent to spy, my father wanted to know if Pèire still had all his faculties. If he chose you as a great protector, then the answer would be no."

"How humorous. If I cock it up, it'll be up to you as a brother to protect Pèire's family."

"I don't consider you my brother."

"Think bonfraires, Perseus. I heard you say the oath, so you're in this too, since I'm calling on you."

"Fine. But please don't tell Senhóra Isabella who I am."

"Why not? She's in this trouble, too."

"Because," Jean-Luc sighed, "however worthless it is, I still have something like pride. I'd rather be taken for an insignificant smith than to be seen by people as a worthless cast-out."

"She wouldn't see it that way."

"It's my name and my honor. Keep it to yourself."

"I won't tell the senhóra," Tomás said. "But I can tell you from experience, she won't like it when she finds out."

After a while, as they jolted along together, Tomás said, "I remember you. At the siege of Jaffa. I lived in the city with my mother. My father sent us to there to be safe, not knowing Saladin planned to attack it."

"But I don't remember you. I remember smoke and garbage and dying dogs and crying women."

"You probably just saw us as street vermin. You and your brother were the only French squires who weren't puking their guts out. You carried arrows and water to a dozen men each. The soldiers finally gave you both turns at the loop holes. My brother and I believed you were valiant."

"It hardly counts as valor. Our father warned us not to drink the water without boiling it."

"You were the only squires who didn't cry your eyes out when we saw Saladin prepare to attack."

"My brother Yves always liked whistling in the dark when there was nothing else to do."

"And you?"

"I pray to the Virgin Mary. I did then. I still do. She protects me."

After a moment, Tomás said, "Maybe the Holy Virgin got you out of Jaffa, but from your story, I don't think the Virgin has done very well by you since Constantinople."

Jean-Luc settled into appreciating the silence as they traveled. But then Tomás began talking again.

"My apologies for that fight at Valerós. I should have done as Pèire asked without humiliating you."

"You won. Your skill exceeds all the pricks in Christendom." Jean-Luc didn't fully accept the apology. "I learned something from it, though."

"Not to leave your middle open when fighting someone smaller than you, which is most of the time?"

"Not to let my feelings get into the fight. You beat me with your overworked tongue, not your sword."

"My sword did fine," Tomás said.

"We'll try it another time when you aren't yapping. Can you fight without talking the whole time?"

"I don't know. I've never tried. But I can teach you how to protect your middle."

"I don't want to learn anything more from you. Your dance is only good for tricks at a village fair. It won't do you any good on horseback or in a melee."

A league later, Jean-Luc asked, "Did you ever do that, let your feelings get in your way during a fight?"

"No, I never have," Tomás said.

"Do you even have feelings?"

"Not usually."

"That's what I thought."

60

Eu Vos Amor

Isabella in the Aude valley
9 days before Pentecost

NO ONE EXPECTED PRIVACY, except the rich who could buy it. Therefore, like everyone else, Isabella had often listened to others' ardors, because there was no choice to do otherwise. At the inn, the woven-reed wall between their two loft-closets gave merely the illusion of privacy. She wrote by rush light, trying not to wonder what kept Tomás away so long and trying not to hear through the wall.

"You didn't need to follow me, Chrétien. I can fetch your rebec by myself."

"Yes, you probably can."

"Are you intending to sing in the dinner hall the whole night once again?"

"What do you think?"

Isabella scratched through a line of the letter she was copying before Durán answered.

"Last night was the loneliest night of my life. Then we spent today talking and laughing together. You got me to tell you everything I've done in my life. When I heard you sing last night, it was as if the angels had taken me to heaven."

"I'm glad you liked it."

"Then you just smiled and said good-night as if I was nobody. And today you did it again. I spent the whole day laughing with you in the garden. These are the two best days of my life, with the worst night ever wedged between. You must know what I'm feeling."

Chrétien didn't answer.

"Did you invite me up here just to torment me? Are you going back to the great hall with your rebec to show off all night? Because if you are, I'm not going to—"

When they stopped talking, Isabella feared they heard her pen scratch as clearly as she heard their breathing.

"No one ever kissed me on the mouth before."

It was quiet again for a long, breathy moment before Chrétien spoke. "And I'm betting you've never been behind a closed door with a real bed, either. You just find who you can on the streets, and they use you and you never see them again."

"Don't be mean. I told you what my life is."

"It breaks my heart to think of it. I'm not toying with you, I swear on my honor," Chrétien said.

"What do you want, then? You just sit there looking at me, while I feel like dying."

"It's like pausing before sipping a truly fine wine. I want to savor the moment."

Durán's voice cried out. It wasn't a word Isabella knew, if it was a word at all.

"Come here, *cor dolç*." He called Durán *sweetheart*. "We don't need to talk now."

She needed to keep her quill point as sharp as possible while writing in the dim light, although she feared the screech of the penknife might disturb them. But then she guessed they couldn't hear anything in the world except each other's breathing. She set the pen down and sipped her wine, listening to the sound of two people falling in love, wanting to weep for envy.

"Can I touch you like this?"

"You can touch me any way you want, *cor dolç*."

"I never did this before."

Isabella lay down on her own pallet and curled into a ball, rocking herself for comfort, feeling a sense of loss for what she'd never had, except for a moment, only as long as a heartbeat, with the donzel Jaume, who had been far younger and even more innocent than Durán. Meanwhile, two voices on the other side of the flimsy reed wall just prayed *ai Dèu, ai Dèu, ai Dèu* into the late night.

She never slept. In the very early morning, while it was still dark, she heard Chrétien again.

"Let's stay together."

"You can't mean it."

"But I do, *cor dolç*. I'll teach you to be a vagabond and a mercenary, and we'll see the world together."

"I'm a goodman who believes in prayer, and you don't."

"I'm taller than you, and that makes about as much difference as the other."

"This must be a dream. Except I'm warm and aching all over."

Jealous beyond reason—not even Jaume had ever spoken so tenderly to her—Isabella paced. The rush light still flamed in its little bowl, and by its dim light she spied that venomous letter from Renoud, the devil's own contrary form of tender speech. She snatched it up and held a corner to the rush lamp-wick until it began to smolder, and then she set it to burn in the brazier, just as the voices nearby rose again.

"Don't you go confessing this to a priest, Chrétien. It isn't a sin. I bet the stupid priest who heard my confessions when I was a Catholic pulled his own wanker after telling me to say a dozen paternosters."

"There's no sin to confess," Chrétien said. "I know you goodmen don't swear oaths, but promise you'll quit your old ways. I want you to be true to me."

Faint laughter carried through the walls.

"This is serious, Durán. Don't lie there laughing at me."

"I'm not laughing. I'm stunned with pleasure. Say it again."

"Promise me—"

"No, say, 'Be true.' It's so exciting. I'll promise, though I have one condition."

"There's no bargaining about this."

"You have to let me say *eu vos amor* whenever I want, even if you don't believe me."

"Why would I stop you?"

"The one time I ever said it, the man beat me half to death as soon as the words left my mouth."

"Come here, *cor dolç*, and say it while you're touching me."

"Wait, there's one more condition."

"This isn't a good time for waiting, Durán. What is it?"

"You can't make me do anything I don't want to. So if you say, 'Come here,' I'll only do it if I want to."

"Of course. We're equals. But that reminds me. I need to tell you a secret before you decide to stay with me."

"But I decided yesterday. Or at least I wished for it so hard that now we truly are staying together. What's your secret?"

"We are equals. My brother Tomás and I, we think we know who your father is."

61

Rendability

COMING TO THE INN at the crossroads, Jean-Luc followed Tomás of wherever-Hell-had-spawned-him. Inside they encountered the inn's mistress, burdened by a bundle of laundry. She pursued Tomás across the great room and up the narrow ladder, and Jean-Luc found he rather enjoyed how she scolded the swordsman.

"I don't like it one bit, senhór. This is a respectable house, and we don't need your like. Who knows who comes in and someone else goes out, thumping around all night. Your squire lit a fire and made the whole house smell of burning leather."

Tomás turned on the woman, a fierce expression on his face. He opened his hand to show her a palm full of silver. She ceased berating him, dropped the laundry bundle at his feet, snatched the coins, and fled. Outside the warren of cells, a thin-as-a-stick lad slept with his head on the rickety door.

"She was friendly when I left. Who knows by now? Wait here, Perseus." Tomás stepped over the sleeping form. "The two pennies I paid him to stand guard was a poor investment, don't you think?"

He didn't close the door behind him as he addressed Isabella of Valerós, the woman within.

.

"You finished your letters, ma dòmna?" Tomás used the gentle voice she'd needed to hear at the woodcutter's cottage, because her whole posture seemed weary. "Was it a hard night?"

"I didn't sleep." She didn't turn around to look at him.

357

"I'll wake Chrétien, and we can be on our way as soon as you are ready."

"Chrétien and his new friend Durán rode out at dawn with merchants headed for Toulouse. He carried copies of the letters for me, and he left his hauberk and sword for you. He said he'd be safer with just his rebec."

"Did he leave a message?" Tomás wasn't surprised by that departure. It fit with their conversation the day before.

"Òc. 'Stay me with flagons. Comfort me with apples.'"

"Ai, he's in love."

"Don Tomás, when were you going to tell me that Durán is my husband Nicolau's bastard son?"

"Today, ma dòmna." Too bad he hadn't warned Chrétien to tell Isabella as well as Durán. "I didn't have a chance before now."

"I see." Her tone was as cutting as a Saracen's knife.

"Perhaps, ma dòmna, you'll tell me what Durán said when Chrétien told him."

"He said, 'Who'd ever guess,' four times. What did you expect? He's like a Great Pyr puppy. He's more excited that Chrétien is teaching him to play the rebec and use a sword."

"He's too old to start that way. Best begin with a quarterstaff."

"You still aren't honest with me."

"I am, I swear it. Chrétien guessed yesterday." Was she about to make him grovel? He could see that this news upset her, yet what sane person wouldn't suspect that a man like Nicolau left a trail or bastards? "You now know as much as I do."

"More," she said. "Chrétien is happier than most of us could ever hope to be. Who were you talking to outside the door?"

"You remember the itinerant smith at Valerós?"

"Yes. And I know he's one of your blasted bonfraires. But he disappeared the night Pèire died. What's he doing here?"

"He's the Viscount de Chartrain's man."

"Pèire told us that. To be precise, he's Gerard's spy. Though he looks like a Whitsuntide mummer."

"I met him at Hugues's camp last night. It turns out only one of Gerard's sons died in Constantinople. The other son was falsely accused of stealing from the Church." Now, to tell her this story without repeating a falsehood while respecting the promise he'd made to Jean-Luc, to protect his secrets. "Jehan the smith has been all over Christendom seeking the men who betrayed the viscount's son."

"It was a long night," she said. "Perhaps I'm not as quick witted as you. Why do I care?"

"Because," Tomás knocked back his frustration, so he sounded rational, "Gerard was one of Miquel's and Pèire's old comrades. He and his sons are also victims of our enemy. Who know how many other poor *baquelars* are out there, thinking God has it in for them when it's just some bastard who hates their fathers."

"I'm too tired for philosophy," she said. "Can Jehan the smith travel with us now that Chrétien's gone? I'd feel safer."

•

Deftly done, to Jean-Luc's way of thinking. Tomás revealed enough but not too much. He could ride with Senhóra Isabella if she believed him only to be Gerard's spy. Which, it seemed, she already knew.

However, Senhóra Isabella's voice reminded him of her foster-sister Felicia. The same accent and rhythm of speech. If there was a plot, Felicia might be in peril, too, though she wasn't a grand-daughter, only a ward, unrelated to Pèire. Or Miquel or Gerard or any other crusader. Her widowed mother had married Isabella's widowed father and then died. Felicia was too insignificant for any enemy seeking to plague those three ancient crusaders.

The bone-thin young man in the hall, roused from sleep, sat up startled when he saw Jean-Luc standing over him. When the lad heard Tomás's voice, panic seized him.

"You can go," Jean-Luc said. "I'll stand watch." And he expected it to be quite interesting.

Tomás burst from the room. "Let's eat breakfast."

He followed the swordsman to a deserted corner of the inn for a breakfast of hot ale and fried porridge.

"Chrétien's hauberk and gambeson might fit you in length." Tomás twitched in agitation while they waited for Senhóra Isabella to join them. "He has a rather fine sword you can use, though I'm sure it's lighter than the Frankish bludgeons you're used to."

"I'll make do," Jean-Luc said. He'd often picked open the seams of a gambeson to make it fit over his shoulders.

"The stable man is seeking a horse for you. And I paid the mistress to find us both clean shirts and breeches in the village. *Per l'amor de Dèu*, I've laid out so much silver at this crossroads, they could add a tower to their church in my name."

"The shirt is much appreciated," Jean-Luc said.

Tomás talked constantly, a stream of words that seemed to come from too little sleep and too much excitement, but all the while he kept glancing at the door, although Jean-Luc couldn't tell if he was nervous or anticipating something.

"I've never ridden so many leagues just to spend silver instead of earning it." Tomás still chattered. "And we've been on the road so long, I'll have to pay a whore for an entire day of picking fleas and lice when we get to Toulouse."

Senhóra Isabella entered the room, looking like a fatigued boy not yet old enough to start a beard, dressed in leather jerkin and hose, her hair tucked into her linen shirt. Burned from the sun, her face and hands glowed red against the white linen undershirt, her fingertips ink-stained. She took Jean-Luc's hands in a Catalan greeting, which seemed gracious in these circumstances, since she was regent of a pair of seigneurial castles, and she knew him to be a lowly spy. The gesture was so touching that Jean-Luc smiled, too, as he clasped her hands. Meanwhile, the swordsman stared at his fried porridge in silence.

"I'm hoping you'll join our journey," she said.

"It's kind of you to ask, but I'm on my way to Toulouse," Jean-Luc said. "Are you returning to Valerós or on to your son's estate?"

"Why would we return to Valerós right now?" Her deep, raspy voice surprised him at Valerós, and now it seemed stronger than her thin, sunburned body could produce.

"You know I work for the Viscount de Chartrain," Jean-Luc said. "Pèire's courier didn't make it through to Toulouse, so I believe Gerard is at Valerós." Although she didn't seem fragile, he didn't want to tell her about fighting crows and the couriers' bones. He didn't expect her reaction.

"Thank God and all the dancing angels!" She brightened, like the sun breaking through at dawn. "He can help Beatriz. She won't be utterly alone. And he has knights to help defend Valerós."

"But…" He'd heard from Felicia how much Isabella didn't want to marry, but he'd also heard none of them would ever go against Pèire's commands. "Aren't you marrying Viscount Gerard?"

She frowned, but it seemed to be her perpetual expression of worry. "I must be at the bishops' court by Pentecost," she said, "because my brother-in-law threatened me and stole my son. But I'll find a way to do what Pèire would, without using a husband to act for me." She addressed Tomás. "The viscount doesn't need to help us the way Pèire asked. Instead, I'll make him a business deal."

"What do you have that he'd want?" Tomás sounded wary.

"Knights trained in the Outremer," she said. "No one has men more experienced in siege warfare than the Valerós knights."

Tomás set down his ale mug and put his head in his hands. "Gerard has his own men. He has no reason to hire you." He glanced at Jean-Luc, as if he wanted support in the argument, but Jean-Luc had already seen enough to know to stay out of it.

"Then I'll go to Narbonne," she said. "One of Pedro's seigneurs must need men."

Tomás said, "The sole word that matters? 'Men.' No one hires mercenaries led by women."

"The sole question for you is whether you choose to remain in my employ, knowing it may be a while before you are paid."

"What do you want me to do?" he cried, sounding like a man in pain. It caused Jean-Luc to pay much stricter attention to what was passing between the swordsman and the senhóra.

"The next time we meet Renoud," she said, "let me kill him."

"You think Renoud is your enemy?" Jean-Luc chose his words carefully, given the anguish in her voice. He'd seen enough of this woman to know she couldn't kill a man.

"You know Renoud?" Her eyes were on him like a hawk's.

"Until yesterday, I thought Renoud helped the viscount's son escape Constantinople. But I learned it was Hugues de Beaurain who helped him."

"How did you find out?" Tomás asked.

Jean-Luc sought an easy answer. "Hugues's wife is an old friend."

"Hélène of Toulouse? That well-known fount of truth?" Tomás sounded scornful.

"You know her?"

"I was with Hélène when Renoud's henchmen did this." Tomás fingered the ugly scar across his cheek. "She must have been busy yesterday, for I talked to Hélène, too."

"You didn't tell me that." Isabella's voice turned to ice in a way Jean-Luc had never heard from gentle Felicia.

"What chance have I had to tell you anything?" Tomás sounded like a placating lover, but then he shuffled his mug on the table, his jaw set. "You didn't tell me that Renoud believes you're marrying Hélène's brother Louis."

"How can Hélène help find your enemy?" Jean-Luc asked. He refrained from stating his opinion of Louis, who at last reckoning owed him seven marks in loans and lost bets.

"She thinks Hugues is Renoud's father," Tomás said. "Which means the Marquis de Beaurain is our enemy."

"No, it's not Hugues," Jean-Luc said. "I've known him all my life. He's an honorable man." He felt Isabella staring at him, but he hadn't revealed what he wanted to hide.

She said, "Tomás, did you discuss Hugues with Pèire?"

"He and Miquel both knew Hugues in the Outremer."

"What did Pèire say?"

"That it couldn't be Hugues. That he'd surrender his immortal soul if it was Hugues."

"Then it's not Hugues." She bit a fingernail, then dropped her hand to rub a blister on another of her ink-stained fingers. "And I can't spend years tracking down an enemy. Valerós and Arracheuse are in peril from Simon de Montfort. Renoud has my son."

"Isabella, things aren't as dire as they seemed yesterday." Tomás offered reassurance while looking desperate. *Ai*, the swordsman was in love. And given how much the senhóra scorned him, one almost felt sorry for the bastard. But only almost.

"I met the king of Aragón in Hugues's camp," Tomás said. "*Bon Dèu*, what a man! When I forfeited myself to him because of that murdered priest, he believed my story, because he respected Pèire so much. Then he put Castell-de-Valerós under his protection. All he asked was rendability."

"*Ai Dèu!* You forfeited Valerós to Pedro? *Fenta baquelar!*" She swore a torrent of oaths only soldiers and street-brawlers used. "You had no right to do that."

Jean-Luc had lived apart from people for a long time, but he still recognized Tomás's signal for him to leave. He did as the swordsman asked. But he was no longer so civilized as to forego listening at the door.

.

"No, Isabella," Tomás said, though surprised at her violent reaction. "I forfeited myself to the king because of that dead priest. He let me go so I can to keep my oath to Pèire. Pedro considers Valerós under his protection. You only render your castles if he needs them."

"Mercy! How can it get worse?" Isabella's voice was filled with despair as she cried for mercy.

"You can trust Pedro. He made me swear an oath as his knight. *Ai Dèu*, he's like Pèire, a leader that you want to do whatever he asks. And he likes me."

"He likes you? He let you forfeit your body to him. Is that also how you got Hélène to talk to you? She'll sleep with anyone with a title or money. She'd fornicate with Gerard's mummer of a spy if he had two bezants to his name."

"Why so much passion, ma dòmna? Did Chrétien and Durán disturb you?"

"Chrétien is welcome to every dram of happiness he can find." Isabella's voice crunched, as if her breath passed over shards of pure fury. "Do not discount my wrath as mere pettiness."

"Isabella, I don't understand." This was as frustrating as their last discussion at Valerós. "What's wrong?"

"What's wrong? A fey Languedoc hawker kisses your brother and gets half of Montcava. You forfeit Valerós to Pedro d'Aragón, when he's the last person who can keep us safe."

Tomás tried the soft voice that had comforted her once. "You're exhausted, ma dòmna. Do you want a nap before we ride?"

"I shall sleep when my enemies are on their knees, begging dark angels for mercy. We need to be on the road. Now."

"But for what sin am I being punished?" And how had he ended up feeling once more like he had to beg her for mercy. "Is it because I submitted to my own king so I'm not hung for murdering that infernal priest?"

"You might as well hang now as later."

"If you're going to be a captain of mercenaries, ma dòmna, then control your feelings. Use the sense God gave you."

"I despise your arrogance, Don Tomás of God-knows-where. I do not want you to make decisions for me."

"Fine. If Marshal Guillem is at Lagrasse, I'll leave you with him. Otherwise, I'll take you to Pedro."

"Listen to me, please. I made a single mistake, leaving Valerós. But I'm not a fool. You and Pèire kept secrets from me. But the problem is greater than just my lost son or your lost estate or the demon that shoots arrows at us."

"What do you mean?"

"Look at this letter you left with me, Tomás. Read it again."

"'We'll burn your cubs.'"

"Forget that part. It's this: 'Your Rock won't help you. God won't come to Aragón, when Aragón is Gomorrah.'" She was seeking his response. "Don't you see? Our enemy is Pedro's enemy. If we go to Pedro, we deepen the danger for all of us."

"Our enemy is Hugues de Beaurain and his ill-gotten son Renoud. Hugues has no reason to threaten Pedro."

"*Petrus* must mean *Pedro*. Why else talk about Gomorrah and Aragón? You must know what they say about him."

"This letter is about Pèire, not Pedro. You imagine things."

"I imagine I'd be better off traveling with a blind donkey-drover, Don Tomás of wherever."

"Cyprus. I'm from Cyprus."

.

Jean-Luc stepped back from listening at the doorway just as Tomás burst into the hallway. He grabbed Jean-Luc's arm as he passed, and then in the yard on the way to the stable, he said. "You lead, Perseus. I'm not fit for it."

"Why me?"

"You have a better title, and you're Perseus in the bonfraires. I'm carrion, fit for crows."

"I have no title. I can't lead."

"But I'm the seigneur of copulating sheep while you're the son of a viscount. If you won't lead, I'll end up hanged for strangling the spiteful Queen of Jerusalem."

"I'll try to help," Jean-Luc said.

"And stop spying. It doesn't become the heir of a viscount."

While they went to ask the stable boy to have their horses ready as quickly as possible, Tomás remained in a state.

"And whatever you think, Perseus, I didn't couple with either Hélène or Pedro last night."

"I didn't think. I'd never ask."

Tomás didn't seem to hear his voice. "But my mother must have coupled with the devil, which is why my life is a leper's hell."

Jean-Luc, in his new role as leader, sought the inn's mistress, who gave him the new linen Tomás had paid for. Then he helped pack the horses, preparing to ride across the Languedoc plains with the two itchiest people in Christendom. A nap wouldn't cool either of them.

At least now he had a horse. And a sword and chainmail. And companions who wanted to be in Toulouse as badly as he did.

Lubos with New Friends

LUBOS TRAVELED WITH NEW FRIENDS. Of course, they weren't really friends, because you can't trust people who say they are your friends any more than you can trust a man who claims he's your brother. Both want to steal from you, pick your pocket, take your food. Or worse. Didn't the great Esau in the priest's story prove that? Damn brothers, anyway.

Back on the plains, there were too many people, and it grew confusing, trying to separate friend from foe. Counting possible enemies felt as impossible as counting the stars. That's why he now traveled with a double-brace of men. He stayed with them once he knew they wouldn't attack him, which also helped him to judge whether others they met were enemies.

But he couldn't stand the smell. Or the noise.

It had been so much nicer in the hills, where he could converse with his real friends in the trees and stones.

No matter. He washed his sword and rubbed it with sand. Aykuna hadn't told him so, but he'd learned that the spirits also lived in steel. After all, when you separate a man's soul from his body, the soul has to go somewhere. When you use your sword to take a man's soul, it makes sense that you get to keep the soul if it goes into your blade.

He wrapped his hand around the handle and touched the blade's edge, feeling the throb of the souls he'd taken.

✦✦✦

PART SIX
Vitriol and Wine

This chant carries my sighs,
With a wish to sing about my dolorous state.
I will never be obedient ....
For now, I am going into exile.
In grand panic, in grand peril,
In war I am leaving my son,
And the vermin nearby will hurt him.

— Guilhem IX
"Pos de chantar m'es pres talenz"

In Part Six

62
The Vale of Roses

Jean-Luc at the Lagrasse abbey
9 days before Pentecost

JEAN-LUC COMMANDED THE LEAD, as the swordsman requested. At Lagrasse, he knocked at the gate of the monastery to ask for the sister house, but before he said a word, the porter heaped a torrent of abuse on him.

"There's no hostel here. We shelter only monks. You'll have to find your board and fodder elsewhere. This isn't a way-stop for marauding knights."

"I'm looking for your sister-house," Jean-Luc said. "We're seeking a woman who has taken shelter in a nunnery."

"We have no sister house. Go see the Fontrevists up the Vale of Roses. They take everyone in, man and woman alike." The porter began ranting. "Though I don't know how much longer the pope will put up with that. Monasteries live under a Rule for a reason."

Jean-Luc waited patiently while the porter castigated him for the travails of put-upon monks perpetually troubled by travelers plaguing their gates. Finally, Jean-Luc interrupted to ask directions to the Fontrevist abbey.

After giving him information, the porter said, "And you'd best warn them that heretic knights are attacking the monastic houses. They probably haven't heard yet."

"What?" Jean-Luc, astounded, hadn't seen evidence in the past months that resentment in the south had led to such bold action.

"Some heretics paid a Moor to kill a priest at Fontfroide just yesterday. He murdered another up in the hills earlier this spring."

"Why would they do that?"

"The Cistercian monks chanted through the sieges last summer. That's why these heretics are out for our blood. They hated the Church and its priests before, but now they'll murder anyone they can find, the same as they kill babies for their heathen rites."

Jean-Luc saw no use in arguing. Instead, he thanked the porter and then fell back with Isabella and Tomás.

"It's another half a day to ride up this valley, the porter said."

Then he repeated the news about the heretic knights out murdering priests.

"*Ai Dèu!*" Isabella cried.

"Pedro knows better," Tomás snapped. "I already explained to him what happened to the priest in Valerós."

"Your king isn't around right now," Jean-Luc said.

"Pedro can't help us," Isabella said. "He's in the same mortal danger we are. And I'm not rendering our castles in exchange for his protection."

After Jean-Luc interfered in the arguments, they agreed to split up: he and Senhóra Isabella would seek Katelina, and Tomás would join them after hiring messengers in Lagrasse to deliver Isabella's letters to Simon de Montfort and Pedro d'Aragón.

.

THE DAY GREW WARM. The sickly sweet aroma of lavender competed with honeysuckle. Dressed as a mercenary, again in someone else's clothes, Jean-Luc dozed in the saddle, daydreaming that he could recover both Felicia and his name. Even Senhóra Isabella of Valerós grew less agitated in the steamy heat, asserting aloud that they'd find the Valerós knights at the end of this day's ride.

But all possible pleasures of a day in May disappeared when they crested the rise and gazed down into the little valley that held the Fontrevist abbey.

Surrounding the low stockade wall of the main buildings, a city of tents and shanties covered the sides of the rocky valley and spilled down into the farmland. The wail of crying children and the stink of sewage wafted up in the same breeze that perfumed the air on the other side of the hill.

"What is it?" Isabella asked.

"Half of Carcassonne, I'm betting."

"Sancta Maria, how can they live like this?"

"By having no other choice," Jean-Luc said. "Senhóra, respectfully, I'd like to be the sole voice to speak with the authorities here."

"Òc, thank you. I agree."

The gated entry into the Abbaye St-Marie de la Vale des Rosa was more like a toll-taker's barrier than the protective gate of a castle. Three nuns argued with people on both sides of their barricade about who should be allowed in and who inside must depart. The Fontrevists offered shelter to refugees in exchange for work on the monastical lands, raising food, tending animals, or helping to repair the abbey. Each person had to swear an oath and repeat the Apostles' Creed to pass the barricade. The nuns told each beseeching party that the abbey had no room for new refugees. However, any suitably tragic story seemed to break the nuns' resistance, and yet more people were admitted to the city of tents on the hillsides.

"Greetings, Holy Sisters, in the name of our Lord and Savior," Jean-Luc said when their turn came to claim the nuns' attention. "We are knights of the Marquis Hugues de Beaurain, seeking a woman who may be here."

"Alas, my lords, it's impossible. We don't know the names of all who huddle here. We can send out among the shanties, and maybe in a few days we'll find her for you."

"We're seeking a noblewoman who might have joined your order. Senhóreta Katelina of Valerós?"

"Òc, senhór." The woman brightened, becoming more welcoming. "She is here, and the knights who brought her. The prioress can help you. Who shall we say you are?"

"Jehan and Sebastián of Valerós."

While a nun went in search of the prioress, he and Isabella said their Creed and swore their oaths. Isabella pitched her voice low and made a convincing boy, aided by the man's arming cap that covered her sun-bronzed hair.

The sisters who tended people inside the abbey barricade were haranguing two despicable-looking travelers who refused to leave.

E . A . S T E W A R T

"You agreed to our rules, senhórs: no drinking to excess, no harassing the women, and regular work. Yet in two days, you've broken all the rules and stolen bread meant for little children."

"*Ai*, thank you, sisters. We carried bread up to sick babies at the end of the valley. And haven't we been working hard in the bitter sun? You can't begrudge a man a sip of wine to refresh his strength."

"You gave an oath, senhór, in Our Lord's name," one sister said.

Beyond them, under the shade of a small cypress grove, another wolfish face stared back at Jean-Luc. A man the size of Yves, familiar yet malevolent.

He touched Isabella's elbow. "Look over there, under the trees. Do you know that man?"

That face had disappeared in the mass of dirty, ragged bodies.

"*Ai Dèu!*" Isabella exclaimed. "It's those rotten crusaders from the toll-barrier who claim they know Pèire Leteric!"

She ducked, hoping not to be seen, but one of them spied her and nudged his partner, smirking. "That sweet squire boy found himself a new master."

The shorter and fatter of the two men squinted into the sun to see Isabella and Jean-Luc. "Guess the boy wanted it bigger and harder than he got from the Moor."

Jean-Luc strode across the clearing, picked up the smaller man, and tossed him over the barricade, where he landed on his backside in the dust. The other man, even more slow-witted, froze in surprise, which made it easy for Jean-Luc to leverage that man's weight and hoist him over, too.

"These kind sisters will send your gear," Jean-Luc said.

He shifted into his most challenging posture, legs spread and braced for whatever they might try, although they were the cowardly, rabbity sort of men who attack only from behind. It cheered him when the crowd in the clearing pointed and laughed as the two wretches scrambled to their feet.

"Thank you, senhór," a woman's voice spoke. "Though we try to solve our problems with words rather than violence here."

Feeling caught out by a censorious mistress, Jean-Luc bowed low to the prioress and tried to recall how to cozen *religieuse*.

"Good day, Mother Prioress. I am a knight of Hugues de Beaurain, and this is Sebastián, the heir of Castell-de-Valerós. We're seeking our friends here."

The prioress was a small, prim woman with a sharp nose and bright eyes, awake to nuances of the events around her. She was no perpetual virgin who had grown up in a convent, but a seasoned business woman who, Jean-Luc guessed from her accent, came to the veil after living as the wife of a lord. From her lips, the common tongue sounded as smooth as any Provençal marquesa might speak.

"Senhóreta Katelina of Valerós resides in our guest house," the prioress said. "However, the senhóreta requested solitude. We must respect her wishes."

"And her escort? The knights from Valerós?" Isabella asked, forgetting either to be quiet or to speak as a man.

"The Valerós knights are a gift from God," the prioress said, "but most have taken ill with camp fever. If you want to wait here until your friends are well, perhaps you can spend time helping our little village."

Jean-Luc said, "You have more than a village to care for, Mother Prioress. You have a city."

The prioress led them along a set of paths among the tents and shanties. "With the warming weather, camp fever has become a problem. The Valerós knights built new latrines and moved people away from the stream, but then the knights fell ill. Thanks be to God, your friends were strong enough to withstand the ravaging fever."

Jean-Luc kept searching for the wolfish face he'd seen at the gate, but the crowd was a mosaic of shaggy, desperate faces. Each time he saw that face, it disappeared again. A troop of dirty children ran past, barefoot and laughing.

"It's the children I worry about," the prioress said. "Sick for a single day, a baby dies. With people crowded together like this, we continue to bury children each morning."

As they passed the tent-homes on the south side of the valley, the prioress pointed out that many women were pregnant.

"When Carcassonne surrendered, the crusaders allowed the citizens to leave the city. However, many women were raped by marauders as they tried to find shelter in the countryside. All winter I worried about how to find homes for these children. Now I worry we will fail to keep them alive."

She led them back up a trail near the stream to the abbey itself. Jean-Luc continued to search out that face, the hairs at the back of his neck tingling with the sensation of being watched. Yet each time he turned around, he found only the myriad unwashed faces of women and children.

"We've begged Simon de Montfort for more measures of grain," the prioress said. "Many lords have sent us foodstuffs, from as far away as Toulouse and Narbonne, though it's often old, rotten grain and moldy cheese. On very unhappy days, I fear the heretics' goal of annihilating life on earth will come true if the armies empty more cities into the countryside."

Looking about the grim Vale of Roses, Jean-Luc considered the injustice that admitted him into the abbey itself. If he'd been born of another mother, he'd be sleeping in filth, eating putrefied grain, and going barefoot into the gorse to search out twigs for firewood, with the slimmest hope of a better life before winter returned.

"We have the creek," the prioress said, "but its waters will be too low come summer to sustain everyone. The sisters are seeking places for people, either as farmers on the plains or shepherds in the upper hills. But most households have already received many relatives and friends when the French forced everyone out of Carcassonne. We have too many with nowhere to go."

Senhóra Isabella turned the color of parchment beneath her sunburn as they toured the camp. Jean-Luc repressed a similar sickened reaction. He'd seen such misery before, but only in the aftermath of a battle in the Outremer, never where Christians had shoved aside other Christians to take their land and their homes.

Isabella said, "We can receive some refugees at Valerós."

Jean-Luc felt relief hearing her proposal but shook his head to remind her that he alone was to speak.

She didn't let him catch her eye. "We don't have provisions to help the people travel," Isabella said. "But if you can arrange that, our villages can take at least two hundred people."

"Thanks be to God! Gracious donzel," the prioress said, "this will surely help us."

.

The abbey in the Vale of Roses was a poorly constructed, half-finished set of buildings, part stone and part timber-and-plaster, and more like sheds than houses. The abbey stood behind a low wall that could keep out only foxes and stray dogs.

The layout of the nunnery imitated more established abbeys, though unlike the Cistercians, the Fontrevists housed both nuns and priests, with a wall down the middle of their abbey, separating their domains. Stacks of stones in the service yard indicated grand ambitions, but the stonemasons' shed showed no sign of activity. Red chickens and white geese roamed the yard, picking at beetles and scorpions on the sun-warmed faces of the builders' stones.

Walking through the yard on the priests' side of the wall, Jean-Luc prepared to meet a man he'd hoped never to see again.

"Master Guillem!"

When Senhóra Isabella called his name, Guillem turned, smiling at Jean-Luc, and then smiling more broadly when he recognized the disguised donzel. From across the yard, he greeted them in the Catalan manner, his arms high in the air, a motion Jean-Luc always mistook for a gesture of despair, although he knew it was to call down blessings from heaven. Then Guillem threw his arms around Jean-Luc, pounding his back. When Guillem let go of the embrace, tears streamed down his cheeks.

"*Senhór baquelar!*" Sir rogue, Guillem cried. "I hoped you'd turn up again, you mangy cur."

Jean-Luc clasped Guillem's hand and smiled, as he pushed aside a rush of feelings, the chief of which was shame.

Father Anselm poked his head out of the infirmary door, seeking the cause of the commotion. Then he rushed to clutch Senhóra Isabella in his arms and he too wept.

They learned that the Valerós knights had endured a hard time. Guillem and Father Anselm had resisted the fever, but then they worked themselves into exhaustion caring for the horses, fetching supplies, and nursing the ten men from Valerós.

Over a meal of potage and dark bread in the infirmary, Isabella said, "I don't understand why you brought Senhóreta Katelina away from Valerós."

"We meant only to leave on the journey Pèire planned," Guillem said. "But Katelina insisted it was Pèire's plan that we bring her here."

"And Pèire had our sworn oath to serve her after he died," Father Anselm said.

"But you didn't pause to tell me of your plan," she said.

"We thought it best," Guillem said, "if you were to stay safely at Valerós."

Senhóra Isabella bit back a response. Jean-Luc silently applauded her. She'd recovered from her morning tantrums.

"We are all done in," Isabella said. "We need to sleep. Then later we'll make new plans."

Guillem and Father Anselm offered a cot for Isabella in the shed by the stables. Jean-Luc pitched up the ladder into the stable loft and sank into the deepest sleep he'd known in a fortnight.

63

Fontrevists

"MORE VINEYARDS, THAT'S WHAT you plant."

"No, peaches," Isabella said. "The bishop in Narbonne will pay their weight in gold."

"Too much risk, *xiqueta*. One frost can ruin the whole season."

She waved toward the lower valley beyond Valerós, where storks flew over the olive orchards, their monster nests a maze of sticks and rushes. "We'll plant in that vale in Arracheuse. It's protected from the winds, yet the sun shines from early morning to late afternoon."

Daylight glared off the whitewashed plaster on farmhouses. Songbirds flitted from cypress to mountain ash.

Pèire shook his head. "Vineyards, I tell you. If those blasted crusaders stay for long, they'll thirst for more than blood and gold."

Isabella woke, not in Valerós, surprised at the darkness. The clamor of work and hum of worship had died down in the abbey.

She dressed in breeches and soft boots, and then crossed the service yard and vaulted the low wall separating the sisters' quarters. She sought the shed that served as the nuns' laundry, where she borrowed a rough linsey-woolsey garment, and then crept along the wooden walls of the hostelry, seeking Katelina.

A figure slept on a servant's cot outside the only cell door that showed light through the cracks. Isabella pressed open the door as quietly as possible. As if expecting guests, Katelina sat in the sole chair in the tiny cell, her hands on the small table in front of her, unadorned by rings or bracelets, and uncharacteristically doing nothing. When she saw Isabella, she motioned for quiet, pointing to the figure sleeping by the door.

"They've honored me with a lay sister as servant," Katelina whispered. "She sleeps soundly. Myself, I don't sleep."

"What are you doing here, Katelina?"

"I help the suffering people outside."

Isabella said, "Go home. The prioress is sending two hundred people to Valerós. Show them the way."

"Leave me be, *xiqueta*."

"No. Why did Beatriz send you away?"

"I came of my own volition. If you're worried, I have my own gold to buy a place in this house. I did not take gold from Valerós."

"Such a thought never occurred to me," Isabella said. "We came to bring you back. Beatriz was in a passion of grief."

"Don't blame Beatriz."

"You haven't taken the veil yet. Come away with us."

"The pope insists this house can have only eighteen women. I must wait for an elderly sister to join her Savior in heaven."

"You don't belong here," Isabella said. "You aren't a Catholic."

"I intend to take a vow of silence. It won't matter to other people what I believe."

"You'll be living a lie."

"I've done that most of my life."

After a long silence, Isabella said, "Everything is in havoc. Renoud snatched Sebastián the day you left. I was attacked when we tried to follow you. Renoud is telling people we murdered a priest at Fontfroide. He claims we're all heretics."

"Everyone in the south is now called heretic." Katelina waved her hand in the same way Pèire dismissed bad ideas.

"The wool shed burned the day we left, too. Now there's no hope we can pay our taxes," Isabella said.

"I can't be part of your world any longer."

"Katelina, please. I don't have anyone I can trust."

"Yes, you do. Don Tomás promised Pèire he'd help you."

"It isn't working." Isabella sank to her knees, laying her head in Katelina's lap. "I killed a man, Katelina."

"Was it that priest?"

"No. Why does everyone think that?"

"I'd do it myself, for the terrible things that priest told you, blaming you for Nicolau's and Renoud's sins." Katelina rested her hand on Isabella's head, her fingers tucked under the head covering, brushing Isabella's temples, as if Katelina couldn't help offering comfort the same as always.

"No. I killed one of Renoud's henchmen. He declared he intended to rape me, but I stopped him before he could touch me."

"And so probably saved other women, too. You don't still believe what that despicable priest said?"

"No."

"Then what?"

"There was blood everywhere."

Katelina embraced Isabella at last. "My poor darling girl."

She let Katelina stroke her head for a moment, but then she got up and sat on the cot again. "But now I know I could kill Renoud myself. Even if it means seeing his blood."

"Stop thinking about murder. It won't help you or Sebastián. Go to Pedro if you can't trust Tomás."

"But Pedro is part of this danger. Whoever they are—the Knights of the Lunate Cross—they mean to harm Pedro. Didn't Pèire see that threat in the last Wolf letter?"

"Santa Maria!" Katelina whispered. "I kept that letter from Pèire."

"Who wrote it?"

"I don't know."

"Can it be Hugues de Beaurain, as Tomás claims?"

"No. Hugues is a true friend to us. It can't be Hugues."

"Do you know the smith who fought Don Tomás before the bonfraires? The one Pèire said was a spy? Who is he?"

"Someone Pèire knew a long time ago in the Outremer."

"He is going to Toulouse with us. Don Tomás thinks Gerard de Chartrain and his sons have also been attacked by whoever wrote the Wolf letter."

Katelina breathed sharply. "We should have guessed that. You must tell Viscount Gerard when you meet him at Fontcours."

"The smith says Gerard never received Pèire's message, so he is at Valerós with Beatriz."

"Thanks be to our Holy Father!" Katelina sighed. Isabella had never heard her friend care so much about divine beneficence. "I prayed someone might take care of her. Don Tomás has enough to do, just caring for you."

"I don't want Tomás to take care of me."

"Don't be foolish. He's the best man to help you."

"But he's a liar and a murderer."

"No. Miquel twisted him into an assassin. Pèire taught him better. And bonfraires cannot lie. What's the real problem, *xiqueta*?"

Isabella sat for a moment. "I can't bear how it feels when that man is near me."

.

"We'll come back at summer's end, on the way home to Valerós," Isabella said. "Please talk to me then, one more time."

"All right, if I haven't taken vows by then."

After kissing Katelina good-bye, fighting tears, Isabella left the hostelry cell. She lingered by the separating wall, waiting for a safe moment to cross over. A white-robed cleric stepped outside the main house.

"Sister," he said in a low voice. "Please serve our Father Abbot for a moment. I must attend to nature's call."

"I can't."

"Just wait by the door."

A voice called from within.

The cleric said, "Please see what he needs. I cannot tarry."

He fled toward the latrines. Isabella followed her courage, stepping across the wall to answer the abbot's call.

"Pare Abát!" she cried. The man in the abbey's guest room was the abbot of St-Féliz-de-Fontcours.

He glanced up in surprise from his meditations, straining to see her in the dim light. "I know that voice, but I can't place it."

"It's Isabella of Valerós. I hope you'll greet me as a friend."

She knelt to kiss his hand and receive his blessing. The abbot's damp, soft hands were swollen, and he'd removed his rings. The flesh puckered around his soft brown eyes, although otherwise the abbot had grown even thinner in the years since they last met. In those old days, the abbot used to put his hand on Isabella's shoulder in greeting, one of the few who cared for her and handled her gently.

Now, after he blessed her, the abbot put his hand on her shoulder again, studying her in the candlelight. Then he gestured where he wanted her to sit.

"And so, child, you've taken the veil? I can't say how much it pleases me. It suits your studious mind."

"No, Pare Abát." She called him Father Abbot, though he was unlike anyone's father, with his soft, kindly ways and his scholarly, myopic religiosity. "I borrowed some clothes, because my traveling garments are ruined. I am surprised to see you so far from home. I didn't know you were abbot here, too."

"We have several daughter houses, gifts to the Fontrevists from lords to preserve homes for their widows and daughters. The prioresses manage each house. I take advantage of their hospitality when I'm traveling. The bishops have kept us all busy this season."

"I'm happy that God brought you here."

"But what brings you so far from home, Senhóra Isabella?"

"My grandfather died. Our family is upset in every way. I came here to talk to a friend before she takes vows."

"I am so sorry to hear of your loss." He touched her hand. "Was it painful? Did he linger?"

"No, it was sudden. Those of us left behind feel all the pain."

"What a tragedy for you."

The abbot spoke in the same tender way as when she lived in Toulouse, his voice tinged now with the rasp of advancing age. In years past, he'd served as a kindly spiritual guide while she lived in hell. On Sebastián's fourth birthday, the abbot showed him more kindness than the boy ever had from the Montcavas.

It struck her that the abbot was the best of messengers for her letter to Simon. She started to ask, but he spoke again.

"Senhóra Isabella, I've been thinking of you with a heavy heart. Your brother Renoud met me yesterday, asking my help with a writ of grievance against you, which he sent to the bishops' court."

"No!" she cried. "*Ai*, Pare Abát, what he claims isn't true."

"God is your judge. If you say it's not true before God, then I believe you."

"Thank you, Pare Abát. Would you hear my confession, like in the old days?" Isabella tried to think of what to say. She couldn't confess about the dead mercenary at Anfos's cottage or about the torment Tomás represented.

"With the Count of Toulouse excommunicated, the clergy isn't allowed to hear confession. But I've always endeavored to serve as your spiritual guide. What can I do to relieve the burdens you carry?"

"How can I believe God is good," that deep anxiety burst from her, "when it's impossible to find goodness in the world?"

"Child, you must hold to the faith as we say it in our creed."

"That's my sin. I often believe more in my own reason than in the faith of our fathers."

"These are grave sins." He used the same words Father Clémence used when she told him how Nicolau and Renoud treated her. "You need more than paternosters to say for such sins. You must retire to a house of women dedicated to God."

"It's a dream of mine to do so, Pare Abát. But for now, I must act for my family. I cannot retreat from the world."

"Since I cannot absolve your sins, I can only offer guidance. Say your Creed ten times in the day, so you always have it in your heart."

"Father, when will the bishops' court consider Renoud's writ?"

"The Monday after Pentecost."

Isabella breathed a sigh. Ten days away, giving her a sliver of time to find ways to stop Renoud. "How am I to prove to the court I'm not a wanton woman?"

"More important, you must prove you aren't a heretic."

"What?"

"He condemns you as a goodwoman who abjures marriage and denies the beneficent nature of our Holy Father and the salvation Our Lord promised."

"He isn't accusing me of wantonness?" She regretted every word of her confession.

"His writ points to that as a symptom of heresy."

"Renoud has sworn falsely. He wants to destroy my life so that he can take my son." *And because I tried to kill him.* She remained bitter that neither she nor God had struck Renoud dead at Fontfroide.

"It's natural for Nicolau's family to want the boy at home. But you say you aren't a heretic. The bishops' court administers justice, not unfair reprimands."

"How do I prove it?"

"What commitment did your grandfather make to our crusade?"

That question startled her. "I'm journeying with our knights to join Hugues de Beaurain at Fontcours. Is that enough to prove I'm loyal to the Church?"

"One can no longer think so, with the Languedoc lords making promises and then switching sides. We've heard that Pèire Leteric helped murder your confessor Father Clémence. And Valerós shelters heretics and schismatics."

"Pèire didn't murder anyone. He was as loyal to the Church and Pedro d'Aragón as any man in Aragón."

"If you are bringing knights to the crusade and swearing loyalty to the Church, it might go well for you."

Isabella clasped her hands to keep them from shaking.

"Pare Abát, will you speak for me in the court?"

"I want to help you, Senhóra Isabella. I'll say what I can in your defense. But only you can help yourself. At the heart of it, you know you aren't living the life of a good Catholic woman."

"How can you say so?"

"You have no husband to help you live the consecrated life Our Lord intended for women. Only a heretic refuses to have a husband."

"I promised Renoud I'd marry by Pentecost. Pare Abát, if you see him, tell Renoud that I am doing as he asks. May I write a letter for you to carry to him?"

The abbot gave her quill, ink, and parchment to write a missive to her brother-in-law. She used it to plead the fiction of her familial goodwill, claiming Tomás carried her away against her will. Once she finished writing lies, she jabbed the quill back into its lovely carved holder. A tray alongside the inkpot held the abbot's rings, and the ruby in his signet ring reflected the candlelight. In an impulsive moment, she let it fall into her sleeve.

"I have nothing with which to seal this." She hoped the abbot would read her fictions. "And I must ask another favor of you. If you encounter Pedro, can you give him a message from Valerós?"

The abbot protested the improbability of meeting the king, because Pedro has left for Narbonne the day before. But she wrote her simple message, this time in the common tongue of the south: *You are in grave danger. Beware Crux Lunata.*

After the ink dried, she folded it into a packet and gave it to the abbot, feeling as the Outremer lords must have felt when they sent pigeons to seek help against a siege.

•

When she returned to Guillem's shed, she found Tomás there, dressed as a Cistercian lay brother. The cowl hid most of his face, but his eyes flashed as she entered, reflecting the glow of the rush lamp. She bit her lip to keep from showing the pure joy she felt at his return.

"Are we speaking to each other again, Sister Isabella?" He touched the sleeve of her stolen habit.

"I talked to Katelina," she said. "She refuses to come home, but an elderly sister must die before she can be admitted here. There is still time to persuade her."

"Shall I speak with her?"

Ignoring his question, she said, "Katelina says our enemy isn't Hugues de Beaurain. She said someone can't be so good and evil at the same time."

"That's the same argument that Pèire used," he said. "I'm still not convinced."

"Katelina agrees with you that Gerard de Chartrain and his family are joined in our peril. She agrees with me that the second Wolf letter is about Pedro." She removed her head covering and pushed back the stray hairs escaping her braid. "Katelina found the first Wolf letter in the Outremer. That means she knew Pèire for a long time."

"More than thirty years," Tomás said.

"It's unpleasant how you know family secrets I don't. Did you put a spell on Pèire?"

"I look like my father."

"And I look like my grandfather, but you tell me lies. Why are you dressed as a monk?"

"To travel easily. Renoud put out the story everywhere that a mad Moor from Valerós is murdering priests."

"It's soon dawn. We can't be seen like this in the abbey." She removed the borrowed habit and folded it while standing in a linsey-woolsey shift. "Bring Father Anselm and Marshal Guillem here, please. I need their help understanding what to do next."

"And Jehan the smith, too."

"All right, if you insist."

After he left, she put the abbot's ring in her leather pouch, hearing it clink against the tarnished piece of brass that had been Nicolau's only gift to her when Sebastián was born.

64
Cavallers de Pedro Rei

Jean-Luc at the Vale of Roses
8 days before Pentecost

JEAN-LUC WOKE BEFORE DAWN and went into the alcove off the infirmary, where he found Father Anselm and Guillem with Benito, the Valerós master-at-arms. They were toasting cheese on a brazier. Guillem rose and grasped both of Jean-Luc's hands in the Catalan way, as warmly as when they'd been friends at Valerós.

"Welcome, my friend. We are lucky you've joined us."

When he offered Jean-Luc bread and hot cheese, their hands touched, and all the feelings Jean-Luc has denied since the night with the bonfraires in Valerós—shame, jealousy, loss, betrayal—cascaded over him. He managed to say, "I'm happy to see you again."

Tomás the swordsman came in then. Father Anselm offered him bread and cheese, but Tomás shook his head. "Senhóra Isabella wants to speak with all of you. Father Anselm, are there cloves in the apothecary? I have a toothache Job himself could not endure."

Jean-Luc trailed behind, walking alongside the swordsman, who had the glazed, mad look of an insomniac. He studied the Moorish madman while the knights listened to Isabella.

"Renoud has denounced me to the Church as a heretic," she said. "I must appear before the bishops' court the Monday after Pentecost to prove otherwise. Pentecost is in nine days."

"How do you know this?" Father Anselm seemed calm, while the others expostulated oaths of dismay.

"The abbot of St-Féliz-de-Fontcours is here. He was my friend years ago, and he saw the writ Renoud sent yesterday."

"First Renoud wanted you to marry his cousin," Tomás said. "Now what does he want?"

"After Fontfroide, he seems to have changed his mind."

Senhóra Isabella told the long story of their troubles. While Jean-Luc heard the story again, his mind first wondered to what he should do, which seemed at first that he should take the horse Tomás lent him and ride straight to Toulouse, pursuing the man who might help restore his name. And then to find his father. But it became clear as he studied one knight's face and then another that all of them were prepared to do whatever Senhóra Isabella asked. And these were his bonfraires; he'd sworn to support and defend them. He needed to stay with these knights for now. He'd end up in Toulouse anyway, but in the time his bonfraires required, not to meet his own need to find a phantom he hoped might save him.

Isabella said, "In April, Renoud demanded I return to Toulouse with Sebastián. The murdered priest brought letters threatening to expose Pèire as a rebel who sheltered heretics." The men muttered, indignant. She told them about being attacked by Renoud's mercenaries, who had seized Sebastián. Tomás describe how a lay brother had been murdered in the Fontfroide abbey by Renoud's henchman.

"We believe a plot arose when Pèire was first on crusade as a young knight," Tomás said. "Someone keeps sending evil against Pèire, Miquel of Morella, Gerard de Chartrain, and their children. Renoud is part of that plot. He started the rumor that knights of Valerós are priest-murdering heretics."

Father Anselm said. "I understand Renoud taking Sebastián. But does he really want to harm you, ma dòmna?"

"Perhaps Renoud is practicing before he denounces his own mother," Tomás said. "He needs to protect the Montcava estates from being seized because his mother is living with the goodwomen."

More remained to be explained about Renoud. The senhóra and the swordsman exchange glances as they shared their tale. Jean-Luc intended to find out the whole story when he next got the swordsman alone.

Marshal Guillem said, "The important thing is to protect you, ma dòmna."

Father Anselm began: "As Pèire Leteric's men—"

"You're Pedro's men now," Tomás said.

"No," Isabella interrupted. "Aligning with Pedro increases our danger." She turned to the others in the room. "One of the messages Pèire received holds a dire threat meant for Pedro."

"Ma dòmna," Tomás spoke evenly. "Simon has a list that asserts Pèire Leteric's family and the Valerós knights are heretics. We must swear ourselves to Pedro and the Church at every opportunity."

"First, we must protect Senhóra Isabella from the charges of heresy," Father Anselm said.

"You are the best knights in Christendom," Isabella said. "But your swords cannot protect me from the Church. Give me your counsel. What shall I do?"

"Do exactly what your grandfather planned," Father Anselm said. "Marry, and then rely on your husband to speak for you."

The swordsman crossed his arms and nodded his head to the senhóra, but Jean-Luc guessed the swordsman got small satisfaction from hearing his advice confirmed. As she next spoke, surprise washed over the swordsman's face.

"The abbot of St-Féliz convinced me of that. The Church insists only hereticated women refuse to marry. Therefore, to protect Valerós, I must take a husband. Marshal Guillem, you are the leading knight, so it should be you."

Guillem blanched. "No. I'm promised elsewhere."

"Not Guillem," Father Anselm said.

"I'm not proposing a real marriage," Isabella said. "Once we meet with Gerard and Hugues near Toulouse, I'll beg their help. By the end of the crusading season, we shall petition for annulment."

"Pedro wouldn't accept such a marriage." Guillem seemed desperate to offer the right counsel. "Ma dòmna, I have no title and no skill to speak for you. Jean—"

At the same moment Tomás said, "Perseus, you—"

Jean-Luc shook his head, warning them off with a scowl. They both knew he was excommunicated, making it impossible.

"Tomás," Jean-Luc said. "It must be Don Tomás."

Father Anselm and Guillem nodded.

Tomás shook his head. "No, it should be Perseus, because—"

Jean-Luc interrupted. "You are Pedro d'Aragón's knight. You are a seigneur, Don Tomás of Morella, Cyprus, and St-Joachim." He repeated the pedigree Tomás had given on their ride from Hugues's camp. "As our bonfraire, no one here but you can do this."

Isabella said, "This isn't ancient Athens where everyone votes. I'm asking you only as counselors."

"And we all agree on the best solution. It can only be Don Tomás." Father Anselm gripped the swordsman's shoulder, like a father assuring his son. "You swore an oath to Pèire, Don Tomás. This is what Valerós most needs for protection."

Between the dismayed bride and the distressed bridegroom, Jean-Luc wondered who felt the most pain. It wasn't toothache that left the swordsman looking as if he'd been punched in the face, or lack of sleep that left the senhóra ghastly pale. But it wasn't his place to admonish the blind to see.

"We'll fix it later when you're safe." Father Anselm put his arm around Isabella. "The usual arguments for annulment can be made."

To Jean-Luc's way of thinking, insanity would be the best argument. Senhóra Isabella was half way to madness from her long adventure, and the swordsman was worse from denied desire.

Isabella drew herself up, looking regal and severe. "I consider marriage the worst of all possible options, but there's nothing else left. God will understand it's both important and meaningless."

65

Peccador

Tomás at the Vale of Roses
8 days before Pentecost

TOMÁS PURSUED FATHER ANSELM, calling his name when the priest went to retrieve the articles of his office from the infirmary.

"Ah, Tomás!" Father Anselm slapped him on the back. "Come along. We can write the marriage contract here, my friend. I have ink and parchment."

Tomás sat at the wobbly little table while the priest prepared his pen. "Father, I'm troubled about this business."

"*Òc*, I feel the same. It goes against my conscience to perform this service when I know you aren't swearing true vows. But it breaks my heart that the Church might harass Senhóra Isabella. She has no other choice."

I can swear a true vow.

Aloud, Tomás said, "I've given my oath to Pèire and Pedro, and now to this woman. If I do any more swearing, God won't believe a word of it from me."

"Do you want to confess first? Will that help you?"

"*Òc*." Tomás said. If any priest in the world might understand him, this one would. "I confess that I stole, though not for my personal gain. I lied, though not to advance myself. I sinned my frequent sin of arrogance in both word and deed."

"These are sins God will forgive," Anselm said.

"Three men are dead by my hand. As if it were a true war, I did it to protect Isabella."

And I burn for what I don't deserve and can never have.

Father Anselm waited for more.

390

"My courage fails sometimes, because my oath to Pèire seems more than I can do. And I blaspheme."

I'm afraid I'll pull her into the hell where I burn, instead of delivering her from evil. And I believe heaven is inside a woman, where I want to be more than in God's true heaven.

Father Anselm waited patiently. Tomás said, "That's about it."

The priest said the usual words and asked the usual responses of him. Then Anselm said, "Your penance, besides prayer, is to take this new vow, so you can keep your first oath to Pèire."

"Father, it's too much."

"You are one of the bonfraires. I know you can endure."

"But I'll be living a lie, marrying a woman who doesn't want me."

Like my father once did.

"We shall write the marriage contract," Father Anselm said. "I'll take responsibility for the lies, and you provide the truths. The first lie will be the date of the nuptial. Do you think the night of the bonfraires meeting is sufficient?"

Tomás said, "No. Make it the day before Father Clémence died."

Father Anselm seemed surprised.

"If you're willing to prevaricate, Father, let's go back far enough to cover every evil."

"Fine. I shall include the usual beginning, stating the authority of the marriage based on the teachings of our Heavenly Father." He began penning the lengthy introduction and the scriptures.

> … Wherefore a man will leave his father and mother and cleave unto his wife, and they shall be two in one flesh. Therefore I, Tomás of Morella, son of Numa of Cyprus, led by the admonitions of my counselors, and supported by faith and prayers, seek partnership through matrimony. According to our most ancient customs, I give to my betrothed, Isabella of Valerós …

"What will it be?" Father Anselm said.

"Everything," Tomás replied. "It doesn't matter."

"Yes, it does. This may not be a real marriage in your mind, but to battle Renoud, you must be cautious about what you say in this contract."

"Give her everything in Morella and Cyprus."

"The custom is to give it in perpetuity, for her free use."

"Do it."

As the priest wrote out the details about the gift, Tomás blurted, "I want to do more. If anything happens to me before we conclude this business, I want Sebastián to have everything else of mine."

"Then you'll have to list it all. But the custom is to give it in parts to all children of this marriage. Acknowledging future children will prove this is a true marriage."

Tomás hesitated. Everything he knew about the laws of marriage came from his father's losses, starting with the notion of a "pall of marriage" that settled over the husband and wife.

"Can you please write, 'All children covered by the pall of this marriage,' and divide it equally among them? Except everything in the Languedoc must go only to Sebastián."

Father Anselm wrote as Tomás described his properties, including the fiefs in Aragón and the Outremer. He saw the priest's eyebrows lift when Tomás claimed the Fontcours estate as his.

Father Anselm wrote at length, then broke his silence. "I don't like this next lie, but we must do it." He forged the date and Pèire's name. "The diocese would be unhappy to know I put God, Pèire's family, and the Church in that order for my loyalties, but so it is."

> Done in Castell-de-Valerós. Made and affirmed by Tomás of Morella, son of Numa of Cyprus. Consented by Pèire Leteric, his seigneur. Written by the hand of Anselm the priest on the second of the ides of April, the fourteenth year of the reign of Pedro II, King by the Grace of God of Aragón.

"You sign here," Anselm said.

As Tomás bent over the table, the priest said, "Did Pèire know you are in love with her?"

"No." He closed his eyes. "It's just a temporary madness."

"Shall I speak to her for you?"

"Please, no. This will all be over soon. Then I'll go home to Cyprus, and everything will be forgotten."

"Are you certain?"

"She needs to be with a man of honor who can take care of her."

"That can be you, Tomás. She suffered in her last marriage. You can show her that marriage doesn't mean terror and pain."

"Father, I barely managed to keep her alive this past fortnight." He paused, it taking a moment to hear that Anselm used the same words Isabella had said about marriage. If Anselm meant to reassure him, Tomás felt even greater fear about what he was undertaking. "She knows what I am and despises me for it."

Father Anselm prepared another piece of parchment to make a copy of the contract.

"Why don't you send the others in here to sign this, Don Tomás? I'll see how many men in their sickbeds are well enough to serve as witnesses."

•

Tomás walked into a crowded chapel. All but two knights proved well enough to walk across the courtyard before matins. The chapel was more like a whitewashed cave, with its low, rounded ceiling, where the scant light from a rush lamp got lost in the curving shadows. Guillem gave Isabella his arm and wrapped her in his long cloak. With her hair under a linen head covering, she looked like a woman again. Father Anselm recited the words of the marriage rite.

It was brief, filled more with silence than with sermons, prayers, or vows, and in each void of silence Tomás fell into a waking dream. *How many days has it been since either of us slept?* There was no consecration of the bride because she'd been married before. Guillem gave him thirteen coins for the priest to bless, and he had his father's ring tied inside his doublet. Miquel leaned against one of the vaulting arches, shuffling his feet in the shadows, never looking up.

Summoning his courage, Tomás dared to look into her eyes while he spoke the vows. His words and her answer got lost in a susurrus of whispers echoing in the chapel vault.

Then they lay prone together before the altar, the cold grit of the stone floor as chilling as the touch of her hand while Father Anselm spread his cloak over them, representing the pall of marriage. As soon as the cloak covered them, she moved her hand away, and he lay shivering alone while the priest said the final benediction. Then they rose and stood before the priest as the leaden grey light of dawn leaked into the chapel.

"With this kiss of peace, I seal this marriage before God," Father Anselm kissed first Tomás's left cheek and then the right, making the sign of the Cross, and then gesturing for the bridegroom to convey that kiss to the bride. Tomás lightly touched her left cheek and then the other. *God help me, I want this.*

Isabella took his hand the way one Catalan knight greets another, looking past him rather than at him. "Thank you, senhór, for the service you do my family."

■

Tomás was left alone with Isabella when Jean-Luc, Guillem, and the priest went to determine which of the Valerós knights were well enough to ride. While writing at Father Anselm's little table, she'd removed the linen head covering and tied the strings of her jerkin as tightly as possible, concealing any sign she was a woman.

"I'm doing what I promised Pèire," he said.

"Sit down. It's intimidating when you stand over me."

He sat on a wobbly stool beside the table, not knowing how to shake off the chill from lying on those cold stones.

"This is the worst of all possible worlds."

"I've heard you say so before, ma dòmna."

"I am now your possession under law," she said. "If you use that power for anything other than to help Sebastián and Valerós, I'll..." She stopped. "I have always found a way to move forward. But right now, I can't even picture myself still alive when winter comes."

"Please trust me."

"How can I?"

"Do the same as Pèire and I did, ma dòmna. We didn't tell each other everything, but we shared enough to work together."

"Why didn't you tell my men the whole story? You left out the part about Eloïse and her bastard sons."

"We can't importune Father Anselm to tell even more lies. He wouldn't be so eager to marry us if he remembered the laws against consanguinity forbid it."

Isabella frowned. "What does incest have to do with us? You aren't my brother or cousin."

"Not incest, ma dòmna. Just affinity. A man can't marry his dead brother's wife. The law comes from Leviticus when priests hectored the Israelites in the desert. As far as the Church is concerned, if Miquel of Morella was my father, then Nicolau was my brother. You have a handy excuse to be rid of me."

Guillem came in and greeted Isabella, stopping her answer.

"The men are ready to go. I suggest we start on the main road to Carcassonne," Guillem said. "My mother has a little house on the way, where we can take shelter."

"Before leaving," Tomás said, "I want to try to persuade Senhóreta Katelina to join us."

"What more can you say?" Isabella asked.

"I need to try. I'll join you on the road."

When they were gone, Tomás returned to the infirmary to retrieve the robe he'd left there. Dressed as a Cistercian lay brother once again, he strode through the deserted service yard to the hostelry. The leaden skies had lightened to steel grey, and priests' voices chanting matins drifted from the chapel toward heaven. He hopped the low wall and slipped into the shadows of the hostelry portico.

"Why did you sign away everything?" Miquel said at his side.

"I've told you time on time. Don't trust a woman with an oath."

"Leave me alone," Tomás whispered. "Go to hell, or wherever you belong."

"You can join me there later," Miquel drawled, lost in the shadows.

The doors of the first two cells stood open, with no one inside. The third door opened as he pulled the latch, and a rush lamp flickered on the table inside, the oil burned down to mere drops. He smelled a familiar ferric tang before he saw anything in the dim light.

She lay on the cot. Long dark hair shot through with grey spilled wildly over the woolen covering. Her arm hung from under the blanket, the tips of her ethereal-blue fingers resting in a dark pool of blood sinking into the pounded earthen floor of the little cell.

For a heartbeat, he felt relieved. *Pèire will be so happy that she's by his side again.* But then he remembered he didn't believe in heaven.

When he bent to lift the hair, his hand grazed the hilt of the knife at her neck. The blanket beneath was drenched in blood. At a tug, the knife came free and he wrapped it in the long sleeve of his monk's robe. He cast about the cell in search of anything that shouldn't be left there, snatching up her prayer book.

He stepped back out to the portico, brushing against Miquel.

"*Bon Dèu!*" Miquel wept, wiping away tears with the back of his gloved hand. "No heaven, but hell is right here."

"There isn't time for that now." Tomás rubbed at his own eyes. He pulled the cowl of the robe over his head just as a handful of priests emerged from the stone-cold chapel. One gestured for him to join them. Miquel raised a hand in greeting and stepped toward them, but Tomás moved as quickly as his robes allowed, sprinting across the service yard and leaping over the low wall of the abbey stockade. He tore off the robe as soon as he reached a grove of trees, and then ran through the gorse to find his own horse.

At the head of the line of Valerós knights, he glimpsed Isabella's hauberk gleaming in the morning sun as she rode between Jean-Luc and Guillem. He hollered for their attention, shouting when he wanted to scream. As he finally came within hailing distance, they paused for him.

"What did Katelina say?" Isabella asked.

"I couldn't make her come with us," he said. He'd gained enough control to look her in the eye as he lied.

Isabella opened her hands in a gesture of surrender. "She promised to talk to me when we come back. We'll try then."

She rode ahead to join Guillem and Master Benito at the head of the line of knights, leaving Tomás alone with Jean-Luc.

"I am the worst sodding knight-errant on God's own earth." Tomás told Jean-Luc about finding Katelina. Even before the benediction finished echoing in the chapel, he was once more lying and keeping secrets from Isabella.

"What good would it do her to know at this moment?" Jean-Luc murmured.

66

Perseus Cuts His Hair

Isabella on the Carcassonne road
8 days before Pentecost

AT THE FIRST BREAK to rest the horses, Isabella stood in front of the knights to explain what she intended, tingling with the sensation that she now led a band of knights like Eleanor of Aquitaine.

"We'll offer forty days service to the crusade. We have no money, so we must rely on the Marquis de Beaurain and the Viscount de Chartrain for provisions. And because our enemies are spreading rumors that Castell-de-Valerós shelters heretics, you must hide your surcoats until we join our friends."

People stirred and whispered to each other at this, but she continued, starting to feel brave.

"I'm asking you to please accept my command as if it were Pèire Leteric's own. I respect your bonfraires. You must help me know when I must especially regard any man's opinion because of his status in your brotherhood."

They murmured again when she said this, but it seemed a good sort of noise.

"Finally, after our forty days' service, I intend to offer the Valerós knights as mercenaries. It's our best chance to restore wealth to Valerós. If anyone doesn't like this plan, now is the best time to ride back to Valerós."

When she finished her speech, Guillem said, "Well done, ma dòmna. Your words hardened the steel in their bones."

"However," Father Anselm said, "if we encounter crusaders, we need a leader who speaks French. I am happy to help, but a priest can't lead you. Don Tomás?"

"I speak French less well than a barking dog," Tomás said. "Jehan can speak for us. But he'll have to shave and cut his hair, since French knights don't go about so ill-shorn."

The smith seemed reluctant, but at last submitted to Father Anselm for barbering, although he didn't let the priest cut the thin braid falling alongside his ear.

"You look like a Greek mercenary." Tomás disapproved.

"Their mercenaries are mostly Turcopoles," Jehan the smith said. "They're all just second cousins of the Seljuks."

"It's the Sicilian Muslims who make really handsome mercenaries," Guillem said. "They're great soldiers and engineers."

"Our Perseus is handsome," Father Anselm said. "But those Sicilian mercenaries don't wear braids either."

"The braid stays. We aren't discussing it," Jehan said.

Without the mummer's rag of hair and beard, Jehan the smith was brilliantly handsome, with a cleft chin and high cheekbones, his blue eyes even more piercing. The oft-broken nose seemed to add to the grandeur of his appearance.

She wanted to join in the camaraderie of the men. "Taken as a whole, this is rather better than my first wedding. At least we get to ride horses."

Tomás made a noise in his throat. He told Guillem he needed to sleep and lay down with the others.

Isabella was too agitated to rest. Jehan was seated against a tree, sewing on the gambeson he'd inherited from Chrétien.

"May I join you?" She longed to ask questions.

He moved to allow her the best seat. "I couldn't refuse any request from you, ma dòmna."

"Everyone looks to you before they agree to what I ask," she said.

The smith shrugged, peering at the sewing in his lap. "As you said, there are levels in Pèire's bonfraires. Luck has blessed me with attaining the level—"

"Of Perseus. Katelina and I spied on the last meeting of the bonfraires. I saw you fight."

"An embarrassing evening for me."

"You were cheated. If these grizzled old knights defer to you, why aren't you leading troops for the Viscount de Chartrain?"

"I am an outlaw among the French. I can't serve as a knight to any lord until I remove the mark on my name."

"What should I call you?"

"The same as you always have. Or Perseus."

"Will you help me lead these men? I can't do it on my own, and Tomás is too impetuous."

"I am at your service, ma dòmna. What do you want?"

"Since they all look to you, help me know how to lead."

"Perhaps you should confer with all of your counselors before giving commands. Avoid the impetuous behavior you complain of in your swordsman-husband."

"Do you think I can trust him?"

Jehan the smith still didn't look up. "He is earnest, ma dòmna. And I find him amusing."

She couldn't get any more out of him, and so she went to curry her horse, stepping past Tomás, who lay sleeping amid the other knights. She still didn't have everything the queens of Jerusalem had, but she now had an army to command and a reckless adventurer as a consort.

67

No Feat, No Fortune

Tomás on the Carcassonne road
8 days before Pentecost

TOMÁS TURNED HIS BACK to the knights, creating a false privacy while he picked open yet another pocket of his gambeson to take out silver sewn in the lining. He felt along the seams, calculating if he had enough to take them to Fontcours, having never financed an entourage of knights. Marshal Guillem had depleted the knights' silver purchasing fodder and provisions at the Vale of Roses abbey. Tomás didn't begrudge it, but the miser in him did not enjoy so much silver leaving his palm to buy more provisions. The marshal promised that his family near Carcassonne could shelter them until the ill knights were in better shape.

After Isabella, Guillem, Jean-Luc, and Benito rode away to purchase food from a nearby villa, the knights who stayed behind surrounded Tomás. Lázaro, the bandy-legged Catalan, spoke first.

"So, Don Tomás, it's the end of your days as a single man, and you ain't bought us a bottle of wine, much less laid out a feast."

"Father Anselm fears rich food is bad for your health." Tomás smiled at the idea of a wedding feast. "And the nuns of the Vale of Roses hadn't a vintage worthy of your refined tastes."

"I've a bit of good red wine." Lázaro held up a bota. "We'd like to drink to your health and your wife's."

"To Miquel's son and Senhóra Isabella," Bonanat said, the tall, thin knight who used to egg Pèire on in his storytelling. "Long life and good health to you."

"Thank you." Tomás bowed in the Catalan style.

The men passed the bota around, saying lines of a Catalan toast in unison between each sip.

Here's to great joy in the getting—
of all the sons you could want—
and daughters too—
and your wife to never complain of it!

It was rather touching, however deluded they were about this sham marriage. As Tomás sipped their wine, he saw them glance around at each other, and someone nudged Bonanat, who toed the ground, nervous.

"We expect you are like your daddy, as we knew him in the old days. We hope you do like your old dad did when he married your mama. Leave your cocksman days behind."

Surprised, Tomás laughed, which wasn't what they wanted.

"If you hurt our Senhóra Isabella, we'll take it off for you," Lázaro said.

"And leave you singing the high notes," another knight said.

"I appreciate the gesture, gentlemen. I assure you, I'm made of the same stuff as my father in that regard."

"Then it's a loss to the ladies of the Great Sea, isn't it?" Bonanat said. "They say Miquel made it around the whole middle sea, bed to bed, without it ever costing him a single penny to sheath his sword."

"Have you seen much of the world, *fadrin*?" Lázaro asked

"I confess I can't measure up to my father in all things." Tomás was amused to be called "lad" again. "I've spent as much time choking my own chicken in battle camps as the next man. But like my father, I never wasted my pay on whores."

The men groaned, like gamblers at dice who see in a final toss they can never win.

"What?" Tomás feigned indignation. "I like good conversation, but not enough to pay for it."

"What were your favorite ports of call?"

Tomás laughed as they called out questions. They wanted titillating, so he counted off a litany of high points on his fingers.

"Though I hated the Venetian merchants, I remember rather liking their wives. The ones I knew had long tongues and long fingers, and they liked to scream, for which I have a personal weakness."

"It's always worth another silver penny for a screamer," Bonanat said.

"Which is why you've owed me three deniers since we were last in Narbonne." Lázaro raised yet more laughter.

"But for a real thrill," Tomás said, "there's nothing like Cilician women. They are fond of soldiers. They sharpen their fingernails in an odd way, and they're small and amazingly flexible. Most men don't make it to that part of the world to find out for themselves."

"I can agree about the Cilician whores, if I remember right," Lázaro said.

"Your memory hasn't worked right since Jaffa!" Bonanat said. The others laughed at a private joke they didn't share with Tomás.

"And did you make it all the way around the Mediterranean?" another man asked.

"Mostly. I haven't explored the dominions of the Almohades. I've never been deeper into the Moors' land than Valencia. As a matter of fact, I've never been deep into a Moor."

"And you part Moor yourself?" Bonanat said.

"The occasion never arose in the company I keep. And now my rogering days are over."

The thundering arrival of Guillem and the others interrupted the party. Despite the weight of gambeson and hauberk, Isabella bounded from her horse and stalked in amongst the knights.

"I want a word with my husband, please. Alone." Isabella's voice dripped vitriol on the word *husband*.

The knights shifted uncomfortably. Tomás followed her down a dirt trail among the hummocks of grass and oak shrubs. She stopped just out of the knights' hearing and stood two paces uphill, forcing him to look up to speak to her.

He said, "I don't mind if you humiliate me, but it won't help you to convince those men to follow you. If you're offended by our talk, they're just playing. They don't know we aren't really—"

"Remember those wretches from the quarrymen's toll-barrier? They are camped near the villa where we bought food," she said.

"They knew Master Guillem, because one was formerly Pèire's knight. Do you know what he has?"

"How could I?"

"A baptismal record he stole from Castell-de-Valerós years ago. Do you know what it says?"

"Òc," Tomás said, "from what I learned the night Pèire died."

■

After the bonfraires' ceremony,
at Valerós

When they left the ceremony, Tomás sat beside Pèire on the stairs. The old crusader talked on, though he had a hard time breathing.

"I didn't listen to Miquel begging me to help him die. Instead I left him in Numa's hands, and I went to my own wife, blind with grief, thinking of nothing but Vidal dead in the desert. I spent a year, crazed, trying to get another child on that poor woman. She suffered so much, losing babe after babe she got from me. None ever lived long enough for her to even hold."

Pèire must be raving, suffering an elision of misplaced time, so the old man remembered his first wife Anglesa, dead for forty years.

"You don't know," Pèire said. "The way you live, you can't know what it is to bury yourself inside a woman every night, praying to God a child will come of it."

Pèire had such a grip on Tomás that it hurt.

"At last we got a child and she kept it. When I felt it quicken and grow, all I wanted was my son Vidal to come back to me, like a fool goodman believing in the migration of souls. I sinned against my wife Katelina then," Pèire said. "I forced her to come back here with me. The pope forbade our marriage. Her Greek church forbade it. But I thought if we could be here, far away in my own land, it might all come right. When our baby girl was born, I lost what was left of my senses and sinned against God and my wife."

"That can hardly be," Tomás murmured. "You're a great man who gave your life for the Cross."

"I'm a small man with no courage," Pèire said. "My girl Melisinda died with her tiny babe Beatriz. I brought my own baby Constanza into this house to take her place. I made my wife Katelina into a servant so I could keep them by me each day. My wife who had been a great lady in Greece and left her own world because she loved me. I made her lie every night beside a monster who's so afraid of the Church and my enemies that I can't let my family even know each other."

"*Ai Dèu!*"

Beatriz—Constanza, or whatever her name was—stood in the doorway. Pèire released Tomás's hand and turned to see her.

"Daughter?" Pèire called to her for the first time.

.

"She's not your sister," Tomás said.

"That vile man claims he buried the baby Beatriz with my mother. Pèire paid him off by sending him to the Outremer as a knight." Isabella wound her arms around herself.

"Beatriz is Pèire's own child," he said.

"And Katelina is her mother? Do the knights know about Beatriz? Of course they'd know."

"Just the ones who came home with Pèire from the Outremer. Not Jehan. Nor Chrétien. I didn't tell them. But if any didn't know, they can see how much Beatriz looks like Katelina. It's amazing you never noticed."

"That's why Katelina left, because Beatriz was so angry. That's why Guillem agreed to bring her to the Fontrevists."

"*Òc.*"

"How could you sit with me holding Pèire, and then leave me outside Beatriz's door, and not tell me?"

"Pèire made me swear."

"The devil take your oath. Pèire's dead. I'm alive. And you let me stand before those knights and make myself ridiculous. I'm not the regent of Valerós. There's nothing for Sebastián up that valley but my father's sheep farm."

"By your Catalan customs, you and Sebastián have a portion of Valerós, as your mother's heirs," Tomás said. "And Sebastián has my land at Fontcours."

"Fontcours is your fantasy." Her words stung. "Why did Pèire do it? How could Katelina live a lie all these years?"

"They were afraid for their lives. And the Church would seize his lands for marrying a schismatic, like they did to my father."

"Pèire never feared anything in his life."

"The whole fabric of his life in Valerós was woven from threads of fear. Pèire wanted to protect you"

"Don't protect me anymore. Tell me what you know so I can protect myself."

He looked down, as if searching the stones might help him find what to say.

"You turn away when you're lying," she said. "What else?"

"I found Katelina murdered this morning."

She went white behind the sunburn, anger erased.

He said, "I found her stabbed in her bed." He slipped the knife and the prayer book from inside his jerkin. "This knife. You see this design in the hilt? It's Greek. And this book belonged to Katelina."

She took the book from him but wouldn't touch the knife.

"Senhóra Isabella?" Father Anselm approached them. "Marshal Guillem told me of your meeting. Perhaps you and I should talk."

Tomás reached out to her, but she put her head on the priest's shoulder. She shuddered in grief, but never wept.

▪

Tomás sat apart from the other men, not wanting them to see how discomfited he was. After a long time with Father Anselm, Isabella came back and sat between Tomás and Guillem.

"Don Tomás, I want you and Guillem to go back and take the letters from those men."

"It's not worth the effort," Tomás said. "They're thieves and liars. No one will ever believe them."

"Father Anselm's name is on the license they have from Pèire. He can't lie if anyone questions him," she said.

"He'd lie if he had to," Guillem said.

"If you won't go," she said, "I'll command Jehan the smith and Benito to do it."

"Father Anselm and I will advise them not to," Tomás said. "We might be pursued, since someone dies by knife whenever we appear at an abbey. There's no time to go back."

She asked Guillem, but he agreed with Tomás, while apologetic for crossing her.

In fact, Tomás intended to return during the night. Alone. The others wouldn't be prepared for the complete housekeeping required. He'd have to practice the arts his father taught him.

■

All the knights except Tomás begged to ride more, but Guillem insisted they stop for the day. They made a real camp in a field the sheep had deserted for summer pasturage. Exhausted, Tomás barely stayed awake through a supper of bread and cheese.

In recognition of their new status, Marshal Guillem made a gift to the bride and groom of his embroidered squirrel-lined cape, ceremoniously covering Tomás and Isabella as they lay rigid beside each other. Exhausted, Tomás slept deeply, then roused in the middle of the night when he planned to ride out and finish that chore. But Isabella was no longer beside him when he woke.

"*Jhezu del tron!*"

Miquel leaned against an oak tree, his empty hands spread before him. He shrugged and shook his head, unhelpful.

Tomás crept among the other sleepers to see if she'd moved her bed, and then he sought the sentry, who turned out to be Jean-Luc, fingering the braid in his hair and staring out into the night.

"Where's Isabella?"

"In your bed, I assume. I've been here only a short while."

"She's gone, and Benito is too."

"Why don't you sleep with your arm around her? Then you'd know if she left."

"We don't touch each other. It isn't part of the arrangement."

"But you want her. Anyone with eyes can see that. Why don't you just take her? She's legally yours."

"Because she doesn't want me, and I'm not forcing myself on any woman."

"Noble. But it appears you've lost her."

"Will you help me fetch her, please? She went after those lying vagabonds, and you know how to take me there."

68

Crucesignati Beggars

Isabella on the Carcassonne road
8 days before Pentecost

IN THE BRIGHT MOONLIGHT, Isabella and Benito sat amid the boulders on the hilltop and studied the swale below. In the clear night, a disorderly campfire illuminated the pair of sleeping figures and their mule and horse grazing together.

"Easy as taking booty from laundry girls in a lost baggage train," Benito whispered. "I'll go around to the other side, so we come at them from two directions. Move in quietly when you hear my signal."

He made a sound like the quick churring of a nightjar, and she answered with a soft *goo-ek*. After Benito disappeared in the shadows, Isabella waited, fingering her leather pouch of mementos. She'd laid her head in Katelina's lap seeking comfort just the night before, not knowing it was for the last time. When Isabella had come home from Toulouse, Katelina taught her how to forget nightmares. By borrowing from Katelina's schismatic faith, Isabella came to believe God had forgotten what happened in Toulouse. Which meant now only Renoud knew about Toulouse. Everyone else was dead.

You must do your duty, the abbot said. Her duty was to protect Valerós against evil arising from generations of secrets. Her friend had sentenced herself to silence in a nunnery and then died alone. Such evil had to come from Renoud. Isabella wanted to weep again. *Too many secrets.*

A small-bird sound floated across the hill, but it wasn't a nightjar. The air around her moved with the sound, so she felt before she saw the armor-clad man appear beside her, as if spirit were made

407

flesh. He was about as tall as Jehan the smith and held a sword in one hand, but merely tipped her head up, as if to examine her.

She didn't have time, and this wasn't the place, to be afraid.

His aventail covered most of his face. In the moonlight, he had dark caverns where his eyes should be. He twisted his head to the side, the way a hawk does when it studies its prey.

"You're the boy my father wants, the one Renoud stole."

He mistook her for Sebastián. This must be the man who took Sebastián from Valerós. And perhaps caused their other woes.

"I ran away," she said.

"*Ai*, brave boy. We must get you to my father. He'll keep you safe." His hand roamed over her head to rest on her shoulder, moving in the jerky, loose-limbed way of an injured man.

"I'd like that." She lied in the same way she had with Renoud. But this time, she had a knife, the one Pèire gave her. She dropped her hand to cover her baldric, the sleeve of her hauberk ringing but hiding her movement as she pulled the knife free.

"I wish I could have you. I want a son, too." The man's voice alternated eerily between a high-pitched whine and a growl, as if his throat had been hurt. He held her chin in his hand again. His face was hidden, but the moonlight shone on the metal studs of his boiled-leather cuirass, which covered his body like a turtle's shell. "You aren't afraid of me, are you?"

She shook her head.

"Good. You were brave before, too. I'd be proud to have you for my son." He held up his sword, close to her face, startling her again. "Can you hear that? The steel is singing the song I want to teach my son. I can't teach it to girls."

"Teach me." She spoke calmly, believing the man to be mad.

"It's an old song. My father taught it to me, before I knew he was my father." He whispered a song. "'I saw the wolf before the wolf saw me. I'll kill the wolf before the wolf kills me.'"

"'God take the wolf and God save me,'" Isabella whispered. "I know that song. My father taught it to me."

"Then we must be brothers." He touched her face. She smelled blood on his gauntlets. This was the man who tossed her from the parapets at Valerós and who likely made every other attempt to hasten her end. His sleeve fell back, and the moonlight shone on a series of lunate crosses tattooed up the pale flesh of his forearm.

At the scent of his hands, fear flowed like poison in her veins. She looked for where to strike, seeking a gap in his armor. In training, Chrétien promised there'd always be a gap. She slowed her breathing, to slow the turning of the spheres so she had time to find where to strike.

But he felt the change in her, and it seemed to wake him from his dream world.

"You aren't the boy my father wants." His whisper became a shriek. "You're supposed to be dead with the other spawn. You can't be my son." His hand clawed at her face, but the gauntlets only rubbed at her skin, as if he couldn't get a grip on her. "The stones and the spawn. I'm supposed to send you all back to the dust, like your mestitz guard."

The voice of a nightjar churred rapidly, screaming in alarm.

A dog snarled and growled, its voice deeper than a Pyrenees wolf. A mastiff appeared from nowhere and leaped onto Benito at the edge of the clearing. Its massive jaws chomped down on Benito's sword hand and held tight.

The ghost-knight, startled by the sound, looked over where Benito bellowed in pain. While he was distracted, Isabella slipped free.

But the sleeping forms proved to be four vagabonds, not two.

"*Bazasa!*" The filthy squat man from the toll gate stood in the moonlight, spitting at Benito. "It's another arrogant Valerós knight, too good for the likes of us."

He held the leash of a second dog that strained and snapped until it got its master's attention and dragged him over to where Isabella stood in the boulders, trapped with her murderer. She put the ghost-knight between herself and the dog, but he followed her, listing like a drunken man dismounting a horse.

"Looks like our Wolf-boy found fresh meat again. What a great hunter he is."

One of the other men spoke behind her. Fear tingled in her fingers and numbing shards shot up her arms toward her heart, but she faced the men with a look of sulky rage.

"What did Wolf-boy drag home?" The fat false-crusader studied her as he slapped his dog's leash into his other hand. With his free hand, he pulled off Isabella's cap. "Bless me for a bleeding devil, it's that Moor's catamite."

"Guess his new master still wasn't enough man for him," one of the vagabonds drawled.

"Looks like he bites," said another.

"Pull King Richard off that Valerós bastard." The false crusader pointed to the mastiff biting Benito. "Else he'll ruin another dog for me, giving the beast a taste for blood."

While everyone watched the dog bite Benito, Isabella held her dagger, covered by the too-long sleeve of her hauberk, ready to attack the way Chrétien showed her. But a dagger couldn't do much with five men standing around her, laughing.

"Our Wolf-boy says he wants to kill degenerate kings, not hunt down a Moor's bum-boy." The man came close, the foul wind of his breath blowing decay and ale on her. He flicked his sword to slice open the top lacings of her hauberk. She resolved that at least one man would die before touching her. "You owe us for the misery we find every time we see you."

"My friends won't take it well if we're harmed," she said.

"We're your only friends now. I think we all get a poke at what the Moor's been having."

Another said, "Not for me. I don't like it secondhand." It was the man with the wen-ridden face, the more stupid of the original two toll thieves. "I'll just get me a suck, I will."

"What are you doing?" the ghost-knight shrieked.

The fat man, surprisingly strong for his drunken state, grabbed Isabella's arm and twisted it behind her, forcing her face down on a boulder. He leaned over her, his fetid breath in her ear. "We'll each take a turn, and I'll go first."

"This spawn is supposed to die," her murderer said.

"There's no fun in that, Wolf-boy," the fat toll-thief said. "Go kill meat for our breakfast if you don't want to play."

He lifted the back of her hauberk with the hilt of his sword. When she felt his calloused paw at her breeches, tugging them down, she forgot the odds against her dagger. She squirmed toward him and slashed at the same time, slicing into his hand, ripping up from palm to elbow.

The man shrieked in pain and rage just as Jehan the smith jumped from the higher boulders and thrust his dagger into the throat of the mastiff. Then the smith hacked with both hands, bringing his sword down onto her screaming attacker, hammering into the soft entry between neck and shoulder. Tomás leapt into the clearing and slashed in the same focused, deadly way as at Anfos's cottage, attacking each man in turn while shouting curses on them.

The fat man dropped to his knees, his head tipping to the side as he fell on Isabella's boot. She jumped away as Jehan the smith ripped his dagger free from the one mastiff and plunged it into the neck of the dog that gripped Benito, killing it in a single stroke.

Isabella held her own dagger out so the blood didn't drip onto her body. All she heard was Tomás's ululating battle cries as he stopped three men from breathing. The smith pursued a fifth man, the disarmed ghost-knight, who ran into the shadows, unhobbled a horse, and galloped away.

•

When Tomás stopped shouting and stood panting, and when Jehan the smith began tending to Benito's wounds, Isabella went to the brook and washed her hands and her knife. She dried the dagger in the grass on the bank. The smith knelt beside her to wash both of his weapons, but he didn't speak or look at her. Her fingertips still tingled from the jolt of fear.

"I only wanted to take care of my own business," she said to Jehan, who didn't answer.

Tomás said, "My wife can't govern her impulses, but I believed better of you, Master Benito. Please return with Perseus so the others stop searching for us. I'll clean this up and join you shortly."

Isabella moved to follow Benito and Jehan.

"My wife will stay with me. To have a private conversation."

Benito and the smith weren't out of hearing before Tomás began shouting at her.

"What in the name of the grievous angels were you thinking?"

"I wanted those letters from him," she said.

411

"And how were you going to get them? By picking his pocket while the five of them took turns poking you?"

"There were only two this afternoon. And they were so drunk then that I thought—"

With a roar, he wrenched off his aventail and dashed it to the ground. Then he began work to bury the bodies, all the while haranguing Isabella, condemning her for a fool. He dragged the men by the boots to a crevasse in the boulder pile and tossed them in without removing anything but their weapons. Tomás, with the same assassin's mask as she'd seen at Anfos's cottage, tore open one man's shirt and breeches and pulled off the boots, searching every fold. He found a few coins that he tossed into the crevasse with the bodies. Then he held up a packet, waving it for her attention.

"Come help. There's not enough soil here to bury these men."

They pulled smaller boulders free and rolled them into the crevasse. When they ran out of movable boulders, they threw stones until they'd created a cairn to keep off scavenging dogs. Isabella panted from the hard work, doing exactly as she was told. She finished by loading the mule with the dead men's weapons while Tomás scattered the campfire with his boot. He buried the cinders in the dust and rocky debris, so the whole little swale was a mess of trampled undergrowth, making it impossible to guess what might have occurred there. He pushed her across to where their horses were hobbled.

69
Kalila

SHE DID NOT WANT to be afraid of him, but Isabella kept checking over her shoulder.

Even after they'd ridden most of the way back to their camp, Tomás still raged. At an arched stone bridge where the road crossed the stream near their camp, they dismounted and walked their horses and the mule down to the water. Tomás twitched with impatience as the animals drank.

"The man who rode away," she hid any timidity in her voice, "he's the same man who tried to kill me at Valerós. And then at Fontfroide."

Tomás stared at her, smoldering, but he didn't speak.

"He mistook me for Sebastián. He said he was supposed to give Sebastián to his father, but Renoud stole him away."

In the moonlight, she saw the muscles of his jaw working. Finally he said, "Katelina was right. She said our enemies are at war with each other."

"All this time, I believed Sebastián was safe with Renoud, but now—"

"What does he look like?"

"I don't know. His aventail was laced over his face. He speaks in growls and squeaks, as if his throat hurts. And he's big, the size of Jehan the smith."

"*Jhezu del tron.*" Anger still rang in his voice. "Do you believe me now, ma dòmna?"

413

"*Òc.* He wants to kill all of us." She couldn't stand Tomás angry, especially angry with her. "He thinks he killed you at Fontfroide. I don't know if he recognized you here."

Tomás nodded in a curt way.

"Let's go," he said. "No use waiting for him to join us."

Their horses ambled up the bank, but the mule balked. She grabbed its lead and began to coax it, talking sweetly in its ear.

"Come on," he said more urgently, slapping the mule's rump so it scampered away. He gave Isabella a push up the bank, but she lost her footing, slipped, and fell back onto him. Catching her, Tomás wrenched her around and pushed her up against the stone wall of the bridge.

"You," he said, "you—"

"I'm sorry."

"Sorry? Every time you leave my sight, you almost die. *Per l'amor de Dèu,* just trust me to take care of you."

"How can I?" Forgetting to be afraid of him, she tried to push him away, but he didn't budge. "There are always more lies. Do you have still more, Don Tomás?"

"Very few, ma dòmna."

"What? What else aren't you telling me?"

He grasped her arms, and when she tried to squirm away, he shook her.

"Isabella—"

"Stop it."

"I can't. I want you safe more than I want salvation. If you died, I swear my heart would stop beating." His voice strangled. "God in the golden heaven knows I burn for you, ma dòmna."

"Sancta Maria. Don't tease."

"I love you so, I could believe I have a soul."

"Stop mocking me!" She tried to free her arms to cover her ears. "I know it's wrong to feel this way, but I did what you asked. I stayed away. I haven't touched you. Don't punish me anymore."

"Punish you?" His hands loosened their grip, but he still held her, his eyes frantic.

"You think I'm weak and foolish. But I'm not. I swear by—"

"Isabella, listen to me." He shook her, gently. "I want you to be my wife. It's all I want on this earth."

"*Ai Dèu!* I thought you despised me." Her faith in her own wisdom drifted away on the breeze. She touched his scarred cheek. He jerked at the contact, as if stung. "I've tried so hard not to want you."

He trembled, making a soft sound, like a man wounded.

"Tomás—"

"I'm the greatest fool on God's own earth."

He pressed his head against hers, murmuring words she didn't understand, brushing her hair with one hand while the other reached around her waist to pull her to him. She buried her face in his jerkin, drowning in the smell of sweat and cloves.

"*Ai Dèu.* Since you first warned me off, I can't look at you because it leads me into temptation. I want—"

"Just ask. I'll give it to you, *kalila*." His fingers caressed her cheek, the way one comforts a child.

"What Anfos and Maria have in their life together. Loyalty between equals." Her voice rasped.

"You have it, on my honor as my mother's son. *Sodalitas, fidelitas, virtus.*" He turned serious. "You must want more from me."

"Perhaps I have it already."

"What? A blind fool who worships you?"

"No, to be a partner with a warrior as brave as Pèire."

He held her out at arm's length, sober. "*Bon Dèu*, Isabella. Pèire showed me what it looks like, but I'm not so good a man."

Their horses nickered. He shivered and looked around.

"Let's secure the horses and find shelter."

They walked the animals back to camp and hobbled them with the others. Jehan and Benito sat guard, keeping company with two other knights.

"There's a shepherd's hayrick a short way up the hill," the smith said. "If you want a safe place to talk."

They walked there, Tomás's arm around her waist, his hand on her hip. He pointed to a thatch-roofed shed near a stand of cypress.

"This is nicer than Anfos's grain crib," he said.

"I won't miss the chickens," she said.

"And I don't miss having my hands bound so I can't touch you." He held her as she'd seen men hold their lovers. "Do you want me to touch you?"

"Yes." She took a breath. "It seems strange after the catastrophe I caused tonight."

"Desire goes well with danger. It helps us forget." His hands and his face buried in her hair, he murmured, making her shiver. "Why did you fall for a fool?"

"Because you're the most arrogant liar with a sword God ever made. And you smell of cloves."

"You'll be an easy wife to please." His hands wandered down to her waist and hips, and he brushed her lips with his. Her tongue touched his, but he broke away to whisper, "Say it's only me who touches you. I long to hear it more than I long for heaven."

"Stop speaking heresy."

"Take this off," he said. "It's worse than heresy to hide your body like this."

He untied her gambeson, then peeled off his own and enfolded her in his arms again. Heat radiated from his shoulders and belly as he nuzzled her hair and neck, kissed her eyelids, her ears, her throat, and each of her fingertips. Then he pulled her down so they reclined against the straw. When his knee and hip parted her thighs, their bodies collided.

"*Ai, kalila.* Get lost with me." He kissed her until her face was damp and her mouth felt bruised and stung of cloves. "Let me make you my real wife." Tearing at the strings of her breeches, he freed them in the same movement as he loosened his own. He brought her hand down to touch him, which startled her so much she closed her legs. Fear shot through her.

"You have to help me, Isabella. I can't just take you."

"*Ai Dèu.*"

"Please. We have to do this together. Help me."

"I can't—"

"Shhh. Let's slow down. Are you afraid?"

"It hurts. It always hurts."

"Not with me. We'll go slow." He cupped his hand over hers. "Do you have any idea," he breathed, "how much I want you?" He nudged with his hip and thigh, then slowly filled her. While he murmured reassurances in her ear, she closed her eyes, breathing the smell of cloves to feel safe.

"Let me worship you with my body, *kalila*."

Sighing, she followed where he wanted them to get lost. She wanted to put her arms around him, to touch his face, but he held her so closely she could only clutch at his hips. When she touched his tongue with hers, he cried out and collapsed against her, his weight pressing her into the straw.

"Yes." Isabella breathed, overwhelmed with the sense of his heart beating inside her body. "Only you."

"*Kalila*." He buried his face in her hair, his jagged breathing hot on her neck. She listened to the brook rambling close by and the wind swirling through the cypress trees. And birds—thrushes, from their song—had wakened before the dawn to call to each other.

"Only you." She put her head on his shoulder.

Moments later, he pulled away from her, kicked free of his breeches and hose, and walked in his undershirt into the nearby stand of cypress.

·

Everything had changed.

Every bit of tissue in his body altered.

Only for one moment, at the end, had his nightmares returned, of being lifted from a woman, beaten half to death, and left in the dark. The unbidden memory sent Tomás out into the trees to be sick. He looked around, expecting Miquel to harangue him, but was alone. The only fear left was what she must think, since he lasted just five heartbeats inside her before spewing seed and then running away like a sick dog.

He went to the stream to drink water. When he came back, she lay in a pool of moonlight, wearing only his long linen shirt. She rose up on her elbow with a beatific smile and gestured with her hand for him to come to her.

"I'm sorry it was like this." He sank down to the straw beside her. He wanted to touch her everywhere the moonlight did, but instead put his arm around her and rested his hand in the wilds of her hair, his chin on her shoulder, as if he were a man who could restrain himself. "You are like a queen. It should be the best bed with the finest linen. I would crown you with lilies."

"You are beautiful." She bent her head to kiss his hand, leaving it wet, and then twisted under his arm to touch him, her small breasts brushing his chest. Her fingers traced the scars, ridges, and lines of his face and then the smaller marks on his collarbone.

"Perhaps before."

"No, still."

Untying his undershirt, she grasped the muscles of his upper arms, avoiding his injury, and ran her hands over his shoulder blades.

"It's as if the moon glows from inside you," he whispered.

She touched his belly and then his chest. Her fingers skimmed over his nipples, making them hard. He shivered, aroused again.

"Let's try it again, *kalila*. I'll be less of an animal this time."

Beginning with her chin and then her collarbone, in the same way she'd explored his body, he traced the lines of hers, stopping to hold her small breasts in his hands. As he bent to kiss her, she lifted her hips against his and circled her fingers around each bone at the base of his spine. He moved his hand to her belly and then felt the hard muscles of her thighs. When he slipped a finger toward that wet heaven, she clenched and held her breath.

He let go. She relaxed again and snuggled up to him. But he, too, wanted to go slowly, to take all the time in the world. Lying beside her, he slowly stroked the magnificent muscles of her inner thighs and wondered why all women weren't encouraged to ride horses. He sought to get her lost with him in pleasure for long moments before he gently slipped two fingers between her legs.

Again, she stiffened at his touch.

He stopped moving but didn't withdraw. With his other hand buried in the copper floss of her hair, he gently turned her head to face him. "Someone hurt you."

The flicker of fear in her eyes broke his heart.

"*Ai, kalila*. No one will ever again hurt you."

She wanted him. With the slight control he had, he entered her as slowly as possible, worrying he must have hurt her the first time; but as his hips met hers, she locked her legs around his thighs. He propped on his elbows to keep his weight off her, cradling her narrow shoulders between his forearms. At every pause, it felt as if she might steal the rhythm away and make it too intense, too soon after too long.

Looking down, he cried out at the sight of the graceful curve of her neck as she arched back when he thrust against her. He bent to kiss her just as her lips parted in a sigh. He wanted to transform her sigh into more but had to stop them both from moving so he could keep control.

Because Isabella lay beneath him in the moonlight.

Her strong, smooth hands on his naked hips urged him toward her, her fingers kneading the muscles of his haunches, a small animal sound in her throat, begging.

She wanted him.

Anguished delight shot up his groin, knocking him breathless, and then twisted around his heart, so he came inside her again.

When he could hear over the roar of his own breathing, he held her close, afraid she'd slip away. He started to speak, but whatever he said would be wrong. Still, he throbbed inside her every few moments, and he felt her pulse where he kissed her temple. When he whispered her name against her hair, she relaxed in his arms, still moving toward him instead of away.

After a long while, they rose to return to camp. "They expect us to be gone," he said. "We just got married. Either yesterday morning or a thousand days ago."

"Let's stop down at the brook," she said. "I need to wash."

His arm around her shoulder, they ambled back toward the knights' camp. "Will you get a child?"

He wanted it to sound like a casual, practical question, but felt his heart beating so hard she must have heard it. They were in too much danger for him to think of giving her a child. He didn't know where such an idea came from.

"No. Remember when I told you how frightful it was when Sebastián was born? I won't have another child. Do I disappoint you? Will you want to annul our marriage?"

"Nothing about you disappoints me."

He now had more than he'd ever dream of, so he could wait until they were safe. Then he'd talk her into changing her mind. Right now, he only wanted his wife's legs wrapped around him every possible moment.

"*Ai, kalila,* you can't get away from me. You're my wife."

70

Constantinople, Redux

Jean-Luc on the Carcassonne road
7 days before Pentecost

JEAN-LUC WAS TENDING A small fire and serving as sentry, the only man awake in the camp when they returned.

The senhóra shook with cold and the swordsman urged her to sit by the fire. Tomás left her for a moment while he retrieved the squirrel cape Guillem had given them as a wedding present. When the swordsman's back was turned, she looked up at Jean-Luc. He saw her world had changed.

"I'm sorry for the trouble I caused," she said.

"It's nothing," he said. "We're all alive."

Her husband returned and helped her to lie down by the fire, cradling his wife's head in his lap. Tomás said, "Isabella met a knight just before we arrived. Or a ghost."

As she lay by the fire, the senhóra described the man: as big as Jean-Luc, in a boiled-leather cuirass and mail-studded gauntlets. "Could it be the same man you fought in the garden, who tried to snatch Sebastián?" she asked.

"It was dark," Jean-Luc said, "like tonight. But it's likely."

For a long time, there was only the sound of the fire and a horse muttering to its friends.

"Is she asleep?" Jean-Luc asked after a long time.

"Yes," Tomás murmured. He pulled the cloak close to her and then rested his arm across her breasts.

"What an enlightening conversation you must have had after I left," Jean-Luc said. "Things changed."

"Yes, everything changed."

"It's for the best."

"Probably not," Tomás said. "This wasn't what Pèire intended, and it isn't what we planned at the abbey."

"A blind man could see this coming."

Tomás laughed, without humor. "And I always prided myself on the acuity of my vision."

"It's what you want, isn't it?"

"I'm only my father's avenging angel. I wasn't bred to want more than a warm bed and food if I can get it. A good fight now and then."

"God grant you can keep your wants so small," Jean-Luc said. "If you succeed, you are a better man than I."

"I already want more. I want her to stay with me."

"Have you ever lived with a woman?"

"I've never coupled with the same woman for more than a week before saying goodbye. I've never slept in the same bed that long."

"Then best of luck to you, man. You'll have to give up being such an arsewit if you hope to keep her."

"Probably," Tomás said.

"No, definitely."

The two men were quiet for a while. Then Tomás said, "Tell me what happened to you in Constantinople."

"Were you there?" Jean-Luc asked.

"No, I worked for the Venetians as far as Zara, where we fought your Franks for three days. By the time captains like you got the streetfights under control, Chrétien and I were too disgusted with the Venetians to stay. We worked in Burgundy for a while."

"You know what happened in Constantinople?"

"I've heard stories," Tomás said. "But I want to hear yours, because the arrow I found in my arm was Greek, as was the knife that killed Katelina. The cuirass Isabella described wasn't made by a Frank or anyone here in the south. You're the last of us to be in the eastern empire. Tell me your story."

Jean-Luc told the miserable story about the Franks' conquest and how he and Yves tried to stop knights and mercenaries from rampaging through the city. He glossed over the burning, raping, and pillaging with brief words. The swordsman understood without needing the details.

"What happened to you?" Tomás said.

He said, "In the confusion and the dark I found my brother Yves. But not until my sword was thrust through him and my hand on the hilt felt his ribs."

"*Jhezu del tron!*" Tomás breathed.

"By the time I got our soldiers out of the church, I didn't know who was with me and who was missing. I spent the night and the next two days fighting fires and looters and carrying booty to the priests, as we'd all agreed before the invasion. Then on the third night, several of Hugues de Beaurain's men searched my possessions and found a pile of booty from that church."

"Did Hugues plant it there?"

"I have no idea who did it, but it wasn't Hugues." Jean-Luc felt a strange relief; the swordsman assumed he was innocent. "First, they condemned me as a thief, and then a heap of accusations came. Some said I killed my brother when he tried to stop me from pillaging. Others said I'd blasphemed God and raped nuns. None of my men could be found to testify about what happened."

"How did you escape being hung?"

"Renoud of Montcava cut my bonds and gave me a horse. Told me he did it because he'd lost a brother too. I believed that I owed him my life."

Tomás shivered violently. "That's not a debt you want."

"But Hélène says Hugues arranged my escape."

"Whose men were in that church where your brother died?" Tomás asked.

Jean-Luc hesitated. "Men from Montcava and Toulouse."

"Renoud's men?"

"Serving under his brother Nicolau. Renoud took command when Isabella's father and husband died."

"What happened to Nicolau?"

"In the church, he pulled his sword on me when Yves and I tried to stop the pillaging. He tripped and I kicked him in the head just as he slashed my thigh open. The last I saw of him, he lay on the steps dead, like my brother."

"Have you considered that Renoud might not feel friendly toward you?"

"After I killed my own brother, I haven't considered anyone's feelings, except my father's."

"These aren't the sort of crusader stories one tells the children."

"You won't tell, will you?"

"Won't tell what?" Tomás said.

"Please don't tell Sebastián his father died a coward's death. There's no use in his knowing any of this."

"Not a word from me. But how do we change your story? Even if we find our hidden enemy, that won't restore your name."

"I'm close to the answer," Jean-Luc said. "They say there's a soldier who was at Constantinople who's confessed to ruining a man with lies. I believe he's in Toulouse. So perhaps it's only a few days until I find the man who can restore my name."

"Good," Tomás said, "then you can help us find and take revenge against our enemy. Whoever that is."

71
Hola, and Farewell

JEAN-LUC DROWSED IN THE saddle. Likely all the knights did, after long nights and the onslaught of spring. Out on the plains the air thickened with the smell of herbs and blooming trees. And bees buzzed everywhere. At the top of a rise, he looked back into the distance from where they'd come. In the far distance, the peaks of the Pyrenees were still covered with snow. However, it wasn't possible to make out where in the higher hills Valerós stood.

"*Ai*, look there!" Guillem rode up beside him, nudging Jean-Luc with his boot. He pointed to a manse atop a hill, the whitewashed house and outbuildings gleaming in the sun, the red tile roofs shiny. "We can shelter there as long as we need. You will enjoy the comforts there, I promise."

However, Jean-Luc felt dismay flood every muscle when the shelter Marshal Guillem promised proved to be a huge domus belonging to his mother. Speaking in his infuriating, friendly way, Guillem said, "When we came home from the Outremer, I brought my mother and sisters from Sicily to Narbonne. My mother—she's called Paulette—married a rich merchant, and now they are all together with my sisters and their husbands and children."

Guillem pointed out the comforts his family offered: a rambling, whitewashed plaster-and-stone manse named Casa de Rossynols, with a host of outbuildings making up a small village. From the welcome Jean-Luc received, the marshal must have whispered to his mother Jehan the smith's true name.

"You do us honor." Paulette took Jean-Luc's hand in greeting. She was about must sixty-five, still pretty in a girlish way, and ecstatic about seeing her son. "My son praises your friendship and your honor as a knight."

Then Jean-Luc was coddled in lordly ways he'd forgotten. Shown to the finest room in the house, he argued politely that it was too much for a soldier accustomed to bivouacs. With apologies, the servants led him to a slightly smaller but still fine room, with its own fire and privy, and smooth white linens on the bed. A manservant offered to tend to Jean-Luc's every need, beginning with a bath, clean clothes, fruit and bread and cheese, and an unsubtle query as to whether he required a woman.

No, he required only solitude.

He lay naked on the linen sheets over a real mattress of feathers rather than straw, his head on pillows filled with down and lavender. The prospect of a lazy day in this manse, waiting for the Valerós knights to regain strength, seemed sinful, decadent. He listened to young boys outside the windows who Tomás had to polish their rusting hauberks. While rolling barrels of oiled sand, the boys schemed to sneak off and swim in the ponds. Scents of mint and cypress and whatever bloomed in Senhóra Paulette's garden drifted through the window, as if it were not possible for places like the Vale of Roses or Béziers to exist.

He fell asleep with the gentle wind caressing him and woke dreaming of Felicia's breath on his bare skin, begging him to stop and then not to stop. He reached out to run his fingers through the silk of her hair and said yes, he'd stay, he'd never leave.

It wasn't a dream; it was the swordsman and his new wife, the sound drifting from their window to his.

Spread-eagled across the bed, the linen damp from his sweat, Jean-Luc felt the breeze as a torturer's lash. The sounds of coupling didn't bother him; he'd heard it in every camp when his neighbors brought in baggage girls. Isabella's voice was a deeper tone, but too much like Felicia's. The rhythm of her speech, the way she pronounced certain words, the turns of phrase. And the too-familiar words of an overly-experienced man instructing an inexpert girl.

When night fell, nightingales competed with the sound of the lovers. It sounded like love. But how can you know? It might feel like love, but not be. It might feel like Divine Grace, and then not be.

Perhaps the goodmen are right: it might be that God is both good and evil.

Perhaps it's only the dark angels who lead a man to believe there is love in this world.

But he'd traveled far enough from Valerós to face truths: he had nothing to offer Felicia. No name. No future.

He had to learn the lesson once again, that he could not have Felicia. He had to stop the wild prayers that the world might prove not to be as it is. The one hope in life he retained was the task that Pèire Leteric forced upon him. He had to clear his name—and then to return his father, for Gerard's own sake, not as a stopping place on the way to a woman he could never have.

∎

Plagued by his own regrets and desires after listening to others' whispered *cançós d'amor*, Jean-Luc was hungry beyond reason. He answered a servant's call to dinner, where Senhóra Paulette had prepared a feast to honor the newly married seigneur and his senhóra. However, Tomás and Isabella didn't appear when called, so dinner began without them.

The servants bore platters of roasted duck smothered in a sauce of figs and black pepper, and then bowls of rabbit stew with broad beans and cardamom. Each of them received a round loaf of bread with the insides scooped out and replaced with *espinacas picadas*—chopped spinach cooked with bacon and goat's milk, chunks of white cheese floating at the top.

At table, Senhóra Paulette seated her husband, François of Rossynols, beside Jean-Luc. François had preserved his Norman good looks; only a few streaks of grey charged through russet hair, cut in the style adopted by many merchants who traded with Venetians and Genoans. The man inspected his plate closely and looked around as voices called his name. *Ai*, the fellow was as near-sighted as a long-eared bat. However, François possessed the same sociable good humor as his wife and shared her wistfully romantic glee at sheltering newlywed lovers.

"There's nothing like a good wife," François said as he helped Jean-Luc to more of the stewed rabbit. "I spent time chasing from one bed to another when I was young, mind you, so I can compare animal pleasure and profound bliss." He sipped his wine. "For my part, I say, 'God bless this damnable crusade.'"

"How is that?" Jean-Luc asked, a shiver of caution running up his backbone.

"I had a wife for twenty-five years who never brought me one stroke of luck. No children, no wealth, and certainly no joy. She fell in with the heretics long ago. Last year, the Church sent my cousin Thedisius, who is clerk to the pope's prelate. I was ordered to put my bad wife aside or lose my land. A fool can decide that easily enough." François paused to refill Jean-Luc's cup and then his own. "Senhóra Paulette and I had been keeping happy company since she first came to Narbonne. When I did as Cousin Thedisius instructed, that left me free to marry Paulette. I'm happy to take her children and grandchildren as my own. Now there's nothing but good cheer among my new family. Therefore, I say, 'God bless this crusade.'"

Jean-Luc murmured his best wishes, not knowing how to respond to a horde of unasked confidences. But then the conversation turned to war instead of love, especially with Father Anselm, Benito, and Marshal Guillem.

Father Anselm started the thread of idea that drew the men nearby into deep discussion. "For six generations, people have been excited to send boys and men off to take up the Cross."

"Yet across the Great Sea, desire for retribution is gathering for every Saracen woman and child killed by the crusaders," Guillem said. "Their anger was salted and left to rise with the pitiless brutality Richard Lionheart dealt when he tried to retake Jerusalem."

"What are you saying?" Father Anselm asked. "Why so bitter?"

"He means Christians can never win in the Outremer again," Jean-Luc said. "Battles, perhaps. But they won't keep their territories or gain local allies. Saladin brought them together."

"You're saying that Christians will never be forgiven. For what Richard did," Guillem said.

"Perhaps I understand." Father Anselm mused. "My friend Simon Ibn Kalil in Cairo said the pope who first preached crusade cast his words to the wind like seeds."

"Generations ahead will reap hatred and retribution in the wake of that wind," Jean-Luc said. Alone too much for too long after Constantinople, he'd had too much time to meditate on what it meant to go on crusade.

François of Rossynols said, "But God wants us to destroy the Saracens' hold on Jerusalem."

Anselm shook his head. "I can't find where our Lord Jesus ever asked us to slaughter innocents in the land where He walked."

"I'll be bolder than Father Anselm," Jean-Luc said. "It's foolish to think that's why the kings and popes sent those boys and men to die. Crusaders were to make the place safe for merchants. And for Frankish barons to seize land where they could live like kings."

"With slaves to fan them and feed them figs and dates and honey," Father Anselm added.

"And the land the Christian kings want most is Egypt, not Jerusalem," Jean-Luc said.

Guillem made a deprecating gesture. "You've grown too cynical. I took up the Cross to fight Saracens so Christians could walk freely in Jerusalem."

Father Anselm said, "I fought alongside you, Guillem. And we both spent time fighting for the sheer love of battle."

"*Ai Dèu*," Paulette said, excited. "Here they come. She looks lovely. Her new lord refused my maid. No one touches his wife, he said. He's her handmaid. It's as romantic as any *cançós d'amor*."

While the couple took the places at table that Paulette offered, Jean-Luc began tallying a score on the swordsman-turned-lover. He awarded one point to Tomás for persevering when it seemed hopeless, and another point for his gift with words of love. Although the man didn't shut up in a fight either. But he docked a point for jealousy when François lingered too long over Isabella's hand. Jean-Luc was tempted to warn him, since jealousy destroyed many lesser men.

Tomás had transformed the senhóra from the leather-and-chainmail boy into a more elegant woman than ever was seen at Valerós. She wore a simple grey silk gown, its sleeves tied with ribbons at the top to show off her long, pale arms, her waist cinched with an embroidered braid. The clinging silk showed how slim she was, which one forgot under a gambeson and hauberk. The swordsman must have done her hair, for no married woman left her tresses to flow down her back, with just a handful caught up on the crown under lace that passed for a senhóra's head covering.

The swordsman, wearing bleached linen, made a great bride-groom, his hand at his wife's waist, a triumphant smile on his ru-ined face. Jean-Luc conceded a point for having dressed her beau-tifully, but he subtracted two points for parading her for the sake of his own glory.

Isabella shyly accepted her host's congratulations, while her husband reveled in the knights' teasing calls. Guillem proposed a toast to their health, and the Valerós knights called out several rounds of toasts before Paulette persuaded everyone to leave off drinking and eat their dinner.

"Marshal Guillem," Father Anselm said, "it's time you tell your story, since God already knows it."

"What is it?" Paulette said.

"Then, Mama, I will tell you." He stroked his moustaches. "I'm married. My new wife Felicia is waiting for me at Valerós."

"You! Married at last, Guillem?" his mother cried.

Jean-Luc, sipping wine, felt his heart stop beating.

"Just barely." Guillem grinned. "Father Anselm united us the morning we began this journey. I'll fetch her to meet you as soon as we finish our business."

"Bring her to stay. We need more here than just your sisters."

"Mama, you must have fifty people in your household."

"But don't you want to be with your family now? My husband has no children. We need a son at here to rule the domus. Tell us everything about her and why you love her."

To keep breathing, Jean-Luc fingered his braid and then caught Isabella watching him. He stopped fiddling, caught at bad table manners, and sipped his wine again. But he couldn't guard his mind. Yves's voice dripped sarcasm.

She vowed to wait like a crusader's wife. Or maybe all crusaders found their wives fell into other men's arms.

430

Though he'd done no better, having fallen prey to Hélène's pleading as quickly as ever.

When the dinner party broke up, Paulette begged Guillem to visit in her apartment. The old knights pounded Tomás on the back to harass him with vulgarities. And Isabella sat down by Jean-Luc.

"You saved my life last night. I didn't thank you properly."

"I am at your service, ma dòmna."

"In the last fortnight I've seen amazing things," she said. "Starving children and murdered soldiers. I met a mad goodman weaver who thinks Jesus once lived in Rennes-les-Bains. I saw a man's face when he was stabbed and knew he'd die in the next heartbeat. Just a while ago, I saw the same look on your face."

"You're mistaken."

She put her hand on his. "Felicia wanted an adventure before she married. I'm sorry she hurt you."

"Guillem is a better man than I," he said. *I don't care who Felicia loves. I don't care whether I live or die.*

Just then, Tomás appeared at Isabella's side, his eyes flashing between his new wife and Jean-Luc. And so, Jean-Luc subtracted another point for jealousy.

Isabella, however, forgot everyone in the room when her husband came to her side. Jean-Luc studied the change in her. Was Felicia altered after they first came together? No, Felicia argued, cajoled, and laughed at him after they became lovers. Then he remembered again: he no longer allowed himself to care about Felicia.

"I'm going to Toulouse in the morning." Jean-Luc spoke to Tomás and Isabella before they could escape to their bedroom. "There's news that I might find the man there who betrayed me. May I take the horse you bought me?"

"Of course," Tomás said. "We're going to Laurac next, to see if Sebastián is visiting Renoud's mother there. Then we'll ride for Font-cours as fast as God lets us. To do as Pèire planned and join the peacekeepers."

"I'll look for Sebastián in Toulouse, too. Then I'll meet you at Fontcours. Please make my apologies to our hostess. I won't see them before I leave in the morning."

He took the senhóra's hand to kiss farewell, as knights did with ladies in the Pays de France.

As Jean-Luc walked away, he felt Tomás's glare still burning into his back.

As if there's even one thing in my life for you to be jealous of.

"Go with God," Isabella called after him.

God has been less than half-hearted about traveling with me.

Such an enormous dark hole waited for him to tumble into. Jean-Luc heard Yves's voice again.

You can be such a fool, I'm forever amazed.

He turned around. "Hey, swordsman!"

Tomás glanced up from where he was burying his soul in his wife's eyes. "Yes?"

"Don't be an arsewit."

72

In the House of Nightingales

Isabella and Tomás at Casa de Rossynols
6 days before Pentecost

"DO YOU KNOW WHO Senhór François is?"

As Isabella asked, she shut the door, leaving them alone at last in the whitewashed room that was their borrowed bedroom. A rush lamp glowed on a table, and the open window showed thousands of stars in the sky. Outside, frogs and nightingales competed to sing the night's music. The room smelled of the garrigue, that mélange of rosemary, juniper, and herbs that she'd breathed while riding through those limestone hills. That perfume had scented each day of the chaos wrought during her unfinished journey.

"Do you mean the randy fellow who gawped at you all through dinner?" Tomás embraced her as soon as she latched the door, his hands drifting up to untie the ribbons at the shoulders of her gown.

"I didn't notice." She wanted to share what she'd learned at dinner, but also wanted to be distracted in the way he seemed intent on doing. "Perseus, when he said goodbye, told me that François is Hugues de Beaurain's brother. At least, he thinks so."

"He's wrong." Tomás kissed her bare shoulder. "Chrétien and I hunted the Beaurain brothers when we fought in Burgundy. One disappeared into an obscure position in the Church, and the other is a spice merchant in Narbonne. There's a half-brother who rides with the marquis' army, but he's too young to have been in the Outremer with my father. Or your grandfather."

Tomás wrapped one of the ribbons around his finger, then pulled it free, tickling her shoulder. On purpose.

"You and I also missed François's story," Isabella said, "because we came to dinner late. Perseus says the happiness of this rose-covered casa results from the Church forcing François to abandon his previous wife, who's a goodwoman."

"A challenge you and I will never experience. Since we came together specifically to prevent that. Shall we go to bed?"

"To sleep this time?" Isabella returned his lingering kiss, a comfort and provocation like she'd never known before. "When was the last time you slept?"

"I prefer to stay awake. Every time I fall asleep, you disappear and almost get killed."

"Not this time. I want—"

A knock at the door, which had a latch, but could not be barred.

The same prickly annoyance that she felt visibly rippled through his muscles. While she tugged her robe up over her shoulders, Tomás opened the door. It was Senhóra Paula.

"My maid forgot the last of her chores." Paulette beamed like she had at dinner, so happy to have them in her house. She offered a gleaming golden silk pillow. "I have a sachet like the ones I made for my daughters' wedding night. Please accept this with all the best wishes of our domus for your happiness and long life."

"You are too kind, ma dòmna." Tomás blocked Paulette from entering the room, while speaking in what Isabella heard as his most honeyed, sensuous voice. "We cannot have found a better shelter for the first night of our lives together."

"Everything is as you'd wish? Our servants provided for your comfort, I hope." She wanted to see into the room, but Tomás still blocked her way.

"Indeed, ma dòmna. This is the prettiest room I've ever slept in. We shall sleep well. And we wish you the best night also. *Bon nuoit.*" Tomás touched Paulette's hand in a farewell gesture.

He closed and latched the door.

Isabella felt free at last to laugh at him, the way she'd often seen Chrétien teasing him. "Prettiest room ever? Or first pretty room where you don't have to worry that a woman's husband might come home and discover you?"

"What?" He seemed genuinely confused.

"Chrétien told colorful stories of your past life when we practiced with blades while our horses rested. I think he meant to warn me off, since you are a known arsewit and degenerate seducer of women. Wasn't that part of the salacious tales you told the Valerós knights yesterday?"

"That seems so long ago."

"It's after midnight, so I suppose it's two days ago now. We've been married that long. Didn't the Valerós knights force you to swear off your old ways?"

"I mean, it's a long time since I lived in that senselessly carefree way. From before this." He brushed the scars on his face. "And now I have what I most wanted since I came to this country."

"And it's two days since I last declared what I most wanted to avoid in this life. Now here I am with a husband, and I can no longer claim it's the worst evil. Perhaps it is its own kind of blessing, beyond saving me from being declared a heretic." She stroked his jaw, barely touching him, because she'd learned it made him shake fiercely while she pressed against him.

"*Aiieee!*"

"Even if my new husband is, as his brother claims, a degenerate seducer of women."

"No. Only you, *kalila*, forever more." He stretched out atop the bed, motioning her to him. "Though it's likely, as Perseus claims, I'm still an arsewit."

"Perseus? Do you know who the so-called smith is? That he was a knight under Gerard de Chartrain?"

"*Òc*, he told me when we met at the French army camp."

"And Guillem knows?" She sat on the edge of the bed.

"Yes. Because Pèire recognized him from the Outremer. But don't pout because I haven't told you. He made me promise not to reveal his name."

"Perseus seems to have suffered deep pains. You see it in his eyes, how he walks. How he seldom smiles. It's the least I can do to respect his request to remain hidden." But she shrugged off for the moment the problem of Perseus's pain. "It's unfair that I am able to enjoy what he most wanted, while Perseus remains denied."

"You mean love? Perseus wants more than that." Tomás held her hand, as if they hadn't passed much further than that. "Also, you now have what you wanted most. You shall lead knights into Toulouse. Then we will rescue Sebastián and destroy Renoud."

"Yes. Now, can we—"

Another knock on the thick plank door. Isabella moved to answer, but Tomás got there first, annoyance traveling across his face and down his body.

Isabella watched her husband cross the room, walking like a predator. There was only the nagging sadness, that she couldn't tell Katelina that she'd got what she wanted. *If you met a warrior determined to live an honorable life? Who'd go into the world as your comrade?*

■

The young servant at the door drew back, alarmed, before Tomás remembered how fierce his face seemed to others. He wrenched his face into a kinder smile than he felt, given the interruption, and applied honey to his voice.

"Hola. It's Sanç, isn't it?" He hoped he remember the fellow's name. In the past day with Isabella, he'd forgotten the rest of the world. "What do you need?"

"Our senhóra asked me to close all the windows. The chickens are facing south in their roosts, and the horses are sleeping with their backs to the north. The tramontane winds will commence tonight, blowing cold down from the mountains. The senhóra doesn't want you to freeze in your bed."

Tomás barred the way with his body. "*Ai,* thank you, to be sung a thousand times by the golden angels. Please send the senhóra our gratitude. I'll tend to the windows."

"The latches can be tricky," the fellow insisted.

"If I can't manage, I'll call you." Tomás wanted Sanç gone, while striving to retain his own buoyant mood despite the interruption of strangers.

He tugged at the shutters, found the hooks holding them open, and reached into the night to yank them closed. In the starlight, skeleton shadows of cypress trees marched atop the ragged hills they'd crossed in the past week. Storks' nests reached for the starry sky from the tops of the nearby olive orchard.

When he finished latching the windows, he returned to Isabella, undoing the buckles on his jerkin.

"I can do that." She touched him, at his collarbone, before grasping the buckles. The sensation flowed through him, like a strange tonic from an Outremer healer who might be a magician, not just a physician. Nothing else took the pain out of his bones like when she touched him.

When she finished with his buckles and string-ties, and he stood bare chested, too aware of scars he didn't like others to see, he untied the strings of her robe, easing it from her shoulders.

"*Ai*, Isabella. This is a pleasure I never dreamed of. Let me see you in the light, *kalila*. I want to inspect my new possession."

"Your possession?" She frowned, but she seemed to know he teased. "You're *my* sworn knight."

"But the law says, you're my property. I want to see what I own."

"You jest."

"Of course. What's this scar on your belly? And this one on your breast? Do you wear padding when you practice with weapons?"

"It's from Nicolau. My first wedding night was not pleasant."

"I won't guess what happened there. But now you're with me. I will never hurt you." He paused. "And I swear I'll kill him for it."

"He's already dead."

"Then I'll kill his brother. And when I see Nicolau in hell, I shall avenge you."

"And what's this scar?" She traced a long white line down his torso. It tickled like the devil.

"*Aiieee*, let's not tell sad stories tonight. Let's see if this feather bed is as kind as we thought it was in the afternoon."

Despite the closed windows, the room was cooling. He lay back on the bed, coaxing her to lie on top of him. When he pulled the soft linen coverlet over them, it settled like the fingers of a thousand angels, smoothing all cares.

•

Midway through whispering how he loved her, Tomás felt her fall asleep, her breath even, shallow, brushing his bare shoulder like an angel passing by. Sleep did not deign to allow him to slip into dreams with her.

He needed to sleep. He wanted to sleep. But he stayed awake pondering what she'd ask in the morning: *What's next?* He'd spent two nights and a day so stupidly in love that he'd thought of only one thing. Isabella. He could make an excuse, especially if Miquel showed up again to plague him, that he was fulfilling his oath to Pèire, to protect his children. And with Isabella, he was moving toward Toulouse and the bishops' court. In addition to gaining a lover he'd never expected, whom he could protect from Renoud's foolish accusation of heresy, the contract Anselm had written for them provided a crucial safety. Sebastián was now his son. Renoud had no more claim on the boy.

The pre-dawn birds had begun despite the rising Tramontane wind. If only he could teach birds to sing to her all day long. *Sebastián is safe. Valerós is safe. We're safe. Nothing can touch us now.* They only needed to come before the bishops' court, show their certified truths, and be free.

Free for him to finish hunting Renoud and then destroy him and all enemies in league with him. He'd die for her along the way, except he couldn't; he had to stay alive to protect her.

"*Aiieee!* Mercy!" She thrashed in the bed, tossing madly.

"Isabella. Wake up. You're having a bad dream." He touched her shoulder, gently, afraid that waking her might frighten her more.

She woke slowly, shuddering, trying to sit up while trapped in the coverlet that she'd mangled.

"*Ai,* I'm here. With you."

"Yes. You're safe."

"I dreamed about Katelina...walking away from me...into the mists that must be heaven. Now I have no friend."

He hadn't seen her cry, except for the sacred night when they cradled Pèire. She turned to him, buried her face in the linens, and cried silently, her body shaking.

He wanted all the dancing angels to grant him the ability to offer comfort.

"*Ai, kalila.* I'm here. I'm not leaving." He shifted, one arm cradling her, the other hand stroking her shoulder, her neck, her hands, like his mother did when they were sick with a fever or needed stitching after accidents. "*Eu vos amor.* You aren't alone."

When she relaxed into his arms and again fell asleep, it was late enough—or so early—that the ovens had been lit. Despite closed shutters, odors drifted in the room, first of burning charcoal, then the yeasty odor of baking bread. He wanted to let her sleep yet gambled against her fury if he let her sleep too far past dawn, when she wanted to ride out to find Sebastián. In the middle of his indecision, someone again knocked on the door. He eased his arm out from where he'd cuddled her, pulled on his small clothes, and snatched one of the linen sheets to wrap his torso.

"Bonjorn, senhór." It was Sanç, who must have slept as little as Tomás had. "Senhór Guillem asked me to bring you breakfast and his messages. He's staying here for a few days, to give three of your knights time to heal. The kitchen is preparing food for your travels, and the stablemen are preparing your horses.

Sanç set a platter of food on the table, peeling back a linen cover that a fastidious person in the kitchen had laid over it.

"And Master Guillem asked me to give you this." Sanç handed him a piece of parchment. New parchment like the wedding contract written at the Vale of Roses. "He says a senhóra of Valerós trusted him with it, but he begs me to say that it is your responsibility now."

Tomás said, "Can you please give Master Guillem my thanks? And our best wishes for safe travels until we meet in Laurac."

When Sanç left, Tomás set the packet aside, to read when Isabella woke. Instead of satisfying his curiosity, he investigated the food. A small platter of thin-sliced cold lamb and a firm white cheese. And a bowl of fruit—strawberries and the season's first cherries. Bread so hot it must have just then slid from the oven onto the wood plank that held it. And a carafe of white wine that tasted like sweet grass in the spring.

He broke off a piece of the bread, then settled on the chair by the bed with a tin mug of that white wine. Now he had the freedom to watch her sleep, without it being a guilty trespass. He tugged a corner of the soft linen coverlet over her barred shoulders. His motion

439

E.A. STEWART

was deft, his fingers never touched her. The linen soft as feathers. Yet the movement woke her.

She blinked twice, smiled when her eyes met his. "Tell me again, *el meu amor*, what you and I decided to do next."

"Like when we waited for Chrétien at Anfos's cottage?"

"Yes. But the story and our chances are better now, aren't they? Now that I have everything I wanted. Except Sebastián."

"Yes, our chances and hopes are better. First, Chrétien is a superb hunter. He's found Sebastián by now and made sure he's safe." Tomás told the improved story. "We'll ride out this morning with the healthy Valerós knights, first to Laurac to see if Sebastián is with his grandmother in the goodmen's community there."

"Sancta Maria. I hope not. Eloïse never offered me a moment's kindness." The dark shadow fell over her face, like it did whenever she spoke of her old life in Toulouse. "But even if Sebastián isn't there, we shall demand that Eloïse tell us who fathered her sons. It may be the only way we can uncover our hidden enemy."

"Then…" Tomás spoke slowly, struck by how they'd come to the same mission, the same goals. "We'll fly to Toulouse, with you leading the Valerós knights. We'll arrive by Pentecost, to deliver our proofs and say our creed. Then you and Valerós and Fontcours shall be free of Renoud's threats forever more."

"And then?"

"I shall finish hunting my…our enemies, while you join the Valerós knights with our…friends at Fontcours. Which fulfills the demands made on Pèire to support peacekeeping this summer. So Valerós and everyone there will be safe."

She sat up and began searching out her riding gear.

"Hold on just a moment, Isabella. Eat breakfast first." He offered the bowl of strawberries and cherries. She refused the wine. "And we need to read what Guillem sent."

He studied words. The form and shapes of the letters indicated that Father Anselm had inscribed it, witnessed by Guillem and Benito. "It's Pèire's last words, written on the Sunday of our Confraria gathering. Pèire declared Sebastián a knight of Valerós, and therefore a man who has come of age."

440

Isabella took it from him, studied it. "Sebastián is the baron of Valerós, responsible for all that Pèire governed. Pèire had no intention of Beatriz inheriting Valerós. Because—"

"Because he feared his secret enemy would come for Beatriz."

"But not Sebastián? Why didn't he worry about Sebastián also? Or is it just—"

"Stop. Pèire didn't make Sebastián the Master of Valerós because you weren't capable. You don't think that, do you?"

"No. No. This is...this is good." Isabella swallowed, seeming to seek her best voice. "I can lead the knights to Fontcours but...it's likely Pèire was correct. That the French invaders won't regard my right to lead. I can't...claim to be master of Valerós."

She studied the words again, what Pèire wanted, what Anselm had written for him. What Guillem and Benito swore to. Her hands shook so hard, she set it down and folded her hands. He couldn't tell if she was struck with anger or another emotion.

"What's troubling you, Isabella?"

"My nightmare lingers. I'm still thinking of Katelina, who carried this from Valerós. She too wanted to ensure Sebastián kept his place in the world." Her voice trailed off, and she shuddered, so he didn't believe Sebastián ruled her thoughts at that moment.

"The way Katelina died," Tomás found his kindest, soft voice, "it happened in an instant. She didn't suffer."

"Yet she was suffering deeply when we last talked. She went to that nunnery because of Beatriz. Because of ancient lies and secrets."

"We're done with secrets now, you and I."

"Yes. Except, Tomás, I need to give you a present."

"What is it?" He yearned for a light, carefree moment, hoping she'd roused from her night terrors and was able to play again. He was disappointed when she offered a packet of parchment. "A letter? I'm sick of secret letters and contracts."

"Read the first few lines, Tomás."

He strained to decipher the tiny writing. "'I thought you loved me. I have given my life for you, without regard for my immortal soul.' Very pretty. Is it a troubadour's song?"

"Read more. I stole it from that murdered priest. It's what you came to Valerós to find, isn't it?"

"*Jhezu del tron.* This is from Renoud's evil father. To Eloïse."

"We're partners now, aren't we? We trust each other, like Pèire and Katelina." She spoke eagerly, throwing her arms around him, holding him closer than he'd ever dared to hope, her breath tickling his ear, a balm over the scars at his hairline. Yes, he'd come to Valerós seeking that letter—a mere fragment, like Hélène said, and not useful. But he'd gained so much more, so much of it unearned.

"Yes, *kalila*, we trust each other." He vowed silently to be worthy of all that had come to him in the past two dozen days. "On my mother's honor. You and I are comrades, Isabella. Like brothers-in-arms whose hearts beat as one."

"Then come on, Don Tomás of wherever you're from now."

"Castell-de-Valerós, if you'll have me as your knight." Every sinew and muscle felt honed, ready to take the offer Pèire gave. "*We need men like you to keep our world in order. Stay here. Join my home and my knights. Make a family.*"

"Excellent. Let's find our horses. We get to ride today, which is a good thing. And the trail leads to my son."

Lubos and the Spirits

WOMEN HAVE BONES INSIDE them, even though they have no soul. Lubos was surprised when his knife scraped across bone, because he thought women were empty inside. But then he remembered the feel of bones under the skin of his little girls. Like little birds.

At his campfire, he tapped red ink at the crescent points of a lunate cross, this one for the woman who died. But that didn't add to the singing voices in his sword, because it was a woman, and they have no souls. And he'd used a knife. A little knife, like only a woman would have.

Counting the crosses, he felt satisfaction at work done.

Still, he shuddered, remember the last touch, when he believed he'd found a true son to take home with him. But it turned out that he touched a woman. Who had no soul but refused to die. Like her filthy protector, who resisted his sword. For comfort, to ward off dwelling on failure, he counted his successes from Père-Izsák's list.

That fancy priest called Pierre, on the banks of the Rhône.

The ugly priest, who had laughed at him in Toulouse.

The French giant who got in his way in that garden.

The decrepit old man in the castle, one of those men who'd scoffed at his father. That took the last of Aykuna's potion.

Two knights who wore the colors of his father's enemies.

That false monk, the twin of the mestitz trash he hunted.

That foreign witch with the long hair and lovely hands.

He rubbed at two of those little crosses. The false monk—that was a mistake, but the man had joined with evil. The one he'd tapped into his arm after the fight in the garden, that man still lived and had to be hunted again, along with the other two men on his list.

Yet he was tired. He ached in every bone from the last battle. He longed for comfort, like when Aykuna stroked his hand and prayed in a heathen language. When she conjured, it took away the pain.

"As beautiful as the angels, that's what you are." Aykuna whispered, stroking his hands. "Like a bird of heaven that I can hold in my hands. We shall call you Lubos."

Lubos stirred at the sound of her voice, dreaming of her again. He wanted to go home. To be with her.

He liked the name she gave him. It sounded like "wolf" in his own tongue. But she said, "It means 'little bird,' which is my favorite guardian spirit. You have powerful spirits who kept you alive through all you suffered. I see them sitting by your side. You'll be my angel now that you're well."

Aykuna, the woman Père-Izsák had found for him, launched into a flight of fantasy about how the world worked. But he still believed as he always had: that women and children have no souls. Women are only given to us by the angels to carry our seed into the future, to make us immortal. But for the first time that he remembered, the spirits had provided a gift of comfort in a woman.

The town where he lived under Aykuna's care lay in a cove on the Dalmatian coast. In three years, she gave him three daughters but no son. Proper propitiation of the earth's spirits brings the gift of sons; it wasn't Aykuna's fault.

"I'm longing for a son," he said when Père-Izsák asked him how he was doing.

"That's what the harmony of creation comes down to," Père-Izsák said. "Fathers and sons."

Lubos had been taught from an early age to call the man Père-Izsák. But after the war, Lubos knew in his heart that this knight-priest was Lubos's real father. He hoped Père-Izsák felt happy when Lubos called the man "Father" and didn't add "Izsák." Père-Izsák ruffled his hand through the curls of Lubos's hair, like a father does his son, and he taught a secret knowledge that Lubos sucked up like a calf takes milk from the teat.

At their last meeting, Père-Izsák said, "Your face has changed. I hardly recognize you. You look like an angel."

Out the door, only daughters played in Aykuna's garden, tending families of little straw-and-wood dolls Lubos made for them. "Children," he called. They came, crawling into his lap like puppies. Père-Izsák put his hands on their heads and give his blessing.

A tawny owl called *hoo-hoo-hoo!*

Another answered *ke-wick!*

Lubos roused at the shriek. The spirits' call reminded him that he was in a strange land, far away from Aykuna and his little girls, where he couldn't return until his finished his chores for his father. He rose and packed his kit, neatly, like his priest-knight father taught him. His horse nickered, answering the spirits in the trees.

Time to ride, to do as his father commanded, to feed the souls of Père-Izsák's enemies to his singing steel blade. And to find a real son to take home with him.

✦✦✦

END BOOK 1 ▪ ACCIDENTAL HERETICS SERIES

Next:
BOOK 2: TREBUCHETS IN THE GARDEN

Heretics' Glossary

A

Affinity (canon law): Kinship by marriage; at the time of this story, affinity and consanguinity restricted marriage to fourth degree relationships. A man, for example, could not marry his brother's widow.

Ai Dèu: O God.

a mal punt: A bad state.

Angevines: The Plantagenet dynasty that ruled from Ireland to the Pyrenees at the time of this story. The Angevine empire grew through the marriage of Henry II and Eleanor of Aquitaine.

aqua vitae: Medieval ethanol, typically made by distilling wine.

aquí, aquí, gat: Here, kitty!

aventail: A chainmail curtain to cover the neck and shoulders.

B

baise-toi, fif: A vulgar retort.

baquelar: Villainous rogue.

barcelonese: A silver coin under the Count of Barcelona.

bazasa: bastard.

bezants: A Byzantine coin.

Bogomils: A medieval Gnostic sect, believing a dualist view of Christianity, seemingly arising in Macedonia.

bon amics: Good friend, or boyfriend.

bon Dèu; Bon Dieu: Good God.

bon día: Good day.

bon nuoit; bona nuèch: Good night.

bon vèspre: Good evening.

bonfraires: A brotherhood.

bonjorn: Good morning.

booty: Treasure; during the crusades, the primary way crusaders financed their armies or paid their mercenaries. Rather than "looting," these cultures considered booty as legitimate plunder.

bordonier: A freeholder who arms and fights, freely, for a baron.

Brabançon: A mercenary from the Low Countries, with a reputation for lawlessness.

brioix: Bread.

C

cançós d'amor: Troubadours' love songs.

cançós d'Arturo: Songs of the Arthur legend.

cançós de guèrra: Troubadours' songs of war.

Candlemas: Feast of the Purification, February 2; one of the pre-Christian fire festivals.

Catalan: In the Middle Ages, a language, not a political entity.

cavaller: Knight.

charogne: Bastard (as an expletive).

Cilicia: An Armenian kingdom on the south coast of Asia Minor.

Cistercian Order: The White Monks, a reformist Benedictine order, who stressed manual labor and a return to the Rule of St Benedict.

comme ça va: How is it going?

common tongue: The Romance language of the Languedoc in the Middle Ages, often now called Old Occitan.

compadre: "Shared parent," like a godparent-godchild relationship.

connard: A French vulgarity.

conrois formation: A tight cavalry formation.

consanguinity: Laws governing the degree of relationship that will prohibit marriage among people with a shared ancestor. A convenient reason for marriage annulment among European ruling classes, since they were all related, and a "fourth degree" relationship could easily be discovered.

convivencia: "The Coexistence," describing the period of relative peaceful coexistence among Muslims, Jews, and Christians on the Iberian Peninsula under Muslim rule.

cor dolç: Sweetheart, an endearment.

cortezia: The southern value of grace and courtly honor.

crucesignati: Crusaders.

Crux Lunata: A (fictional) secret brotherhood, whose symbol is a lunate cross, featuring lunar crescents at each terminus; a pagan symbol; war tokenism imported to Europe by returning crusaders, adding the Islamic crescent in heraldic and other symbols.

cuirass: A rigid armor covering the torso. At this period, it was still made of leather.

D

debauchery: In its archaic definition: a knight going astray from his allegiance or duty.

deniers: A French coin.

Deus vult: God wills it! (a crusader cry).

Dieu de la miséricorde: God of mercy.

domus: Household; specifically, the larger economic household of a titled landholder.

don: A courtesy title for a gentleman from the landed classes.

donzel: A young gentleman, in training for knighthood.

duenna: A governess or chaperone.

E

el meu amor: My love.

Endura: The goodmen's so-called sacrament or practice of death by fasting, an ascetic suicide.

eu vos amor: I love you.

F

fada: Fairy.

fadrin: A lad, a term of endearment.

faitdits knights: Southern knights who have no lord, who have foresworn their previous oaths.

fenta: Excrement.

Fontrevists: Members of the Order of Fontevrault, whose abbeys included separate communities of men and women, led by a monastery abbess.

francimand, francimandalha: Frenchman.

Franks: Colloquially, at the time of this story, a reference used by Muslims and others for Western European people.

fustian: A heavy cotton fabric.

G

gambeson: A padded jacket worn under armor or worn alone as a defensive covering.

garderobe: The inner privy of a castle.

goodmen, goodwomen: A reference to the people whom the Church called heretics; now commonly called Cathars.

Greek fire: An incendiary of naphtha, pitch, and sulfur.

H

hashishiyyin: An abusive term referring to the Nizari Ismailis in Persia and Syria.

hauberk: A chainmail shirt.

hé, connard: Hey, jerk (but using an anatomy reference).

hereticated: Having decided to adopt a heresy.

hola: Hello.

Hospitallers of Jerusalem: A Christian military order, founded in Jerusalem to care for sick pilgrims; later given a charter for defense of the Holy Land.

I-J

Il n'y a pas de quoi: It is nothing (a response to "thank you").

Je n'en ai rien a foutre: I don't give a rip (using an expletive).

Jhezu del tron: Jesus in heaven.

jongleurs: Medieval minstrels, who sang the songs of the troubadours.

Juan Zoquette: John Chump.

K

kalila: Sweetheart, an endearment.

Knights Templar: A monastic crusader military order, the most elite of the crusader armies.

koupepia: Stuffed vine leaves, as prepared on Cyprus.

L

Latins: Colloquially, how the Muslims referred to the invading Western Christian armies.

lay brothers: A non-ordained member of a religious order, typically doing manual labor and managing secular affairs.

loophole: A slit in a stonewall that allows light and ability to shoot arrows while protecting the defender.

M

ma dòmna: My lady.

maître forgeron: Master smith.

mangon: A catapult design first used in Roman times.

mangonel: A large siege engine.

maricón: Derogatory reference to a gay man.

marquis, marquesa: A lord (and his wife) whose land is on a frontier border, and so must be a capable defender.

Mater mitis, sed viri nescia: "Pray for us, O Holy Mother of God, that we may be made worthy."

mestitz: A person of mixed heritage.

mignotta: A prostitute.

Monsenyor: An honorific, such as for a king.

Moors: People from northern Africa who settled on the Iberian peninsula under Muslim leadership. Colloquially at the time of this story, a person of mixed heritage with a dark complexion.

morabatin: Gold coins in Aragón. A horse cost about 100 morabatins.

N

Nizari: At the time of the Crusader states, a legendary assassin cult.

Normans: Descendants of the Viking Northmen who settled Normandy, and later invaded Britain in 1066.

O

òc: Yes.

Outremer: The lands across the Great Sea, where the Crusader States were founded and other territory seized by Christian invaders.

P

Pare Abát: Father abbot.

paratge: A concept in Troubadour culture of kinship and justice, more than honor: natural balance, harmony, "what is right."

Parzival: From the Arthurian legend, the knight who heals the Fisher King and goes to the Grail castle with Galahad.

peccador: Sinner.

per l'amor de Dèu: For the love of God.

petraria: A rock hurler powered by a bow.

Petrus mortuus. Petrae disiectae: Peter dead. Peter's descendants dispersed.

poulain: A colt; colloquially, a pejorative used by Latins in the Outremer to describe children with crusader fathers and local mothers.

punxor: Prick.

Q

quiquid: Whatever.

Qui s'ho creu: Who'd believe it?

R

Ransomers: A monastic order of knights in the Crusader states.

rebec: A medieval stringed instrument, imported into Christian Europe via Andalusia. At the time of the crusades, it was likely referred to as a lyra.

religieuse: Women in a religious order.

rendability: A practice, at the time of this story, of a king (or other leader) demanding that an independent lord make castles available to the king, in exchange for the king's promise of protection.

renrén: Fool.

S

Sancta Maria: A woman's oath, calling on Saint Mary.

Saracen: Colloquial term for Muslims used in Europe.

schismatic: For members of the Holy Roman Church, a common way to refer to members of the Eastern Orthodox Church.

scrofula: Tuberculosis of the neck; colloquially, part of an insult.

seigneur: A man of rank who rules lands and a household.

Seljuks: Fighters from a Turkish-Persian empire.

seneschal: A steward.

senhór, senhóra, senhóreta: Titles of respect.

simony: Paying for an office or position in the Church.

Sodalitas, fidelitas, virtus: Latin motto of the *bonfraires*: fraternity, fidelity, virtue.

squire: In the southern lands, a fighter of rank between knights and foot soldiers, for his lifetime. In the southern world, squires did not rise to become knights.

surcoat: A long coat worn over others clothes or armor.

T

troud'cul: Vulgar reference, involving body parts.

Turcopoles: Mercenary mounted archers in the Crusader states.

V

va te faire foutre: A vulgar retort.

Venetians: The instigators and financiers of the so-called Fourth Crusade which changed course to conquer Constantinople.

viscount: A European noble rank, above a baron, below a marquis.

W–Z

woad: A plant used to create a blue dye, grown as a cash crop around Toulouse.

xiqueta: Child, an endearment.

Place Names

Valerós, Fontcours, Montcava, and the Vale of Roses exist within the world of *Accidental Heretics*, but nowhere else.

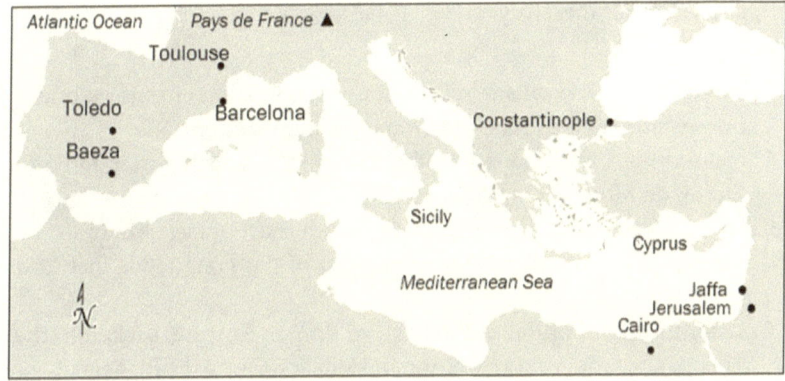

Crusaders' World, 1210

A

Aleppo: One of the oldest continuously inhabited cities. In Syria, at the end of the Silk Road, and now undergoing new travails, Aleppo was besieged twice by crusaders but never conquered.

Antioch: A city on an important trade route, conquered early in the First Crusade. Multiple successive crusader rulers battled over the city until it was abandoned in the face of the Mongol conquest.

Aquitaine: A duchy in what is now southwest France; then, a key portion of the Angevine empire under Henry II and Eleanor of Aquitaine.

Aragón: In the mid thirteenth century, a union of the Kingdom of Aragón and the County of Barcelona established the dynastic Crown of Aragón, with tributaries across the Languedoc at the time of this story.

Aude: A river in the southwest of what is now France that flows from the Pyrenees to the Mediterranean.

B

Barcelona: A territory on the Mediterranean, now approximately the political entity of Catalonia; Pedro II held the title Count of Barcelona.

Béziers: A Languedoc town that controlled most of the east-west trade route, and that was infamously burned by the invading crusader-terrorists in a massacre.

Bram: A fortified town in the Languedoc attacked by the French crusaders in 1210.

Byzantium: The Greek-speaking Eastern Roman Empire, with Constantinople as its capital, including Macedonia, Greece, and part of Turkey at the time of this story.

C

Cabaret: Castles and villages north of Carcassonne that formed a center of resistance to the French early in the Languedoc crusade.

Carcassonne: A fortified city in the Languedoc, which surrendered to Simon de Montfort in 1209.

Cilicia: An Armenian kingdom on the south coast of Asia Minor.

Corbières hills: Foothills in the southwest of the Languedoc that lead up to the Pyrenees.

Constantinople: Capital of the Eastern Roman Empire, sacked in the Fourth Crusade; ruled by Norman lords for the next fifty years.

Cyprus: A Mediterranean fiefdom conquered by Richard the Lionheart, who then saw it as not worth the bother and sold it to the Knights Templar, who then sold it to Guy de Lusignan.

D–F

Dalmatia: A region on the eastern Adriatic coast, portions of which were under the control of Venice in 1204.

Edessa: An Armenian city, ruled by various Crusader lords and under frequent attacks by Turks. First of the Crusader States to be lost.

Famagusta: Tomás's home on Cyprus.

Fontfroide abbey: At the time of this story, a Cistercian monastery near Narbonne.

H–J

Holy Roman Empire: The successor in central Europe to Charlemagne's empire, including during the late Middle Ages parts of Germany, Burgundy, Italy, and Bohemia.

Iconium: An ancient city in Asia Minor, now Konya, Turkey.

Jaffa: The southern part of what is now Tel Aviv, captured after the First Crusade, conquered by Saladin, and then reclaimed by Richard Lionheart. After fighting off Saladin, the crusaders held the city until 1268.

Jerusalem: Captured by the crusaders in 1099, recaptured by Saladin in 1187, traded back and forth for several decades until finally captured by the Mamluks and lost forever by the crusaders.

L

Lagrasse: A town in the lower foothills of the Pyrenees, centered around the abbey of Sainte-Marie de Lagrasse.

Laurac: A village in the Aude valley.

Limoux: A town in the Languedoc, on the river Aude.

M

Maine: A province in France, under Norman and Angevine control until lost to King Philippe in 1203.

Montpelhièr: A walled city in the Languedoc, near the Mediterranean, with the second oldest university in Europe.

Morella: A town near Valencia, taken from the Moors by El Cid, lost again before finally becoming part of Aragón in the Reconquista.

N

Narbonne: A rich Mediterranean port in the Languedoc that was the seat of the bishop and home to a significant Jewish community.

Naxos: A Greek island in the Aegean Sea, alternately under Byzantine and Venetian rule.

O–Q

Outremer: The Crusader States, the land overseas.

Pays de France: The historic personal domain of the king of France; most of this area became the province Ile de France.

Peyriac-de-Mer: Site in the Aude region of a Cistercian monastery.

Poitiers: A county in west central France, whose county governed the Aquitaine and Poitou.

Provence: A county on the Mediterranean under the rule of the counts of Barcelona.

Quéribus: A stronghold on the Aragón frontier in the Corbières hills.

R

Ramla: The city where Saladin and Richard I signed a treaty, when they each had too many other troubles to continue battling over Jerusalem.

Rennes-les-Bains: A spa village in the Corbières hills.

Rhône: The major river running from the Alps to the Mediterranean.

Roussillon: A county in the Languedoc, under the Count of Barcelona at the time of this story.

S

Sicily: A Norman kingdom during much of the Crusades era, after Normans conquered the Arab rulers of Sicily and southern Italy.

St-Gilles: Site of a Benedictine abbey to the east of Montpelhièr.

St-Sernin: A Romanesque basilica in Toulouse.

Syria: An Arab land in Western Asia, with districts captured, recaptured, and carved among Turks, Seljuks, Byzantines, and Crusaders.

T–Z

Termes: A stronghold castle in the Aude valley, attacked by Simon de Montfort in 1210.

Toulouse: A county and a city in the Languedoc on a major trade route between the Mediterranean and central France, whose count owed allegiance to the king of France. The city was one of the largest in Europe at the time of this story.

Zara: An island in the Adriatic where Venetian and French mercenaries rioted in rebellion, while camped and awaiting ships to advance of the crusade to conquer Constantinople.

About the Author

E.A. STEWART is an American writer whose *Accidental Heretics* series explores intrigues in France and Spain in the thirteenth century. Annie Stewart worked as a technical writer and project manager in Pacific Northwest software companies.

Ms. Stewart lives and writes in Seattle.

www.eastewartauthor.com

Author's Notes and Acknowledgments

THANKS TO: Ajax Bell, Elizabeth Bjorkman, Laurie Cropp, Phyllis J. Hatfield, Don McQuinn, Daj Oberg, Jacyn Stewart, Susan Urban.

NOTES: I began this series with a strong idea of the story arc and then chose the historic period with the thought, "I always wanted to learn more about the Albigensian Crusade."

This ended up being like the ancient maps that label a whole quadrant with "There Be Monsters." By the time I finished the first six months of research, I worked with a few basics that shaped the actual arc of this story.

First, everything I knew about the Middle Ages in Britain and France was of little use. The part of Europe that's not Languedoc-Roussillon wasn't feudal, didn't speak French, and was a wealthy, cosmopolitan region, chiefly because of the trade advanced by the first century of crusades. Women inherited property. Women of upper classes ruled politically and economically.

Next, I began working with Laurie Cropp, whom I met when she left her medieval scholar life behind. She emphasized how, beyond the troubadour poetry that survived, an early renaissance was underway in this part of Western Europe. The advances of Muslim-world scientific and medical knowledge came to Europe because of the increased trade and movement around the Mediterranean. Universities were being founded in Paris and Montpelhièr.

Now, how to understand the thinking of people living in the thirteenth century Languedoc. Beyond the surviving poetry and civil records, it's hard to find records of everyday life and ordinary people's actual religious beliefs. For a deeply literate culture, the written record is missing—because of the "crusade" and the subsequent Inquisition. Most information about what the so-called Cathars thought was recorded under extreme duress one hundred fifty years after the Church first requested military action to crush the Cathar communities. I've used the following analogy to explain why I don't rely on the recorded interrogations at Montaillou. How close (and divergent) are the beliefs and practices among people attending an Anglican parish church in an 19th century London suburb versus people in 2015 who belong to a nondenominational church in northern Idaho?

Finally, I'm a writer in the twenty-first century with pacifist, egalitarian, anti-imperialism tendencies. My characters are part of a colonizing warrior culture in a stratified culture, living under the stress of a foreign invasion. It's 1210 when this story begins, and these people believe that the attack of the French invaders is dangerous, but it's a temporary problem. The Count of Toulouse will settle his quarrels with the Roman Church and then life will return to normal. They cannot see that their entire culture will be destroyed over the next seventy-five years.

But this is only Book 1 in an adventure through the early years of this venture of peace and faith. Here are a few books you might enjoy if you want to learn more than you can find on Wikipedia.

·

The Cathars: Dualist Heretics in Languedoc in the High Middle Ages by Malcolm Barber, Pearson Education Ltd., 2000.

Ermengard of Narbonne and the World of the Troubadours by Frederic L. Cheyette. Cornell University Press, 2001.

The Perfect Heresy: The Revolutionary Life and Death of the Medieval Cathars by Stephen O'Shea. Walker & Company, 2000.

Medieval Warfare Sourcebook by David Nicolle. Arms & Armour, 1997.

About the Accidental Heretics Series

Lost in the Languedoc Crusade

Find this series in your favorite online store
or ask your independent local bookseller.

ACCIDENTAL HERETICS SERIES
Book 1: *Bone-mend and Salt*
Book 2: *Trebuchets in the Garden*
Book 3: *Crux Lunata*
Book 4: *Song of Valerós*
The Mad Woman of La Catalane: A Novella
The Blue Door… and More Accidental Heretics Tales

LEGENDS OF VALERÓS SERIES
Wheel and Serpent: 1
Traitor: 2
Hero: 3

To learn more about
the Accidental Heretics series, visit:
www.eastewartauthor.com